The Battle for Eire

THE BATTLE FOR EIRE

Kieran Wasserman

iUniverse, Inc.
New York Lincoln Shanghai

The Battle for Eire

Copyright © 2005 by Kieran Wasserman

All rights reserved. No part of this book may be used or reproduced by any means, graphic, electronic, or mechanical, including photocopying, recording, taping or by any information storage retrieval system without the written permission of the publisher except in the case of brief quotations embodied in critical articles and reviews.

iUniverse books may be ordered through booksellers or by contacting:

iUniverse
2021 Pine Lake Road, Suite 100
Lincoln, NE 68512
www.iuniverse.com
1-800-Authors (1-800-288-4677)

ISBN-13: 978-0-595-36860-0 (pbk)
ISBN-13: 978-0-595-67428-2 (cloth)
ISBN-13: 978-0-595-81270-7 (ebk)
ISBN-10: 0-595-36860-3 (pbk)
ISBN-10: 0-595-67428-3 (cloth)
ISBN-10: 0-595-81270-8 (ebk)

Printed in the United States of America

Preface

"They are here!" cried one of the village women. She ran through the village square, in the center of town, stumbling upon a stone as she did. Fearghus burst out of his house behind his brother, who dashed to her aid, helping the middle-aged woman to her feet.

"You must calm down!" he said. "Who is here?"

"The Romans!" she cried, sobbing uncontrollably. "The Romans have come at last! After all these years, they are attacking at last!"

"But the Romans had no intention of attacking! I can't understand why they are here. What did you see?"

"They're landing one of their ships!"

By now, Fearghus had reached them, wearing only a short tunic. He brushed his long, unkempt hair out of his eyes, and looked inquisitively at his older brother, who, as a warrior of the village, was dressed in traditional armor, including a crimson cloak. "What is going on?" he asked. "What danger befalls us?"

His brother's expression was grave. "Nothing of your concern!" he said. "These are matters for warriors to attend to."

"Yes, but what is happening?" Fearghus pressed indignantly. He took much offense at his brother's prejudice.

"The Romans, you foolish herder! The Romans are attacking! I knew they would come sooner or later! Now we must march to the sea, and drive them back! As the accounts go, they already have laid waste the fisher's houses! I must go now!" he answered.

"Please take me with you!" Fearghus pleaded. He wished very much to become a warrior. Now, just as he desired, a conflict had arisen. It was a conflict that needed him. If he did not fight now, he wouldn't ever.

But his brother pushed him back. "You are no warrior!" he bellowed. "Now go get me my weapons!"

Fearghus, like a slave, followed his command, and turned back to their house, a modest wooden hut, sealed inside and out with mud and thatch. Pulling back the cloth over the door, he looked inside, scanning the walls for his brother's arms. His search took him inside the house, where he conducted a more thorough search. Then finally, next to his bed of straw, he beheld the long spear of his brother, very near to his own staff, a tool he used to herd sheep in the surrounding hills. The two items were very different. On the left, his brother's spear was long and smooth, whilst his staff was rather gnarled and weak. The broad head of the spear gleamed in the faint light in the hut, whereas his staff was hidden in darkness. It was a mark truly of the difference between the two brothers.

He was not generally a very strong man. Instead, he was lanky and fair-skinned, his hands soft and unbroken. His older brother, Feidhlimidh, was quite his opposite. Fiedhlimidh's body was strong, and muscular, and also very dark. He was brought up as a fighter, training with the village elders from a very young age. Fearghus, on the other hand, was neglected, for so weak and timid he was. Now, he was merely a shepherd, tending the flocks of the villagers, including his wealthy brother, in the inland hills.

He snatched up the spear and dashed out to his brother, who had procured a shield from the common armory of the village. It was a round, oval-shaped pavise, marked with Celtic designs. The spear that Fearghus gave to Feidhlimidh completed his costume of a warrior, and now he looked quite a sight. His broad shoulders were well protected by round pauldrons, and a breastplate made up of only a single bronze piece protected his chest. He wore a bronze helmet that complemented the rest of his garb, and it displayed a closed face, so that his eyes were hidden in shadow, and his nose was covered.

Fiedhlimidh now went to the center of the square. "Join me!" he shouted. "Join me! The Romans have come across the sea at last! We must fight for our freedom! We must stop them from advancing! Join me now and fight!"

Many warriors, nearly twenty by Fearghus's count, had been preparing for battle just as Fiedhlimidh had. Now, they all advanced to him in the center of the village, wearing similar armor and all carrying spears and shields. They were quite a sight. All the numerous points of their lances bobbed above their heads, and their helmets glinted in the sun, which had emerged from the many clouds in the sky. All at once, they began a great chant, a great cry before the commencement of battle. It was an ancient and wonderful tune, set to the words of the most ancient of warriors, whose name is not known. It went:

Sound the horns of battle,
Amongst the fields and trees,
Above the mighty mountains,
Across the stormy seas!

Call one and all here,
The warriors and the slaves,
The archers and the spearmen,
The axe-men of the caves!

For Eire we battle,
For Eire we die!
In the name of Eire,
We sound our battle cry!

Even Fearghus, a lowly shepherd, was stirred by this rousing chorus. He shouted until he was hoarse, with the rest of them, holding aloft his staff as the others held their pikes. Standing well away from them near his hut, he still felt a part of their rally, and a sensation of pride stirred in his breast. "For Eire!" he chanted with them, "For Eire!"

At last, Fiedhlimidh came to him, as the others moved to depart. "You should tend to your beasts," he said. "We should like to have a feast, when we return victoriously from battle."

Fearghus nodded. "It shall be as you say," he said. And with that, he left the village and all of its warriors behind, running to the hills with his staff.

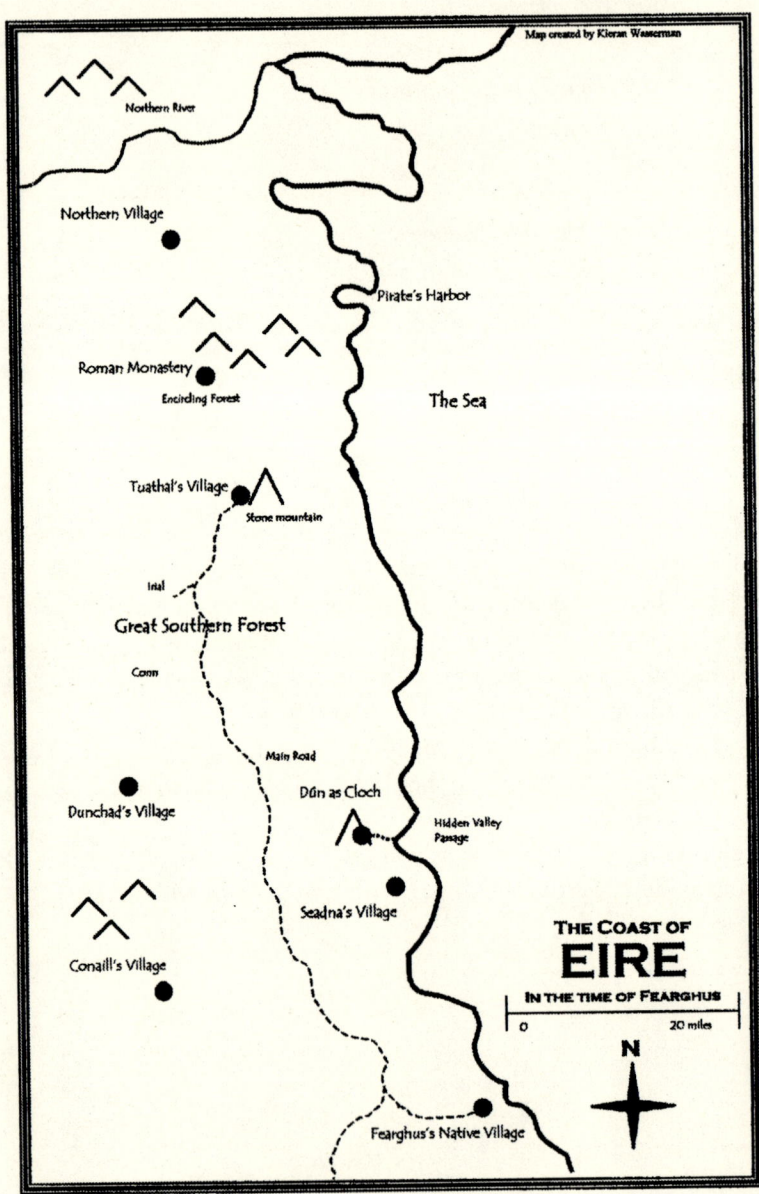

Chapter 1

A Warrior is Born

As far as the eye could see, sheep dotted the rolling green hills of Fearghus's large plot of land in Eire. He was leaning on his staff dazedly amidst the bleating of his flock, standing on a low hill in the middle of a great, green grassy land. Yes, this was Eire, the land of the Celts.

He was immensely bored. Certainly, he did not enjoy standing here, idly, while his brother was out fighting on the coast. This was the work of slaves! He did not want to be here, defending a flock of lowly sheep, he wanted to be on the coast, beyond the rolling green hills, and the river, and the village. He wanted to be out on the beach, with a great lance in his hand, thrusting it into whatever dirty Roman dared to come near him.

But no, he was standing here, with nothing but a rotted old cane in his hand, fighting not Romans, but rather the heads of strong willed sheep. And on top of that, it was beginning to rain! He did not even care to look up while the first drops of rain began to pour. Soon the sun was gone, and, a sad, cold rain set upon him and his flock. This was really terribly degrading. But very quickly, all was interrupted.

Suddenly, lightning blazed across the sky. For the first time, Fearghus peered up into the darkening clouds. In the black, swirling storm he could see what appeared to be two intersecting lines, one shorter than the other, etched into the clouds, blazing white like the sun. He wondered what this image was, being so oddly shaped and all. Was it a sign from the gods, or was it quite simply a natural phenomenon?

Fearghus gazed downwards, for a second, but then, suddenly, the ground was coming alive! Shrouded in the darkness, the ground a few paces away was rippling like the sea. Not knowing what else to do, Fearghus held his ground, snatching up his staff in his fists. The dark wave was quickly moving towards him, with alarming speed. It was almost upon him now.

Suddenly, the sky was rent with lightning again. Fearghus looked up quickly, and while the flash blazed in his eyes, he suddenly noticed a peculiar feeling coming over his feet. He looked down, and in another, lesser flash, he could clearly make out the shapes of many thousands of snakes slithering across the ground. Upon this sight, he gave a great cry, and jumped straight up into the air. Now he did whatever was possible against these ugly creatures. He began to jab his staff into the earth and stamp his loosely clothed feet on the ground.

Soon, however, he noticed that as he smashed the reptiles' heads, none even dared to bite him. In fact, they seemed almost as if occupied by another matter too serious to deal with him. Slowly, Fearghus withdrew his stamping, and very quickly now, the last few snakes passed him, slowly picking their way through the mound of dead snakes at Fearghus's feet. What an odd spectacle, he thought, that so many snakes should pass him by without at least attempting to bite him.

He turned around and looked at the wave of reptiles. They were headed east, towards the sea and towards the villages.

Fearghus began to run. He was going to go right through those snakes and warn the villagers. Nearly stumbling a few times, he ran over the slithering snakes, disregarding all of the snakes that he killed along the way. He had to take long strides in this mass of serpents, to keep from slipping.

Soon, he was ahead of them, and he began to sprint faster and faster, until the thatch of the village began to appear. There were a few men walking about the streets, clothed in robes, and as Fearghus ran by, one of them shouted, "Hey, boy, what's going on! Did a wolf get one a' your goats?"

Fearghus turned around abruptly and said, "No, just a couple thousand snakes,"

"That's crazy!" retorted the old, bearded man. "Impossible! Where do you get these stories from!"

"They're as true as your beard is long," Fearghus responded, calmly. "And those snakes are headed this way," he added.

"Maybe he's right!" the other man prodded, shakily.

"Hold your tongue, Flann! This boy is crazed! Can't you tell?"

"I certainly am not! But don't worry, the snakes are harmless. They just slither right past you," Fearghus told him. "Well, I've got to go warn the rest of the village before they get here." He turned and ran.

"Wait just a minute there, boy! I won't have you starting a panic!" cried the old man. Fearghus had scarcely turned around when the man struck him with his walking stick. Fearghus spun on his heel, brandishing his staff toward the man.

Suddenly, Flann cried, "Look, a lone snake dares to enter the public square! He's headed right for us!" And with that, Flann took off running as fast as he could. But Fearghus stopped him.

"They are harmless, Flann. I saw them myself," he said.

"No, I don't have to listen to you," cried Flann, "If we hesitate, the snakes will get us all!" And he broke away from them and ran, crazed, into the night.

"I'm not finished with you, boy, we still have a score to settle!" And the old man swung his cane mightily at Fearghus's head.

Fearghus parried and returned a blow with his staff. The old man blocked it and swung again, hitting Fearghus's thigh hard. "Respect your elders, boy! May the gods take you for this sin!"

Suddenly, more snakes came into the light. They were coming in droves now, quicker and quicker, until the square was filled with them. The old man didn't notice them in all his hurry to beat Fearghus. "Look, they are here!" cried Fearghus suddenly, pointing to the ground. But the old man would not hear him and struck a deafening crack to his head.

Staggering, Fearghus dropped his staff and slipped on a snake. He fell down hard, and dazedly looked up. The old man pointed his cane at Fearghus and cried, "By the power of Sucellos, I curse thee, boy!" And then as Fearghus looked on, a snake appeared literally out of nowhere, threw up its head, and bit the man dead by the heel. Breathing a last, painful breath, the man toppled like a great tree under the axe.

Fearfully, Fearghus struggled to his feet and ran for his life. As he passed the East Gate, Flann appeared out of the shadows and seeing his friend dead in the street, he ran about wildly, calling "The Snakes! The Snakes! They'll kill us all!" to the villagers.

Fearghus spun around, and running into the midst of the snakes, he snatched Flann by the arm. "We must run, Flann! We must save ourselves while we can!" Fearghus was quite evidently struck with the idea that the snakes had now become hostile.

"No!" cried Flann, pulling away. "If it be the will of the gods, then I shall live!" and he bravely ran back into the square, stamping on the snakes. Even as

Fearghus watched, though, a snake pulled up and bit Flann in the heel, and Fearghus stood there, horrified, as the figure of Flann crumpled to the ground next to his friend.

Now Fearghus was scared. He turned and ran, trying to leave the snakes behind. But suddenly, as he got to the end of the street, a bolt of lightning struck the ground, and everything went black. His knees buckled, and he hit the ground hard.

When he awoke, Fearghus was still lying on the ground, stupefied. The sun shone warm above, and not a sound save the happy twittering of birds could be heard. He wrinkled his face in the warm sunlight and struggled to his knees. But suddenly, as if coming out of a daze, he realized that his right arm was numb. It was not moving! He looked down as the pattern of broken light through the trees danced upon his pale limb. Nothing seemed to be wrong. His arm was perfectly full and smooth; there were no apparent bruises upon it.

Putting all of his weight upon his left arm, now, he pushed himself up to his wobbly feet. Righting himself, he stared down the street and into the deserted village square. This didn't seem odd at first, but there was nothing there. No crumpled bleeding bodies. No dead rotting snakes. There was nothing but some green weeds growing up through the uneven blank cracks of the pavement. But as Fearghus looked on, these weeds seemed to glow. They were so enticing, the beautiful glowing green plants. Fearghus ventured toward them, somehow hypnotized by their brilliant light.

Presently, he came upon them and reached his hand out to touch one. He now noticed that these were some kind of clover, shamrocks to be exact. The whole square now glowed with their brilliant light, long shadows of each little pebble and twig stretched across the ground in the steady green light. Then his fingers made contact with the soft leaves and the whole world exploded with blinding white light. Trying to shield his eyes, Fearghus staggered back and tripped upon the pavement and fell, the white light burning in his eyes. Planting both his arms in the ground, he hoisted himself up and leapt at the source of the light, giving a great cry of anguish.

He slammed into the ground with a deafening thud. All of the mysterious light was gone, and he was lying, facedown, with a mysterious weight pressing down on his body. He got up and grabbed his staff, and looked about the deserted town. In the lazy morning sun, he leaned his head upon the top of his staff. Suddenly, a sharp pain shot through his cheek and blood flowed down his neck. He quickly withdrew his staff from his face and looked down at it. It was no longer a staff, but a great lance, with an array of smooth gems all about it, and a blinding silver head fixed at the top, his blood gleaming upon the point. As he looked down at the shiny hardwood shaft, he noticed something else. His hand was clothed in a fine leather gauntlet, decorated with elaborate gold and silver embroidery at the bottom. His fingers strained against an array of golden rings fixed about his hand.

As he looked down his hand, he noticed a large, glimmering cuff fixed about his forearm and an elaborate crimson tunic set loosely about his shoulders. There was a strong bronze breastplate on his chest and the long, jeweled hilt of a sword jutted out from his belt. There was even a heavy golden helmet strapped to his head, and a small round shield of steel on his back. Fearghus nearly lost his breath in awe of this amazing transfiguration. His arm was strong again, as well, and his whole body was bursting with hard, chiseled muscle.

Presently, he looked up and again surveyed the deserted city. The early morning sun bathed the dusty streets and thatched roofs with its beauty, and the trees swayed in a light, salty breeze. Fearghus thought to himself for a moment. Shouldn't he go thank the gods for this? Surely the village temple would be open. He briskly jogged down to the thatched hut and drew back the curtain about the door. The smell of death greeted him. He crept inside and let the sunlight pour into the temple. In the faint rays, in the back of the temple, the golden statue of Sucellos gleamed. Fearghus, hesitantly, with his lance raised, crept toward the statue. Suddenly, he tripped over something. Looking down, he could make out the figure of the old magus, the keeper of the shrine, rotting at his feet. He had two huge holes in his white head, and black, dried blood stained his holy garments. Fearghus could not look at such a terrible sight. Stepping over the corpse, he came upon the ghostly shrine and reached out to touch the feet of Sucellos, the ruler of the gods.

As he did so, he noticed behind the statue what appeared to be two white, glowing sabers, and like Roman pillars they sat on either side of the holy statue, framing it in the white light. Fearghus stopped and withdrew his hand immediately, raising his lance in uncertainty. Then, as if on cue, the two sabers closed about the statue, and darkness enveloped the head of Sucellos. All of a sudden, two red eyes opened simultaneously in front of him, and they were the eyes of a great snake. With a start, Fearghus plunged his lance into one of the eyes and bolted out of the temple with his back turned. When he got out into the street, he spun around and drew his blade for the first time. The sharp edge of steel hissed against the mouth of its scabbard. In its blinding light he almost couldn't see when the great serpent leapt out of the temple door and coiled itself in front of him, reeling back its head to strike.

And it did. Fearghus had barely just enough time to jump out of the way before the two huge sabers pierced the ground where he was standing. Again facing the creature, he noticed his lance protruding from its eye, and the point, now black with venom, was sticking out of the back of its scaly head.

Now he had to do something quickly before he was dead. Realizing the hopelessness of the situation, he gave a great cry and charged with his sword raised, swinging the clean metal in the warm air. He ran right to the serpent's belly as it raised his head for another strike and then swung his sword hard into the snake's soft skin, through the soft, slimy flesh and the slippery hard bones, cutting a deep gash that exploded with black, venomous blood. Prepared for this, Fearghus sprang off of his feet, out of the way of the wound, and hit the ground hard as the snake's head again struck the ground with amazing force. Now blood was pouring in gallons out of the serpent's belly, and a foul stench filled the air. The serpent was reeling now, his head swinging about with the big lance through it, while his bloody belly dragged venom across the dusty street. Fearghus stood clear, his sword angled down, its former shine drowned in thick blood. He backed up in awe of the great snake, writhing back and forth, and he dared not approach it.

Presently, the snake crumpled to the ground and let out one last angry hiss before it was expired and its one eye closed with a great heave. Fearghus reluctantly drew up to it and fixed his hands about the shaft of his lance. He pulled with all his might until the lance began to slide smoothly through the flesh of the reptile. Suddenly, when the head of the lance appeared, the one eye opened, and searing venom shot out of the dead eye, covering Fearghus's gauntlets and burning his forearms. He staggered back in extreme pain, but in all of this, he just winced and leveling his lance, he cast it at the other eye. The lance stayed true and slid right into the beast's head several inches in the precise middle of the eye. Fearghus was concentrating so hard on this that he did not even notice his arms. The venom was sliding right off of them. He was completely unharmed. He looked up, short of breath for all this luck, and noticed that with both eyes gouged out, the snake had subsided once more. With not a care in the world, Fearghus brought his shield up about him and yanked his lance free.

Now Fearghus left the street momentarily and walked down to the shady meadow by the river. Propping his lance and shield against the trunk of a tree, he took his sword down to the bank and cleansed it of the blood in the sand. He placed it back in his sheath and looked out over the glimmering water. A light breeze danced across the cool stream as small fish swam about, picking at little plants and pebbles on the bed. There were many shamrocks here as there were in the street, along the riverbank where some of the snakes had drowned last night.

Sitting there, enjoying the beauty of the river, Fearghus began to think about what to do next. The town was deserted and destroyed with the corpse of a huge snake in it, many people had been killed or had fled the village, and above all, Fearghus was clothed in the finest armor and was arrayed with the finest weapons he had ever seen. This thought led to an even stranger thought: was he now to become a soldier? Had the gods blessed him in this way so that he could go forth and help his brother fight the Romans? Was it his destiny to fight and kill like this? Certainly with such experience as this large serpent he was more than qualified for a place in the fighting. He was excited now. His blood rushed through his body as he realized this and his hand, unknown to him, grabbed the hilt of his sword tightly. This certainly seemed like an admirable field. After all, that's what he had wished for in the field yesterday while he watched his flock.

This thought suddenly brought pain to him. He had left his sheep unattended in the hills last night during a rainstorm! He sprang up and snatched up his things. Beginning to run, he noticed that his feet, too, were arrayed with this nice dress. They were fitted in tough, leather sandals strung to his lower legs tightly. He was literally flying across the ground now, his cape stretched out behind him in the wind. He jumped across all the rocks and roots that crossed his path in the forests and meadows, and in no time he had reached the top of the hill where he had been last night.

He looked down at the rolling hills and attempted to find any sign of his sheep. But there was nothing but the hills and the trees in front of him. Now he had lost his flock and he would starve. But then again, he thought, while looking down at his lance, now he had lost his flock and he had found his sword. He could, if he had to, earn his keep fighting. Now proudly, he stood up and gazed across the hills once more, like a great sailor on the bow of his ship.

Suddenly, something caught his eye. It was nothing more than a glimmer, a spark of light in the distance. But it could have only come from the smooth, shiny blade of a sword or the edge of a shield. This was it! Fearghus was going now, to see what ever lie beyond that hill, to start a new life of bravery and valor! With that, he leapt off of the hill and landed upon his feet below, his sharp lance clasped menacingly in his hands. He started running again, toward the hills, the breeze blowing through his long hair. Then he remembered the drop. He stopped just in time, to avoid falling down the steep cliff that he had just reached.

He had been here before, but he had never gone past it. Now he looked straight ahead, across the flat plain before him, and what he saw brought him much anger. What he saw were Romans.

There was a whole legion of foot soldiers in small, neat columns, waves of them marching in the distance. Their helmets and shields glimmered in the sun as did his, and upon the head of one, Fearghus spied a huge plumed feather. They were certainly an imposing force. Their splendor and number would surely drive away any Celtic folk that they came near. But not him, he would never be afraid of those swine.

Now Fearghus decided to take down his helmet and weaponry and wrapped them in his cape. He turned to his right and looked down the cliff for a way down. Soon he spotted some stones and footholds and hoping his bright colors would not attract any attention, he scrambled down the wall and leapt into the brush below. He raised his brown head above the bushes and scanned the terrain. This was rare grassland, with tall wheat and grass growing all about. He knew that if he could move through this easily enough, he very well would not be spotted. He crept through the tall grass, on all fours like a dog, stopping every now and then, in case anyone saw his movement. He moved very cautiously, sometimes only making any move at all when the wind upset the grass above his head. Soon he was nearing the edges of the Roman camp, and he withdrew his weapons from his cape and refitted his armor. He leveled his lance and flitted behind a thick tree, while the Roman closest to him looked away. But the Roman had seen Fearghus's cape. It was red like his own, so he did not suspect much, but nonetheless approached the tree, speaking in what Fearghus supposed was Latin, very different from Gaelic.

Now Fearghus made up his mind, and swiveling around the trunk of the tree, he stuck his lance right into the throat of the man. The stunned Roman crumpled to the ground with not a sound as his mouth overflowed with hot, sticky blood. Fearghus gathered his cape about him and spinning back around the tree, he looked at the head of his spear. It was stained black with the venom of the serpent, and he dared not clean it, for this venom would kill his enemies with even just one prick of his lance. Now he decided he would go kill the man with the plumed feathers in his helmet, since he was no doubt the leader. Then he would escape and gather a great force to destroy the unorganized legion. Peeking around the tree trunk, he noticed that all he could use for cover would be the few other trees in the area, and also, as he looked on, there was a great silk litter parked within the camp. The Roman with the feathers was standing near this litter, no doubt guarding the man inside.

Fearghus fancied at the idea of there being an important man inside the litter who he might kill as well. Now he ran behind another tree that was close by, but he couldn't see any more trees close enough to him. He would have to kill at least three of the Roman soldiers before he could have a chance at the closest tree. Presently, he decided on one of the men, and he cast his lance. The man hadn't even gotten a chance to fall when Fearghus pounced upon the other two with his sword, slitting their throats. He quickly snatched up his spear and leapt to the other tree before more soldiers noticed him.

What he saw when he turned the other way made his heart leap with joy. There was a paddock of livestock near this tree, and along it he could creep right into the heart of the camp! On all fours once again, he stole past a number of the sheep before any started to bleat. When they did, he stopped and dropped on his belly as the Roman shepherd tried to steady them. Then Fearghus looked up. Right at the edge of the loose wooden fence was a sheep with some very odd markings on it. He had seen sheep like this before. He somehow recognized the coat of the sheep. Suddenly, he remembered. This was one of his own! The Roman swine had stolen his flock! This idea gave him a start and his muscles tightened.

As he lay there fuming, the sheep suddenly dropped dead in front of him. Suddenly all of the other sheep became very distressed and began mulling about and giving frantic cries. He had accidentally touched his sheep with the tip of his lance. Now they broke the paddock and started running all over him; The Roman shepherd gave a call of distress and Fearghus heard the footsteps of many soldiers coming to his aid. With so many sheep running on top of him, he stood up and thrust his lance into the shepherd. It was now or never. He had started this battle, and now he would have to finish it.

He brought up his shield and reluctantly threw the lance aside, drawing his sword. Swinging it above his head, he hacked down the first man that reached him and thrust the point of his sword into the second. Now a third man delivered a crushing blow to Fearghus's shield, and he reeled around and slashed the man's face. Swiveling back around to meet a new attack, Fearghus slit the soldier's throat with the sharp edge of his disc, and plunged his sword into the man behind him. There were quite simply too many men now, and new soldiers appeared and sliced into his legs and back, and little lines of warm blood ran down his body as he continued to hack down the disorganized band of attackers.

Suddenly, as he drew his sword out of one man's stomach, the soldier with the plumed helmet called aloud and all of the attackers withdrew. Fearghus, his blade gleaming with the gallons of Roman blood he had spilled, now stood in front of a huge column of archers, each one with his dart drawn back and ready to release, and each one aimed at him. Now the man with the plumed helmet spoke. "This man has committed a great crime against the Roman Empire in his action of spilling Roman blood." He said in a clear, cool voice, "Since he is not a Roman citizen, the penalty for this action is death. But realizing his great ability, I have decided that he shall become a slave under my household." This was met with a great murmur from the crowd of soldiers gathered there, and a great cheer rose among them as the archers began to close in on Fearghus. He threw down his sword and raised his arms in a sign of submission to the Romans. He had failed in his attempt to upset this legion and would now be a slave of these swine.

The archers broke into shorter groups and led Fearghus closer to the center of the camp. As Fearghus walked, he suddenly realized that the cuts and bruises he was covered with were miraculously gone, and he was healed of the fighting. He did not know what this meant, but the fact that he could bleed at all was reason enough to submit to these men around him. It would not be this day that he would fight.

Fearghus was stripped of his weaponry and was forced to march with the column of archers in chains. Anger was still on his mind, and disgust, disgust about how the Romans had treated him, laying their filthy hands all about him and taking away all of his hope. They were not too heavy on him, but the long trip to the ocean certainly was.

On the command of the centurion, a small group broke away from the legion and turned back on the path through the forest, which was now rutted and broken by many horses and wheels. Fearghus just trotted along in his sandals. He knew every stone and branch in these woods like the back of his hand. This was his home and he knew, as sure as the sun would shine, that he would return to this happy place to fight again. He looked straight ahead, as the harsh stones of the horse's hooves defiled the fair earth of Eire. He just kept his mouth shut and walked in a straight line, not giving heed to anyone about him.

Presently, the column came to a halt and the soldiers reclined on the soft earth, taking turns guarding Fearghus, who was kept upright. A number of the men jogged over to the nearby stream for water, while others cast lots for the coins and trinkets they carried with them. One man sat down near Fearghus. "Sure is unfortunate that a boy like you should come to such an end, out here in his own country," he drawled, in a heavily accented Gaelic tongue. "I was from these parts, once. I lived down near the beach. Well, that was before the Romans came," he continued, "They killed our men and raped our women. Then they took me for their army. I've served under Rome ever since."

"Haven't you ever thought of rebellion? Surely there are men among you such as yourself," Fearghus responded with his far superior Gaelic dialect.

"Quite surely I have," said the man, "but there is no use. The power of Rome stretches throughout the known world, and such a rebellion would be as a fly that tries to kill a wolf."

"But," Fearghus countered, "what if there is a demon within that fly…one that can kill the wolf."

"Don't get your hopes up, boy. There is no wolf stronger than Rome. No fly of our design could penetrate the skin of the Romans. Any attempt to bite would lead to our utter destruction!" the man muttered in his poor tongue.

"Surely you do not doubt my ability," Fearghus said calmly. "If you but spare this fly of the whip, then maybe the demon within him may come out."

The man sat there, brooding. Then suddenly, as if from no where, he drew his blade and cut Fearghus loose. He pointed his dagger at Fearghus's throat and shouted loudly, "This man has cut his bonds loose, and has attempted to escape! Now he must die!" and as he stood there a great cry rose up from the men as they gathered their arms.

The men gathered about Fearghus and the man in a crescent, their swords drawn and ready. Suddenly, the man withdrew his sword and sweeping it mightily about him in a circle, he hacked down a number of the men, who were caught at unawares. Then he drew a short dagger from his belt and tossed it to Fearghus. Between the two of them, they began to whittle down the surprised men. When a soldier's sword sliced the man's arm open, Fearghus leapt in and plunged his dagger into the man's chest. His wounded friend spun around and hacked down another guard while Fearghus stabbed unrelentingly into the mass of enemies.

Within minutes, all of the men were dead. As the last soldier made a futile attempt to prop himself up upon his sword, a great sigh of relief swept through Fearghus and the man. Fearghus and his friend were badly wounded though. The man hobbled on a lance he had acquired from one of the men, the bandaged stub of his leg hanging listlessly. Fearghus had been slashed a number of times by the blades of the soldiers, and blood ran down his back where it had earlier that day. They could not go on.

As he had expected though, Fearghus's wounds healed very quickly. Even so, he stayed with his friend to the last breath. "It's a miracle!" cried the man in a hoarse voice, observing Fearghus's healing wounds.

"Yes, it is a miracle that we have escaped," Fearghus told the man softly. Then, as he looked on, his friend reclined on the trunk of a tree and expired. With a broad Roman sword, Fearghus dug the man's grave in the soft earth and covered the hole with a mound of sweet-smelling soil. Upon it he set the man's sword and helmet, in memoriam to his late friend's heroic actions.

Now, with a heavy heart, Fearghus took with him a broad sword and shield. Wrapping himself in a long, red cape, he bounded off into the dark forest, in search of aid.

Long and hard, Fearghus padded through the green woods. His load was light upon his back, and the undying power of anger and hate propelled him faster than he had ever gone before. The wind blew in his face furiously as he slipped through the bushes, into the west, where help might still be found, a village or fortress that the Romans had not yet defiled, into the sunset where one last ember of the dying sun might soon be blown back to life.

Then the night crept over him like a rippling black cloth and shut out the light of day. He slowed down and halted beside a tree. He knelt down and gathered some brush in his fist. Off the blade of his sword, the last rays of sunlight shone upon the brush in his hand warmly, and Fearghus noticed that there in his hand was a shamrock. Now he struck a small flint stone in his tunic with the blade of his sword, and the brush caught fire.

Then as the shamrock became engulfed in the flames, a very strange thing happened. It suddenly began to regain its color, and as it grew greener and greener the light about it grew brighter and brighter. Soon it was too bright to see. Fearghus staggered back in the white light and very quickly a familiar heaviness came upon his body. When he opened his eyes, the splendor of his former dress glittered in the light of a huge bonfire. The dull Roman blade had become his sword, and a large dead branch nearby had miraculously become his lance. His power had been restored.

That night, the great bonfire did not die. It had a particular warmness about it, and Fearghus huddled by it, thinking to himself about these things. Certainly now it was certain. The gods had selected him to be a great warrior and a protector of the land, and they had given him the gifts of immortality and great weaponry to go about doing it. Fearghus had made up his mind. Now, in the best interest of the gods, he would go forth and gather up a great host against the Romans, and by the power of the gods he would destroy them under an open sky. And their poisonous blood would flow back into the sea where it came from, and the land would be rid of their curses.

With no fear now, Fearghus slept in great content. The warm light of the everlasting fire washed over him and he had many wonderful dreams. In the morning, the fire had left, with no sign remaining. Fearghus gathered up his weaponry and jogged off down the dry trail of the forest. Today was a very cloudy day.

Fearghus took in the sights and sounds of the forest as he lightly padded along the rocky path. His armor seemed almost too bright and splendid to be a part of this world. Little brown birds flitted around above his head, while small frogs and toads scuffled about in the leaves. Sights like this almost caused Fearghus to put a little good-spirited swagger in his step, but the matter on his mind was too important. He was now very determined to get back at the Romans for what they had done to his people.

Fearghus decided he would stop back at the village for a while, and if there was no business to settle there, he would just continue to go inland until he reached another one. Now it was still a long way to reach the village, and Fearghus had not eaten for nearly three days. He would have to eat very soon. There were probably a great number of wild animals in the forest, and all he had to do was find one. Even with his great muscle and endurance, hunger burned inside him. He longed for a leg of mutton or a plate of corn bread.

So, Fearghus looked down at his jeweled lance and stepped off of the beaten path, and into the thick brush. Even with his strong leather sandals, Fearghus's legs were scratched and poked with the bushes and debris that littered the overgrown forest floor. As he picked through the trees, he tried not to lose sight of the thin forest trail, but he soon realized that he would have to leave it in order to find food.

Soon, he found himself chopping away at the tangled branches in front of him with his long sword. He was now very far from the trail and his only hope was to find some kind of clearing in the forest where he could go about his hunting. It was nearly impossible to find anything in this kind of foliage, though. The light above him was quickly disappearing in the increasingly dense canopy of leaves. Nonetheless, he continued to clear away the branches.

Suddenly, there was a break in the leaves in front of him. Through it, he could see the gloomy sky rising up in front of him. It was just the usual, dull, cloudy Eire sky, but as he looked on, he began to see a trail of smoke flowing up from the ground. This was no doubt a sign of human civilization, perhaps a village or city. In any case, these people would have food and drink ready for him. Although he had never been in this area of the forest, he knew that these people, whoever they were, would be friendly.

He cut through some more low branches and the dullness of a cut wooden wall began to appear in his path. It seemed to him an isolated building, closely put to all of the trees about it, and from the outside, it looked almost deserted. Thick ivy and clover grew right up to the edge of the hut, and a rotting wagon, overgrown with foliage, was parked some distance away from the front door of the house. These signs suggested the absence of any residents, but the loose column of smoke coming through the roof told Fearghus that someone was here and that that someone had a need of fire right now.

Slowly picking his way through the clutter of plants on the ground, Fearghus, not taking any armed precaution, made his way towards the door of the hut. Suddenly, he stumbled into a depression in the ground running with water. Looking down at the small stream, he noticed that it was very warm on his feet. In fact, in the sunlight, a fine mist was blowing off of it in the breeze. Fearghus knew this could only mean one thing. The occupant of this hut was a smith of some sort. This man would have the means of producing any thing from chain links to heavy metal armor. But in this light, he could also be dangerously armed with things such as spears and daggers. Fearghus would not arm himself right away in the interest of possibly benefiting from this man's trade. He could use this forging facility to supply his rebellion.

Now he swept his cape back, exposing the jeweled hilt of his weapon and his smooth armor, and standing upright, he marched right to the door of the hut and beat on it calmly with his fist. No one answered. Fearghus held his ground and beat the wooden planks all the harder. As he listened, a great scuffling came from within the hut and the column of smoke above Fearghus's head disappeared. Fearghus knew now what he had to do to get this frightened man out. He withdrew his hand from the door, and spoke clearly in his native language. "I am a friend," he calmly recited into the coarse wooden door.

Fearghus heard footsteps approaching the door, coupled with the sound of clanking chain mail and heavy swords. The door opened very slightly. In the small slit between the door and the wall, a small, red-faced man peered out. Below, Fearghus could see that he was girt with a shimmering, broad long blade, and, more to his discomfort, the man had a huge crossbow leveled at him. The huge, black point seemed almost too large for the small stature of the balding man.

Fearghus did not draw, nor did he run away. He held his ground and tried his luck at conversation. "I am Fearghus. I do not come to harm you. I come from the village not too far from here. I have just escaped from the harsh treatment of the Romans, and I seek shelter."

"Romans! There are Romans in these parts, you say?" the man asked, in a primitive drawl of Fearghus's Gaelic language.

"Yes, not but a few leagues east down the road here. I have very recently broken away from a full column of the swine," Fearghus replied calmly.

"Come, in, tell me more about your adventures," the short man panted, opening the door wider and lowering his weapon.

Fearghus, keeping his chin up, strode into the small edifice, looking around. Almost immediately in front of the door there sat a rough, slanting table, surrounded by short, sawn cedar stools. Atop the table sat a flask of mead, and a large, sloppy map of linen paper. The whole room was full of gleaming bronze and iron swords, as well as a great number of spearheads and daggers. Upon wooden pegs, here hung some of the greatest size battle axes Fearghus had ever seen. The man certainly had a nice, cozy place here, with a great earthen mantle in the middle and a comfortable bed of hay. "You must be a smithy, my friend," Fearghus said.

"Why, yes!" the man replied, wringing his hands. "But surely I cannot match weapons of your quality," he added, looking at Fearghus's jeweled sword and lance.

"Maybe not," Fearghus responded, sweeping his cloak about his weaponry. "But I think you'll do very well."

"What do you mean, oh great one?" the humble man asked with quick, sloppy bow.

"I think you can help me supply my rebellion, my friend," Fearghus replied, sitting down heavily on one of the stools.

"A rebellion? Where is the sense in that?" the man stuttered, unconsciously groping at the mantle of his forge. "It would be too dangerous!"

"Yes, it would, but I need your help, for the good of Eire," Fearghus told him, rapping his knuckles on the table.

"I will be honored to accommodate your request, oh great one, but I still cannot push myself to participate in such a foolhardy quest." The man's face seemed to be getting redder with every word.

"But you must, my friend," Fearghus retorted, his voice getting louder. Suddenly, the man snatched up his crossbow again and leveled it at Fearghus's chest. This was a very sudden turn of events for Fearghus, who now had to think of a way of escaping. His eyes locked upon the man's snarling face.

"You cannot fool me!" he shouted very surprisingly. "Get out of my house!" he continued. Now Fearghus had to think of something quick. His eyes darted back and forth across the room. Then they fell on his lance. If he knew this magic well enough, then his idea would work. Slowly, he got up and walked toward the door.

"I mean you no harm," he calmly said. Now he slowly slid his fingers around the shaft of his spear and spun around to face the man. "If you help me, I shall give you my great lance," Fearghus recited. The man's face dropped, and he slowly lowered his black arrow. He looked around at the coarse walls of his cabin and sighed.

"What is it you ask of me?" he asked. Fearghus strode forward and placed the long lance into the man's hands and sat back down.

"I wish to carry away from here a multitude of weaponry from your store, to supply my rebellion. All I ask for, in return for this gift, are a wagon and about three hundred swords within it. Will you help me defeat the Romans?" Fearghus's eyes concentrated on the man's face. Slowly, the man's lips curled into a grin as he looked at the lance.

"I shall," he almost shouted, "I certainly will help you." Now he dropped the lance and ran back to the forge. He began to gather huge bundles of clanking iron swords upon his shoulders. Then he ran out side and threw them into the rotting cart. His red face scrunched up under the weight of this task. He repeated this several times until the entire bed of the wagon was covered with the white wrapping cloth. Then he stopped. "Will that be all?" he asked, panting in the sun.

"No, my friend," Fearghus replied, "If you will, I will pay fifty pieces of gold if you will fit new wheels upon the cart."

"Right away," the man responded. Fearghus watched him as he disappeared into his house, and then emerged with a large axe. Fearghus frowned at the rusty, dull blade, not even a drop of sun glinting off of it. "This will take a while," he informed Fearghus. Now he hurried over to a very large tree, and began to hack at it with his axe. The large, awkward tool took mere chips out of the sturdy trunk.

"Please, allow me," Fearghus said, and took the axe from him. Now he stepped back and swung the axe with all his might. In a flash of green light, the axe slid right through the wood like a blade through churned butter. With just one blow, the tree gave way and, creaking violently, it fell.

"How did you do that?" the man said, stupefied. He stumbled back, his eyes fixed on the fallen timber. Next Fearghus positioned himself again and with two great blows and two flashes of light, he hewed out an even log, just big enough for the four sawn wheels to be cut from. Now, in yet another feat of strength, he picked up the log and handed it to the man. There was an obvious sense of amazement in the stranger's eyes as he dazedly dropped to his knees under the weight.

Stuttering, he slowly struggled to his feet. "I'll get to them right away, sir," he said in a muted, heavy voice. "The wheels, that is…" he added, painfully turning his head to face Fearghus. He slowly stumbled his way over to a small clearing next to the wooden wall of his shed and the great log rolled off his knees to rest upon the dry earth. Fearghus looked around and observed that this little clearing was adorned with a great many tools and forged items. Large stacks of clean, white lumber lined the outer limits of the flat land and mallets, chisels, hatchets and pickaxes lay in heaps about the great log.

Fearghus watched as the stout man snatched up an expertly forged saw and began to cut the first wheel with renewed vigor. He sat down on a wooden stool and pulled up his leather apron. His eyes squinted in the cloud of sawdust and he began to pant heavily. The rays of the sun began to appear in the dust and Fearghus saw the man in a new light. He would be a great warrior and a true friend to him in the future.

Soon, the man had sawn three more wheels just like the first, and sat gazing at the rough bark. "I'll have to rub these down, he sighed, puffing into his fist. Not even getting up now, he leaned over and groped for a large grinding stone, half buried in the earth. Now, grabbing one of the wheels in one hand and the stone in the other, he began to furiously sand the wheels, scraping away the bark and exposing the young, smooth wood below.

Within an hour's time, he had finished all four wheels. All four looked the same, sanded to a clean white finish. Now the man lumbered over to his piles and drew forth four even flat slats of wood, and very quickly had trimmed them to fit the diameter of the wheels. Next, using the width of one slat, he skillfully found the midsection of the slats and marked them with the tip of a small knife from his cloak. Stacking them neatly off to the side now, he smiled and disappeared into his hut.

A few minutes later, he emerged with the wheels, the slats nailed in, and a set of sanded wooden rods leaning upon his shoulder. "Let me help you with that," Fearghus said, and quickly stepped forward and lightly picked up the front end of the old wagon. The man only smiled and setting down his load, he slid one of the wooden axles into the frame of the wagon. Then he nailed the wheels on with strange pins of his own design.

Soon the wagon was ready. Sturdy sawn discs now replaced the delicate rotting wheels, and the bed was filled with an array of proud metal swords. Fearghus walked over to the man, and, praying to the gods, he reached into his cape and just like he had expected, his hand drew forth a velvet bag of fifty gold coins. "Here is your payment, friend," he said as he handed the bag to the man. The coins had appeared spontaneously and rather magically within his robes, just as he had hoped. The gods certainly were granting his every wish as he dreamed it.

"Keep it to yourself," the stranger said, gently pushing the bag aside, "and call me by my name, Conn."

"Well thank you very much, Conn," Fearghus replied. Then he turned and walked towards the wagon. He paused for a second. "Conn, might you have a bit of rope with you?" he asked.

"Of course I do," said Conn, and disappeared into his house. He returned a few minutes later with a good length of tether and handed it to Fearghus. "Now, you had better get going before it is dark," Conn told him and patted him on the back.

Fearghus fastened the rope to the front of the wagon, and positioned it over his shoulders. He pulled the wagon out of the mud, and found a space between the trees in front of him. "Good bye, Conn!" he shouted, not too loud. Then he lowered his back and pulled the heavy wagon out of the clearing. Immediately he discovered a need to draw his sword, and began to hack away at the edges of the footpath furiously. "The road is but a few miles away!" Conn shouted behind him, "You're headed in the right direction!"

Fearghus smiled and pulled the cart even harder. Soon the sound of Conn stirring grew fainter and fainter, and soon he was all alone, noisily struggling his way through the dense woods of Eire. He was making great progress he thought, and the load about his shoulders never seemed so light. The cool breeze of night began to sooth his face, and as he looked about at the rough trees and dark green foliage, he noticed, a short distance away, a tan, dusty road, like a river of white sand in the dark forest. Now, with all his might, he wrenched the cart from between two trees and burst into the lane, nearly stumbling. He looked around. The road was like a deep chasm. Above his head he could only but see a narrow strip of the darkening sky. The brilliant light of dusk barely touched his face as he gazed up to the heavens.

Presently, he found a break in the trees by the side of the road and there hid his wagon. With a sigh, he placed his sword back into its sheath and prepared to sleep in his armor. Still alertly looking about, he walked over to his wagon and, skillfully hiding its contents, he drew forth a section of the white cloth that covered his store of swords. Then he pushed away some foliage and prepared a sleeping place hidden behind his wagon in the trees.

For good measure, Fearghus drew his sword and set out to cut down some tree limbs to further hide his wagon. He stumbled a few yards into the woods and looking above him, he hacked down a thick, sappy limb from a beech tree. When he had done this, the limb fell heavily upon the earth at his feet. He took a step forward and suddenly halted. It felt like he had just stepped upon a bit of cloth.

He slowly looked down. Right under his sandals, gray and rotting, covered in black scars, was a human arm, clothed in a dingy black sleeve.

This would be no matter except that, as Fearghus looked on, he noticed a ring. It was a square, flat-topped, golden ring, with a strange symbol on it. It appeared to be a serpent. Suddenly, it came to him. This was the symbol of a division of the druids. Fearghus was horrified to be looking at the hand of a magus!

Oh how horrible that a respectable servant of the gods should come to such an end! Who could have done this? The Romans had done it, of course. They had killed a holy magus and tried to hide the body in the woods. Now more than ever, Fearghus wanted revenge. He wanted to get back at these invaders for what they were doing to his people. This was a very serious matter now.

Presently, Fearghus covered the hand with dirt using his broad sword and continued cutting down the tree limbs for his wagon. He hacked at them harder and harder, his grip growing stronger with his fury. Soon, he had cut quite a sizable amount of branches. He turned around and sheathing his sword, he dragged the huge limbs back to the wagon by the side of the road, and began to place them. He put the first huge branch across the top of the wagon, hiding its load, and leaned the remaining limbs beside it, making a thick cover of leaves for him to sleep behind.

Finally, he pushed the section of white cloth against the trunk of a tree, wrapped his cape as somewhat of a cloak about him, and laid back to rest. He set his helmet beside him and looked up to the highest tree. Just barely, he noticed, he could see the great violet sky above, just peeking through the dark branches. The stars were just coming out, and it seemed to him that the brightest one was looking right down on him. For a moment now, he slowed down, and his anger left him. Tomorrow he would begin his rebellion, but tonight, he would rest under the great heavens, the realm of the gods.

Chapter 2

▼

The Battle Begins

Fearghus awoke to the sun piercing the high limbs of the trees, searing his face with its brilliant light. He struggled to his elbow and looked about at the beautiful sunlit world. Right away he snatched up his helmet and adjusted his belt. He had a lot to do today. He scrambled to his feet and quickly began to push away the branches from the wagon. They were like twigs in his hands. Under them, the sword-filled wagon sat contentedly upon its sawn wheels.

Not wanting to waste any time, Fearghus grabbed the rope on the front of the wagon and with a grunt, he yanked it out of the woods. Now he began to pull it down the road, planting each foot in front of the other, taking his time. The entire world around him looked the same, just harsh brown trunks and green leaves right up to the dusty road. Wispy clouds hung like curtains in the narrow sky above, as the sun broke through the dreary forest canopy like a knife. But as Fearghus looked on, he noticed something was wrong. Just over the edge of the trees he could see a vast plume of smoke towering up to the sky. Such a thick, black type of smoke, it could only mean one thing. A building was burning down.

Fearghus decided it would be best to go investigate this, and so he turned to the side and once again he pushed the wagon into the forest between two trees. Then he drew his sword. He knew this could be trouble, and possibly with the Romans, so he would have to be prepared. His sword glinting in the light of dawn, he ambled towards the edge of the road.

Suddenly, an arrow zipped past his ear and smashed into the trunk of a tree in front of him, splitting the wood. Fearghus only stood there as the shaft vibrated next to his head. Then suddenly, in a flash, he spun around and brought his sword up to his face. An arrow zinged off of his blade, falling to the forest floor. Bringing down his sword, he found himself looking straight at the point of a black Roman dart.

"It's time to go back, my slave," the man on the other end said. Fearghus then knew that this was indeed the Roman with the plumed helmet. There it was, the red feathers blowing in the breeze, the helmet of a Roman centurion.

Fearghus was filled with rage now. His sword seemed suddenly feather-light in his hands, and within his gauntlets, his knuckles turned white in his grip. "Lay down your arms, slave, and proclaim fealty to your master," the centurion pressed. But Fearghus would not listen. In one split fraction of a second, he flung himself to the right and brought up his left arm, catching the black arrow in mid-air, right of the head. Warm blood began to dribble down his forearm as a splitting pain pierced his wounded palm. But this did not delay him. Just as fast as he had dodged the arrow, he sprang up again and swung his blade full around him. The speed of his swing was hardly affected when his double-edged blade shattered not only the bow but also the nose of the centurion, who had barely any time to throw his head back. Now blood ran down the man's face, and he drew his short dagger and charged.

In a hard, strained swing, Fearghus parried, bringing his sword up to his chest. Then it was his turn. In an intricate move of his hands, he slipped his way past the sword of the centurion and slashed the leather armor of the man to shreds. Blood already pouring down his face, the centurion suddenly lunged at Fearghus. His great fist was suddenly upon Fearghus's wrist, and his sword pointed at his throat. Fearghus's own blade hung uselessly in his loosening grip, while the angry centurion scrunched up his face in both anger and agony. "Now it is time for you to die, you foolish peasant!" he cried, and plunged his sword into Fearghus's neck.

But suddenly, the pain was gone from Fearghus. The sword splintered upon his skin. By the power of the gods, he would not be able to die! Now, for the first time, Fearghus discovered a look of fear upon the centurion's face. He drew back his shattered blade and his mouth opened wide in amazement. Now he knew he had to do something quick. He suddenly withdrew his hands and fixed them around Fearghus's neck. "In God's name, I shall slay thee here today, you wretched slave!" he cried, tightening his grip. But Fearghus's neck was as if made of steel. The man's fingers strained in vain upon his muscles.

Then the centurion tried something different. After one last futile attempt to slice open Fearghus's skin, he leapt up and ran as fast as he could in the other direction. He dropped his sword and tore his cape off and his great helmet, and humbling himself before Fearghus, he made for the other side of the road. Now the anger had reached its peak in Fearghus. And now was time for the magic of the gods to come through again. He picked up a branch from the ground and cast it at the centurion. Just as he had expected, in midair, the stick turned into the golden spear that he had left at Conn's abode and the lance went right through the man's back and split the tree in front of him with great force. Fearghus watched as the man slowly dropped to his knees and began his last few labored breaths, his hands laid flat against the huge hole in his flesh. Finally, he fell forward upon his knees and expired.

Suddenly, lightning rent the ground and thunder sounded above. A huge, blinding bolt landed upon the centurion. The limbs of the bolt splayed out and their small, white hot fingers slashed at the trees violently. Fearghus was thrown back by the blast and hit the trunk of a tree with a hard thud. When he righted himself, he could see huge fires blazing on all the ground about him. The centurion was completely gone. Not even a drop of blood remained from the previous fight. Not even a smoldering bit of cloth or flesh.

Now, Fearghus got up and putting all his trust in the gods, he walked right into the flames. As he had hoped, the fire had no effect on him. Now he boldly strode over to the other side of the road and grabbed the shaft of his lance. Spontaneously, a huge bolt of intense pain shot up his arm and engulfed his whole body. He looked down and saw the spear gleaming, white-hot like the lightning had. And he also discovered that he could not withdraw his hand from it. Painfully, he jerked it loose from the tree and staggered out of the flames.

Was this the work of the one God the centurion had been talking about? Was He getting revenge upon him for killing one of His people? Now his clothes were burning in the fire and his armor was being seared off. There was only one thing to do. He stumbled his way out of the fire, and crouching down, he prayed to the gods. Maybe they could help him defeat this God of the Romans. And slowly, as if by magic, it worked. As the flames began to go out, Fearghus became increasingly tired, and fell asleep upon the ground, still clutching the spear.

When he awoke, the sun was shining again like it previously had, and a cool breeze blew through the hollow forest, whistling as it pleased. Fearghus now lifted his head and looked about. The armor upon him seemed as if reshaped, and new, stronger muscles strained against it. His sword remained girt at his side, as before, but one thing was missing. Grasped tightly in both hands, where previously was his lance, was that branch which he had originally cast at the centurion. Fearghus looked in amazement at it. Where was his jeweled spear?

Quickly he let go of the stick and then snatched it up again. Nothing happened. Then he picked up another branch that was lying nearby at the edge of the road, but still, he did not see his great lance. The God of the centurion had stolen his weapon from him. Now he would have to use what remained to him to fulfill the wishes of his own gods. Fearghus quickly jumped to his feet and drew his sword, the blade burning bright in the heavy sun of midday. Almost playfully, almost childishly, he thrust it in the air and swung it about, giving a great battle cry of his own design. He was back, and stronger than before.

In the blinding light of the sun, something suddenly caught Fearghus's eye. It was that same plume of smoke he had seen before, rising above the tops of the trees. Fearghus's grip tightened on the hilt of his blade. He knew a building was burning and that the Romans had something to do with it. Now, just as he had done before, he decided he would cut his way right through the forest brush and reach that distressed house.

With nothing more to settle, Fearghus set his mind and literally lunged at the forest, hacking down branches from the very start. His blade flashing in the muted rays of the far away sun, he made quick work of all of the little, dried out branches that clouded his path. He was moving much faster than he had with the wagon behind him. He did not fear death, or the thought of getting lost. What drove him on now was an intense anger, one deeper than he had ever felt, one directed right at the Romans and their corrupt religion.

From time to time, he was able to look up through a break in the thickening forest canopy and what he saw made him almost sinisterly happy. The plume of smoke lay right in his path, getting closer and closer, growing higher and higher as he walked towards it. It was getting close to possibly a large battle or a small skirmish. Fearghus's sword was thirsty for Roman blood, and he was confident where it might find some.

Presently, a large clearing came into sight. Within it Fearghus spied a large wooden shack. Then it came to him. This was Conn's forge! He had found his friends abode once again, and from it came the large plume of smoke that had brought him so much concern. Now Fearghus raised his sword and slowly began to circle around the smoldering walls of the forge.

Finally, he came around the corner and saw what this battle had left. Quickly Fearghus began counting. Lying dead upon the dirty, unkempt ground were twelve Roman soldiers, each with a black iron sword stuck in him, angled straight up. As Fearghus neared the front door, he spied a thirteenth soldier, a proud centurion like the one he had just faced. He was leaning over a barrel, his plumed helmet dented and lying upon the ground, the feathers smoldering. This one did not have a sword pinning him to the ground. A large black arrow, the size of a small lance, stuck out of his side, gleaming with fresh blood.

Suddenly, as he looked on, Fearghus noted that the man was not entirely dead. His feet began to move, and his knuckles grew white as he hopelessly clutched the rim of the barrel. Fearghus raised his sword as Conn's slippery arrow slid out of the man's bloody wound. Raising both hands over his head, he aimed and thrust his blade down into neck of the soldier. The body gave a small jump, and expired, sliding off of the barrel and thudding on the ground. Fearghus withdrew his sword, and finding one of Conn's black swords nearby, he pinned the man to the ground in a like fashion as Conn had done to the others, and walked towards the door, prepared for battle.

He decided it would be smart to rush the men inside, so he ran now, and kicked the door open, jumping into a crouched position, his sword flung wide, swinging around violently. But no Roman blades met him. It was only Conn, sitting upon one of his sawn stools, happily enjoying a flask of mead and trying with a little trouble to reload his huge bow. "Come in, come in!" he cried, wiping his lips upon his sleeve. "I've had a run-in with a few Romans, you may've noticed," Conn said, grinning over his bottle. "Take a seat!"

"Thank you, Conn." Fearghus replied, and came to rest on another identical stool. "I saw the smoke and came running," he told Conn.

"Well, you must not have run very fast, for these men have been dead for a while," Conn humored.

"I had a little trouble too," Fearghus replied.

"Eh, you been using that spear a' yours? I thought you'd taken it back."

"Not exactly, friend," Fearghus countered.

"You'll find some way to pay me back," said Conn with an even bigger grin.

"Well, friend, I was wondering if you'd do me another favor," Fearghus said as he pulled his money bag back out of his cape. "Can I have a look at that map of yours, Conn?"

"Sure! Of course you can!" Conn muttered, bringing the flask back to his lips. He took a long sip and leaned over the crooked table, turning the map towards them. "Well, over here, a few miles north, is the house a' my old friend Irial, a timber man. He's very nice, but also very messy. He'll have a large clearing around his house." Conn pointed at an intricately drawn house on the scrap of paper in the middle of a large break in the blanket of trees depicted.

"Can he give me any aid in the case of an emergency?" Fearghus prodded.

"Well, he won't fight for you, if that's what you're asking," Conn told him. "But he's sure to have a warm bed and a stomach-full of good food." Now Conn looked back down at the map. He pointed at a large group of drawn houses and small huts. "This here is the village, as we usually call it. To some, it's just a few houses full of superstitious lunatics and cowards. But I know better. There's a man there named Tuathal. He can help you coordinate your rebellion. You'd be a smart fellow to go to him."

"This man, Tuathal, lives quite a bit away, doesn't he?" asked Fearghus.

"Well, yes, if you go by foot, that is. But if you drive over, its only a short distance."

"Conn, how do you suppose I will get there before a heavier invasion is set?" Fearghus asked.

"I thought you might ask," Conn muttered. "You don't think these Romans walk on foot either, do you? I have a Roman horse strung up in the woods just over a few paces, and I can rent him out to you…for a small price."

"That sounds great!" Fearghus roared, and spilled forth his magic golden coins all over the table. "Take all of this, Conn. It should do." Conn's face erupted with pleasure as the coins glinted in the front door's light. As he grabbed fervently at the money, making little stacks, Fearghus walked leisurely out of the hut and looked around. It didn't take long before he noticed a large white stallion tethered to a small sapling, a few feet into the forest cover. Gently stroking its finely groomed mane, he slowly untied it and led it into the clearing, guiding it around the mess of corpses littering the ground.

He decided that with the tether, he would have enough rope to make some kind of a makeshift harness for the animal. He was just beginning to head back to the footpath when Conn burst out of his shack. "You might need this, Fearghus!" he yelled drunkenly, swinging a large battle-axe in the air. Fearghus, still holding the tether, stumbled over to Conn and snatched it out of his shaking hands. "I'd thought you might want it…when the Romans come after you," he muttered. "Made it myself, even cut the wood," he added with a grin. He was not too afraid of Fearghus's jeweled weapons now, and nearly seemed to be boasting his workmanship.

"Thank you, Conn, and may our paths meet again." Fearghus strained, bowing his head quickly. Then, with a wave, he turned on his heel and strode towards the trees. Fearghus was already several paces into the path when Conn's door slammed with ringing finality. The path he was taking was the one he had cut for himself with the wagon only yesterday. Soon he would again reach the dangerous road and then it would only be a short walk to the woods where he had left the wagon hidden.

It was still close to midday and Fearghus's step only quickened as he neared the brightly-lit thoroughfare. He had now become accustomed to the clip-clop of the horse's shod hooves on the hardening earth. As he finally came to the end of the trees and stepped out into the sandy road, he could hardly believe the splendor and radiance of Conn's axe. Of course it paled in comparison to Fearghus's higher grade of magical weaponry, but it was special, a gift from a close friend. And of course, even a brawny Roman soldier would think twice about attacking a man with this kind of weapon. Fearghus smiled at the sight of the hefty steel blade swinging back and forth in front of him as he walked.

Looking up into the blazing blue sky, he turned north and tugged lightly at the fair beast, instructing it to continue to follow him. He knew that his wagon with all of its supplies was only just a mile away, and that on the beaten road he would have very little trouble reaching it.

Soon, as he thought he had almost reached his destination, the soothing sound of the horse's hooves became muffled. Very far away, he could here the sound of another horse, and this one was galloping. Also, as it neared him, he could hear the pained sound of a man shouting at his steed to go faster, and then, the man's heavy breathing. And the voice he heard, as he had already half-expected, was in Latin.

Fearghus knew he had to do something to escape. And soon it came to only one thing. He would have to ride his horse. Although he had never any experience doing such, this was his only chance to avoid a very nasty death. He had seen other, richer men ride their mules and asses, and it didn't look very hard.

So, with a deep breath, Fearghus set both hands upon the beast and leapt up upon its back, awkwardly righting himself. Then, with his fists wrapped tightly around the shaft of the axe and the tether, he roughly kicked the horse in the side. The animal reared slightly and with a great neighing, it began to bob up and down as it sprinted. Fearghus was knocked back by this at first, but holding steadily on the tether rope, he was able to hold on as he bulleted down the road. He didn't look back, but he knew the man would be upon him now. He just crouched low in his seat and looked straight ahead.

Then, it hit him—his wagon was coming up on the right and very fast. He thought about dismounting, but this seemed all too foolhardy. But it did seem smart to stop. Now, breathing heavily, he almost drunkenly pulled up on the tether and pulled it around to face in the other direction. The Roman was right upon him. His red cape and feathers blowing violently in his wake, another

Roman centurion was headed right for him, swinging a huge barbed pike above his head. His eyes were fixed fiercely upon Fearghus, and as he neared, his lance came up, level with Fearghus's breast, aimed right at him. Fearghus realized that if he didn't do something quick, he would be run right through with the spear. The gods had let him bleed before, and burn before, and feel pain before, and he was not going to let that happen now. Upon their honor and his, he would take down this man. He would fight.

Now he suddenly had an idea. The great blade on his axe would do good to help him in this situation, he thought, but not with the ominous pike of the centurion bearing up on him. He needed the whole axe, and quickly, before it was too late. Just as the centurion neared him, he snatched up the long weapon in his one hand and with a flick of his wrist, he tossed the axe level with the rider. The shaft came up to the abdomen of the Roman and with out even breaking skin, it caught the centurion and sent him hurtling back to the ground, his horse running from under him.

Now, of course, it was all about Fearghus and his sword—and it was to be a quick skirmish. As soon as he had cast his axe, Fearghus had drawn his blade. Now, with it swinging above his head, he grabbed it in both hands and leapt off of his steed. Then, jerking his chest forward in midair, he plunged his sword downwards, right through the man. His blade plunged down in the earth to its hilt, upon which Fearghus's left and right hands slowly eased their grip.

Presently, Fearghus let go with his left hand and drew his weapon out of the ground as if out of its sheath, blood gleaming on its shiny surface, and plunged it back down into the road, cleansing it. After sheathing his blade, Fearghus leaned over and lifted his mighty axe up to his face, and in a strange way, he thanked it for being there. He had so much gratitude for Conn's generosity he could burst.

Now he had to hitch up his wagon to the white horse. Presently, he tossed his axe and his new pike into the bed of the wagon and gripping the wagon's tether tightly, he jerked it out of the woods. All this time, he had barely noticed the centurion's horse. It was still there, even after its master's death, munching on a few shrubs growing in the path. This horse could be useful.

Soon he got to work on stringing up his horses. He decided now that he could use the centurion's lance for other things. Tying the two ropes he had from Conn to the ends of the lance, he then tied the shaft of the lance to the necks of the two horses using the reins of the Roman soldier's horse. Then he knotted the ends of the two thicker ropes tightly to the hilts of two swords that he had fixed in the wood of the wagon bed. Then, straining his brain for more ideas, he made girths out of the tough leather saddle blanket that belonged to the dead soldier and fastened them tightly to the ropes. He was ready to go.

He sat himself up in the bed of the wagon and poked at the two beasts with the long shaft of his battle-axe. Slowly, he was able to convince them to start pulling with a little fierce prodding. The two exhausted animals began to trot, and Fearghus grinned in his awkward position. It wouldn't be too long before he would reach the village now, and there he could get a real wagon and supply his rebellion with the swords he now carried. From now till dusk he would just sit here, rapping the handle of his weapon on the rumps of the horses, quickly getting closer to the village.

Slowly getting to faster speeds, Fearghus was confident that he would see the village before the day was up. The horses were trotting along nicely, and his makeshift harness seemed to be holding well. He was certainly getting there faster than if he had walked. Fearghus was also confident that he wouldn't be seeing very many Romans, either. And anyway, who could stop him? He had the strength of the gods in him now, and he feared no one.

Soon, the sun began to sit low in the sky. Fearghus was very tired now. However, he knew that it was now or never, and with constant vigor, he kept on poking the horses. As the day continued to wear on, Fearghus never lost hope. He thought now that he would be very near to the village. But then, his hopes were dashed.

As Fearghus rounded a sharp twist in the winding road, he suddenly began to hear small rustling noises in the trees. And there were so many of them, that it caused him great alarm. He stopped abruptly and looked around, peeling his eyes for danger. And danger walked right up and hit him in the nose. In some of the dense bushes, he caught a glimpse of a Roman crimson cape. This was very unorthodox for Romans to be attacking this way, but he knew these particular Romans well. They had tasted his blood and the blood of his country, and they knew what to look out for. Their leader was obviously very accustomed to stealth fighting, and very likely was formerly a foreigner to Rome.

Now Fearghus knew he was in trouble. If he didn't move quickly, he would be overrun with any number of lances and arrows. Then it became clear to him. He only had one chance. Drawing two long swords out of his wagon, he slowly leaned forward and simultaneously, he stuck the extreme tips of each one into the rumps of the horses. Both of them reared, and bolted forward, nearly catching Fearghus off guard. Then the race was on.

Almost immediately, rows and rows of clean, glittering lances shot up in low arcs, some hopelessly missing the speeding wagon, others splintering on the sides and the tough sawn wheels. Fearghus was gladder than ever that he had refitted the spokes of the wheels with hard wooden discs. Countless armored foot soldiers now began to step out onto the road, leveling ominous longbows with Fearghus's crouched figure. Immediately, Fearghus drew his sword and ducked into the bed of the wagon. Then, suddenly, he popped up and swinging his sword above his head, he severed a well-aimed arrow in mid air and then with a great yell, he cut down the first archer his wagon came to and ducked back down. Now it seemed like hundreds of arrows were zipping over his head, some splitting the side of his wagon with amazing force. But then came the ultimate test.

Fearghus looked up for a second. And what he saw horrified him. The archers, now, were shooting their arrows in high, lightly strung arcs. Now he would have to think of some way to protect from above. Even as he looked on now, an arrow found its mark and clanked against the hidden swords in his wagon. Now it was time to make a stand. Suddenly Fearghus noticed the wide blade of his battle-axe and its worth.

Presently, Fearghus dared to put up his head. And, as he had expected, a shower of arrows zipped right to his face. But they were not so lucky as to hit him. The broad flat face of his battle-axe scrambled the arrows easily. Now with the slight advantage, Fearghus suddenly withdrew his shield and with a great strain of muscle, he swung the blade of the axe wide to the right, easily slicing through the soft leather armor of the archers. But as he did this, something very bad happened. An archer from the left notched his dart true and the arrow plunged into Fearghus's lower back.

Blood began to leak down his cape as a splitting pain rang through his body. He had never felt such agony. Wait a second, he was not supposed to be able to feel this. What ever happened to the healing power of the gods? How would they let an arrow pierce his skin? Now he was forced to duck down again. He was beginning to feel dazed now, and then, another problem came to him. A huge clatter of wheels and shod hooves led Fearghus to believe the Romans were giving chase. And now, he realized, his horses were beginning to slow down.

Just for a second, he popped his head up and saw the problem. The two horses were bumping into each other, and they were becoming annoyed with one another. Thinking as hard as he could, Fearghus thought up a solution. Just barely extending his head above the side of the wagon, he pushed the head of Conn's battle-axe over the front. He slid it down in between the two horses, and both gave a whinny of pain as the sharp double-sided blade made bloody gashes in their sides. Fearghus gave a cry of his own as the two simultaneously pulled away from each other and began to sprint faster. Fearghus was quite sure now that he had cleared the range of the ambushing archers, and now he picked up his blade again and sat up in the carriage.

Keeping the axe in the same position, he spun around to get a look at the Roman pursuit. There were about ten gallant soldiers, lances at the ready, their capes whipping about behind them, crouched down in their leather saddles. Each one had a look of intense anger upon his face, as years of training and hardship came to a point. Fearghus was not daunted by the bobbing lance heads, or by the shining helmets of the soldiers.

His arrow wound was feeling worse and worse, but that did not scare him as the riders drew up beside the wagon. As one man came up and hopelessly missed with a plunge of his pike, Fearghus had no trouble shifting his grip and hacking him down with a swipe of his menacing blade. Now all of the riders seemed to simultaneously bear down on him. One man dared to take aim and cast his lance at Fearghus. The shot fell short, and the lance fell flat upon the bed of the wagon, the head clanking against the bundles of swords. Now this man drew his dagger and galloped ahead of the others. Seeing this, Fearghus picked up the polished shaft of the soldier's lance and ran him through with it. The man screamed as his own weapon pierced his light armor. His steed slowed as blood ran down his chest violently.

Now Fearghus was in trouble. Five of the deadly lance heads were suddenly within striking distance, and a whole legion of Roman cavalry seemed at the ready, in close pursuit. Fearghus could barely hear himself in the frenzied stampede. Now Fearghus had only one option. He took up his axe and swung it in a full, fluid swing, all the way around him. The blade hissed as it sliced through the flesh, bones, and armor of the fierce soldiers. Then Fearghus did what he had never dreamed of doing. He laid down all of his weapons, and pulled up a thick bundle of iron swords about him, spreading the hard metal to a thin layer.

Fearghus had just barely pulled his head down under the bundle when what seemed like a thousand spears and broad swords crashed down on the metal. Countless lance heads and the points of swords stabbed into his skin, as huge numbers of shallow wounds spilled blood all about the white cloth. Huge, crushing blows bent and warped the swords in the bundle, bruising Fearghus painfully.

He had nearly given up all hope when suddenly, the wagon stopped. Now he was really in for it. Every muscle in Fearghus's body twitched as he waited for the final crushing blow to end it. All the gods had failed him and now he would pay for his mistake. But suddenly, he noticed, nothing was happening. The wagon continued to sit at a standstill and the gallop of horses' hooves had now faded.

Fearghus was driven to emerge from his shield. The white cloth was turned a terrible crimson in his blood, and the whole wagon was filled with countless splinters and holes of the great ambush. Now Fearghus slowly leaned over the side of the wagon. There, lying in a huge pool of blood, were his two horses, both run through with spears and arrows and daggers, covered in already blackening wounds and gashes, still tethered in the flimsy harness.

Fearghus had survived the ambush, but was now left with great loss. He now sat bleeding in this break of the violence, his wagon falling apart and his animals dead. But still remained his weaponry and armor, and his blessed strength, and most importantly, his life. Now it was time to walk. And even with his wounds he would not give up now. If it were the gods wouldn't heal him, so be it.

As he leaned over the edge of the wagon, the rotting wood split and broke. Fearghus hurtled headlong into the bloodstained road. He was pained to get up and pull, but he decided to choose this trouble over that of possible capture. Now he thought that at least he could reach the village down the road by sunset. Slowly and increasingly painfully, he continued to set his feet in the earth and dragged the delicate wagon down the road.

Several times he looked up into the waning sky. He was moving slower than he had counted on and his wounds began to sting with infection. Now the sun sank low in the sky. Fearghus began to lose hope. He knew that if he did not reach help soon, he would expire. The cursed sun burned his bloody wounds as it dropped. Fearghus cried drunkenly as it abandoned him. He knew also that he would never find help in the darkness of night.

He now had a new enemy: time. Death had raised its axe and it was striding towards him as fast as it dared. And now, as Fearghus struggled to move his wagon a few paces, he could do nothing to stop it. He drunkenly cried out and lunged forward with the rope now, and wearily crumpled down on the dusty road. Suddenly the dreaded darkness began to set in. The dratted sun had withdrawn from the world once again, and the trees grew taller in their evil intentions to blot out visibility. Fearghus's teeth gritted. His fingers dug into the earth and tightened around his sword as the pale glow of the high moon glinted off of it.

Now his fate became sealed. A weak, moaning wind howled through the trees. The owls and bats began to screech as they searched for their carrion. The great world of the darkness was coming to life just as he was losing his own. Now a new thing found its way into his head: anger. Anger at the gods for using him as a pawn against the might of Rome, and anger against Rome itself. And now anger drove him. It filled his aching muscles and lifted his mind. His legs came to life and his arms reached out into the darkness.

He struggled to his feet. Silent as the air around him, he staggered forward, his sword drawn, swinging freely. It cut into the ominous dark, letting all around him know what they were dealing with. He continued to stagger over the road, and turned a corner. Now his vision blurred. A great, blinding light was coming towards him. Maybe it was a Roman scout out searching for him, or a local farmer. Or maybe, just maybe, it was a gate. The great gate to the heavens, welcoming him to honor and glory in the halls of the gods.

Now weariness was slipping a black cloth over his eyes. The axe of the executioner was falling. He had to get away from it. He had to slip away from under it before it was too late. He took a few more steps and collapsed into the light. And it caught him. Two arms came up and caught him. Now he was warm and safe in the light and it welcomed him. Its blinding radiance enveloped him in its splendor, and Fearghus slept.

When he arose, more lights hovered around him. He grinned in the heavenly warmth. But then it came to him. He was not dead. As his vision improved, he discovered that he was lying in a loose bed of miscellaneous cloth. Wooden walls greeted him. Linen bandages were wrapped tightly about his wounds, and a small basin of water rested on a table next to his bed. He painfully sat up and dipped his hands into the cool, refreshing liquid and rinsed his weary face. Suddenly, the smooth wooden door of the room opened.

"I see you're awake, my friend," a coarse but gentle voice said. Fearghus looked up and beheld a tall, fairly muscular man, with a short beard and dull eyes. "I am Irial," he said with a slightly better dialect than Conn.

"I have heard of you, Irial, from a man named Conn. I hear you are a man of lumber," Fearghus responded, smiling at his fairer speech. "I am sorry to have disturbed you at such a late hour last night."

"It is of no consequence, friend," Irial told him.

"I am Fearghus, from a village not too far from here, close to the sea," Fearghus sighed. "I received my wounds during a narrow escape from an ambush from the Roman cavalry. I have left behind a wagon filled with many weapons for the purpose of a rebellion to the Romans."

"You no doubt have received those such things from Conn," Irial remarked.

"Why yes, Irial...by the way, how do you know him?" Fearghus asked curiously.

"Many long years ago," Irial started, "Conn and I lived in a very small settlement, many miles away on a beach south of here. We came here because a Roman vessel landed in our village. We just barely escaped."

"I see," Fearghus responded. "Will you help me with this rebellion? Conn has already fought a great battle against the Romans. They move north along the road."

"All I can do is help you along the way. We must flee to the village and seek shelter and men there. But even all the men of the village cannot withstand a whole Roman Legion."

"They may not have to," Fearghus told him. "Is there some other village or town we may reach, possibly a larger one? We must order a full evacuation of the forest."

"There is a religious settlement, a parsonage or monastery, built by the Romans not far north along the coast. It is populated with timid Roman men in dark robes. If we can reach those stone walls before the Romans do, we may be able to hold it long enough to let more help come. It is our only chance."

"So we will slaughter innocent religious men?" Fearghus asked.

"No, we shall simply drive them away. They have no right to our land anyway."

"We'll depart at sunset. Do you have any beasts or vessels to help us get there?" Fearghus asked.

"Yes, I own three mules and I can supply a good wagon for the way," Irial muttered.

Fearghus looked around Irial's house. It was messy, as Conn had described it. Miscellaneous wooden items and scraps littered the ground. Half-made stools and yokes and wheels were all over the place. Also, Fearghus noticed, the floor was wooded, quite adversely to most other buildings that Fearghus had seen in Eire. While most other places were of sod or clay, Conn and Irial's huts were expertly put together with chopped wood. Of course they paled in comparison to the marble halls of Rome, but Fearghus really felt comfortable here. Irial had a two-room house, with a bed and lots of homemade furniture.

"I can give you something to eat, if you'd like," Irial said. "I've some smoked boar meat in the back."

"That'll be fine, Irial, if its not too much trouble," Fearghus responded.

"I'll be right back," Irial said and grinned as he left the hut. Fearghus decided to get up. All of his clothes and many panels of his armor were pierced with countless bloodstained holes. However, he dared not change his ethereal garb. He was still confused about why the gods had not healed him and his supplies as they had already thrice before. Were they angry with him? He shook his head and stared down at the floor.

Momentarily, Irial reappeared in the doorway with a jug of goat's milk and a platter of cooked meat and vegetables. "Here you are, Fearghus," he said, "Now, tell me more about your adventures." Fearghus told him all about his travels, starting with the tale of the giant serpent and including his capture and escape by the Romans. He told him all about his relationship with Conn and his battle with the Roman centurion. Irial was especially attentive to Fearghus's account of his weaponry and strength. "So, you really think you've lost your invulnerability now?" he asked with a sigh.

"Yes, I do," Fearghus responded, "and I can bet you my missing lance has something to do with it."

"Well, the good thing is you're still here to tell me about it, Fearghus," Irial said. "And until you find that lance, I can help supply you with food, transportation, and water…. Anyway, where do you suppose it is?"

"That's a good question, friend," Fearghus said. "Before I could find it almost anywhere. In a cane, or even a tree branch. But now, who knows where I might find it." Fearghus took large bites out of the meat and ate heartily. He hadn't eaten food for a while. The vegetables tasted very good. Before, he somehow did not hunger at all, but now, the emptiness inside him nearly drove him mad.

"I suppose you'd like to go get your wagon now," Irial said and broke the silence. The platter of food had disappeared quickly.

"Thanks, Irial. It should be just down the road from here," Fearghus choked through the last mouthful of meat. He rolled out of bed as Irial disappeared and wrapped his torn cape about him. Soon the two were off.

When they returned, the sun was just rounding the top of the clouds. Irial was straining at the front as Fearghus wearily pushed. "There's a lot of swords here, Fearghus," Irial gasped. "We had better get them into my wagon right away." They came around to the side of the building. Irial's wagon looked quite different from Conn's. It was much smaller, but still much sturdier. The wheels had thick spokes and the bed was smooth and level.

They slowly began to load Irial's wagon. Fearghus removed the damaged bundle and sorted out all of the bloodstained wrappings. Soon Irial's wagon was filled to the top. Subsequently, the day passed quickly. Before he knew it, the sun was again setting below the trees, burning Fearghus's eyes with its red light.

Now it was time to leave. Bringing plenty of food and water with them, Fearghus and Irial boarded the wagon. Two of Irial's mules were harnessed to it with a thick wooden yoke. Now, in the deepening dark, Fearghus and Irial set out to reach the village. It would only be a short drive to the group of houses. Soon it was too dark to see, and Irial lit torches for them to hold. "You really think we're going to make it?" Irial asked as they galloped along the wide road.

"I know we'll get there," Fearghus told him. "It's just what happens when we do get there is what I'm worried about."

"I don't think the Roman monks will put forth much of a fight. Besides, what weapons have they?" Irial reassured him. Fearghus knew it well, too. It was the Romans he feared. Both Irial and Fearghus knew the forest very well. They both had passed this road, but still, Fearghus knew nothing of this village, or of the strength of the Romans in these parts.

It was deathly dark as the trees began to thin, shying away from the path. The village would not be far away from these parts. The large wooden torches left a trail of blazing light in their wake, as the wagon continued to speed to the village. The road became rockier, and a few times the wheels jumped on the stones.

Suddenly, fear greeted Irial and Fearghus. As they eased up on a shallow hill in the road, a large crowd of soldiers came into view. There were many torches ablaze, bobbing up and down over the men. In their flickering light, Fearghus, with a jump, beheld the glint of golden helmet and silver spear, of sharp blade and thick shield. A Legion of Roman soldiers was marching on the village! "Quickly, put out the lights!" Fearghus cried, pulling on the reins. Irial leaned over, and with a start, he threw both torches over the wagon.

"What'll we do now, Fearghus? The village is but a mile from here!" Irial yelped, panicking.

"We will go around them and warn the people," Fearghus said. "We must save them!"

"There is a stone mountain right over there," Irial started and pointed at a large black mass against the dark sky. "If we can make it there in time, we can ride around it and reach the village."

So Fearghus drew up the whip and turned the mules around. Soon they were racing under the low branches of the outer forest, the ominous stone mountain looming up against the black sky. The road was rough and torn with roots and ravines. Fearghus looked up, letting the cold breeze refresh his weary face. The clouds overhead were gathering. A rotten, gray cover thickened, blotting out the stars in a sinister haze.

Fearghus cracked the whip with vigorous anger. His dreams of rebellion lie just around that stone mountain, if he could reach it in time. Irial's sturdy cart bounced up and down, swerving from side to side as it sped through the trees. Fearghus gritted his teeth and looked straight ahead. His torn cape whipped out behind him as the first few drops of rain began to fall.

Now the mountain was upon them. The wheels of the wagon clattered as they slid onto a slippery stone path. Towering above Fearghus was the tallest, most ominous mountain he had ever seen. A fearsome stone path had been hewn out of the mountainside by ancient stone-wrights. Water began to slide down the steep mountainside, washing across the path like waves of the great ocean. As Fearghus guided the cart up the path, the rain only thickened.

The path wound steeper and steeper, until the other side of the mountain became visible. The cart had risen to incredible heights. Fearghus momentarily stopped the cart. From the top of this landing, Fearghus and Irial could see all the plains and hills of Eire stretch out before them. Just ahead, nestled between two gentle green hills, was the village. All the little lights Fearghus had expected had undoubtedly been washed out by the storm. However, as he looked on, a huge host of torchlight was moving towards the little settlement quickly. Fearghus's anger rose as he watched the hundreds of bobbing flames break upon the hills along the road like the sea striking rock. They were almost upon the village. He knew that from now on he would have to make no mistakes. The lives of all the villagers were at stake.

Suddenly, the wooden wheels squealed. The water was washing the cart off of the road. Fearghus snapped the whip violently. The mules finally started pulling, just in time. Fearghus continued fervently to coax them up the steep path. It was quickly becoming harder to move on the slippery path. Footholds were becoming scarce as their height rose.

Then, disaster set in. The wagon halted. The mule's hooves scratched the stone with futility. The path was too slippery and too steep. Now the wagon began to roll backwards. Fearghus cried aloud as his dream began to slip away from him. He had to do something.

Suddenly, Fearghus jumped out of the wagon and ran ahead. "We shall make it!" he cried and snatched the wooden yoke in his arms. The wagon stopped rolling and Irial jumped out. Fearghus strained with all the might the gods had given him. He was almost at the top now. Every muscle strained and lengthened as Fearghus toiled. His anger continued to drive him. He was performing yet another huge feat of strength as he had done before.

Unfortunately, Fearghus was forced to stop. He suddenly realized with great fear that his strength had found its end. His arms weakened dangerously. Irial, at the back of the wagon, cried aloud. "Fearghus! We must go on! We are almost to the top of the mountain!" Fearghus could not let his friend down.

Now he gave it his all. He dug his feet into the stone and heaved with all his bodily strength. Lightning split the sky. Fearghus looked up. The sky had suddenly declared war on the ground. A great wind stirred, blowing his garment about and refreshing him. Then, the gods came out of their hiding and their fury rent the world with fire. A huge bolt of lightning struck the wagon, and it seemed to Fearghus that it came alive. The wooden craft suddenly leapt up into the air, still burning in the lightning, and landed on the other side of Fearghus. It had reached the summit and now was headed down the mountain, with both the animals intact. Fearghus was the only one of the two men close enough to catch it. He lunged at it and landed in the bed, hard onto the bundles of swords. Now the wagon was racing down the other side of the mountain.

To steer, Fearghus improvised and leaned in different directions to keep the wagon from swerving off the mountain. The mules were half running, half sliding down the wet stone. The cold, wet wind sprayed in Fearghus's face violently. He was moving so fast, his stomach had jumped into his throat.

The bottom of the mountain was coming up fast. Fearghus was lying on his belly, looking straight down. Presently, he righted himself and snatched up the reins. He was now on a steep ramp, headed right for the village. Then suddenly, he noticed something else that dismayed him. The columns of Roman soldiers lie directly in his path. He tried to rein up the horses but they could not seem to brake on the slippery path. Fearghus was reaching the bottom of the mountain quicker than he liked.

The mountainside sat right up next to the village. The end of the winding path sat almost directly parallel to the sloppy wooden gate of the village wall. As Fearghus looked on, the Romans drew up and set a human blockade in a crescent about it. Fearghus could only grab the sides of the wooden wagon as he hurtled towards the soldiers. He knew he would have to fight now. His wagon would be shattered by the collision and he would be alone in a crowd of angry Roman foot soldiers.

Fearghus drew his sword and stood up in the wagon as it came upon the blockade. Now he prepared to jump out, but suddenly, a terrible wind pushed him down on his back. As he looked on, all of the Roman's torches blew out simultaneously, and quite eerily. A fearsome darkness set on the land for a split second until, suddenly, a bolt of lightning ripped through the silence. It landed right in front of Fearghus, in the middle of the darkened Roman blockade. What happened gave Fearghus a start of joy.

The Romans directly in front of him were thrown back in the blast, and in the short light of the strike, Fearghus saw his path clear. In the utter darkness, Fearghus's wagon swept through the Roman army and slid under the gate. "Close the gate! Close the gate!" he cried to the villagers standing on top of the wall. Immediately several men in long robes armed with spears came out of the shadows and swung the large wooden door shut. The few Romans that had gotten through were scattered in the host of village guard.

Fearghus's sword was already out. He jumped out of the wagon and his blade literally blazing in the light of torch and candle, he made short work of the remaining Roman invaders. Now he was safe, but only briefly. As soon as he had sheathed his sword, he heard the crash of Roman axes on the wooden gate. Now the whole town was stirring. Several people were already rushing towards him with torches. "Invasion! Invasion!" Fearghus cried drunkenly, "Hide the women and children! Men to your arms! Men to your arms!"

As soon as the townspeople reached him, Fearghus started talking. "I have brought arms for a rebellion! Bring these swords to your kinsfolk! I seek to see Tuathal!" At this a soft murmur rushed through the crowd.

"We will bring you to Tuathal," one bold villager started, "if you tell us your purposes."

"Rome is raiding the coast of Eire, and now a great host of them gathers even at your own gate! I have brought swords for your fighting-men…"

"We cannot fight men such as them! Who are we to stand up against Rome?" the man snapped back.

"We shall not fight, you fool! We shall ride to the monastery in the north!" Fearghus bellowed.

Chapter 3

For Eire

The preparation began right away. Within a matter of minutes, the villagers turned out several wagons and horses, which were quickly loaded with food and supplies. Meanwhile, Fearghus was led to a large wooden hut in the center of the village. On either side of the front door stood gruff-looking men in animal furs with huge pikes at their sides. The villager spoke up again. "The honored magus Tuathal," said he, and made a sweeping bow towards the door. Fearghus looked around at the village. Most of the houses were of sod or wood, with uniformly straw roofing. It was a small village, with a well in the middle of a central square. The people of this village were better off than those of other settlements, with the luxuries of water and a sturdy wall. They were doubly blessed to have such an esteemed magus as Tuathal at the head of their people. Fearghus stepped inside.

Fearghus took only a few steps and humbled himself before the robed man. Tuathal was the first to speak. "I have been told that a renegade Roman legion threatens the safety of my people. Is this true?"

"I am afraid so, oh honored one," Fearghus said with his head bowed low.

"It was always clear to me that Rome had no intentions of invading Eire," Tuathal reasoned.

"It has been my understanding that these soldiers want to avenge the death of a missionary," a villager piped in.

"These men have been here for months," Fearghus told them. "They plan to destroy our people."

"Whatever the case, we must drive them back to the sea!" Tuathal said. "As possibly my final command to you, I hereby appoint you, Fearghus, the leader of our effort to evacuate to the monastery. You seem a fit choice for this service, since you have suggested this trip." And with that, his slaves began to strap on his leather armor. Fearghus watched as one man tied a large sword to Tuathal's belt. "Prepare my chariot! We will do war!" Tuathal shouted, and a great scuffle of feet and chains rang throughout his wooden hall.

Outside, shouts of "Fire!" and "Invasion!" greeted Fearghus. He noticed on a happy note that his wagon was cleanly empty of swords. Huge burly men scurried about like mice, each swinging one of Conn's blades. On a sadder note though, Fearghus noticed that the wooden wall of the village had been set fire. Even as he watched, Roman javelins sailed over the low barriers. Suddenly, Tuathal was out in the public square.

"Retreat! Retreat! Women and children to the chariots! We ride to the north!" he cried. Huge crowds of women and little children ran as fast as they could to the waiting carriages, their cloaks and hair whipping out behind them. The men had already prepared a multitude of wagons and carts to transport them out of the small settlement. The wagons quickly began to glide out of the back entrance.

Now it was time to fight. Fearghus gulped as he turned towards the gate. Countless armed men now gathered around the battered wood. As Tuathal drew his chariot up to the men, the sound of Roman axes grew louder. Huge chunks of wood splintered and flew in various directions as gaping holes appeared.

"Kill them!" Tuathal cried from his chariot as countless Celtic lances and arrows found their marks in the damaged door. Suddenly, the Romans returned their long-range attack. Roman arrows zinged off of shields and helmets, as many lances and pikes plunged through the villager lines.

Spontaneously, the wooden frame of the door collapsed, and the initial attack began. Bold Roman foot soldiers collapsed as the villager's spears rained down on them. Suddenly, all attention was on Tuathal. He had given a great cry and had plunged his chariot into the Roman lines. Fearghus drew his sword. He had to go defend the magus as he made his bold attempt to sway the Roman movement. He ran right through the men and jumped, swinging his sword over his head.

Fearghus hacked his way over to Tuathal's chariot. A few of the men followed cautiously. The old magus was swinging his dagger back and forth, slitting open Roman throats and arms. Fearghus himself was putting forth quite an effort as the Roman soldiers overran his comrades. Roman blood spattered upon everything in this terrible fight.

"Fearghus!" Tuathal cried, "Go with the women and children! My men are now tied to this fate! Go forth and live! Take some of my men with you and retreat!"

"But, oh honored one..." Fearghus started.

"There is no time to waste! Go now!" Tuathal cried as a Roman soldier swung at him hard. Fearghus turned and ran as Tuathal's chariot's wheels splintered. He did not want to see the man die. He sprinted hard. As the burning walls began to collapse, Fearghus ran for the remaining chariots. As his small band of followers ran to prepare his chariot, Fearghus turned around and looked at the doomed fighters. As he looked on, the wooden arch above the gate toppled and crashed down on the men, smothering the remainder of the villagers.

Fearghus's chariot was ready. He took one last gaze over the flames at the menacing Roman soldiers. Above the burning wreckage, like a dying ember, Tuathal gave a great cry and swung his dagger above his head, disappearing into the mass of invaders. Now the Romans were running across the deserted town square. "We must go!" cried one of Fearghus's attendants. Fearghus turned on his heel and leapt upon his chariot as the first few javelins sailed above his head. He snapped the reins and suddenly, he was off.

The path of a chariot was a very fast one. Fearghus had never ridden with such smoothness and control. He was standing on a leather platform stretched between two quick, speedy wheels. It was like riding on air. He looked over his shoulder. The Romans had been quick to abandon the chase as soon as the town was deserted. Fearghus gazed with longing as the straw roofs of the huts in the village disappeared in the distance.

The curved delicate wheels of the chariot sliced through the thick grass of Eire, skipping across the flat stones and pebbles strewn about. Fearghus's horse snorted and whinnied as it danced across the lush turf. He was racing across Eire as fast as he dared, in a last attempt to reach the stronghold of the Roman monastery, before the remnants of his rebellion would be crushed.

As he glided across field and forest, a great number of things raced through Fearghus's mind, as well. He remembered with pain the memories of Tuathal and Irial, both likely dead in the wake of the Roman attack, and he began to remember his previous life. So much had changed since the gods had performed this miracle upon him. This scene, with the world rushing by so fast, was nothing that Fearghus could ever have imagined would happen to him.

The sun began to inch its way up into the sky as Fearghus rode on. Very soon, he knew, he would reach the coast of Eire. He had been there not too many times in his life. His native village was only but a few miles away from a stony inlet of the sea. Only those few fishers and shipbuilders among his people knew the sea very well. They would live and eat by the edge of the sea throughout their lives. However, the Romans had recently driven them from their homes. A Roman vessel had been split upon the jagged rocks of the bay and had stormed the helpless villagers. Even now, Fiedhlimidh could very well be on that beach, fighting the shipwrecked swine. Fearghus did not want to consider the other possibility that may have befallen him.

Fearghus was beginning to tire of the excursion when suddenly, the air became thick with the dust of a well-traveled road. A few sparse trees now lie between Fearghus and the vast expanse of the sea. The large trees rushed by, the brilliant blue sea flashing in between their thin trunks. The brilliant rising sun nearly blinded Fearghus as it reflected off of the water. The other chariots filled the air with a choking haze as the band of villagers raced to safety.

Now Fearghus began to realize that the dusty road was quickly becoming a sandy beach. The chariots slowed as the wheels struggled in the deepening sand. Steep white cliffs rose on the horizon. Fearghus's grip tightened around the leather reins of his craft as he neared his destination.

A cool breeze from the sea refreshed Fearghus's weary face. The sun flashed off of his attendant's helmets. Presently, one of them slowed his chariot and drew up aside Fearghus. "We will reach the monastery in a short bit," he shouted above the sound of the horses. "The women and children wait in the forest a little ways away."

"We shall announce our intentions and climb the monastery walls, to begin with," Fearghus responded. "Anyone who disagrees with our claim shall die."

This statement brought a slight frown to the man's face. "It shall be as you say. We owe you our lives, and thus our allengiance," he replied, and returned to the front. Now the white cliffs were getting closer. Fearghus squinted as a large valley widened in front of him. Around the stony depression was a large forest, like a ring about the center, where stood a large stone city on the flat earth. Fearghus gazed at the plumes of smoke and the comfortable stone houses of the monks. The monastery was the ultimate site for the besieged rebellion to set up its headquarters. Irial had been correct about this place.

Now a steep rocky path led quickly into the gloomy encircling forest. Fearghus eased his tired horses down the hill. The thick trees of the wilderness loomed up quickly. Now Fearghus began to see where the fleeing women had halted their travels. Under the canopy of trees, a short way down, a strangely large fleet of chariots and wagons lay idly about. The colorful garments of the women stood out in the thick foliage. The few men that had escorted the evacuation now joined Fearghus's own entourage.

The camp was very secretive. No fires were to be built, and no loud noises were to be made. Every man and woman crept about softly, eating the dry fruits and breads that had been brought. The men sharpened their swords and washed their weary bodies in the streams of the forest as they prepared for the monastery invasion.

Fearghus walked back up onto the ridge and surveyed the valley, squinting in the dawn. One man that had assisted with the evacuation joined him. "The gate appears to be open," he started, spinning around to face Fearghus. "We could rush them in our chariots."

"These monks know this forest well, no doubt," Fearghus replied, "Possibly a surprise attack would not be too foolhardy."

The man stroked his chin as he looked about. "Maybe some sort of diversion," he said slowly. "A diplomatic run to the gate may be able to cover for a rear jump on the walls."

"That is a very good idea," Fearghus told him. "I shall appoint you to lead the gate campaign. By the way, what shall I call you?"

"My name is Tadhg," the man replied and walked back down to the camps. Fearghus looked ahead into the shimmering valley. His hands formed fists as he prepared for this new adventure. His sword, in itself, seemed ultimately excited as well.

Presently, the horses were tied once again to the chariots, and the women and children drove deeper into the woods. Fearghus and the men took a different route through the forest. Their well-armed chariots delved even deeper, getting ever closer to the monastery.

It was hardly worse than he had ever seen, but Fearghus did not enjoy the trip through the gloomy woods. The dense trees and brush bore down on him like the black blanket of night. The utter darkness of the deep forest seemed to have an effect on all of the men. However, the thin ring of trees around the monastery came to a quick end.

Directly in front of him, through the green sunlit leaves and dark tree trunks, were the tall stone walls of the Roman monastery. The men behind Fearghus slowed their horses and dismounted their noisy craft. Some brandishing their weapons, they gathered about Fearghus's chariot.

Fearghus turned to the men and gave them their instructions. "Tadhg shall lead the excursion to the gate," he boomed. "All others shall follow me around to the north wall. Bring your weapons, but do not use them. We shall merely drive away these religious men. All who do not heed our request shall die at our hands."

With that, Fearghus jumped off of his chariot and beckoned the men towards him. "We shall leave immediately." Then he turned to Tadhg. "You may select your own men. Do not launch your chariots until I wave my cape to you from across the clearing. Stay here until I give the signal."

Fearghus then turned, and decisively started the journey. His men followed close behind, all making an extra effort to quiet their clanking swords and luggage, so as not to alert the monks in the monastery nearby. They were creeping along with sometimes only a few yards of trees and brush between them and the open clearing. The stone walls of the monastery were always in sight. Fearghus was to lead them to the whole other side of the forest, taking the shortest route imaginable.

The journey tolled on uneventfully, until the silence was suddenly broken. A man from the rear of the party had captured a monk wandering around in the forest. Fearghus was disgusted at how the Celt had drawn his dagger up to the harmless man's throat. "Leave him to me," Fearghus told him. The man reluctantly loosened his grip on the monk's brown robes.

"You are a Roman, I presume?" Fearghus asked. "We have seen your people before..." he continued, the men murmuring.

"Yes, I am a citizen of Rome, but most importantly, a faithful servant to God. Have you heard of my God?" the monk asked in weak Gaelic tongue. Fearghus slapped the man upon the cheek.

"A Roman patrol has plundered our villages and killed our people. We want nothing to do with your God," Fearghus shouted. "Our intentions are to take over your residence here, as you have done to our own lands." At this the monk broke free of the man and attempted to escape. "Kill him!" Fearghus cried, his voice cracking in the still air.

Arrows sliced through the dense forest, splitting trees and chipping stones. Celtic weaponry cut countless holes in the monk's robes as he scrambled upon a rock formation. "Forgive them, Father," the monk cried as the warriors bared down on him. Fearghus watched as one of his men put an arrow through the man's side. Blood stained his robe as he collapsed upon the rocks.

"He's still alive," one of the warriors said. The men began to drag the wounded monk down to Fearghus.

"You men shall go forth and deliver him to Tadhg," Fearghus told them. "He may be instrumental in the dismantling of the monastery." Quickly the men had left. Now the slightly smaller party was getting even closer to the rear wall. Soon Fearghus and his warriors were rounding the final bend.

"Prepare your ropes and hooks," Fearghus instructed his men. "Use you swords to scare, not to kill," he continued. The capture of the monastery was about to begin. Fearghus waited by the edge of the forest, lying on his belly, watching for Tadhg to appear on the opposite end. Every muscle in his body twitched with anticipation.

Momentarily, Fearghus spied some movement in the bushes ahead. He heard the quiet prancing of horse's hooves and saw the glint of a sharp Celtic blade. Tadhg had moved his men into an attacking position. Fearghus now did what he said he would do. He stood up, coming clearly out of his hiding place, and swished his brightly colored cape about him.

Almost immediately, Fearghus saw Tadhg burst out into the clearing in his chariot, and disappear out of view, heading towards the gate. Subsequently, the other men who had chariots and those who didn't slowly crept out of their hiding places, yelling fiercely and swinging their weapons above their heads. Fearghus signaled for his men to also leave the forest cover and ducked back down, listening to the conversation.

"We seek shelter behind your walls!" Tadhg shouted above his men. Now Fearghus's men began to cast their ropes atop the wall. "Give us food and shelter and no one will be injured!" Tadhg continued. Suddenly another voice joined in. It was that of a monk.

"I am the abbot of this monastery," the monk said. "We shall be pleased to accommodate you if you lay down your arms and proclaim friendship with us," the cool collected voice of the abbot bellowed.

Fearghus was very excited now. His men were beginning to climb the wall.

"We shall fight for this place then!" Tadhg yelled up to the man. Now the abbot was very distressed.

"We mean no harm to you, friends..." the abbot stuttered nervously.

"We have fought Romans before, and we shall now have our revenge!" Tadhg cried, skillfully using scare tactics. Tadhg even went a step further by ordering his men to cast their lances over the walls of the monastery. This was almost too much excitement to handle! Fearghus burst out of his hiding place, and within minutes he had himself scaled the stone walls of the religious settlement.

When Fearghus would have thought the abbot would surrender or hide, his voice again came smooth and soft over the walls. "Your cursed people shall not enter this realm of the lord! Our gates just as the gates of heaven shall remain shut to you!" Fearghus was angered as well as pleased by this remark. Now it was time to capture the monastery.

Fearghus gathered his men about him on the deserted catwalk. All had their swords drawn and ready, and all with the burning fire of hate and rage in their eyes. "Take as many prisoners as you can. We shall lock them within their own shrine," Fearghus told them. Then suddenly he was interrupted. Tadhg was speaking.

"We shall not enter through the gate, oh unfortunate one, we shall climb the walls!" Tadhg cried. A great force awoke in Fearghus. In one fluid movement, he stood on the edge of the wall, in view of all the monks below, and raising his sword high into the air, he gave a great cry. "For Eire!"

In a huge display of force, his men rose up behind him and like ants they swarmed down the wall with their ropes, snarling like animals. Fearghus himself took the long way down, running to the nearest tower. On his way down the spiraling staircase, he suddenly heard a scuffle from down below. As he continued on, the balding head of a monk appeared in his path. "Oh please, don't hurt me!" he pleaded, kneeling at Fearghus's feet and performing a strange gesture in which he touched his forehead, shoulders and chest.

Fearghus felt a pang of guilt for the misfortune of this helpless monk. "There are ropes on the north wall," he explained to the monk, and stood aside for the man's passage. He paused as the man shuffled by him, dragging his robes.

Suddenly, Fearghus heard his body collapse on the stairs. He turned around and there, standing above the murdered monk, blood gleaming on his dagger, was Tadhg. A sinister smile crossed his face as he recognized Fearghus. However, Fearghus was not so pleased. Some kind of animal awoke in him. His face reddened as anger rose in his chest.

Before Fearghus knew it, his sword was swinging about him. His mind was set on only one thing: revenge. He cried aloud for the death of the innocent man, and dazedly, he plunged his sword into Tadhg. He had not even realized what he had done, when Tadhg crumpled to his knees before Fearghus's gleaming blade. "I am sorry…" he stuttered, as Tadhg gave him a pained look.

Now Fearghus was confused. He had killed one of his own men for the life of a Roman monk. He looked down at his sword. It was an instrument of evil, twisted and gnarled and black in Fearghus's sight. He cast it down and wept.

Outside, even more confusion was setting upon the monks. Countless robed monks were running back and forth bleeding with immoral wounds and bruises. Even more lay dead, killed in cold blood in the square. Now Fearghus was filled with even more rage over his people's folly. His blood was burning hot with anger.

Suddenly, a monk ran by Fearghus, a Celtic warrior tailing him with a small hatchet. Only a few feet away from Fearghus, the hatchet sailed true, and cut down the terrified religious man. The monk fell to the ground dead. Fearghus's anger kept on building as the warrior retrieved his hatchet and aimed it at another man. His rage had reached his peak. Now knowing exactly what he wanted to do, he snatched the man's axe as he swung it behind him and hacking as hard as he dared, he buried the hatchet in the man's flesh.

A great silence set upon all there as the Celtic warrior fell to the earth dead. All the men stared at Fearghus with looks of disgust and anger. But Fearghus spoke to them. "The death of an unarmed, helpless man shall result in the death of the murderer. Are we as lowly as animals? Did we come here to kill innocent men?" Fearghus's words resounded throughout the bloody square, and his warriors lowered their weapons to hear him. "I have made this same mistake, too," he continued, "and it is wrong, under the laws of any of our gods. We shall not kill these men, we will just take what is ours, which includes all of this land."

Almost instantly, all of the daggers were sheathed, and all the bows lowered, and peace again came to the once happy place. The warriors began to clean the battlefield, and the blood of the fallen monks dried under the sun. Fearghus and all his men had just undergone a serious mental transformation. They were no longer ruthless murderers, but kind, moral people, living more closely to the laws of the gods.

All of the monks, who seemed almost as if they had just realized a fault or error of theirs, quickly gathered their possessions and their dead, and rode out into the forest while the monastery gates slammed shut. Fearghus felt especially happy when the warriors agreed to release the prisoner that had been captured earlier. As Fearghus surveyed the work, one man dared to speak with him. "I never saw it your way, until you showed me," he said slowly, "I feel we have accomplished something good and right. Before, I lived by the edge of my sword, but now, I am beginning to realize that there is more to a good man than a sharp blade and a thick shield. Thank you."

Fearghus was equally as awestruck as this man was. He just looked straight ahead, in deep thought, as the warrior bashfully returned to his work. That night, there were no drunken celebrations or fireside tales of adventure. All of the Celtic warriors seemed to have a deep reverence for the monastery and its buildings and especially for Fearghus himself, their new leader.

Fearghus felt very warm and happy. He and his closest attendants stood upon the wall as the sun sank below the horizon, and the balmy air relaxed the warriors as they cooked their provisions in their campfires. Soon a peaceful night was settling on the monastery.

Presently, a warrior came to him. "Fearghus, the women and children have nearly reached the monastery, and it has been requested that you see to it that they get within these walls safely." Upon his request, Fearghus found his way down the wall and rode out through the open gate into the night, bringing with him his weaponry and a small guard of his men. The large band of women were slowly making their way in the dark through the forest, guided by a number of Celtic scouts bearing torches and bows. It was not long before Fearghus and his men reached them.

One of the scouts sighed and rode up to Fearghus. "I am Colla, at your service," he said and bowed graciously. "We had nearly lost ourselves in this forest when you arrived."

"Colla, have you experienced any resistance involving Roman soldiers or missionaries?" Fearghus asked attentively. He was very concerned about the movement of the Roman renegades.

"No, we have had a fairly comfortable excursion, although the womenfolk are very distressed about the dark. We began to make our way over here..."

Suddenly Colla was interrupted by a blood-curdling scream from one of the women. Immediately Fearghus snatched up a lance and guided his horse to the back of the group. Now all of the women were panicking, huddling together and crying.

When Fearghus reached the back of the caravan, only one of his eyes noticed the bloody corpse lying on the ground. The other eye was delving deep into the darkness, where Fearghus knew a Roman scout was fleeing for his life. Without even flinching, Fearghus cast the lance into the night, and heard the soldier scream as the weapon punctured his body.

The scout had picked off one of the women with his bow, and the poor soul had fallen dead to the ground. Fearghus had the deepest sympathy for this innocent woman, and without pausing, he dug a shallow grave in the dark with a knife, and laid her to rest. "Flee! Flee for your lives!" Fearghus cried, boarding his horse. "The Romans have found us! Flee to the monastery before it is too late!"

Fearghus knew he had slowed the Roman attack by killing their scout, but he also feared that they would have other men out searching. He knew his only option was to order an immediate rush for the monastery walls. Within seconds, the whole party was racing through the forest, at increasingly dangerous speed considering the darkness. Fearghus brought up the rear, the eerie night air blustering in his face.

It was not long before the screaming women and children entered the clearing. Now it was easier to move as the torch light of the guards lit up the white stone walls around the gate. The caravan sped through the open gates, the thunder of horse's hooves growing louder on the packed earth. As Fearghus himself glided across the ground, he looked behind him. Suddenly, from the depths of the forest, a Roman barbed arrow lit with fire shot up into the sky, and in a long arc, it barely missed Fearghus as his horse galloped to safety. The hearts of all that saw it jumped as they realized what this arrow meant. The Romans had followed them to the monastery and likely now lurked in the encircling forest.

The gate began to swing shut even before Fearghus was through it. The warriors had already left their campfires to see what was going on, each one armed. Many of them were now being reunited with their spouses and children, while others comforted the widows and orphans among the group.

"The Romans have found us, but this time, they shall not break through the gate. We shall hold this position until more favorable circumstances," Fearghus shouted. The men responded with cheers and shouts, holding their axes, javelins and swords aloft.

The women and children were quickly escorted to food, fire and shelter, while extra guards were posted atop the wall. Fearghus discovered that a sturdy log cabin had already been accommodated for him with such amenities. Although most of the Celtic warriors of the village had been lost in the sacking of their homes, still a good force of Tuathal's men were wrapped around Fearghus's finger. Fearghus slept contentedly, knowing that he was safe under the protection of his own rebellion.

In the morning, Fearghus and the others were up with the first light, back up atop the wall, watching for a Roman attack. Sure enough, as soon as the rays of the sun dipped down into the valley, what looked like several hundred plumes of smoke rose from the forest canopy around them. "It's an old trick," Colla said. "They are bluffing."

"Should we send out any scouts or patrols to keep us informed of Roman movements, or is it too risky?" Fearghus inquired.

"I should think not," Colla responded. "It would not be too hard at all to send forth a few of our more skilled spies. Good idea, Fearghus." Then Colla's voice dropped. "Maybe you would like a try?" he asked.

Fearghus agreed and Colla prepared his horse for him. "There must be some back exit," Colla said as he tied a saddle onto the animal. "I will send with you two of my favorite scouts," he continued. "Try to stay out of the way of any Roman soldier you see. We don't want any fighting, just information from you."

Fearghus was pleased that Colla was such a helpful friend. He was so inexperienced at leading a rebellion, or for that matter a group of armed men, and Colla was making it much easier for him. Fearghus was learning more and more about the art of hand-to-hand combat as well as long-range fighting. He also was learning how to ride horses better every day.

Presently, Fearghus and two other men shining in polished armor, bearing fine swords and lances rode forth from the monastery. They were making their exit through a small arcade in the side of the wall, which had been sealed with iron bars and a thick door. Colla had selected a section that did not have too many plumes of smoke directly in front of it. "Still be cautious, they may actually want you to head this way," Colla had instructed them.

There was very little danger immediately in the open clearing, Fearghus noted. The Romans clearly were very concerned about their own secrecy. Fearghus was amazed, in fact, that he was able to ride in clear view of the forest cover like this with no worries.

The three men passed quietly into the shade of the forest and walked their horses cautiously ahead, their ears and eyes peeled for any sounds or movements. The sun illuminated the leaves above, and the world seemed quite cheerful in all that was happening.

Nothing new seemed to be taking place right now. The world was quietly carrying on, and everything seemed fine. Soon, one of the scouts spoke. "We should split up, and explore in different directions," he suggested.

"That seems like a good idea," Fearghus responded. So, the three men spun their horses around and trotted off into the dense forest brush, each going in a different direction. Fearghus kept looking back and forth, searching for a Roman scout or camp.

Suddenly, he heard voices in the distance. At this he slowly dismounted his horse and crept low into the bushes. The voices sounded Latin, but then, as Fearghus strained his ears, he heard another language. One he understood. It was a very familiar Gaelic-speaking voice, and it sounded distressed.

Fearghus crept forward as quietly as he could and quickly recognized the scent of a wood fire. A number of Romans were no doubt camping here, but Fearghus was still curious as to origin of the Celtic man. When he was close enough to the small clearing, he raised his head and scanned the Roman camp through a thick shrub. Then his gaze fixed on one man. Lying there in chains, covered in scars and bruises, was Irial.

Now Fearghus had to think of something. Irial would have valuable information about Roman movement and strength. He had to find some secretive way to rescue his friend. Violence was not the only option that crossed his mind, though.

Fearghus was lightly armed, with his sword and a short spear, and could very well take on the occupants of this camp. However, he feared that any attempt to do this would result in the death of Irial, or the rousing of a nearby group of soldiers. Then Fearghus had an idea.

He tried to make eye contact with Irial, who, luckily was facing in Fearghus's direction. Fearghus waited till the Romans were looking the other way, and then he made himself visible. Irial nearly jumped out of his clothes when he saw his friend. A look of pain and anguish, but also of hope crossed his face. Fearghus tried to communicate his intentions to the nervous prisoner, who seemed to interpret them easily.

Fearghus realized he would have to kill to get what he wanted, so now he began to put his plan into action. There were four Roman foot soldiers living in this camp. The one closest to Fearghus was sitting upon the ground, sharpening his sword on a stone. Two of the men were also reclined on the ground, nibbling apples and biscuits. The smoldering remains of a fire pit lay in the center of the clearing.

The soldier, however, that Fearghus wanted to concentrate on, was Irial's guard. The tall, menacing soldier was standing upright next to his prisoner, with his back to the forest. Fearghus crept around the clearing until he reached the man. Very carefully, he walked up behind him and slit the man's throat. The guard made almost no struggle whatsoever, and Fearghus quickly dragged him behind a tree and got back down into the bushes. At this, Irial played his part in the rescue. "I suppose my guard has gone for a little stroll," he shouted to the others.

Soon, another man began talking in Latin and got up to replace the first one. The other two were not alarmed and continued what they were doing. Irial suddenly said, "The sky is *clear* of clouds right now," looking upwards. Fearghus knew what this meant and acted accordingly. Adjusting his position in the forest, he disposed of this man in a similar fashion as the first. Now the other men were becoming alarmed.

The two soldiers had become very suspicious now, and they drew their blades. They were angry at Irial, and began to think he might have killed their friends. Both of them started shouting in Latin and brandishing their weapons. They were coming directly at Fearghus.

Suddenly, Irial, who was lying on the ground, did something very risky. He reached his legs out and tripped up the first man, who dropped his sword and sprawled across the ground. This was Fearghus's only chance. Jumping out of the bushes, he cast his lance into the neck of the soldier who remained standing, and on the follow-through, he reached to his belt and drawing his sword, he plunged it into the back of the fallen Roman soldier. All four men had now been killed, and Irial was free.

The Roman soldiers had not taken the precaution of restraining or tethering Irial, but had still chained his arms together. This would present a problem for Fearghus. "We have already captured the monastery, my friend," he told Irial.

"Yes, I have heard about that," Irial responded. "It pleases me. There are not very many soldiers here at the moment. However, more are on the way."

Fearghus became very alarmed at this news. "We should get back to the monastery quickly and tell the villagers this," he said. Fearghus dried his sword in the grass. He was now seeing a whole new side of Irial. Soon the two of them had found Fearghus's horse again, and began the trip back to the center of the valley.

Suddenly, an arrow zinged past them, missing Irial closely. Latin voices filled the air as the chase was on. Fearghus kicked his horse into a gallop, as the dense forest brush burst with the beating of hooves. The Romans were giving chase.

Fearghus's lance was out in a flash. One Roman rider was catching up. Just as the horses came into the clearing, Fearghus swiveled around in his seat and cast his lance into the soldier's steed, missing him to the bottom. However, the effect was just as devastating for the Roman.

Now Fearghus was nearing the walls of the monastery. As he reached it, he yelled up to the men atop the wall. "Romans riding from the west! Open the gate!" And at that moment, a rain of arrows poured down on the band of Romans from the wall. The men screamed as they fell from their horses, dead to the ground. Now Fearghus rode back around to the gate, which was creaking open. He had a slight jump on the Roman pursuit now. However, as he looked behind him, he spotted several more horses and chariots gliding out of the forest.

Fearghus's horse, tiring from the weight of both men, finally galloped through the narrow opening in the gate. The Roman riders turned aside as the Celtic archers aimed their weapons. Fearghus had narrowly escaped death. When he was safe within the walls, Colla was right there to meet him. "Who is this that you have brought?" he asked. He was very curious about Irial.

"This is my friend from the southern forest, Irial. He had accompanied me before I reached your village," Fearghus told Colla.

Now Colla turned to Irial. "Do you have any information for us from behind the Roman lines?" he asked with a loud, authoritative voice.

This didn't shake Irial, though. "Yes, I do," he said calmly. "The Romans do not have very much manpower, at the moment," he continued, "now we just have about fifty men to deal with."

"This is pleasing news," Colla remarked warmly and patted Irial on the back.

"However," Irial said, his face growing darker, "reinforcements are on the way from the village. They'll be here in four days at least." This statement brought a frightened look to Colla's face. Fearghus knew this fear, too. He knew right away that the Celtic warriors would have to find help quick. Now Fearghus saw a completely different look on Colla's face.

"I want every able-bodied man out here right now!" Colla cried. "We shall strike first!"

Right away, the whole monastery burst with excitement. Horses whinnied, as they were strapped to their chariots. The air was filled with the sounds of swords being sharpened and forged. The sky darkened as the remnant of the village warriors prepared for battle.

Meanwhile, Fearghus and Irial were shown to their quarters, and provided with food and mead. As Irial and Fearghus sat down over a good meal, Irial again spoke up about his travels. "Right after you jumped on the wagon, I was sure I was going to die," he muttered. "As I stumbled down the mountainside, I could hear the Roman axes chopping at the village gate. I feared that you would be dead, as well."

"I am sorry for leaving you, my friend," Fearghus responded. "However, all is well now, luckily."

"Yes, after we defeat these Romans, it will be," Irial chuckled as he chugged down a flask of mead.

"Colla, whom I'm sure you have met, is a very foolhardy warrior," Fearghus told him. "He is attempting to kill the Roman scouts that have brought you here."

"He had better watch out," Irial responded. "My captors are a nasty lot. Their leader is a fierce soldier. It will be a tough struggle."

"What do you think of our chances during a possible siege?" Fearghus asked, turning the conversation around.

"This establishment appears to be quite secure," Irial responded, "but in the face of a Roman Legion, you cannot hope to live but to seek for outside help." Now Fearghus became nervous.

"Are you to say that we are doomed?" he asked loudly. He nearly spilled his plate of food as he jumped.

"Isn't there any way to find outside help, Fearghus?" Irial pressed apologetically. "We could ride to some village nearby, and…"

"There isn't a village within fifty leagues of here," a voice said. Fearghus and Irial looked to the door. There, standing in full armor, was Colla, tall and menacing. "We will ride into the forest at sunset. We shall crush the Roman scouts quickly, before we are overrun."

Fearghus stood up and brandished his blade. "Colla," he began, "I shall ride with you. However, it has come to my attention that we are doomed to be overrun if we do not seek immediate help."

"Yes, so I have heard," Colla responded with a sigh. "And, though I regret this decision, I have found a way to get help."

"How goes this method of rescue?" Fearghus inquired attentively.

"We are close to the coast," Colla began, taking a deep breath, "and along these coasts patrol some of the fiercest pirates this side of Britain. They use some of the fastest craft on the waters. A pirate ship is designed for speed, you see."

Now Irial piped in. "And how do you know of these such things?" he asked ruefully.

"Once, I was a pirate," Colla said longingly. "A very risky business, pirating is. It is a fearful profession. Pirates are crooks, you may already know. Well, once, I was one of those crooks. I know every corner of the sea, every nook and cranny of the land, every hoard of gold and pearls."

"So, you can help us?" Fearghus asked.

"Yes, do you have old pirate friends that you can persuade to help us?" Irial inquired, gazing up at them.

"I am afraid not, my friend," Colla responded. "We shall ask nothing of these robbers and murderers, save only their ship."

"Are we then to sail down the coast in search of help?" Fearghus asked, already half-knowing Colla's answer.

"Yes, Fearghus," he said. "We will take control of a pirate ship."

"But wait a minute, Colla. Where and how will we do such a thing?" Irial asked.

"There is a harbor, not too far from here," Colla told them. "A deserted place. It is frequently the host of one or more pirate ships. We shall attempt to take one there."

"But how do we fight pirates?" Irial pressed irritably.

"I was hoping Fearghus here could help us with that," Colla responded slyly. "However, my men are ready to ride immediately. We must get through the Romans before we can fight them, this time. I shall leave someone else in charge while we ride to the sea." Suddenly, both Fearghus and Colla turned and fixed their eyes upon Irial.

"Oh no, you shall not lure me into your trap," Irial said, backing up. "I don't want to fight."

"You have to fight, Irial," Fearghus recited, "for the future of Eire is at stake."

Outside in the square, the fighting men were bringing their horses together slowly. Their horses whinnied as they gathered their arms together for the great battle. Inside, Fearghus himself was very busy strapping on his armor. So much was rushing through his mind as the time neared for him to depart. This was all new to him. He feared the nasty reputation of the pirates, and especially, he feared for his life and the life of Eire. His hands tightened about the handle of his blade as he envisioned this fate.

The men outside began to chant as their swords slid into their scabbards and the points of their spears pierced the air. They were becoming more violent as Colla was stirring them, and it seemed to Fearghus that they had forgotten him. But even Fearghus now felt this anger towards the Romans. A great excitement rose up in his chest, and his breath grew heavier.

Presently, the murmur of the fighters died as Colla appeared to them upon the balcony of the Roman church. "We shall ride at sunset!" he cried. "We shall defend our homes, our children, our flocks, and all of Eire!" he cried violently. This brought the soldiers back to their cheering.

Inside, Fearghus's hands worked faster as he heard these stirring remarks. He was ready to fight the Romans. He had been waiting too long; his sword was thirstier than ever for Roman blood, and Fearghus was confident he would reach it soon. His vigor for war had been renewed. Now he, too, wanted to shout and whoop down below on the ground.

Suddenly, Colla thrust Irial into the sight of his warriors. "I am sorry, men, for I will not be leading you into battle," he shouted, looking back and forth at his host of fighters. The warriors responded with a low sigh. "However," Colla quickly continued, "I have someone else to fill that position. He is Irial of the great southern forest," he called as Irial cringed in front of him. "He has just narrowly escaped from the Romans, and knows our enemy well."

With this, Colla turned and left the balcony. "We shall still have to fight the Romans, no doubt," Fearghus said as the man approached him.

"That is to be seen, Fearghus," Colla responded. "Whatever happens, we must escape to the sea before the sunrise."

Now Fearghus had to hurry. He strapped on his armor and buckled his belt tightly. The sun was nearing the edge of the white cliffs in the distance. The great battle for the monastery would begin soon. Donning his helmet, he rushed down the stairs of the church and joined the warriors below. Under Colla's direction, a great war chariot had been prepared for him. "Is everyone present!" Irial called weakly over the crowd.

"Yes…now let's get going!" cried one of the warriors.

"Open the gate!" Irial bellowed as the man next to him raised a crimson standard far above his head. The huge mass of smooth wood slowly creaked open. Irial twitched as one of the lookouts atop the wall blew into a horn of seashell. He was new at this type of thing, but Fearghus trusted his friend to coordinate a good battle.

Beside Fearghus, Colla stood tall in his chariot. His cape fluttered out behind him as the former pirate hardened himself for battle. "We shall stay only briefly to fight," Colla instructed him over the beating of hooves.

"I shall be ready!" Fearghus told him, carefully holding his stance upon the chariot bed. The war party was moving slowly right now. It was a good choice for Irial to avoid a violent charge at this point. The Romans were nowhere in sight. Fearghus sighed as the unorganized band of Celtic warriors neared the forest.

Suddenly, the clean sound of a Roman bugle rent the calm air with panic. The forest in all directions suddenly came alive with the zing of arrows and the beating of shod hooves. The Romans were going to charge the warriors if they didn't do something quickly.

All of a sudden, Irial took a chance. He drew his sword, and rearing his horse high in the air, he cried, "Fight now for your freedom!" and rode out in front of the Roman chariots. His statement was met with the hiss of the sword and the crack of the whip. The Celtic warriors all suddenly chose their directions, and rode headlong into the Roman charge.

"Come with me!" Colla cried, signaling to Fearghus. He was headed east with a great host of warriors at his heels. Unfortunately, Fearghus noticed, the Romans had blockaded this side of the clearing as well. As his chariot pummeled into the mass of soldiers, he drew his sword.

He swung his blade about, hacking down the Roman foot soldiers and violently slashing their horses. Beads of blood flew into the air as his sword hissed through flesh and bone. Colla had not completely stopped his horse in the bloody fray. He was frantically trying to hack a path through the men for him and Fearghus to escape. His face widened as both Celtic and Roman warriors fell to their death.

The Roman forces were stretched thin around the warriors. Irial had been correct about their number, and as Fearghus looked on, also correct about their ferocity. The battle had lasted longer than he had thought.

Soon it was clear to go. Fearghus began to turn his chariot around. He gave one last look across the field as Irial, still wobbling atop his horse, thrust his blade back and forth above the Romans. Then, he suddenly realized that Colla had already disappeared into the forest. Without further delay, he snapped his reins and charged into the woods.

Chapter 4

▼

Out to Sea

Almost immediately, Fearghus felt the effects of the black, darkening forest. His chariot seemed increasingly louder as it got farther away from the fighting. The crack of his whip resounded through the empty woods. He gratefully now threw his bloodstained sword useless to the floor of the chariot.

Suddenly, the wheels of his wagon stopped as they collided with some kind of barrier in the road. Fearghus got out of his chariot and discovered the bloody corpses of a number of Roman foot soldiers. Just ahead, the light of the young moon glinting off of his helmet, was Colla. Dark and menacing in the gloomy forest, his sword gleamed with spilled Roman blood. "I am pleased to see that you made it through," Colla started.

"I see you've had some problems to deal with yourself," Fearghus responded, glancing back at the corpses.

"Yes, they gave me a few problems," Colla admitted, pointing to a large array of Roman arrows fixed in the front of his chariot. Fearghus was glad that Colla was such an experienced warrior. He was really helping them get things done. "We should get moving again," Colla said.

The two warriors cleansed their weapons and refreshed themselves in the nearby stream before moving on. When the wheels upon their chariots began to turn again, Fearghus ventured to ask Colla a question. "When you were a pirate," he began, "did you bury or hide any treasure?"

"That's an odd question to ask," Colla said, turning to face Fearghus. "Yes…I did."

"Well, where is it, then?" Fearghus pressed.

"The treasure of a pirate is very sacred to him," Colla retorted, fiercely. "I wouldn't dare to reclaim it."

Fearghus could feel how exasperated Colla was, and so he did not ask any more questions. The two men were slowly making their way out of the forest, and the white cliffs of the beach rose up in front of them, illuminated in the moonlight. Soon Fearghus could see the great, black, sea, stretching out to the farthest point imaginable. The clean white light of the rising moon shimmered in the surf. It was the most beautiful sight he had ever beheld. As the calm waves collided with the soft sand, Colla pulled up next to Fearghus.

"Do not become too attached to the sea, Fearghus," he said. "It can do many terrible things to a young man like you."

Fearghus pulled away and cracked his whip again. The chariots glided over the white sand as the men entered new territory. "Where are we headed?" Fearghus asked.

"A few miles north, just over that mountain," Colla responded, pointing ahead to a great stone mountain similar to the one beside Tuathal's village. "Now, we have about three days to find help and get it back to the monastery. We must hurry."

Colla sped up as the mountain loomed ahead. The balmy air of the night warmed Fearghus inside and out as the two men neared the huge, jagged rock. "The harbor is close now?" Fearghus asked.

"Yes, it is very close," Colla said as he slowed his chariot. Fearghus did the same as Colla scanned their surroundings. "Now, this is a very foolhardy stunt that we're going to pull. I don't want you to do anything stupid," Colla told him. "Follow me."

Colla stepped off of his chariot and pulled out a short dagger from his belt. "Take off your noisy weaponry," he told Fearghus, "We don't want to be seen."

The two men crept slowly through the deep sand, going around the mountain. Soon, they had rounded the rock, and Colla stopped abruptly. "Here, take this," he said, handing Fearghus a longbow and a quiver of arrows he had brought with him. "I'm terrible with the bow," he said, "How about you?"

Fearghus looked down at the smooth wooden rod. "I'll manage," he responded. Fearghus had never wielded a bow before, but, he now remembered, he had shot at birds with a small one when he was a boy. He was not afraid of this weapon.

Below them, a huge drop down a steep cliff, was a hard-packed grassy turf. On it were stacked a multitude of boxes and barrels, no doubt filled with stolen goods. The whole place looked quite a mess. As Fearghus lifted his gaze, he beheld a great wooden wharf jutting out from the land, into the shimmering water. There were no ships here at the moment, and the secret pirate's cove seemed desolate and abandoned.

"It looks safe," Fearghus whispered.

"Looks can be deceiving," Colla responded, sliding a large length of coiled rope off of his shoulder. Fearghus sat there and watched as he tied the end of the string to a large boulder on the side of the mountain and prepared to rappel down. "Watch your step," Colla said as his head disappeared over the cliff.

Fearghus was hardly scared by this task, though. He had himself rappelled up the walls of the monastery. How hard could it be to go down? Apparently, it was quite a magnificent feat. Fearghus's feet slipped back and forth as he struggled down the cliff. Colla waited below, his dagger in his mouth.

"Keep quiet," he told Fearghus. Colla crept slowly in between the boxes and kept low behind them. "I think there might be someone here," he whispered, pointing towards a rundown wooden shack near the water's edge. Fearghus's heart stopped as Colla's dagger flicked out. He got up and boldly, he crept right over to the shed.

Fearghus followed cautiously as Colla burst into the building and came out with a bloody dagger and a sack of money. "That's everyone who's here, at the moment," he told Fearghus. "We'll have to wait a bit before a ship comes." Fearghus was surprised that Colla had taken the coins from the pirate guard. "Help yourself, Fearghus," he said, "it's all stolen, anyway."

Fearghus was amazed at the huge quantity of money and exotic treasures that filled the harbor. Countless barrels and cages filled with food, coins and animals lay about everywhere. A particular gold cross especially impressed Fearghus. It seemed very familiar to him. It was the same cross that he had seen in the clouds above his field, many days ago. "Where do you suppose this comes from?" he asked Colla, holding up the treasure.

"It is the symbol of the Roman religion," Colla responded. "You may have seen one on the roof of the monastery church." Fearghus was very disturbed by this statement. He was very confused as to why this symbol had flashed before his eyes before.

"Colla," Fearghus said, "you have fought the Romans before?" Fearghus was ultimately interested in this artifact. He still did not know what the future held for him.

"Oh sure," Colla responded. "Whole fleets of Roman ships are swarming around Britain as we speak."

"What does a Roman ship look like, anyway?" Fearghus asked. "I've never seen one, save only once, split upon the rocks near my village."

"Those Romans sure did a number on your village, didn't they, Fearghus?" Colla asked.

"Not entirely," Fearghus muttered.

"Well, a Roman ship has a broad, square sail, and several oars jutting out the sides. It is one of the largest ships to navigate the sea, as well. You don't want to cross paths with a Roman boat," Colla told him, answering his first question.

"How do all the oars move the ship?" Fearghus asked curiously.

"Slaves, my friend. I am sorry to say so, but the Romans use prisoners of war to move their boats," Colla responded. "They get these slaves from small, helpless villages like your own, and clap them in chains."

A great anger arose in Fearghus. Now he really wanted to get revenge. He wanted to kill. He wanted to stab his sword into the soldiers that would dare to enslave his people. His heart beat faster as he envisioned his kinsfolk in chains. His vision blurred as he grieved for his persecuted family.

Suddenly, his thought was interrupted by Colla's voice. "Pirates! Take cover!" he called. Fearghus spun around. In the distance, gliding like a ghost through the deep fog, was a tiny black sail, fluttering in the wind. An eerie, terrible feeling came over Fearghus. The pirates were coming for him. He froze as the ragged sail came out of the mist. The keel of the ship glided closer and closer. The darkness of the night enveloped him and held him fast to the ground.

"Get down!" Colla cried, jumping upon Fearghus. The two men crawled behind a large box as the wooden ship crawled into the desolate harbor. "What were you doing?" Colla pressed, his dagger at the ready.

"Oh, nothing," Fearghus responded, clumsily stringing his bow. His muscles tightened as he heard the wooden wharf creak under the feet of many men. Fearghus still wasn't sure how Colla expected to take the ship, but he kept his hopes up.

Suddenly, his hopes were dashed. "Have any ideas?" Colla whispered. Fearghus strained his mind for an answer. Somehow, he couldn't think of a safe way to hijack the ship. However, he realized the importance of this mission, and he kept thinking.

Momentarily, he had an idea. Just as when he had attacked the monastery, he would now use a distraction to lure the pirates away from the ship. To put his plan to use, however, he would have to move to a different location. Still crouching now, he crept over to the edge of the stack of boxes and peered out into the night.

The men he beheld looked dirty and greasy. They wore hardly any clothes, and their unshaven, nasty bodies were covered in animal skins and leather. Many of them had tattoos and earrings. Fearghus cringed as he spied one of them, a menacing, bald man, with a huge curved scimitar tied to his belt. These men were brutal savages. "By the way, what do the pirates use to turn their oars?" he asked Colla under his breath.

"Enslaved Romans," came Colla's answer. This statement didn't surprise Fearghus, though. He was pleased, in fact, that the Romans were treated in this way.

Now it was time for action. The pirates had, for the most part, left their ship, and now began to work among the stacks of boxes on the shore. Fearghus looked around wildly for more cover as a strange mix of Gaelic and British voices grew louder.

Signaling Colla, he crawled out into the open, and then quickly scurried behind another stack of barrels. He was trying desperately to get closer to the pirate ship, without being seen. Luckily, this time, neither of the two men was spotted in the darkness. "We need some kind of distraction," Fearghus told Colla when he caught up with him.

This remark brought a grin to Colla's face. "You see these here," he said, pointing into an open box. "These are fireworks, smuggled from the Far East. They'll make a great distraction with the addition of fire."

Fearghus looked at the little brightly colored canisters in the box. He did not know how, but he knew these little cylinders would help them distract the pirates. "I have an idea," he told Colla, looking down at his bow. "Let's go."

He inched his way closer and closer to the shore, jumping in between stacks of boxes. His heart raced as two pirates holding torches paced back and forth between them and the water. Fearghus suddenly realized that he would have to get as close to the sea as possible before he could execute his plan. In a daring, risky attempt, he and Colla finally reached the last pile of crates, and turned their backs to the water. "What now?" Colla whispered nervously.

"We wait," Fearghus replied, and drew two arrows out of his quiver. "Colla," he said, "can you cut me a few lengths of cloth from my cape?" he asked his friend.

"Sure," Colla responded, and flicked out his dagger. Fearghus watched the pirates attentively as Colla sliced furiously at his cape. "Here you go," he sighed when he was done. "I still don't know what you're doing, though."

"You'll see," Fearghus reassured him. The look of confusion on Colla's face did not subside, though, as Fearghus wrapped the red cloth around the heads of his arrows. Colla didn't know it, but he had a big surprise in store for the pirates.

When he was done, Fearghus continued to wait there and watch the pirates, while Colla's patience melted away. "What are you doing?" Colla asked.

"I'm waiting for just the right moment," Fearghus responded. Then his expression changed. "Quiet down!" Fearghus gasped, as one pirate walked right up to their stack of boxes. The light of the man's torch cast a long shadow over Fearghus's head. Fearghus stopped breathing as the man finally turned his back on them. He signalled to Colla to stay put and slowly stood up behind the man. Now his plan was coming together. Trying extra hard not to draw any attention, Fearghus put the head of the arrows in his hand through the flames of the man's torch.

The cloth caught afire, and Fearghus dropped back down behind the boxes, and hurried himself, notching one of the flaming arrows to his bow. Now it was time to test out his skills with the weapon. The pirate in front of them had already begun to walk away, and it was now or never. Fearghus knew he had to get this arrow off before it went out. "Oh, I see what you're doing," Colla said slyly.

Once again, Fearghus stood up, and looked across the ground, until his eyes found the box of Oriental firecrackers a few yards away. Then, as quickly as he dared, he drew his bow up to his chest, aimed, and let go of the shaft. Before the arrow even hit the ground, Fearghus ducked back down and braced himself for the explosion.

The type of explosion he heard was not the kind he thought he would. Instead of the sound of crackling fireworks, he heard the voice of a Gaelic-speaking pirate screaming. "Intruder! Intruder!" he cried. Fearghus realized he had obviously missed the box of firecrackers and notched the second arrow quickly.

The second arrow began to go out as Fearghus jumped up. In a split second, as he glanced across the grassy ground at the box, he saw the pirate with the torch standing there with his first arrow in his hands. It was the bald pirate with a wolf's pelt around his shoulders. And, before Fearghus thought to release the second shot, the pirate saw him. "There he is!" the man cried.

Suddenly, the world was in slow motion. As the arrow on Fearghus's bow went back, the man's finger lifted up to point at Fearghus. Fearghus read the angry, brutal look on the man's face and a pang of fear hit him. The world seemed to be bearing down on him. Fearghus was conscious of every gleaming trickle of sweat on the pirate's head. He saw every ball of torchlight growing larger, surrounding him like a pack of wolves. Every nerve, every pinpoint of flesh on his body screamed as the veil of death swept about his eyes. And then, suddenly, there was his arrow. His arrow was there to save him. As it zipped to its target, the world grew faster and faster.

The flaming head of his target got closer and closer to the box of firecrackers. Then, suddenly, Fearghus realized that he had missed his target. Instead of the fireworks, his dart plunged into the flesh of the pirate. The pelt around the man's shoulders burst into flame. Fearghus's mood was suddenly lifted when the pirate began to scream as his skin was seared in the fire.

Right away, Fearghus knew he had succeeded. Before it even happened, he knew what was going to happen to the man. He whispered to Colla to wade into the water as the pirate fell on top of the box of explosives. As the fire caught the canisters, Fearghus and Colla were already waist deep in the harbor.

Fearghus looked behind him. He had never seen a firecracker go off. The Orient was almost a myth to the people of Europe, especially in Ireland. He wondered how these had found their way here. But it didn't matter. The fireworks were so beautiful. Red and green sparks showered the corpse of the pirate.

Some of the fireworks had found their way into the air. Fearghus and Colla ducked their heads under the water as the spinning wheels of fire illuminated the harbor. They still did not want to be seen, yet.

Now it was time for the second part of Fearghus's plan. The pirate ship was only a short swim away from where he and Colla were standing. The water of the harbor at night was uncomfortably cold as they began to move. On the shore, a state of utter confusion had set upon the pirates. Fearghus turned as he swam and chuckled to himself as the grimy pirates ran back and forth, their scimitars glinting in the colored light.

Fearghus and Colla had to stay a good distance from the shore. The pirates were frantically emptying out barrels and running to the sea to fill them with water to put out the fire. This presented a problem, but Fearghus knew that no pirate would have time to look for them in such a dire matter. They would not see them anyway, here in the shadow of the ship.

Fearghus glanced over at Colla. He looked more like a pirate than the ones on shore, with his dagger fixed in his uneven teeth. Suddenly, he signaled to Fearghus to follow him. Now the two men were getting further and further from the shore. Fearghus was confused as to where he was being led.

Then it all became clear to him. Just ahead, like the thick trunk of a sapling, was the anchor rope. Fearghus treaded the water as Colla began to climb up the soggy tether. When he was halfway up, Fearghus followed suit. The rope was not altogether hard to climb, he discovered. The coarse texture of it helped him grip better and pull himself up. He had left his bow on the beach, he suddenly remembered. However, it was of no consequence. The pirate's ship was no doubt filled with any number of swords and lances.

Momentarily, Fearghus reached the railing of the deck and Colla pulled him up. "Here you have it, my friend," Colla said. "This is the *Silverbeam*, one of the fastest pirate ships that sails these waters. I've been on this very ship a few times myself."

Fearghus was amazed at the beauty and skill demonstrated in the architecture of this vessel. Now he was not sure whether this or the fireworks was more beautiful. He was in awe of the beauty of the world of the sea. "It's a wonderful ship, Colla," he said.

"Don't say that, my friend," Colla called from the other side of the deck. "The life of a pirate is far from glamorous."

Fearghus walked over to the captain's quarters. In the back of the ship, this room looked especially nice, being above the ship. It was skillfully crafted of wood, and sported many windows. As Fearghus admired its beauty, he noticed the door was open. Suddenly, the fear that had long since left him returned.

Before he entered, he crept over to a wall and snatched up a large harpoon. He feared for his life as he penetrated the enclosure. Inside, there was a low bed against the wall. Fearghus breathed a sigh of relief as he spied the figure of the ship's leader asleep under the animal pelt covers. The man looked even more savage than the other pirates. His hair was wild and matted and he sported a coarse beard and several tattoos. Beside his bed sat several kegs of ale. "Okay, get up!" Fearghus yelled, prodding the pirate with the harpoon. "We're taking over this ship!"

Suddenly, the pirate burst out from under his covers and drew two jagged daggers from his belt, swinging them about above his head. Then he spoke in a gruff Gaelic tongue. "You'll have to get through me first!" he cried, thrusting his daggers forward. Fearghus drew up the heavy harpoon and parried. The steel blades of the knives notched the soft wood.

Now the pirate attempted to rush him. Fearghus saw this right away, and swung the handle of the tool around and cracked it on the man's head. This did not slow the pirate, though. Before Fearghus could do anything, one of the daggers came up and sliced a long gash in his arm. Now he was afraid.

Making no attempt to attack, Fearghus burst out onto the deck and pointed his spear forward. The pirate jumped aside. "We've got trouble!" Fearghus yelled. Suddenly, Colla jumped out of nowhere and plunged his dagger into the pirate's arm. The man spun around and punched Colla in the head. "Go pull up the anchor!" Colla cried.

Fearghus dropped his weapon and ran back to the tether rope. He knew this was not a one-person job, but he was confident in his own physical strength. Grunting in the pain, he heaved the anchor up, length by length, until it was hanging just beside the deck. Then, looking around, he found a large wooden post to tie it to.

Meanwhile, the two pirates aboard continued to battle. Fearghus feared that Colla was overmatched. Still weary from pulling the anchor, he snatched up the harpoon again with his blistered hands and rushed into the fight. Right away, Colla saw him and drew out of the scuffle. "You have lost, Bressel," Colla said. "You cannot win today."

"That is true, old friend," Bressel said. "I shall not win *today*."

Suddenly Bressel turned and ran. Before Fearghus had a chance to kill him, the pirate had reached the railing of the ship. Fearghus cast his harpoon, but the man jumped, and his spear missed the man over his head. Both splashed into the dark water below.

"I have already untied the boat," Colla said. "We've got to get moving before the pirates start coming back to their ship. Let's go talk to the slaves down below," he remarked slyly and brandished his bloody dagger.

Fearghus followed Colla down underneath the deck to where the slaves sat in chains. Here under the floor, almost thirty dark-haired Romans were sleeping on small wooden benches. Jutting out from the wall, next to each bench, were the wooden handles of many oars. Fearghus was horrified at the conditions the slaves were living in. Given only a small loincloth to wear, the men's backs were covered with bruises and whip markings. "This is how any ship you can find runs," Colla said. "In a Roman ship right now, our people are sitting in the same chains."

Fearghus felt guilty for the persecution of these Romans. Even so, he knew that the future of his own people depended on their captivity. He just leaned against a wall while Colla coordinated the escape. "Get up, you filthy swine!" he snapped, poking the point of his dagger into the weary men. Slowly, the slaves awakened and grabbed at their oars. Fearghus winced at the sight of blood trickling down the arms of one of the helpless men. "Fearghus, I want you to coordinate the rowing, for a while," Colla said. "We'll need a great deal of speed to get out of here. Watch me."

Fearghus stood up and watched Colla as he snatched up two wooden mallets and began to pound them on a wooden post. Suddenly, in unison, all the slaves began to row. They followed the beat of the hammers, and the ship began to move. "Go check the topside, Fearghus," Colla said. "They'll be suspicious, now."

Fearghus spun on his heel and leapt up the stairs to the deck. Smoke filled the air. He noticed that the former sound of crackling fireworks had now been replaced by the clamor of angry pirates on the shore. Running to the back of the boat, he nearly fainted. The water was filled with at least twenty small rowboats full of angry pirates in close pursuit. Fearghus would have to fend off the attack from behind.

His heart nearly stopped when he realized he didn't have a weapon to fight with. He had left his sword behind on the beach. However, this was no problem, as Fearghus soon realized. As a rain of arrows shot over the railing, Fearghus picked one up. Just as he had expected, the sky flashed green, and the arrow morphed into his own blade.

Fearghus turned and ran behind the mast, trying desperately to shield himself from the terrible arrows. Then he realized he could not hide for long. Several grapple hooks flew up in the air, barely missing the railing. Soon, he noticed, one caught the edge of the deck and held fast.

Now he had to think of yet another way to escape from this trouble. But it wasn't the time for a complex solution. Fearghus had to act fast. He hardened himself for battle, and ran out to the deck, swinging his blade ferociously.

To start with, Fearghus kicked the grapple hook off of the deck. However, there were several more at this point, and the faces of angry pirates began to appear above the railing. "We've got even *more* trouble!" Fearghus called, thrusting his sword in and out of the attackers. The steady beat of Colla's hammers down below got faster and faster.

Now the pirate ship was moving quicker. Fearghus nearly lost his footing. The small rowboats began to pull away, some even capsizing in the impressive wake of the ship. The escape was nearly complete.

Fearghus was in trouble, now. As he stood there, three pirates simultaneously burst over the railing of the ship and drew their scimitars. Fearghus remained confused as to where they had gotten these exotic weapons. However, this was no time to think about this. Right away, his own sword came up to defend him. It was hard to parry the multiple attacks of the three men, but it was no problem for Fearghus's ethereal blade.

The sound of clanking metal rang through the cold air as the snarling pirates swung their weapons about uselessly. Fearghus quickly realized how superior he was to these men, and finished the fight quickly. Thrusting his sword into the belly of one, he slashed the other two to ribbons, until all three weary fighters fell back over the edge of the boat, their eyes closing in agony.

Right away, Fearghus dropped his bloody sword and ran down to where Colla was fiercely pounding his mallets. "Everything's fine, now," he told the exhausted man. "I'll have a turn at this."

"That's good to hear," Colla responded. "Just don't tire them out. We need these men to get where we're going."

Fearghus took the heavy hammers from Colla and began to pound them. The weary slaves beside him didn't care to look up as the transition was made. Fearghus realized that it was a very easy job to regulate the rowing in this manner.

It was a very disturbing sight, watching the slaves toil endlessly at their oars, sweat cascading down their ragged, bloody backs. Fearghus realized that he was having a lot of trouble concentrating on his hammering while he thought about this. This certainly was not the kind of condition he would want to be in. Even so, he knew that he had to keep these slaves rowing like this. It was vital for his and even their own escape.

Fearghus just sat back on a sawn stool and closed his eyes, listening to the beat of his hammers. It had now become routine, listening to this sound. For the first time in many hours on end, Fearghus finally realized how tired he was. His hands relaxed, swinging the hammers slower, and slower, and he drifted off.

"It's a beautiful morning!" came Colla's voice. Fearghus jumped as he woke up. He had fallen asleep. He was extremely embarrassed that he had done this.

"I'm sorry, Colla…" he started, rubbing his eyes.

"That's alright, my friend," Colla reassured him. "We don't need to row anymore. There's a strong wind sweeping down from the north. We're on our way!"

"I'm pleased to hear that," Fearghus mumbled, righting himself upon the stool. Around him, sleeping just as soundly as he had been, all the slaves were resting, the handles of their oars pulled in out of the water. This brought pleasure to Fearghus. He dreaded the chore of pounding hammers for them.

"Let's go up on deck," Colla prodded. "I'm sure you'd like some fresh air after last night." Fearghus was pleased at this remark, as well.

Up on deck, the haze of night was still set about the ship. To the left, beyond the horizon of the sea, was the beautiful dawn. The orange rays of the sun pierced the gray clouds of the night and pushed them away beyond Fearghus's sight. It was yet another beautiful sight to see in his travels. "Even in such a breathtaking world," Colla said, "there is still evil."

"Colla, do you remember our talk about your treasure?" Fearghus asked.

"Yes, I do," Colla responded. "And you'll never know where it is."

"I was just a bit curious," Fearghus pleaded.

"A lot of people are curious about things they *don't* know about, Fearghus," Colla explained. "Now that I *do* know about pirating, I realize that it's nothing special."

Fearghus thought long and hard about these words. They had a special meaning for him. He still didn't know what his purpose was, or why he had been blessed with this strength, and this sword. He didn't know even if he was supposed to be fighting the Romans. Just for a moment now, he thought really hard about this. What was he put on this earth for?

"I suppose you'd like some breakfast, Colla chuckled. I'll go get some food from the back," he shouted, and jogged back behind the captain's quarters.

Presently, the two men relaxed themselves over a hot meal of stew and vegetables on the deck. The light, salty breeze of the sea cooled their tired faces and excited Fearghus. He felt refreshed and ready for more fighting.

"Now let's just hope everything goes our way from now on," Colla said.

"Colla, do you suppose Bressel will seek revenge on us?" Fearghus asked, sipping a glass of wine from the bedroom.

"I've known Bressel all my life, dear friend," Colla started, "and he's the nastiest pirate I've ever seen. He'll be back, I'm sure of it."

"So this is the *Silverbeam*, as I've heard," Fearghus said. "Have you been aboard this vessel, before?"

"This was my first ship, Fearghus," Colla explained. "Bressel here...well he taught me how to be a good pirate. It's a beautiful ship, ain't it?"

"Yes, very," Fearghus replied. "By the way, how are we going to get ourselves enough soldiers in time for the Roman attack?" he asked.

"That's a very good question, my friend," Colla answered. "You see, I came from a village not too far down the coast here. 'Twas those pirates that took me from it."

"So you really think that your hometown will stand beside you, after you went off and became a thieving pirate?" Fearghus asked cautiously.

"I can only hope so, my friend," Colla sighed, putting down his empty bowl.

The day tore on boringly. There was so little to do on a pirate ship. Fearghus and Colla squandered much of the day away sharpening their swords, eating, and catching up on sleep. When the wind died down, they took turns pounding the hammers for the slaves down below, and made quite a bit of progress for the day. Soon, the sun was beginning to disappear behind the rocky coast of Eire.

"We'll keep moving through the night," Colla told Fearghus, as the last rays of the sun disappeared. "We can take turns guarding the vessel during the darkness."

"Alright," Fearghus replied, yawning. "I'll take the first shift. I'm not tired, anyway."

Fearghus tightened his belt and sat down in the front of the ship, crossing his legs. In the sky above, gray, gnarled, wispy clouds wove their way through the blanket of stars. The ocean calmly washed against the steep cliffs on the shore. For these few moments, the world of the ocean was at peace, but not for long.

At length, in the misty fog ahead, Fearghus began to see strange shapes. At first, they seemed to blend in with the white fog, but Fearghus knew better. As they got nearer, he was able to distinguish two square sails, lightly fluttering in the breeze.

This was a Roman sail, he knew right away. In the middle of the gargantuan white canvas, he easily recognized a religious cross, painted red. An intense anger set over his body. "Romans to the east!" he cried, drawing his sword. He gritted his teeth as the lights of the cabin on the deck came nearer. "Romans!" he cried once more, brandishing his blade. Across the water, on the other ship, he heard Latin voices begin to whisper.

Suddenly, he was knocked to the deck. Colla was on top of him. "Don't make a sound!" he gasped. "We don't want to be seen!" Fearghus tried to slow his heavy breathing as Colla removed his hand. "They have more to fear from us, than we from them," he whispered. "You see that big black sail, up there?" Colla asked, pointing upwards. "Well, as soon as they see that, we're okay!"

Fearghus lay down upon his sword, desperately trying to hide it from the moon above. Colla wrapped his black cloak about them. They would be in dire danger if the Romans suspected any weakness. Right now, they would let the black sail of the pirates do the talking.

Fearghus watched the smaller Roman vessel slowly drift by. Now more Latin talk was heard on the other ship. The Romans were discussing something. Fearghus just hoped that they were not talking about him.

Unfortunately, he was the topic of their discussions. When the two ships ran alongside each other, a great murmur rose up among the Roman sailors. Then, a great torch was lit on the side of the vessel. "Let's get out of here!" Colla cried suddenly, stumbling to his feet. Fearghus snatched up his sword and leapt for cover.

When he looked behind him, he saw a huge spear, which looked rather like an oversized arrow, crash into the deck, splintering the wooden floor. However, what scared him was that the point, as large as his head, was ablaze. He scrambled to his feet as the dry deck caught afire.

Suddenly, Colla was behind him. "We have something similar, on top of the bedroom there!" he cried. "I'll put out the fire! Take this!" he shouted, handing Fearghus a large torch.

Fearghus didn't quite know what he was supposed to do, but he knew where he was to go. Sprinting as fast as he could, he climbed up a ladder to the flat roof of the captain's bedroom. On top of the room, there was a huge wooden catapult, tied fast to an iron ring. Beside it was a pile of large boulders, with a strange substance on them. Fearghus knew what this was for. Without even thinking about it twice, Fearghus lifted one of the projectiles onto the burnished catapult. "Light it afire!" Colla cried down below.

Fearghus looked at the torch in his hand. Now it was time to strike back. Slowly, he placed his torch on the stone, and drew his sword. "Take this!" he cried, and cut the rope.

The huge wooden catapult hurtled forward, nearly ripping off the roof of the cabin. A great sense of relief washed over Fearghus as the fiery boulder whistled through the air. "Good job!" Colla shouted. "Now get down here and fight!"

Now the Roman ship was burning. Across the narrow chasm between the two vessels, the enemy sailors were screaming and running about. This only enlivened Fearghus more as he jumped back down to the deck.

"Come on!" Colla cried over the hiss of his sword. In front of him, several Roman soldiers swung their weapons back and forth swiftly. Fearghus plunged into the attacking men, hacking with his blade.

Suddenly, Fearghus noticed quite a few more Romans jumping onto his ship. "There are too many!" he cried, panicking.

"Hold your ground!" Colla responded. "We'll pull through!"

Fearghus continued to parry and slash as Colla left the fight and sprinted down to the oarsmen. "Get up, you filthy slaves!" he snapped, pounding the mallets as hard and fast as he dared. Slowly, the ship began to gain speed.

Suddenly Fearghus realized that the ship was going backwards. Colla had ordered the slaves to row in the other direction. The Roman ship now was beginning to pull away. Fearghus breathed a sigh of relief as the attackers ceased their onslaught.

Then a very extraordinary thing happened. The ship began to turn. "Hold on, Fearghus!" Colla cried from under the deck.

Now the vessel switched directions. "Faster! Faster!" came Colla's muffled voice. Fearghus braced himself. The nose of the ship was pointed straight at the other boat.

Finally, the last soldier fell to his knees before Fearghus's feet. "What are you doing?" he shouted.

"We're going to sink their ship!" Colla yelled, his hammers pounding strenuously hard.

Now Fearghus heard the voices of the Celtic slaves upon the other vessel. "They're going to ram us!" one shouted to his comrades. Fearghus felt sorry for these innocent men. As the two ships neared each other, he bowed his head for them.

"Get down here!" Colla screamed. Fearghus shook himself awake and leapt down into the hold of the ship. Down below, the Roman slaves were pulling their oars furiously to the sound of Colla's mallets. "Get a hold of something!" Colla yelped, looking over his shoulder.

Then it hit. Fearghus was knocked off of his feet and he hit the floor hard. The ship jolted back and forth as it slid through the enemy vessel. "Bring in your oars!" Colla shouted, brandishing his dagger in front of the slaves. The men obeyed and pulled their paddles all the way in from the outside of the ship. The front of the ship was tipping upwards as it ran over the Roman boat.

"Have you ever rammed anyone, before?" Fearghus asked.

"Of course!" Colla chuckled. "We pirates have to protect ourselves, don't we?"

"I just hope you know what you're doing," Fearghus muttered.

"We'll be fine," Colla told him. "We've likely now stopped a sea attack on the monastery."

"Let's just hope we find help in time," Fearghus said, struggling to his feet.

"I'll see my village in only but a day or so," Colla reassured him.

Soon, the ship leveled off again in the water, and a soothing calm set upon the two men. Colla stopped pounding the hammers and left the slaves to sleep. "Let's get back up on deck, he suggested.

Up above, the stars were beginning to come out. Fearghus and Colla walked over to the railing and peered out into the misty sea. "We've gone from fighting pirates to fighting Roman soldiers," Fearghus sighed. "Will our work ever stop?"

"The work of a warrior never ceases, my friend," Colla answered. "Death shall forever be the only exit."

"I wish it were different, Colla," Fearghus continued, looking down at his bloody blade.

Behind them, still burning above the water, was the corpse of the Roman ship. Only but a few planks of wood and bits of cloth still remained of the once proud vessel. "I'm glad we were able to defeat them," Fearghus said, smiling.

"We haven't defeated them yet," Colla responded.

This remark went straight to Fearghus's heart. What was to become of him? Was he still to live by his sword? What was his *real* purpose? Fearghus feared he would never know the answer.

"I'll take the watch, for now," Colla said. "You go get some sleep." So Fearghus dried his sword and retired to bed.

Fearghus had a hard time waking next morning. He was so exhausted from last night's skirmish. And on top of that, Bressel's bed was extremely comfortable.

It was a very strenuous life, running a pirate ship. Colla had to constantly go up and check the sails, and when the wind died down, there was always the task of pounding hammers for the slaves to row by. Even more tiring was the need to set out a watch during the night.

"Get up!" Colla shouted from the deck outside. Fearghus was almost too tired to open his eyes. "We'll be there soon!" Colla cried. Fearghus had to force himself to get out of bed.

"Do you really know where we're headed?" Fearghus asked, rubbing his eyes.

"My village is getting close," Colla bellowed. "But we must hide this ship from them before we land."

"Do you know a good place to do so?" Fearghus asked, squinting in the light of morning.

"There is a stream, down the coast here," Colla responded, gesturing towards the rocky shore. "I think we can hide our vessel in a large cave near that river."

"I'll go get ready," Fearghus told him and set to work bathing, clothing and arming himself while the ship continued to float south down the edge of Eire.

In good time, the mouth of a wide river became visible up ahead of the boat. "I'll go man the rudder," Colla told Fearghus. "You can get ready to drop the anchor."

Fearghus ambled down the outer deck until he came to the coil of rope supporting the anchor. He was becoming happier with each step. This ship had become a prison to him recently, and the thought of leaving it behind, if only but for a short time, simply delighted him.

Quickly, the ship began to turn, and before he knew it, Fearghus heard Colla pounding the hammers down below the deck, forcing the slaves to row up the current of the river.

The ship crept slowly up the stream, making barely any sound. Here and there, along the banks of the river, several trees grew closer and closer to the water. Their reflections danced across the blue water of the stream, painting the beautiful picture of spring before Fearghus's eyes.

"It's just ahead!" Colla shouted from the back of the boat. Fearghus turned and beheld a great black cave, the entrance towering above their sails. It had an eerie sense about it. Fearghus could barely see even a few yards ahead into the dark abyss. "We'll have to light up a few torches, Fearghus!" Colla cried.

"I'll get right on it!" Fearghus responded, and walked into the captain's bedroom to find some. When he returned with the lights, the boat was already enveloped in darkness. Fearghus had a hard time finding Colla, still holding the rudder in the back of the boat.

"Go drop the anchor, Fearghus," the pirate said. "We've found the shore."

Fearghus handed the man a torch and hurried back to the front of the vessel. Then a very strange feeling came over him. The air in this cave smelled very strange. It smelled like death. Everywhere, there was a hint of rotting flesh.

Suddenly, Fearghus was able to recognize this scent. It smelled very similar to the great snake that he had encountered in his own village many days ago. But this time he was trapped in the darkness of the cave. "Let's get out of here!" Fearghus cried.

"Don't fret, my boy!" Colla called. "We're in no danger. This is just another pirate's cave. I've been to quite a few in my day."

"There's no one here," Fearghus said. "I'm suspicious about this place."

"Well, don't be," Colla answered. "The exit's just a short walk away."

"By the way, does this cave go any further?" Fearghus asked.

"Yes, it is more of a tunnel, if I must say. It leads all the way to a great mountain far away. It was said that all the snakes of Eire gathered at that mountain not more than a week ago. It's been abandoned ever since."

"You don't suppose that the snakes have come down here?" Fearghus asked, twitching with fear.

"Of course not!" Colla stammered, strapping on his belt. "Now let's get off this damned ship!"

Fearghus only felt more scared as Colla pushed a plank of wood against the stone banks of the river. He did not trust this place. It brought back too many fearful memories of his past.

Soon, both of the men were standing on the shore. "I still don't like this place," Fearghus almost whispered.

"Come on, let's go!" Colla shouted, jogging off into the darkness with his torch. Fearghus reluctantly followed him.

As he walked through the blackness, Fearghus stepped on something. It was fairly soft, he noticed. When he crouched down to see what it was, his heart sank. Below him, smelly and rotted, was the corpse of a serpent. "Hurry!" he cried, sprinting as hard as he could.

"Cool down!" Colla yelled, slowing his pace. "You're right, this is a strange place," he commented. "Look up."

Above Fearghus's head, the ceiling of the cave stretched far and wide. But that wasn't the peculiar thing about it. As Fearghus looked on, he noticed that the entire inside of the cave was overgrown with green foliage. "These are shamrocks," Colla whispered. "What do you make of this?"

"I've seen plants like these before," Fearghus said. "We'd best get out of here before something happens."

"What do you mean, 'before anything happens'?" Colla asked.

"Trust me," Fearghus responded. "This plant is almost as if magical. We'd best move on."

"I know what you're talking about," Colla sighed.

"What's that?" Fearghus asked. He was very curious.

"Oh, nothing…" Colla told him. "Let's get going. The exit is just around this corner."

Soon Colla had led them to a large crack in the wall, bursting with sunlight. "We'll reach the village soon," he reassured Fearghus.

Chapter 5

Love and War

Outside, the world was bright and beautiful as Fearghus had hoped. The land was covered with rolling green hills and was overgrown with grass and shrubs. "Colla, are you sure you know where you're going?" Fearghus asked at length.

"Of course I do," Colla answered. "The settlement is just over that hill," he continued, pointing straight ahead.

"Do you really trust your kinsfolk to believe you after all this time?" Fearghus asked.

"No, I don't," Colla explained. "But I do expect them to believe *you*."

"How do you expect to even approach them, anyway?" Fearghus asked.

"I'll find a disguise," Colla responded briskly.

Presently, the thatched roofs of the village appeared on the horizon. "Right there, where I thought it would be!" Colla shouted, strutting about.

The two men continued to walk straight at the village, not hiding themselves, until Colla stopped them. "I'll come in after you," he said. "You go ahead and establish some common ground with them. Ask for the local magus to come forward."

"Alright," Fearghus whispered, and crept towards the wooden fence of the settlement. The people of the village took little notice of him, at first. This surprised him, because he looked so different from them. The farmers and fishers of the town looked extremely impoverished. Their huts looked more like lean-tos, and they wore sparse, filthy clothing. Even so, Fearghus knew these men would be good warriors.

Gathering up his courage, he ventured to speak with one man. "I must see the magus, right away," he said, bowing to the dirty farmer.

"Who are you, to be crawling around these parts? We want no business with you rich people," the man snarled.

"We are in a very troublesome situation, my friend. I must see the magus!" Fearghus pressed.

"He'll be down at the shrine, a bit away from here," the man answered, looking down at the ground.

"Thank you so much," Fearghus said, and bolted through the village square. The villagers walking about seemed almost stunned as he ran by them in his armor and cape. They had never seen such good fortune in the possession of one man. They wanted to know more about this wealthy warrior.

It was a fairly large village of wooden and earthen homes, but Fearghus had no trouble finding the shrine. He already knew that it would be the largest and most decorated edifice in the whole lot. Inside the building, the magus sat there, facing the wall, his eyes closed in prayer.

Fearghus knew that he was supposed to pay a bit more respect to the man than he did, but this was still a very dire matter. As soon as he entered, he spoke to the Druid in a gruff, troubled voice. "I am Fearghus, from the north," he began. "My people are being persecuted by the Romans."

"Sit down, my friend," the magus said. "Now, tell me about this problem."

"There is a Roman monastery, far north of here," Fearghus told him. "My people have captured it and now hold it from the attacking soldiers. We need more men to fight, lest we be overrun with these men."

"Who am I to send my unfortunate men off to battle?" the Druid said. 'What is there to gain, and what is there to lose?" he asked.

"Everything," Fearghus said in a low voice. "We will lose our land, our shelter, our lives."

"I still must doubt your purposes, I am sorry to say," the magus responded.

"I beg with all of my strength for your aid," Fearghus bellowed, humbling himself. He was not going to give up now.

"I'm sorry, but I cannot send my people off to fight a hopeless war. We will stay here and continue with our lives," the Druid responded.

Suddenly he was interrupted. Outside in the village square, a great uprising was taking place. Fearghus turned and left the shrine to see what was going on. What he saw certainly did not please him.

"He is back to betray us again!" one of the villagers cried. "Let us do away with this pirate!"

One of the farmers had recognized Colla. Apparently, his disguise was not quite strong enough.

Now Fearghus faced an even bigger problem; his guide and companion faced death if he didn't intervene fast. "Stop this ruckus!" Fearghus shouted, sweeping his cape back.

Simultaneously, all of the villagers ceased their violence and stared in awe at Fearghus's arms. Almost like children, they feared Fearghus and his power. His attire established a strong presence among them. They would listen to him now. "Now who is this?" Fearghus asked, pointing at Colla. "What has he done to you?"

"Many years ago," one villager said, "he betrayed us and became a pirate."

"That is quite a fair reason," Fearghus responded. "However, how do you know of his continued treason? Is he any longer a pirate, as you call him?"

"It is of no consequence!" the man snapped. "He will always be a traitor to us!" he shouted, pumping his fist.

Now the expression on Fearghus's face became cold and menacing. "I shall take his fate into my own hands. This man will suffer for his mistake."

This only angered the man more. "And what claim have you to his life? We shall do the punishing around here."

"I have a very good reason, my friend," Fearghus retorted. "Pirates killed my parents, to put it bluntly," he pressed.

"Fine!" the man shouted in a gruff voice. "Go now and do with him what you wish. We shall let you avenge your kin," he explained.

Fearghus strode forward and snatched up Colla's wrists in his grip. "I won't be long," he told the villagers, and disappeared into the cover of the forest.

When they were both safely out of site, Fearghus loosed his hold. "It's too much of a risk, Colla," he said. "Go back to the ship and wait till I return with the men."

With that Fearghus spun around and walked back towards the village. "You might need this!" Colla suddenly shouted. Behind him, Colla was holding up his bloodstained dagger. "It'll convince them better of my death."

When Fearghus returned to the village, the angry men were waiting for him. "You won't have to worry over him anymore," Fearghus assured them, holding up Colla's dagger.

"That's fine with us!" one of the men answered happily.

"By the way, my friends," Fearghus began, "do you realize that your lives are in danger?"

"Oh, what do you have to tell us now?" one of the farmers said, obviously exasperated.

"I don't believe you've ever heard of Rome, have you?" Fearghus asked.

"I have!" one of the men responded. "I come from Britain."

"Very good," Fearghus responded. "Then you must know how they treat people like us."

"They hate us and we hate them. It's much safer here in Eire, I'd say," the man told them.

"Then would you believe me if I said that they had come here?" Fearghus asked, looking around at all of the villagers' faces for some sign of agreement.

"How do you come by this?" one of the farmers snapped.

"I've just sailed down the coast here from a Roman monastery. My men have captured it and now are desperately trying to hold it from the Roman soldiers. We need your help," Fearghus pleaded.

"I don't believe you!" the man retorted, spinning around to leave.

Suddenly another thing interrupted Fearghus. "Pirates! Pirates!" a villager cried, running as fast as he could into their party. "I've just seen a pirate ship down the coast here! We must hide to save ourselves!"

Now Fearghus was in trouble. Why would Colla do such a stupid thing? It would have been much safer to stay hidden inside the cave. There was no chance now of convincing the villagers to come with them. The only option would be to get back on the boat and escape.

Fearghus started running. Right away, he noticed the black sail of a pirate ship gliding towards the shore. The pirate ship was moving closer and closer to the beach as the villagers fled for their lives. If only they knew that the ship wasn't dangerous, that the man on board wanted to help them.

Then Fearghus realized something. The pirate ship began to attack. As the vessel began to fire its catapults at the shore, he knew that this wasn't Colla. Now an even greater chaos set on the people.

The pirates had followed them here. Fearghus would have to do something fast before they attacked the village. Thinking as hard as he could, he set his mind and drew out his blade. "Hide the women and children!" he shouted. "Prepare to fight!"

The villagers shouted and whooped, rallying around their new leader. "Hold your ground!" Fearghus shouted to them all, as their doom grew closer. The pirates were beginning to launch their boats. Some had already set foot on the land.

Many of the villagers, Fearghus noticed, didn't even own swords. Some of them wielded bows, pikes, tridents, even short daggers and wooden stakes. His fighting force didn't look very good, but he knew they would fight to protect themselves. "Get ready!" he cried.

Now the pirates were upon them. Fearghus started the battle by thrusting his sword into the first man, and the others followed with what they had. For a moment, there was almost as if a lull in the battle. Not many of the villagers had been hurt in the recent scuffle, but Fearghus knew they would in the near future. Now, more than ever, Fearghus wished he had Conn's gift of a battle-axe. He had left it back in Tuathal's village by the mountain where Irial was first captured.

"Watch and learn," Fearghus told the men. "These pirates don't stay together. We'll be stronger if we hold close to one another," he continued. His advice was met with a cheer of approval. He smiled to himself at this, for his plan was coming together.

Now the group weathered the second charge. This band of pirates was a bit more skilled and fierce, but with almost no loss, the villagers once again came through the struggles. Fearghus was becoming increasingly proud of his men.

Suddenly, his hopes were dashed. As more and more men hurtled out of the pirate ship, another one appeared behind it. The men would be swamped if any more of Bressel's men came to his aid. Now the villagers began to curse and throw down their arms. "We can't fight so many men!" one of them screamed. We must go comfort our families before we all die. This is hopeless!"

More and more of the men began to throw down their weapons and retreat. Fearghus's army was leaving him! Now he could only think of one thing to do. "Charge!" he cried, swinging his sword. The few men left to him raised their weapons in a like manner and rushed towards the two ships with him.

The men met the attacking pirates head on and temporarily, they crushed them. However, more were pouring out of the first ship, and the second was getting ever closer to the shore. "We may die, but we'll die with honor!" Fearghus told his men. He knew that this handful of villagers wouldn't leave him.

Just as the fighting started up again, Fearghus noticed something. The second pirate ship was headed right for the other one. As the battlefield cleared for a moment, he ran forward to see this phenomenon. Then it was all clear. This wasn't really another group of pirates, this was Colla and the *Silverbeam*!

The men cheered as Colla's ship crashed into the other boat with a sound like an earthquake. Every plank of wood, every string creaked and strained as the two vessels met. Colla was ramming Bressel's ship. They were saved!

Huge chunks of wood littered the ground. Fires caught on the pirate ship. It was truly a spectacular sight to see a boat being rammed. Fearghus had never seen such a magnificent display of raw power and destruction. Now the pirates ashore fell back as they saw their only lifeline fall to pieces. Fearghus just stood there in awe, while his men rushed ahead to slay the remnant of the pirates.

Fearghus scanned the two boats back and forth. Then he saw something that disturbed him. As the pirate ship slowly sunk, Fearghus spied someone swinging on a rope from it to the *Silverbeam*. Colla was the only one on the ship, besides the slaves, and now he was in grave danger. "Come with me!" Fearghus shouted to his men, running to the beach. "My friend is in trouble!"

Quickly, Fearghus boarded one of the pirates' rowboats and pushed off. His men followed him in the other boats. Now he began to pump his oars vigorously. He had to reach the *Silverbeam* before Colla was hurt. Colla wouldn't be suspecting of the attacking men.

Soon, he bumped into the side of the boat. There was a length of rope in the rowboat with him, and improvising for a grapple hook, he tied it to his sword and cast the weapon over the railing. The sword caught the edge of the ship and held on the wood.

Up above on the deck, Fearghus was pleased to hear the sounds of a struggle. He was happy to find that Colla was still alive and fighting. The man he was fighting with was Bressel, Fearghus discovered.

He pulled himself up and lunged onto the deck of the vessel, his sword back in his hand. Just in front of him, Colla and Bressel were locked in a close sword fight. The two men seemed very evenly matched at this level. He would have a hard time getting himself into the skirmish.

Fearghus tied down his rope to the mast, and his companions began to pull themselves up. One by one, his small army flooded the deck of the ship. Even so, the duel between Colla and his former master raged on in their midst.

Now it was time for action. Fearghus lifted up his sword, and strode towards the two men. "Colla! I've brought help!" he shouted. Colla spun around to see his friend.

Right away, Fearghus knew his mistake. "No!" he cried as Bressel plunged his blade into Colla's stomach. Now Fearghus had lost his greatest companion. Bressel stood their, his bloody sword poised and ready, over the body of Colla.

Feargus didn't even watch Colla crumple to the deck. Both of his eyes were fixed on the man who had killed him. For a moment, he suddenly became his sword, and his sword wanted Bressel's blood. Not nearly even thinking about it, he leapt forward and taking his blade in both hands, he cut Bressel down, and knelt down behind his fallen comrade.

"I'm so sorry!" he sobbed, cradling Colla's head.

"It's on the Isle of Man…" Colla gasped.

"What's on the Isle of Man? What?" Fearghus pressed.

Colla opened his eyes and looked up at his friend. "My treasure," he whispered, and expired.

Fearghus did not have time to mourn for Colla. Quickly now, he laid his friend in the cabin and went out to meet his followers. "This is my ship now, and I'll have each and every one of you join my ranks," he told them. "Go round up whoever else you can find to help."

After disposing of Bressel's mangled corpse, Fearghus walked over and leaned on the railing. Outside of the ship, the remains of the pirate's ship were smoldering in the seawater. Standing there, he thought long and hard about his adventures. It was almost too much to bear, seeing his friend go like this. In the few days that he had known Colla, he had grown to love the man.

Soon, the villagers began to come back from the shore. "We've picked up a whole bundle of men," one told him.

"That's good news," Fearghus responded, still gazing longingly at the water.

Soon all of the men had boarded the *Silverbeam*. One of the fishers dared to speak with Fearghus. "We're all ready to go," he said. "I've been on a few ships before. Shall we shove off?"

"Go right ahead," Fearghus told him. "I'll go look out for danger," he continued and walked off towards the mast. When he got there he climbed the ropes up to the top of the big black sail and sat down on the crossbar of the mast, holding on tightly. The sea ahead looked desolate and plain.

Soon the ship was moving at a good pace. The villagers had regulated the rowing down in the hold, and the deck was crawling with warriors. It was a much easier life for Fearghus, with the villagers doing everything. Right now he could enjoy the salty sea breeze blowing in his face. A great length of time passed.

Soon, on the left, the great cave came up. Fearghus cringed, thinking of what lurked in that darkness. He hoped he would never have to go in there again. He feared terribly the renewed threat of the snakes and the effects of the shamrocks. He did not want to undergo any more magic, and he clung desperately to his current state.

Presently, it was time for supper on the deck. The villagers had prepared what little food they had brought with them, and Fearghus was treated to a good parcel of meat. Once again, he felt safe with his men, just as he had in the monastery before the Romans came.

"We're planning to row through the night," the head of the villagers told him. "By the way, I'm Seadna, at your service."

"I'm very grateful for your help," Fearghus told him. "I'm glad you have agreed to help us fight."

"Well I'm doubly as happy that you've warned us of this disaster!" Seadna chuckled.

Fearghus was pleased at this type of attitude in his men, but he still feared for the future of Irial and the villagers under his control. If they didn't make it in time, the monastery would very likely fall to the Romans. Every mile that they rowed in the sea made one step further to his goal. They would not tarry anywhere during this trip.

Soon, the atmosphere on the boat dropped into the festive mood of drinking and merrymaking. Fearghus loved this nightlife. It was all so new to him, though, and just as well with his men, too. They were all embarking on this strange journey together, and making the most of these times.

As he sat there drinking and laughing with Seadna and the others, Fearghus got to thinking about Colla's last words. He had stated that his treasure was on the Isle of Man. Fearghus didn't rightly know where this island was, but he remained confident he would find it. Before, he was so curious as to where the prize was, but now he had bigger problems to deal with. Even so, he still wanted to know just what Colla's treasure looked like. He regretted that he did not have any more time with the former pirate.

"Approximately how much time do we have, anyway?" Seadna asked him, at length.

"I'd say we have about a day and a half," Fearghus told him. "We'd better keep on rowing from now on."

"Yes, we'd certainly better!" Seadna remarked. "By the way, how many Romans do you expect?"

"A whole legion," Fearghus told him. "That's Roman talk for a great deal of men."

"I only hope my men can help. We really should defend ourselves better…" Seadna responded.

"Did…uh…you know Colla personally?" Fearghus ventured, changing the subject.

"He was always a very bad person," Seadna answered, his voice becoming low and serious. "I wonder how he managed to put such a show on for you?"

"Oh, this ship was stolen," Fearghus pressed. "Colla has been out of the business for a while now."

"That's good to hear," Seadna sighed. "It's a shame that he's gone, at the hands of his former master."

Fearghus nearly choked on his drink. "Wait a minute…how do you know this?"

"I sailed on this ship many years ago," Seadna reminisced. "But I got out before it was too late."

"You were a pirate, too?" Fearghus asked curiously. "You mean, you know what Colla's treasure is?"

Seadna looked hard into Fearghus's eyes. "I'm sorry, friend, but I cannot speak of it," he whispered. "Colla has a deep, dark past behind him. It is not for you to hear."

Fearghus felt quite offended by this remark, but he dared not press Seadna for information. Colla's treasure likely wasn't for his eyes to see. "Thanks anyway," he told Seadna and walked off.

Fearghus had trouble sleeping that night. He once again found himself lost in the world. He still didn't know why the gods had given him this task, or even if this was what they intended. He hoped that he was using his sword correctly, and that he was fighting the right enemy.

The next morning, the deck was buzzing with excitement. Few of the men had ever served as warriors or guards, but they were a fierce and brutal people. Fearghus only hoped that the men at the monastery would have enough weapons for them, and that the monastery was well.

The party would likely reach the shore by sunset. From there it would be a short drive to the encircling woods. A great feeling of fear and hatred was set in the heart of every man. Each warrior knew of the risk of this fight, and of its benefits. All of them had already signed on for good. There was no going back.

The day wore on uselessly, while the party prepared itself. Fearghus's plan was coming together slowly but surely, and this pleased him very much. However, by the end of the day, a great problem had arisen.

"The plunder from the pirate ship provided quite a few swords and pikes, but we are still very badly equipped," Seadna told Fearghus. "How do you expect to fight the Romans?"

"We will fight the Romans with swords, my friend," Fearghus reassured him. "I've decided to ride for the great forest shortly. I have a good friend named Conn in those woods. He'll have enough weapons."

"Shall we land then?" Seadna pressed, readying himself for action.

"Yes, and right away. I only hope that Conn remains alive," Fearghus responded. "I shall not try to take very long."

The villagers had brought with them only two horses, plump slow animals of the field. Fearghus would take only but one other man with him, and he chose a fisher named Finghin. According to Seadna, who remained charged with the task of leading the other villagers, Finghin was a brave warrior from the Celts of the western side of Eire. He had never seen or heard of the Roman Empire, but was already developing a fierce brutality towards its name.

Long before the sunset, Seadna steered the ship to harbor on the gentle stone beach of the southern forest. Fearghus had never been to this part of Eire before, having only explored the west of the woods, but he knew that if he could reach the road, he could find Conn's house easily.

Seadna's men had already prepared their horses. Right away, before he even knew it, Fearghus was galloping down the plank of wood to the shore, bursting into the trees, Finghin at his heels. Both men were heavily armed for the excursion, ready to fend off any hostility.

The forest was thinner in the east, and Fearghus was pleased at the progress he was making. Before the night, he would very likely find the road, or even reach Conn himself. He was quickly becoming accustomed to the art of horse riding, and it was a comfortable feat to him now.

Now Finghin spoke up for the first time. "Have not the Romans plundered this forest already?" he asked.

"Why yes, they have been through here, but my friend Conn is a tough warrior. He will still be there, at his house," Fearghus told him. "He lives a great bit west of the road, buried in the thick forest cover."

At length, the sparse trees grew thicker, and the ground was choking with tangled foliage. The road was not far now, and Fearghus's horse slowed in its exhaustion. What little light was left of the dying sun could hardly be seen through the dense canopy of leaves, and darkness was creeping up on them.

Now Fearghus's only hope was to pray that the Romans had not reached the monastery yet, for alas, his aid would be late to its side, for his lack of weaponry. Even so, he was confident that once he had the supplies, the return trip would be short and decisive. In the favor of the gods, the walls of the monastery were not breached just yet.

Fearghus breathed a sigh of relief as the dusty road came into view. His horse and Finghin's were tired, and the road offered safety and relief to their wandering. "Now if I'm not mistaken," Fearghus reasoned, "we landed close to the south of the forest. I think the old footpath to Conn's house should lie to the north, on the left. Let's not tarry here long."

The two men began to gallop along the road to the north, constantly watching the thick brush for a break. The forest was extremely dense along the path, and this was good, so as to distinguish it from the trail. Fearghus still didn't know how far south they had wandered, and how far this trip would be. It could take a long time before they would find Conn. In his own wanderings several days earlier, he had entered this place from the south anyway.

Fortunately for him, the trail came up very quickly in front of them. It was Finghin who spotted it. "Looks like a trail over there," he shouted. "There are slashes and broken branches all over the trees."

And indeed it was the work of Fearghus's sword. "I'll go investigate," he told Finghin. "You stay here and watch out for any Romans."

And with this Fearghus drew his sword once again, and hurtled into the forest. Just ahead, the familiar smell of wood smoke greeted him. It was normal for a smith to need fire for his trade, but not this much. Right away, Fearghus's fears came true. Out in the clearing, he beheld only a great heap of smoldering wreckage. The smell of smoke now became the smell of death as Fearghus inched forward. Lying about, charred and mutilated beyond repair, lay several dead bodies. Luckily, as Fearghus looked on, they all appeared to be Roman soldiers to him. Conn had likely escaped with his life and was not far from here.

Now it was time to salvage what was left of the once great forge. Fearghus shouted aloud to Finghin to come out into the clearing, and began to clear away the blackened wood of the house. Behind the wreckage, he immediately was able to distinguish several sharp blades of steel, untouched by the burning. There were great quantities of weapons, big and small, buried in the devastation. By the time Finghin reached him, Fearghus had filled his cape to bursting with swords and spearheads. "I'm sorry about your friend," Finghin said when he reached Fearghus. "I'm sure he was a good man."

"He's not dead yet!" Fearghus shouted, pushing aside the wreckage. "Now help me gather these weapons!"

Finghin shut his mouth and knelt down beside his leader. "What'll we do then?" he asked curiously.

"You'll have to take these swords back to the ship on foot, using your horse for the weight. I'll stay here to help my friend," Fearghus instructed him.

Within minutes, their plan was put into action. Fearghus and Finghin, tripping and falling all over the place, slowly carried the packs of swords over to the horses. These were pack animals anyway, and very accustomed to the task of carrying heavy loads. Right away, Finghin was off into the thick forest brush, his horse straining behind him slowly. Fearghus, on the other hand, was galloping north down the road, his eyes peeled for signs of Conn.

The sun was setting quickly, and Fearghus remembered with pain his previous experience riding a horse on this road. Just days ago, he was riding this same length of road, wearing the same cloths, but, oddly, on a different quest. Back then he wasn't short of time, and Conn wasn't in danger.

Soon, it became evident that he would not find Conn, for the darkness of night was enveloping him. His only hope for shelter lie but a short distance ahead at Irial's house, though it, too, was probably burned to the ground.

In complete darkness, finally, Fearghus and his horse, both exhausted, stumbled into the clearing of Irial's house. The smell of smoke greeted them, but it did not scare Fearghus. Right away, he recognized that the house was in very good condition, and that the fire instead was coming from the chimney of the house.

Inside, the warm light of a dying wood fire danced across the bare walls. This made Fearghus wonder just who was or had been here. The house looked just as he had left it several days ago before riding to the monastery.

Soon, it was quite evident that no one was here. The bed in the back of the abode was messy, and the smell of meat hung in the air, but Fearghus knew that whoever these things were from, by now, was gone. Somehow, standing there, he knew it was Conn who had been here. It was too bad that he had missed his comrade like this.

Quickly tying his horse fast to a tree, Fearghus retired to bed and rested himself for another harsh day of travelling. He needed to recuperate. It would be a long ride to the monastery from here, and a dangerous one, full of angry Romans and bloody skirmishes. As he watched the weak embers of the fire slowly fade out, he prayed once again to the gods for Conn's safety.

Early the next morning, Fearghus was quick to his feet. As the sun rose over the edge of the clearing, he was immediately working at feeding and watering his horse. All about him, the craft of Irial the lumberman lay about. Fearghus was pleased to see a sturdy wooden wagon by the side of the cabin, fresh and new in its making. This contraption would likely prove very useful in the journey ahead.

Fearghus filled the cart with a variety of supplies, including food, cloth, and even bringing with him a few daggers and javelins from Irial's store. His horse refreshed and replenished, now it was time to leave. If he hurried, he could reach Tuathal's destroyed village by midday.

It was much easier riding through the morning like this, as he had done with Irial before. The world was bright and wonderful as it had been previously, and the Irish sun shone warmly on his face. However, beyond this shimmering forest lay in waiting his greatest enemy: Rome. Even in such a world as this, he realized, his men could be in terrible danger, and his rebellion be hanging in the balance. All depended on Seadna and his pirate ship to provide help and weaponry.

Presently, the trees of the great southern forest began to thin. Soon there would be nowhere to hide, and his sword would provide his only protection. He had to be careful, because in all likelihood, the enemy occupied the village, and he would not be able to ride through.

Now, on the horizon, the great stone mountain rose up. Fearghus dared not climb that obstacle again. Even so, the sight of it brought him back to warm memories of his first visit to the village, which still remained just on the other side of the rock, burned to the ground in the wake of the Roman onslaught. It likely promised no shelter, or food for that matter, and was even more likely infested with Roman soldiers, but it still remained, and that mattered alone to Fearghus.

Within minutes, he was nearly upon the village. The charred remains of the wooden walls still lay about smoldering, and not even one house could be discerned in the blackened mess. Luckily, the Romans had not tarried here long, but Fearghus still kept his guard up for stragglers. With his sword drawn, he jumped off of his wagon and began to pick through the irregular planks of wood.

The corpse of the once great village now had very little to offer. Fearghus found next to nothing worth salvaging in this place, save a few weapons and spare wagon parts. The Romans had either burned or plundered the rest. Fearghus now would have to ride to the coast, and follow it to the encircling woods of the monastery, a good day's ride away. Conn wasn't anywhere in sight.

Then, suddenly, as Fearghus pushed away the wreckage of Tuathal's shrine, he found what he was looking for. There, jammed between two heavy logs, nearly untouched in all the burning, was Conn's battle-axe. It warmed Fearghus's heart to see this weapon again, after so many days. It brought back painful memories of Conn's near death and his generous help. Fearghus pulled hard and yanked the shaft out of the wreck and the shining head into the sunlight. Now it was time to continue to the monastery.

As Fearghus loaded his wagon, he began to hear a whimpering behind the wall of one of the huts. It sounded strangely like a human, but Fearghus hoped that it was a wild animal or something. Nevertheless, he kept his blade out, and crept towards the sound.

He was greeted by a deluge of glinting swords and helmets, and nearly missed the first parry with his weapon. In front of him, covered in soot and blood, stood or for that matter limped, two Roman foot soldiers, both lightly armed with broad swords. They had been left behind for dead after the sacking of the village, and now were rotting to their death. Fearghus was quick to finish them off with a few thrusts of his blade, and as they crumpled to the floor, the mysterious weeping resumed.

Fearghus sheathed his sword, and crept forward once again, his eyes peeled for any life. His search lasted longer than he wished, and just when he was about to give up, a bit of cloth caught his eye. Right away, he pushed aside a large chunk of wall and beheld the strangest, but yet the most beautiful sight of his life. Curled up like a sleeping dog, covered just the same in soot and injury as her guards, was a frightened Roman maiden, wrapped in a colorful cloak.

Immediately, Fearghus was filled with sorrow and guilt at the peril of this innocent lady. Before he even knew it, he found himself kneeling down by her side, cradling her head. At first, she struggled in his hold, but Fearghus just clapped his hand over her mouth and told her to be silent. She probably would not understand his speech though, being purely Roman in heart and mind.

In a way, it was really the woman who was taking Fearghus prisoner, instead of the other way around. Fearghus knew she was afraid of him, but he also knew that he would have to take her with him, or else she would starve. Pushing her silky dark hair away from her wild eyes now, he picked her up and stumbled back over to his wagon. She was so tired, the poor thing, that she didn't dare even try to jump out of his arms. In fact, she seemed nearly to sleep by the time the cart began to move.

Now Fearghus was embarking on a different adventure. He had never felt this way before, especially about a Roman. Now instead of hate and excitement, a warm feeling of love stirred in his breast. For now, he would try to divert this feeling for the matter at hand, but there was no escaping it in his heart.

When the village began to disappear beyond the horizon, Fearghus slumped back and turned to the maiden lying peacefully in his cart. "Hello, I am Fearghus," he told her, in the only tongue he knew.

Now, to his surprise, she began to move. "I am Agnos, a Roman citizen of Britain, for your information," she muttered in a remarkably fluent Celtic tongue Fearghus recognized from Seadna's British men. "I am only half Roman, put bluntly," she continued. "Why do you look so amazed?"

"Oh, I'm sorry," Fearghus stuttered, trying his best with her dialect. "I thought you would be speaking Latin, or some other strange speech."

"Well, I've lived in Britain all my life, working with my father among the savage natives. He's a missionary, you know, and he's taught me to speak Gaelic," she told Fearghus.

"Then how do I come by you in a place like this?" Fearghus whispered, almost shyly.

"My father's been working in Eire recently, and was killed in a coastal village. This has proved to launch a violent raid of the coast by Roman ships. I've no choice but to march with these men. Much thanks for rescuing me, anyway. I'm sorry if I scared you a bit, at first."

These words went straight to Fearghus's heart. It likely was his village or the next that had killed this woman's father. And in cold blood as well. He had a hand in it, as did his brother. How could such a beautiful creature be related to the Romans? It wasn't fair. Now Fearghus was even more confused with his purpose and fate. "Don't worry, I don't mean to hurt you, fair lady. But I must tell you now that I am a Celtic warrior."

Agnos cringed at these words. A look of fear came over her as she scanned Fearghus's muscular body, finally resting her eyes on his sword. "Did you kill my kinsfolk?" she gasped, backing away.

"Only but to avenge my own..." Fearghus whispered, caressing her. "To avenge the blood of my own family."

"I won't have anything to do with you!" Agnos suddenly shouted, standing up to her full height. Fearghus didn't listen to her. He simply snatched the girl up by her waist and threw her over his shoulder.

"Now, I said I don't wish to hurt you!" he snapped, throwing her back down in the bed of the wagon. "You're going to have to come with me to the monastery, or starve!"

Suddenly, he realized he had said something wrong. "You've infested our monastery, now have you?" Agnos screamed. Now her anger was escalating even more. "Leave me be!" she pressed, lifting up a dagger from the bed of the wagon. Fearghus tried not to flinch in the face of this weapon, but Agnos really was getting dangerous.

She was clutching a rope around her neck. Even in this scary time, Fearghus kept his cool and noticed a familiar shape hanging from it. "That is a Roman cross, isn't it?" he asked.

"What do you want with it!" Agnos retorted, looking down. Now was Fearghus's chance. In the split second that she looked away, his large hand came up and coiled completely around her small wrist. The maiden gave a yelp and dropped her weapon. "Let go, you savage!" she cried, bouncing up and down in agony.

"Not until you agree to come with me!" Fearghus said.

"Just leave me alone!" she shouted, turning the other way.

In a few minutes, Fearghus got the wagon back moving again. The woman now had become silent, after Fearghus had tethered her to the wagon. She just sat there fuming as the cart rolled slowly through the thick grass. Fearghus had a good feeling about this girl. She was certainly a sight for sore eyes.

Luckily for Fearghus, the chariot tracks of the original escape to the monastery remained in the grass and sand. By the time the trees cast long shadows east across the shimmering land and sea, Fearghus was coasting down the beach trail, as he had done before with Tadhg and the rest, only this time, he rode alone but for Agnos. Maybe a day or two before, the Silverbeam likely had sailed by this length of land, carrying much needed help to the villagers at the monastery, and hopefully Conn's swords as well.

For now, Fearghus remained content to follow the pleasant sandy beach of Eire, as the sun sank lower and lower. So lucky was he to be able to relive this experience once again, and with someone such as Agnos by his side. Even so, his happiness was clouded over by the fate of Conn. The smith was nowhere in sight. Fearghus had long since given up on this original mission, but he still mourned the loss of another great comrade.

If Conn still lived, Fearghus knew, he was very obviously riding north like him, trying to outrun the Roman onslaught. Maybe he was camped out in the wilderness, or maybe rowing along the shore. Either way, he had eluded Fearghus's grasp. Fearghus had nearly forgotten about Conn when he'd discovered Agnos, but there remained no easy way to search for Conn anyway. He would first have to get back and help secure the monastery before anything else. Then there would be time for Conn.

Gripping Conn's axe tightly now, he picked a spot on the beach where sharp jagged rocks and boulders towered over his head, hiding his wagon from the rest of the world. Here, he pulled the cart up to a halt, and unloaded Agnos and the necessary supplies for a night's rest. The girl seemed rather tired and weak, exhausted from the arguments earlier on. She hadn't spoken for a good length of time.

Right away, Fearghus lit a fire with driftwood and began plucking a chicken he had discovered behind Irial's cabin. Meanwhile, Agnos curled up in a crimson blanket and leaned against a rock far away from the warm fire, still speechless and wary. To Fearghus, she seemed dark and mysterious in the shadows like this, and he would not have that. Pausing in his work, he got up and squeezing her tightly in his huge arms, he kissed her on the cheek and set her down in front of the fire. "Now don't be afraid, I still don't mean to hurt you. Come get something to eat!" he chuckled warmly. His chicken was nearly done roasting in the flames.

Agnos, still not speaking, ate voraciously her share of the meat. Fearghus was surprised that such a small woman could stomach so much food, but it was all for the better. While they ate, he tried to make an extra effort to make sure she got most of the food, and she just took the greasy chicken and ate it with her eyes angled down. She likely had not eaten in days, being trapped in the village for so long.

At length, both of them were finished eating the remainder of the provisions, and Fearghus prepared a bed for Agnos with the cloth he had taken from Irial's abode. When the light of the fire had died and was replaced with that of the moon, Fearghus tethered Agnos's leg to his own, and drifted off to sleep under the stars.

The next morning, Fearghus, once again, was up with the first light. At his side, curled up in all the blankets he had to offer, Agnos was sleeping beautifully and peacefully. Fearghus found himself struggling to get up and away from the maiden because she was such a nice thing to look at. She had the fair skin and fierce eyes of a Celt, but the dark hair and chiseled face of a Roman.

Then Fearghus reached out to touch her. Her skin was smooth and soft. Soon, she began to wake up, and Fearghus drew his hand back as fast as he could, hoping she didn't notice him. When her eyes opened, they looked longing and innocent. By this time, though, Fearghus was up and about, preparing the wagon for the rest of the journey.

Today Agnos appeared much more outgoing, As soon as she was up, her mouth was open. "I'm sorry I was so violent before," she nearly sobbed. "Please forgive me."

"You are forgiven," Fearghus told her. "And if you really must leave, I'll let you. I'm sorry about your father. However, you have to understand my side of the argument."

"I understand. My father and I have worked among your kind for years. It is not out of my grasp to think that you have feelings, too," she replied warmly, smoothing out her wrinkled cloak. Fearghus was quite happy that she felt the way he did. This was the beginning of a wonderful relationship.

Immediately, Agnos set to helping Fearghus gather up the camp, and even helped feed the horse. As a result, Fearghus had the wagon loaded faster, and the wheels began to turn right away. Both he and Agnos had comfortable full stomachs to start the excursion, and both brought with them a high morale. Fearghus only hoped that this feeling would persist longer. He knew very well that he would likely be fighting to protect the monastery as early as this evening, risking his life and Agnos's. He felt sorry for her. After all, she was only an innocent religious person, not a brutal soldier, and caught in the middle of a war. Fearghus's war.

In the distance just ahead, Fearghus easily distinguished the white cliffs that he had seen previously before reaching the monastery. Before, these rock formations had been a beacon of hope and safety, but now, they served as a warning for the danger to be. Romans, and many of them, lurked just beyond this next hill. A whole Roman legion was probably here by now, knocking on the door of the once peaceful monastery. Fearghus feared for his life, but tenfold more for the life of Agnos, and also for those of Irial, Seadna, and the whole lot of brave warriors, especially Conn. He still did not know just how he would reach the safety of the fortress alive. The whole forest would be teeming with angry soldiers, just waiting to strike.

When the great valley appeared below, Fearghus stopped the wagon just short of the crest of the hill and turned towards Agnos. "You'll get hurt if you ride with me," he stammered, looking down. "I don't blame you if you want to go down there with your own people. I am sorry, but I must try to find a way to safety by myself. I cannot go any further with you."

Agnos didn't say anything right away. She was looking down as well, her hair covering her face. She was thinking hard, and Fearghus knew it. Then, she straightened up and looked Fearghus in the eyes. "I realize the risk of staying with you," she said slowly, squinting in the sun, "and I have also thought of the risk of returning to my people. Either way, I go where I do not belong. But, if I really think hard about it, I understand that I do belong somewhere, and there is not doubt, it's with you."

And at that moment, all Fearghus could think about was Agnos, and how much he had grown to love her, and it all came to him. Just a few seconds suddenly became a lifetime, and Fearghus's lips met hers. It was such a short instance, really, but to Fearghus it meant everything to him. He really loved this woman.

The task ahead of them suddenly became greater. Both were short of words for a moment, and then Fearghus snapped the reins and brought the wagon over the hill, and out into the dangerous valley. Down below, the whole forest was visible, bright and beautiful, but with a dark haze of smoke about it. This was the smoke of a thousand campfires, and the first herald of bitter battle.

The light salty breeze of the ocean would now be befouled with the stench of death, and the work of the gods be burned and gnarled by war. In the encircling forest ahead, Fearghus would risk everything for himself, and his love. A great puzzle, really, was what lay ahead, and every piece of it had a hand against him.

Chapter 6

Thieves

Fearghus slowly guided the wagon down the slope until the shade of the trees overshadowed him. Then he stopped once again and turned to Agnos for help. "How do you suppose we should go about getting in there?" he asked, trying not to sound too unsure of himself.

Agnos looked at him and thought to herself for a moment. "Well, isn't there another way than through this forest?" she countered, leaning back on her arms. "This is obviously not the way to go."

"Only in the north end, on the opposite side of the gate, there is a steep cliff," Fearghus answered. "But I still don't know how we'll make it."

Agnos leaned closer to him. "Let's give it a try up there," she said softly. "It's our only chance."

Fearghus knew it as well as she did. Their speed mattered more than their secrecy, and the forest path would not allow for that. In just a few minutes, he was back atop the hills, and lightly walking his horse around the perimeter of the valley, near the seacoast. He kept the wagon a little ways out of the way of the valley slope, to avoid being seen down below.

Just ahead, dark and scary as night, the *Silverbeam* held anchor in the murky water. It pleased Fearghus to see that it had had safe passage to these waters. Hopefully, its occupants had made it down to the monastery below without harm or loss. The sight of it gave Agnos a start, but Fearghus reassured her that the ship was in the hands of friends.

"That's it up there, is it?" Agnos asked, pointing to the left at a stark white rock face.

"Yes, that's where we'll attempt to enter. The forest is thinnest over there," Fearghus responded.

"I hope we both make it through!" Agnos gasped, swallowing fearfully.

"Take this," Fearghus said suddenly, holding out a steel sword of Conn's design. "It'll protect you." Agnos reached out and fitted her weak hand around the hilt.

"I'll use it well," she said, and laid it down beside her seat in the bed of the wagon. "Now let's get moving before they come out here and see us!"

Fearghus snapped the reins again and the wagon started moving faster towards the north end of the valley. As they neared the danger point, Agnos appeared more wary and slid back into the rear of the wagon. "I'll hide back here," she whispered, and disappeared under a bundle of cloth and tools. Fearghus turned around and lifted Conn's battle axe, scarred and pitted with all the arrows it had deflected, and laid it lightly atop Agnos's back, shielding it from harm. He would rely on his own sword to protect himself.

Now he steered the wagon around to face the forest. It was time to risk all he had. Drawing up a long spear from the bed of his wagon, he jabbed it into the rump of his horse and ducked down behind the wood. Just as had happened in the southern forest before, Fearghus was attempting to run right through a Roman line in a wagon. Last time he had done this, he was greatly injured, but now, the forest ahead remained thin and forgiving. The trip through the woods would be quick and decisive.

As fast as could be, the worst was over and Fearghus poked his head up. The wagon now was zipping down the bleached slope of the cliff, hurtling into the clearing of the monastery. Behind him, like a noisy waterfall, several Roman chariots gave close pursuit. They had appeared out of nowhere and were moving much faster than he was. Now he would have to make a run for, it, lest be skewered on a Roman javelin.

Suddenly, up above, quite a few Celtic archers appeared on the wall. "Open the gate!" Fearghus shouted hoarsely, swinging his sword about in the air. Arrows flew over his head in both directions, barely missing him. Now he was being run down like a deer.

When he neared the gate, the southern end of the forest suddenly burst with enemies. In the front of the monastery, the gate remained closed, to Fearghus's surprise. Instead, Irial stood atop the arch, waving a colored banner above his head. "We cannot open the gate now!" he shrieked, signaling Fearghus to him. "I shall open the back passage instead!"

This remark displeased Fearghus greatly, for now chariots and horsemen guarded the back of the fortress heavily. All the while, too, the Roman infantry was marching to the front gate. Fearghus had no where to go, looking back and forth wildly. He had fallen right into the Roman's trap. The help from the Celtic archers and spear-throwers atop the wall only endangered Fearghus more.

As the Romans closed in, Fearghus could only so much as stop the wagon and brandish his sword. His life would come to a close any minute, as well as Agnos's. He had failed in his mission to find the safety of the inside walls. Now Irial was speaking again. "Go to the back wall!" he shouted.

Fearghus, realizing the hopelessness of the situation anyway, snapped his horse into a gallop and charged at the Roman cavalry, a lance in each hand. Like the hacking of a sword, his wagon hammered into the Roman lines and his lances splintered in the chests of two soldiers. After this, Fearghus picked up his sword and drove his horse harder, until he once again reached the steep white cliff. Then, he wheeled the cart around full circle, and prepared for another charge. Just ahead of him, the small door in the side of the wall that he'd used before was wide open, and while two warriors lay dead at its base, a third stood there behind a thick wooden shield, beckoning him forward.

Now Fearghus's last hope was to hack his way again through the lines, and somehow get himself and Agnos safely through that door. He had scarcely begun this when a great shout rose amongst the infantrymen on the south side. Something had happened over there, and somehow, Fearghus knew it was good. He quickly swerved to the left, dodging a few lances and arrows, and his wagon not nearly holding up, he careened over to opposite side of the monastery. What he saw, as he had hoped, pleased him.

Ten brazen riders, covered in coarse animal skins and such, were hacking their way through the thick carpet of foot soldiers, shouting wildly. They rode on small, quick horses, and bore with them long, merciless pikes. They seemed to be on his side. Fearghus watched them for a minute, his attention completely centered on them.

All of a sudden, he noticed something. A very familiar man was riding at the head, and he looked as fierce as any of them. It was old Conn himself, swinging a short axe about as wild as a frightened bull. Surely the gate would open for these brave men. Fearghus had never seen this side of Conn before, and it amazed him. Now this was the brave warrior he had anticipated. The Roman foot soldiers were gobbled up in his onslaught, and now the chariots were wheeling around to meet them. Just as the gate began to swing open, Fearghus saw his chance. Spinning around, he prepared to make for the back passage once again.

When he did this, he just barely had time to duck as a charioteer swung a sword over his head. But that wasn't what surprised him. Just as a feeling of relief came to him, Agnos sprang up out of her hiding and plunged her sword into the man. This both scared and delighted Fearghus. Now more than ever, he feared for her life, and he ushered her back down as the remaining horsemen met them. He didn't know whether this decision was the smartest he could make, but he had no time to think about it.

Swinging wide of the remaining riders, he maneuvered the wagon over to the small door, which still lay open. Braking his horse hard, he spun around and dug Agnos out of the junk in the back. Right away, the guard with the shield dropped it and ran to his aid, taking the frightened girl into his own arms and back towards the passage. In a hurry, Fearghus threw a bundle of swords over his shoulder and leapt onto the ground, where the guard was sprinting for safety, Agnos over his shoulder.

Quickly, Fearghus caught up with them. The Romans were coming back for them now, and the open door was just paces away, when the guard suddenly took an arrow in the back and fell headlong into the wall, dropping Agnos on the dusty earth. Without delaying another second, Fearghus scooped her up and literally leapt into the passage, as more arrows zipped by his ear.

When he had safely locked the door, he carried Agnos and his swords one in each arm, and limped out into the light of the square. On the other side of the monastery, still roaring with excitement, Conn's riders were celebrating with the other warriors. No one even noticed Fearghus as he threw down his load, save Seadna and a few of his men. "Well, I'm glad to see you made it!" Fearghus said, embracing his comrade. "Just in time, huh?"

"Oh no, we had to fight our way through. We'd have lost all our men had it not been for you. Thank you, Fearghus, our casualties were light." Seadna responded, grinning. "Now, who is this next to you?" he asked, gesturing to Agnos.

Fearghus had barely opened his mouth when Agnos cut in. "I am Agnos, from Britain," she said, tucking away her necklace.

"She is a friend of mine," Fearghus said, clapping his hand on Seadna's shoulder. "I rescued her from the Romans."

"That's good," Seadna responded. "Now that you're back, we can plan our defense."

"I'll get right on it," Fearghus told him. "Finghin, show the lady to her quarters."

When Agnos had disappeared behind the group of houses, Fearghus spun around and went off to find Irial. The whole camp was abuzz with the news of Conn's triumphant entry, and every man went with a spring in his step about the settlement. The group was much larger now, and Seadna's men were making many friends among the host of Tuathal.

Fearghus found Irial standing atop the wall, looking out over the forest, his eyes hardened and fierce. "I'm happy you were able to make it in safely," he sighed, turning to his friend. "We'll do much better now with your aid."

"Thanks, Irial…" Fearghus started, gazing out to the Roman camp ahead. "I've been meaning to ask how the first battle went."

"We took some loss, and they lost some men. It was a good shot for both of us," Irial reminisced, gripping the wall harder. "Now, I'm just not sure how we'll defend ourselves. Do you have any idea how we'll feed and water all of these men?"

Fearghus hadn't considered this problem before. The provisons brought over by Tuathal's men had likely vanished by now, and the *Silverbeam* wouldn't have brought enough for a full-scale siege. Even so, Fearghus had a few good ideas. "For now," he said, stroking his chin, "we can fish for our food. I've a mind to set Conn's cavalry and a good parcel of chariots out to the pirate ship to pick up some food in the sea. Many of the men I've brought over are fishers."

"But if we are seen riding up to it, the Romans will become suspicious and burn it down!" Irial reasoned, his breathing getting harder.

"Not if we man and arm the ship permanently," Fearghus countered. "It would mean a lot less men, but it's worth it. I'll put Seadna in charge of the fishing. If the fighting remains this calm, we'll get our fill of food. It's quite fortunate that Conn is here, no doubt."

"Yes, it is," Irial agreed. "I thought for sure that he was dead."

Fearghus's plan would go into action later on, but for now, he was given the run of the monastery. Down below in the courtyard, the action had subsided and all of the men had retired to their quarters, laughing merrily. The Roman army outside was picking up its dead, badly wounded in the recent skirmish. For now, all seemed well, but Fearghus knew that the pinnacle of his war lay just ahead.

Now, his first task, it seemed, was to go speak with Conn. He had not seen the kind blacksmith in many days, and he still remained curious as to where he had found his companions. According to some of the men, he was quartered in the front of the monastery, near Irial and Seadna's lodgings. When Fearghus walked through his door, Conn was sitting there, drinking and laughing as he had many times before, just as carefree and jolly as he formerly was. "Thanks for the help, Conn," Fearghus said, startling the drunken blacksmith.

"Oh, I didn't see you there, my boy!" Conn shouted, getting up out of his chair. "How's life been treating you, lately?"

"Much better, with your aid," Fearghus replied. "By the way, how *did* you acquire those men?"

"They're just some friends from the west, many leagues across Eire. I rounded em' up after you left. I thought I'd better get myself a rebellion of my own, if you know what I'm talkin' about," Conn chuckled back.

"Well, I'm much obliged for the help," Fearghus remarked warmly, sitting down next to his friend. "But don't they look a bit like savages?" he asked.

"Well, I suppose that's what you can expect from burglars," Conn said, staring blankly at the wall.

"Wait a minute!" Fearghus bellowed, "These men are thieves?" he asked, jumping off the stool with the hilt of his sword out.

"The finest in Eire, they are, but don't be alarmed, I got em' on a short leash," Conn retorted, straightening up in his seat. "They were the only guys I could find!"

Fearghus settled down and reclaimed his chair. "I'll still have to tell Irial about this," he said, resting his hands on the table. "He's a brave warrior, now, in case you didn't hear."

"Well then!" Conn burst, bouncing with laughter. "Irial a warrior! Now I've seen everything!"

Fearghus swept his cape back over him and stood up. "You haven't seen anything until you've fought in a full scale battle," he bellowed, turning to leave. "I'll see you later, Conn!"

After he left Conn's bungalow, Fearghus quickly found Irial again and warned him of the nature of the new arrivals. "I'll post a guard at their quarters," the man said, thanking Fearghus for the information. "Now you go get some rest for tomorrow. All of our lives will be at risk come the next sunrise. As of now, we are on full alert!"

Fearghus heeded his friend's warning well. He knew just as well as every man how hard the next few days would be. Many of his courageous rebels would lose their lives in the future. No one was safe, not even Agnos. Now Fearghus could only hope that his plan would work, for the best and for the gods.

Presently, Fearghus decided to retire to his quarters. He had gone through so much recently, and would need a good lot of sleep before the siege inevitably came tomorrow. For now, he would go back to his bungalow and see Agnos again. A night with her would be just the thing to calm his troubled mind. Tomorrow, the trouble would come, and he would be ready for it.

Inside the hut, Agnos was already asleep on Fearghus's bed. While he was out, she had tidied up the place, even cooking a meal of stewed vegetables for him. After eating his supper, Fearghus woke the girl. She was just as happy to see him as he was to see her. "Oh, I'm sorry…" she stammered, getting up off of the cot. "I see you liked it," she continued, gesturing towards Fearghus's empty bowl.

"I like everything about you," Fearghus laughed, slumping down on a chair. Agnos was really a very beautiful lady. Her hair was long and thick, never tangled or dirty, and her face was innocent and sincere. She had delicate, careful hands, and sleek, shiny legs. With a modest but curvaceous body, she was everything Fearghus dreamed about in a woman.

Now Agnos turned the conversation back around. "Do we have a chance to defeat the Romans?" she asked. "I mean…do we have a proper plan for doing so?"

"Well, we do," Fearghus responded, "but I just don't know if it will work."

"At least we have each other," Agnos said, looking him in the eyes.

Fearghus had already removed his heavy armor. "Yes, we do," he remarked, and swept Agnos off of her feet.

The day after was just like Fearghus had hoped. A great calm had set upon the monastery during the night, and the fresh morning air filled all of the men with renewed vigor and high morale. As of right now, though, the sun was blotted out by a group of gathering storm clouds. They formed just in the same manner, Fearghus noted, as the Romans assembled outside.

Now, more than ever, he wished for Agnos to be his wife. It was just such a bad time for something like this to happen, but they would both take it in stride with the terrible war. During the subsequent hardship, they would try to hold fast to their love and their country.

Without waking Agnos, Fearghus got out of bed and dressed himself outside. The leaders of the fortress, including Irial, Seadna, and Conn, seemed to be the only people awake at this time. Fearghus found them standing upon the wall, staring out into the great valley and the encircling forest. "I'm glad you've come," Seadna remarked, standing aside for his friend, "Have a look!"

Fearghus was instantly sent into a state of awe at the sight. Far away, past the forest, the entire ridge was black with Roman soldiers. Like little ants, they began to weave in between the trees of the forest, moving like one solid object, twinkling in the muted light of the sun. "We'll manage for a while," Conn said, squinting. "I just don't know how long we can hold out."

"They've got us outnumbered two to one," Irial added, "but we have stone walls, and most important of all, we have Fearghus."

"What can I do?" Fearghus asked, flattered by the remark.

"You're the whole reason we're fighting," Irial responded. "You've saved us all with your good timing. I'm sure you'll think of some way out of this."

"I hope so," Fearghus said, looking around at them all. Then he remembered something, and opened his mouth to talk once again. "Seadna, may I speak with you privately?" he asked eloquently.

"Go right ahead," the man responded, leaving his position on the wall. Fearghus led him away to the corner of the catwalk, and thought about what he wanted to say.

"Now I believe that you are a friend of Colla's...am I correct?" he said, looking at the ground. When Seadna nodded, he continued. "Well, from previous experience, I have come to believe that Colla has something in common with me, and I mean to ask you if my assumption is true."

Seadna was shocked. "Of course, my friend, I would be pleased to help you," he said.

Fearghus got right to the point. "What happened to Colla when he was a pirate? I must know," he asked the man.

Seadna's expression became grave and serious. "When Colla was a pirate," he began, "it was a common practice, and still is, to capture young Roman boys on the coast of Britain, for use in slave trading and hard labor. Well, one day, Colla caught a very peculiar young boy, and..."

Suddenly he was interrupted by the shrill sound of a bugle. "Ready your arms!" Irial shouted, and Seadna suddenly was sprinting back down to the ground, his sword flashing out in front of him.

"What was that?" Fearghus yelled, jogging down behind him.

"I'll tell you later!" Seadna replied, disappearing into a crowd of confused warriors. Outside, the Romans were very obviously making some kind of a run at the gate. Fearghus hoped it was not too serious an occasion.

Now Irial was behind him. "Go help your men prepare for battle. The Romans have challenged us early!" he said. Fearghus quickened his pace and leapt the remaining flight of stairs, going in search of Tuathal's warriors. He found them mulling around in a huge group on the west side of the building. Now it was time to take command.

"Form ranks!" he shouted, drawing his blade. "Stand up straight and be ready to fight!" he added. The men obeyed and within minutes, the warriors of the destroyed village had formed a menacing and swollen battalion of fierce fighting men. At their helm, Fearghus stood, his teeth gritted and eyes squinted. He was ready to fight.

Irial standing in the center, the entire force of Fearghus's rebellion gathered in a giant crescent shape. On the right of Irial stood Seadna, his band of warriors from the *Silverbeam* stretched out behind him. And on the left, Fearghus led a large group of Tuathal's infantry. In the middle, though, proud and cunning, Conn commanded the cavalry and the group of chariots needed for the trip to the pirate ship. All stood still in the awe of the great moment, everyone's eyes focused on Irial.

Even including Rome, this was simply the greatest assemblage of raw power Fearghus had ever seen. At the beginning of his travels he had never imagined seeing such an awesome display. Now Irial began to speak, loud and clear. "The time has come, my friends, for action. We will hit the Romans, and they will hit us, but we *will* hit harder!" he bellowed. And now his whole army erupted with a cheer of approval. "To Conn and his riders, I wish luck on this next mission," he continued, nodding toward his friend. "And to Fearghus and his fighting men behind me, so do I wish you luck as well!"

And with that the battle literally began. Only but a few minutes after his words, the sounds of Roman arrows flying over the wall echoed across the monastery. Irial gave a great battle cry, and charged forward. Just as his men reached the gate, the great doors swung open to let them by. Already, the men atop the wall were throwing their javelins against those of the Romans, and men were beginning to fall on both sides. In the advance, Fearghus's battalion became the last to exit the monastery, coming behind the forces of Seadna and Conn, who were bound to ride to the *Silverbeam*.

The fighting remained light at this time, but Fearghus didn't doubt that it would be tougher soon. Immediately, Irial ordered Fearghus's men to strafe to the right, and Conn's to move left, allowing both forces to meet the Romans head on. Irial had chosen wisely, for a small charge from the Roman cavalry met Conn and his thieves, while avoiding Fearghus's lesser infantrymen. These Romans had thick and heavy shields, both a benefit and problem to their own fighting force.

Now it was inevitable: Fearghus's sword was out, his heart racing, and his fate sealed. He was leading his men in a counterattack straight at the thickest part of the Roman army: the infantry. In the Roman infantry, Fearghus noted, there were just about two types of formation. A looser one allowed for more versatility and movement, but a more tightly packed group demonstrated power and strength. Today, Fearghus, personally, would be pushed up against a solid wall of Roman shields.

To start with, Fearghus decided that it would be smart to send Tuathal's small band of remaining horsemen out to break the first Roman lines, and then, and only then, would he loose his men on them. Soon enough, his plan was put into action and the five riders of Tuathal's force galloped ahead to their likely deaths. As Fearghus continued marching forward, it pleased him to see all of them meet the Romans, but the battle afterwards was not so glamorous. Even so, by the time he himself had made his first stroke, the Romans had been softened up greatly by the martyred riders. Fearghus felt guilty for the deaths of these men, but realized that it was simply a part of war he had to deal with. Each had taken nearly ten lives in place of his own and that of his steed.

At first, the Celtic warriors literally ran over the Romans, stabbing and slashing, but a spirited charge from the soldiers behind badly wounded Fearghus's lines and got the enemy right back in the fight. The two warring parties were all too evenly matched, and this stressed Fearghus and his comrades all the more. Today, the best side would win, and the bravest warriors prevail. Feargus only hoped that the gods of Eire were looking upon him with favor.

Across on the other side of the battlefield, Conn's men were having almost no trouble. The Roman cavalry, momentarily, was breaking, and many of the chariots had already ridden through into the encircling forest. Only Irial remained with a small band of riders now, hacking down the helpless Romans. Only a few casualties were lost in this stage of the battle. Unfortunately for Fearghus, the Roman foot soldiers in front of him were a bit luckier. As Fearghus's men continued to fall, Irial channeled more and more horsemen towards his lines.

At length, Fearghus's efforts began to pay off. Parrying and thrusting his sword about in all manner necessary, Fearghus noticed that the men ahead of him became flustered and unorganized. As Fearghus's men gained on them, the Roman soldiers began a full-scale retreat. Halting his men for a moment, Fearghus prepared to fight one last time. "Whoever dares to accompany me now, come forth! Let us chase these men like dogs!"

And so Fearghus spilled more Roman blood on the field. Nearly half of his men behind him, he drove forward one last time. The slower men left on the field could only hope to turn around and put their shields up. In a last bloody skirmish, flesh and bone hissing against Celtic steel, the battle ended. When arrows began to fly from the remote cover of the forest, Fearghus turned his warriors around and sent them back to the gates of the monastery. The badly wounded Roman forces wouldn't attack any more.

As the great gates slammed shut, the first buzzards appeared. They had smelled the tempting odor of Roman blood and wanted to sample its taste. Fearghus had no time to worry about the rotting carcasses outside, though, he was extremely nervous about the results of the fishing trip. It was a very important mission. After the *Silverbeam* was armed, the pursuit of food and supplies would become much easier.

In the aftermath of the first great victory, the soldiers of Fearghus's company became spirited and rowdy. They were fired up after the fighting and looked forward to enjoying the rest of the day with food and drink. Irial, on the other hand, looked always to the worst. With two of his greatest war heroes out in harm's way, he only felt worse. Like Fearghus, he too, could not find happiness in the victory. The fighting, really, had just begun.

"I give you much credit, my friend," Fearghus reassured him, "It was a wonderful achievement."

"But only a fool would celebrate such a trivial event," Irial muttered. "The worst is yet to come."

"Then let us just hope and pray for the success of our comrades," Fearghus said. "There is not much else we can do."

His words were very important, if at least only to him. Now Fearghus could not continue his conversation with Seadna. He still wondered what Colla's treasure was, but nonetheless, he knew that it would help him. Without Seadna's help, he could not hope to find it, though. Something inside him told him that the treasure had something to do with his own magical transformations, he just didn't know what. Colla had acted very peculiar back in the cave, and Fearghus knew why, or at least hoped he did.

Now it was again time to relax. There was nothing more to do at the moment, so Fearghus set out to find Agnos. To his surprise, she was not still resting in his quarters, but rather was in the church, nursing the wounded men from the recent battle. The whole building was filled, it seemed to Fearghus, from wall to wall with cots and injured warriors. Agnos was running about, applying bandages and carrying water to the men. When Fearghus reached her, he brushed back her hair and gave her a hug. "I'm so glad you've made it!" she sobbed. "When the fighting started, I just got so frightened!"

"No need to worry now," Fearghus reassured her. "I've got you."

When the men working around them noticed the two lovers, one of them spoke. "We'll handle it from here," one said, turning to Fearghus. "You two can go off and enjoy yourselves."

So Fearghus and Agnos left the Church behind, and went back out into the courtyard, which was bursting with excitement. The men that remained from the battle were quite happy, and had already begun their merrymaking. With a nod from Agnos, Fearghus decided, with her, to go join the men in the building that had become some sort of a banquet hall. Inside the edifice, a large table flowing with meats and drinks filled up the entire room. At the head sat Irial, still relatively sad and dismal, and around the table near him sat Finghin and the remains of Seadna's men, as well as a good number of Tuathal's guards.

Fearghus and Agnos found themselves a few seats on the long side of the table, and both helped themselves to the generous libations. There was much conversation going on in this room, and Fearghus listened in, curious as to the response of his men after the battle. Presently, one of the more sober of the warriors spoke up. "This fighting is hopeless! I say we flee from here at our first chance!" he bellowed to a cheer from his comrades.

Now another responded. "You should be ashamed of yourself!" he shouted, slamming down his cup. "We should all be proud to defend our lives and land!"

Suddenly, a new voice, and a gruff one, joined in the argument. Right away, Fearghus knew it was one of Conn's burglar friends. Before he knew it, the brazen thief had leapt atop the table, his dagger drawn. "You will get us all slain!" the man said, standing up menacingly. "I say we desert this place and take what riches we deserve before we are dead! Who's with me?"

Now nearly half of the men around them sprung to their feet, shouting. The others slowly crept back into the shadows, afraid to stand for their own beliefs. Slowly, the rebels drew their weapons. Fearghus had to act now.

Pushing Agnos down underneath the table, Fearghus leapt onto the table and placed his sword on the burglar's throat. The men behind him gasped and turned to run. Irial himself became still, standing now behind his seat, a wild and frightened look creeping across his face. Even so, his former authoritative look remained. He was now powerless to stop the mutiny, though. Only Fearghus's sword stood in its way, and it wasn't moving any time soon.

Now the thief's eyes met Fearghus's, and they were cool and menacingly calm. "And who are you to stop us?" he whispered, turning to face his opponent. "You are only but one, against a multitude at my back."

"It is you, I am sorry, who must suffer, my friend," Fearghus responded slyly. "Just try and stop me."

Now the rebellious warriors about him moved in closer. Many of them had their swords out, and all wished to end Fearghus's life. He should have known that a burglar could have caused this. His life in danger, Fearghus spoke again. "You just want to take advantage of us, don't you?" Fearghus said, looking at his men. "Once a thief, always a thief."

Suddenly, a look of fear came over the man's face. His comrades now began to fall back. Fearghus had discovered his secret, and he knew it. "Don't listen to him! I am no thief!" he cried, holding his ground. "He is the thief! He wishes to take all our lives!"

Now the man brought his dagger up and pointed it at Fearghus. "No, just yours," Fearghus said, and plunged his sword into the man's throat. Suddenly, a splitting pain shot through his body. Behind him stood one of the rebels, a bloody sword poised in his hand. A deep wound had been cut into Fearghus's back. Now he became dizzy, and fell to his knees. The world was closing about him.

As the pain escalated, Irial's voice pierced the darkness. "Kill him!" he shouted, leaping onto the table. "Defend your country and your leader! Stand up, lest we all die!" he continued, rushing ahead. And with that, the hall burst with violence. Fearghus squinted. All around the hall, several duels had sprung up. Upon every rebel sprung a warrior, and upon every kill sprung an avenger. The sound of clashing metal rang throughout the room. At every moment, new warriors found their way in and chose a side. Fearghus's war was crumbling, and at the center now, he lay dying.

Now blood was spilling all over the place. Nearly Fearghus's entire back was covered in it. The pain he had once felt was gone, and was now replaced with a dazed, nearly unconscious feeling. The material world was becoming blurrier, and darkness crept up upon the edges. This was death, and Fearghus knew it. Above his head, the battle between Irial and his killer raged on. Without his lance and with it his immortality, he would soon slip away from this place.

Suddenly, the world was split with white light. Fearghus was blinded by its brilliance, and he suddenly felt better. It seemed to come down from the ceiling of the hall, down from the rafters, and a violent crack accompanied it. Was this the afterlife? Was he home to the gods at last?

This thought made Fearghus feel quite happy, for a moment, but then his hopes were dashed. Even as the light strove on, his eyes shut. Unwillingly now, he quickly fell unconscious.

As he awoke a feeling of great warmth and being greeted him. He was lying on the bed of his quarters, Agnos's gentle voice above. When he chose to open his eyes, her happiness seemed almost immeasurable. "Oh Fearghus! You've made it!" she screamed, jumping up and down. Almost immediately, their lips were once again locked. Agnos literally pounced on him.

Suddenly, Irial was there, restraining Agnos. "Get off of him! He's very hurt!" he stammered, pushing the girl aside. Then a look of surprise filled his face. Fearghus hopped out of bed and embraced his friend. "You're alive!" Irial observed.

"I do hope everything has gone well," Fearghus said. "I wasn't gone too long, was I?"

"It only matters that you're back," Irial answered. "The rebels have been subdued. The bolt of lightning that struck you also knocked them unconscious. They will likely now wake up, too. I should have known that those burglars would be trouble. I'll have you lead an excursion to the ship to deal with them right away."

Fearghus only smiled. "That's good to hear," he responded softly.

That night Fearghus was happier than ever. Now, he reasoned, his health was back, and his forces had regrouped. It would not be too long from now when he would see Seadna, and then he would go in search of Colla's treasure. Fearghus had just undergone yet another transformation, and he didn't know just where the gods were leading him. Maybe Seadna could help him find out.

The next morning when Fearghus woke up, Irial and the others were already waiting outside his door with chariots. In a flash, he had his armor on and his weaponry at hand. Today, he would take care of Conn's thieves, and find Seadna once more. Leaving Agnos behind sleeping in bed, he now snapped the reins of his chariot and bolted off towards the gate.

The Romans seemed not so responsive this morning. They were hiding deep in the back of the forest, licking their wounds. In good time, the group of chariots passed through the thin grove of trees in the north and sped out into the foothills. Just ahead, the *Silverbeam* was out in the sea, fishing in the shallow water. The men on board probably didn't know it, but their lives were in danger. When the shore was reached, Irial dismounted his chariot and waved a red banner to the ship.

At first, the vessel was unresponsive, but soon it began to come closer. "Get ready, men!" Irial told them. "We'll storm the ship! Spare Seadna and his men!"

Fearghus was relieved that the men aboard the *Silverbeam* had acknowledged them, but then his hopes were dashed. As the vessel neared the shore, a loud shout arose amongst the men and suddenly Seadna was flung overboard, into the surf below. Now the whole ship had exploded with violence. Fearghus and the men on the beach could only watch in horror as the villains attempted their coup.

But Fearghus wouldn't give up now. Before anyone else knew it, he had removed his armor and was submerged in the salty water. He was going to swim out and rescue Seadna. The waves were tough, at first, because of the boat, but Fearghus fought through them. It was all too important to find his friend, the only man remaining who could tell him about Colla's mysterious treasure. Fearghus had to save the former pirate before his heavy armor carried him below the water. On the shore, Irial's guard panicked and fell into a state of chaos.

When Fearghus finally reached him, Seadna was unconscious, just over his head as he plunged into the surf. Without delay, he brought the man's head above the water and paddled back to the beach. When he got there, the warriors helped him drag Seadna ashore and remove his armor. As they watched, Fearghus thrust his palm into Seadna's chest, and he resumed breathing. "Thank you," he sputtered, looking up at them all. "Now let's get back our ship!"

Immediately, it seemed to Fearghus, nearly half of Irial's men had plunged into the sea, each sprinting, sword in hand, to the aid of the *Silverbeam*. Fearghus, however decided to stay on the beach. Right now he wouldn't risk his life trying to win an already lopsided battle. Irial and Seadna by his side, he stood behind a short row of archers and put his armor back on.

Soon, the fighting on the ship subsided. With Irial's help, the burglars aboard the vessel were subdued. Now the *Silverbeam* pulled in closer to let the warriors off. With them came Conn, who had been betrayed by his men, and a great deal of fish. Fearghus greeted the smith with grave words. "Your men nearly overtook us back at the monastery," he muttered, patting Conn on the back. "Their rebellion has led us to question even you, their leader."

A wild look crossed the man's face. "I shouldn't have even spoken with them. They had tricked me into believing they were reformed. This won't happen again!" he sobbed.

"So long as it doesn't, Irial and I can control the fishing trips from now," Fearghus told him, turning to leave.

Then another problem suddenly found its way into the present. Just ahead of Fearghus, a column of swirling dust was the first herald of a huge band of cavalry. The Romans had discovered them, and now looked to take advantage of their folly. There would be only one escape here: the *Silverbeam*.

As the huge line of Roman soldiers began to appear over the crest of the hill, Fearghus ordered a full-scale retreat. "Back to the ship!" he cried, pushing the men around him backwards. "Get back into the vessel! I'll hold them off!" he continued, mounting his steed.

He had brought with him Conn's great battle-axe. It would be a useful tool when fighting mounted soldiers like these Romans. Now he could only pray for his safety and his life. The ship now had received his message and was slowly rowing its way back to the shore, and the warriors on the beach were scrambling back to it as fast as they could. But the Romans were advancing too fast. Taking a strong position at the edge of the sand, Fearghus prepared to meet them in battle, all by himself.

To start with, a man from the back of the pack rode forward and made a symbolic charge towards Fearghus, his sword raised high above his head. Fearghus simply held his ground and swung his axe through the man's stomach. The Romans were getting angry now. Almost immediately after this occurred, a bugle sounded and the battle began. The sound of almost a hundred horses pounded in Fearghus's ears, and his grip tightened. For the good of all of Eire now, he would protect his men.

After a long and horrendous charge, the Romans finally came upon him. Prepared for this, Fearghus brought up a thick wooden shield he had brought and blocked several javelins that had been thrown at him. Now it was his turn to fight. Just as the line of riders began to pass him, he swung his axe full-circle, catching three Romans by surprise.

Now more warriors replaced the ones he had slain. Luckily, these men were distracted by Fearghus, and did not attack the men rushing to the pirate ship for shelter. Using the stout shaft of his axe as cover and its sharp blade to attack, Fearghus slew several more men in a similar fashion as he had done before.

Suddenly, the skirmish took a turn for the worse. With still more men on the beach, Fearghus was overrun with soldiers. The Romans had formed tighter ranks now, and this made it much harder for Fearghus to defend himself. In just a minute, he would try to make a run for it. He would have to hold off the attack for just a while longer.

Soon, as more and more soldiers passed him, Fearghus realized the hopelessness of the fight. The ship had once again placed a wooden ramp on the beach. The Roman soldiers had now seen this, and were making a mad dash for the ship, passing by Fearghus in huge numbers. The *Silverbeam* would have to pull away, now. As the remaining warriors hurried aboard, the men pulled the boarding plank up and pushed off with the oars. Fearghus was left behind on the beach, and there was nowhere to go, except back into the water. There was only one chance left for him.

Swinging his axe about him as hard and swift as he could, Fearghus spun his horse around and kicked it into a gallop. He would swim to the *Silverbeam* if he had to. He had no choice now but to make a run for it. The world around him was darkening with the dust of the Romans horses. Man and beast choked in the foul air. Just ahead, his ship was moving further and further from the shore.

Soon enough, Fearghus caught up with the Romans who had chased the boat away, and coming up behind them, he brutally hacked them down with his axe and sprinted by, hurtling towards the water as fast as he dared. Just behind him, the thunder of a hundred horses followed in close pursuit. Countless arrows and javelins whizzed by him, zipping through the hot sticky air like wasps, each one with enough of a sting to end Fearghus's life.

Fearghus hit the water. He kept his horse moving as fast as it would, but still, the sea slowed him down. A salty mist of water from down below stung his eyes as he stared ahead to the back of the *Silverbeam*. If only there was more time! The water got deeper, and his horse slowed to a walk. As Fearghus moved ever closer to his ultimate goal, an arrow slammed into the back of his steed, making a sickly sound of severed flesh and blood. The animal reared and whinnied in pain. It was all Fearghus could do to hold on to its mane.

Now he was up to his knees. His horse would drown if he drove it any further. He would have to advance just a few paces ahead before he would reach the ship. Ducking more arrows and such, Fearghus kicked his horse one last time. Just behind him, the thunderous clap of disturbed water heralded the advancement of several Roman foot soldiers.

In the knick of time, Fearghus was there. His horse just barely with its nose above the water, Fearghus turned around and swung his great axe in a full half-circle behind him, dispatching two soldiers swimming just behind.

Just as more men were catching up with him, Fearghus brought his axe up and swung it into the back of the ship. The thick metal blade easily caught in the tough wooden planks. The deck of this ship was not too far above him, with him on top of this horse, especially. Just above it was the railing, also made of thick wooden logs. He would have to hoist himself up there.

The men behind him were hacking at his horse now, as he planned his jump, and the injured animal was sinking lower and lower in the water. With no time to lose, Fearghus leapt off his horse and hanging onto the edge of the ship, he spun his body around, knocking the man directly behind him unconscious with his boot. As the man's head disappeared under the water, Fearghus grabbed at the thick shaft of his axe and pulled himself up and over the railing. He hit the deck hard, on his stomach, and leapt onto his feet.

His axe had disappeared into the surf below with the force of his jump, but his life remained unharmed. Several fishers from Seadna's company immediately greeted him. Among them was Finghin. "I'm happy that you've made it," he said, leading Fearghus towards the main cabin.

"I'm just happy that we made it here in time!" Fearghus muttered, "A serious disaster could have occurred!"

As they advanced to the door of the room, Finghin's face became grave and solemn. "We've taken some casualties," he said, in a low voice.

Inside, several bodies were laid out on the floor, many of them dead or dying. Fearghus's heart sank when he realized that more than half of them were his own men. He had not gotten here fast enough to save them.

Suddenly, his thought was interrupted. Outside on the deck, several warriors were shouting. "The Romans give pursuit, master!" one of them told him. Fearghus dashed out onto the deck, scanning the landscape in all directions. Just ahead, getting nearer and nearer to them, five small boats were close behind them. The small rowboats were cutting through the water much faster than the *Silverbeam*. This had happened before, when the pirates had chased them, but now Fearghus had a better plan.

"Row backward!" he called to the men down below. "Every man or lance and arrow to the sides! Be ready!" he continued, himself snatching up a javelin. When he reached the back end of the boat, he smiled as his plan worked. As their ship moved backward, the Roman boats were forced to steer to the right or left to avoid it. Within seconds, every enemy soldier was gobbled up in the rain of projectiles from the side railing of the ship. His plan was a success.

Subsequently, the world calmed down, and the ship moved further out to sea. Now another problem arose: how to get back on the mainland safely. Right now, the *Silverbeam* was well out of range of the Romans, but still the enemy held the beach, the only safe spot to land the ship for miles.

Then Fearghus had an idea. The pirate's secret harbor wouldn't be too far north of here. If they could land there, then they could skirt around the Roman lines and ride back into the encircling forest safely. The only problem would be holding the harbor from its inhabitants. At least, Fearghus realized, they wouldn't have to deal with the likes of Bressel anymore.

Irial was skeptical at first, but Seadna convinced him. Fearghus was happy that the former pirate was here. Seadna, like Colla, would prove to be useful in this situation. Almost immediately, he ordered the change of course, and the *Silverbeam* started its journey back home.

To plan for the entry, Fearghus met with the leaders of the boat in Irial's cabin. With his friend also sat Conn, Seadna and Finghin. Seadna started the conversation right away as Fearghus sat down. "Our sail will work as a good disguise," he said, "At least until we land."

"Then what'll we do?" Irial asked.

Now Fearghus spoke. "Seadna, you and your men can coordinate the maneuvering and defense of the ship," he said, to a nod from Finghin and his leader. Then, turning to Conn and Irial, he said, "We will plant our forces on the shore, and gather together our chariots and wagons before leaving. We may, or may not have to fight right away."

"If you can break away fast enough, we should have no trouble," Seadna responded.

The four generals thus sent their men forth from the room to prepare for the operation. Even before Fearghus and his comrades had left the cabin, the warriors had begun to prepare their wagons and horses, and bring out their weapons, for defense. Seadna had appointed Finghin to operate the catapult just above them, and had posted archers around the vessel's perimeter. Meanwhile, Irial's riders gathered together in one thick mass on the deck, awaiting the dropping of the exit ramp. Each one had with him a horse, some riding theirs and some being pulled on chariots and wagons. They were all ready to fight, just as well as to flee.

At length, Fearghus recognized the wooden wharves of the cove from afar. They would land in just moments. Seadna saw them also, and ordered his men to roll down the black sail. Every man on board stayed as quiet as possible as the ship glided into the harbor. Luckily, there weren't any ships here, at the moment, but Fearghus knew there were likely some pirates.

"The pirate ships will be here by sundown," Seadna said, as the two men looked ahead. "We've got to make this a fast transition."

"We can only hope that there is no opposition here already," Fearghus muttered, squinting in the low sun.

"Don't worry, my friend," Seadna said. "If you can make it up that slope over there, then you'll be safe."

Fearghus looked to where Seadna was pointing. The harbor, of course, was set in front of a steep rock face, he remembered, but he had not previously noticed the sandy hill to the right of it. The obstacle would slow them down, but not too much. He would just have to drive the horses up this one hill, and then he would find a forgiving flat plain beyond it, stretching all the way to the great valley and the encircling forest.

Just before the ship landed, Fearghus joined his friend Irial. "I'll hold up the rear," he said, turning back around. Just as he reached the back of the group of warriors, the ship lurched to a halt. Before he knew it, the ramp had dropped and Fearghus was swept out into the clearing with his men.

Chapter 7

▼

Journey to the Unknown

The huge crowd of wagons hurtled down onto the wooden wharf with amazing speed. Fearghus had chosen to ride on a light, two-wheel chariot. Coming up behind the large mass of warriors, he brought with him a long spear and his own sword. He thought it would be extremely important to protect the group from behind in the instance that any pirates would give chase on the steep hill. He was confident that once again he could hold off the warriors' enemies.

The clatter of the horse's hooves resounded through the cliffs of the cove. All about Fearghus, wooden crates and barrels lay about, just as they had been before with Colla. Fearghus had never seen the clearing in broad daylight, though. Scanning the area with his eyes, he recognized with a chuckle the large black spot that he had made in the dusty earth when he had ignited a crate of firecrackers so long ago.

Suddenly, the harbor burst with violence. Fearghus strained his eyes to see up ahead, where Irial led the group. The party had stopped for some reason, and when a Celtic horse reared and fell to the earth, Fearghus knew why. "Keep going!" he screamed, maneuvering his chariot to the front. When he reached Irial, he was shocked to see that the general's guard had been gobbled up by a fierce band of grimy pirates. Irial himself was in dire danger, hopelessly trying to fend off multiple attacks from the savages.

Fearghus knew exactly what to do. Riding forward to intercept the enemies, he spoke to the men: "Ignore them!" he screamed, hacking down the pirates. Finally the men realized the importance of speed and once again brought their horses to galloping. Fearghus finished off the pirates and waited until the warriors had passed him before continuing. Just as he had expected, several arrows from behind zipped by his chariot. The pirates were giving chase.

Just ahead, Irial was guiding the party to the foot of the slope. The barrels had slowed their movement enough, but this would really hurt their progress. When the group of warriors had all reached the hill, Fearghus swiveled around and brought up his lance.

None of the pirates present in this cove had horses, but they were still coming fast on foot, letting off arrows and spears by the dozen. Fearghus only hoped that he could hold them off while Irial's men struggled through the loose sandy soil of the dune behind him.

In the glistening water ahead, the *Silverbeam* had repositioned itself alongside the rocky shoreline. It was a beautiful sight, with its flags flying and the clouds behind it. However, Fearghus would soon have to leave it, for now his plan was going to occur. Squinting in the intense light of dusk, Fearghus saw Seadna standing upon the bow of the ship, waving a banner above his head.

Fearghus bent down and picked up Irial's crimson banner from the bottom of the chariot, and waved it high above his own head. Instantly, a huge ball of red fire sprang from the catapult aboard the *Silverbeam*. Just as Fearghus had secretly planned before, Seadna and his men were to burn down everything in the clearing. Every crate, every barrel, every ship was to go.

While the first shot crashed into a huge crowd of barrels, another fiery boulder was launched, and then another. The whole cove was burning up. Fearghus smiled as those pirates left to attack him were turned back by a towering wall of fire. He had planned this just right. There were no trees in the area, just sand and stone, so the fire would not spread. When he returned even as early as tomorrow, every trace of the thieving pirates would be erased.

Suddenly, Fearghus noticed that the fire was spreading quicker than he had expected. Taking his last chance for a safe exit, Fearghus waved back to Seadna on the ship and kicked his horse into a fierce sprint for the sandy slope ahead. He just barely got himself onto the hill when the barrels closest to him exploded with flame. The air behind him was extremely hot and sooty. As Fearghus continued the harsh climb up, he heard the screams of his enemies burning down below.

When he reached the top of the hill, Fearghus turned to look one last time upon the magnificent *Silverbeam*, which now was pulling away from the dangerously flammable wharves, still firing its catapult. Fearghus would look forward to seeing Seadna again and hopefully soon.

Just ahead, Irial and the others were waiting for him. The men kept their horses still until Fearghus rode up to the front where Irial was. "That was a plan well executed," Irial said warmly, congratulating him.

"Well, I think it will be a bit *cooler* back at the monastery, don't you?" Fearghus joked.

"Of course," Irial responded, and moved his horse ahead. Once again, Fearghus waited for the huge mass of riders to pass him before he followed. He was quite happy that the men had successfully retrieved food back to the stronghold of the monastery. Also, he was glad at the acquisition of the pirate's harbor. The cove was surrounded by steep stone cliffs and would be extremely hard to invade. Fearghus was confident that it would prove a good site for storage as well. Now only remained the task of completely exterminating the pirates. Right now, though, he would leave Seadna to take care of that. The disguise of the *Silverbeam* as a friendly ship to the pirates would again prove useful, likely, as would the cover of night.

The trip back to the encircling woods would be a short one, luckily. They were following along the same path that he and Colla had taken so many days ago. The sea now was to their left, as they rode south, and thus the sunset was to the right, just where they were heading.

It wasn't long before Fearghus spied the low trees of the encircling forest in the distance. Just a short ride southeast of here, likely, the Romans were slowly regrouping after they had failed to capture the *Silverbeam*. Fortunately, Fearghus's group of warriors was heading into the forest at a point far north of the beach. The familiar white cliffs of the valley surrounded them, and the monastery down below seemed beautiful and warm. Inside, the men of Tuathal who had been left to guard the settlement would have food and drink for them, but best of all, Agnos would be there to welcome Fearghus back.

Fearghus was happy that his plans for rebellion were coming together so well. He had successfully coordinated a plan for food for his men, and had secured a stronghold. Only two questions remained to be answered: was he to ultimately defeat the Romans, or simply hold his people from them? And also: was this what the gods intended for him? He hoped soon to answer both of these concerns, and discover his purpose and also, maybe, his magical lance. Right now, though, he would once again retire to the monastery after a long day of fighting and adventure.

The group of warriors quickly stole their way through the thinnest part of the forest and dashed out into the clearing. The Romans were nowhere to be seen, probably because of the recent skirmish at the beach, and so they had no trouble making it to the gate of the fortress.

Fearghus was displeased to find several rotting corpses strewn about the front gate, accompanied by the presence of several arrows and javelins fixed in the ground and the gate. More than half of the twenty bodies were Roman, but this was still a hefty price for the outnumbered Celtic warriors. Some kind of skirmish had also been fought here, while they were gone.

While Irial's men loaded the bodies onto their wagons, Fearghus followed his friend into the monastery. Behind him followed several wagons filled with fish for the other warriors, and then came the wagon carrying the casualties of the recent trip. When the gates had closed, Fearghus assisted in the distribution of the fish to the hungry warriors in the courtyard, and afterwards set out to find Agnos. Behind him, Irial drew a thick woolen cloak about him and resumed his usual watch atop the catwalk. The sky above was becoming darker and darker, much earlier than usual. Thick, gray clouds covered the moon, and the stars were all but lost.

The first thing Fearghus did was walk to his cabin, to find Agnos. His bungalow was far back to the right, one of the largest of the group of rooms, but still modest and comfortable. As he walked by the huge mass of earthen and wooden buildings, he nearly ran into several warriors and their wives, bursting out of their cabins to gather some fish from the wagons out in the middle of the courtyard. Everyone was gathering for a big celebration, to worship the gods for their good fortune.

When Fearghus reached his cabin, he heard footsteps inside, and stood aside from the door, waiting. When Agnos burst through the cloth covering, and looked wildly about to see where everyone was going, Fearghus crept up behind her and snatched her up in his arms. "I'm back!" he shouted, and twirled her about. "I've brought home food for us!" he continued, planting a kiss on her cheek.

And so the two of them hurried off to join the warriors in the courtyard. When they arrived, several bonfires had already sprung up. The men were merrymaking and cooking their fish on the tips of their swords and spears. When Fearghus approached them, he chose to sit down with Conn and his friends, closer to the front gate. Agnos shyly crawled up behind him, and wrapped one of Fearghus's blankets around herself. The fish that Fearghus had brought back were stout and slippery. After successfully cooking his first fish, Fearghus broke it apart with his sword, and handed half of it to Agnos.

Agnos ate her share of the meat voraciously, as Fearghus expected her to. The whole encampment had been hopelessly short of food for days. Agnos was unsuccessfully trying to hide her hunger, hanging back in Fearghus's shadow.

At length, all light in the sky had disappeared, and the red light of the fires covered every building and cast long shadows throughout the courtyard. Now it was really time to celebrate. The warriors brought out their last gulps of mead and ale and drank far into the night. Then one of the men took up his lyre, a young warrior of Tuathal's company by the name of Aodh, and he played a tune for the men.

It was not long before a number of the married men began to dance about, circling around the campfires happily. When Aodh finished the first tune, he set to another, and yet another. Soon enough, the drunken warriors began to dance, and as more and more of the men joined in, Fearghus turned around and helped Agnos to her feet.

Now dancers of every age and origin began to celebrate. Some followed intricate steps and rhythms, twirling about with their hands in the air, but others were content to do whatever they liked, ranging from hopping up and down to running back and forth wildly.

As he and Agnos danced their way into the center of the courtyard, Aodh finished the previous song and struck up another sad, longing tune. And as he played, he sang:

> *Alas! O Eire, the sea strikes you down!*
> *The heavens are shut and the forgotten gods frown!*
>
> *For the Romans have come, with shield and sword,*
> *The heralds of death, are here to kill more.*
>
> *Alas! Fair warriors and servants of good!*
> *Take up your arms and fight, as you should!*
>
> *Defend your flocks and your fields of wheat,*
> *Protect your families; never you sleep!*
>
> *And so the King has told us all:*
> *Let us instead take them as our thralls!*

> *Let us lift him up high, and curse him not,*
> *It is Fearghus the King, the King of Eire!*

When Fearghus heard these lines, he didn't know what to say. He was flattered by these words of praise, but somehow, he didn't quite feel comfortable. And so, without stopping, Fearghus saluted the crowd about him and continued to twirl Agnos around. And Aodh continued:

> *He fears no man, nor demon or beast,*
> *He has delivered us all, to this great feast.*
>
> *The Sea steps aside, the mountains shudder,*
> *The world fears him, like no other.*
>
> *His sword cuts through steel, his lance pierces gold,*
> *His strength outlasts the great heroes of old!*
>
> *So raise your glass, and fill your cup!*
> *For this is Fearghus, the King of Eire!*

After Aodh ended his hymn, Agnos was pulled away from Fearghus as the warriors surrounded him, and the men hoisted him up above their heads. The drunken crowd was shouting praises to its new hero. Fearghus did not realize how much respect he commanded from his people. This was a big surprise to him.

The festivities didn't last long, though. Just as Fearghus had expected, the clouds gathering in the sky burst with rain. The sudden downpour slowly extinguished the bonfires and softened the earth. Fearghus was nearly dropped back onto the ground as the warriors hurried to light their torches and grab their pails and helmets.

Fearghus didn't know it at first, but the coming of rain was vital to his rebellion. The camp had been low on water for days, and every warrior, including Fearghus, remained thirsty as well as dirty. The rain would help the effort greatly, and coupled with the recent delivery of fish, the men within the monastery walls were in better shape than ever.

Suddenly Fearghus found Agnos again. Her tunic was soaked, and held tightly to her form, and Fearghus's wet blanket was draped about her shoulders. Fearghus let out a cry of joy and once again snatched her up in his arms. Her wet hair whipped about in his face as he spun around happily. Agnos had a huge grin on her face, and so did Fearghus. Without delaying a second, they shared yet another kiss, this time in the rain.

All about them, the warriors were carrying out their barrels and buckets to collect the rain, and stripping off their armor and cloaks to wash up in the rain. Fearghus did the same, as Agnos watched, and enjoyed the situation to the fullest.

By the end of the storm, the group of men had filled up countless barrels with water, and not one person had left to their name an article of dry clothing. The night air, though cold, was fresh and clear. Everyone's morale had been lifted, and everyone's stomachs filled.

Fearghus allowed Agnos some time in the cabin to start a fire and change her dress. When he was finally allowed in, she was wrapped up in the bedcovers, her soaking clothes hanging upon the wall near the flames. Fearghus did the same with his cloak and tunic, and the two of them enjoyed the warm light of the fire together.

When Fearghus woke the next morning, only one thing was on his mind. He had been thinking about it for days on end. He was still curious, not only as to the location and properties of his magical lance, but also concerning Colla's treasure on the Isle of Man. Only Seadna, though, could help him find it. But also, it was only Seadna that could successfully pilot the *Silverbeam*. The former pirate was well out of Fearghus's reach, for the present.

As Fearghus dressed himself for the new day, he knew right away just where Irial would be, and he knew that he should go join the man. Leaving Agnos's clothes by her side on the bed, he strapped on his light armor and walked over to the stairs.

Sure enough, Irial was standing there atop the wall, staring ahead blankly. When Fearghus joined him, he turned to face his friend. "Luck has been on our side, so far," he said.

"Yes we have been quite fortunate," Fearghus responded, resting upon the wall. "We must now hope that the Romans don't fare the same."

"You've certainly become popular, recently," Irial continued.

"I suppose...," Fearghus said, trailing off a bit. Then he ventured to ask his friend a few questions. "Irial," he stammered, "I was wondering if you really think that we can win this fight."

Fearghus could tell Irial was thinking very hard about this question. Finally, the lumberman spoke. "I'm just not sure," he reasoned, leaning harder on the stone. "I think it is possible, but we may need more help."

"We've done well so far," Fearghus responded, staring intently at his friend's expression.

"But I'm afraid we're too weak, and the aid we need just isn't there for the taking anymore," Irial complained. "We can't hold out much longer."

Fearghus was quick to respond. "What if right now I told you a way that we could get help?" he asked.

"It just isn't possible," Irial responded.

"Oh, but it is!" Fearghus nearly shouted, grabbing Irial tightly by the arms. "It all has something to do with my armor. Didn't you think it a bit strange when I came to you clothed in all this, and with this sword?"

"Of course," Irial replied, "but it isn't strange to carry a weapon in my neck of the woods!"

Fearghus got right to the point. "All of this stuff," he started, gesturing towards his clothing, "It isn't mine! It was a gift from the gods, if you will."

Irial looked at Fearghus very strangely. "It's magic, then?" he asked.

"Yes!" Fearghus shouted back, "And I think I know where there's more!"

Right away, Irial called together some of his most trusted men, and began a meeting concerning Fearghus's proposition. Unfortunately, none of Seadna's seafaring men could be present, but it was important that the other warriors be in on this scheme, as well. Fearghus's initial plan called for several trained fighters, looking for adventure and enough mariners to man a ship, hopefully the *Silverbeam*. Irial was all for, it, as Fearghus expected, in addition to a great number of the warriors present. Each one remembered Aodh's song the night before, and hailed Fearghus as something of a god. Fearghus was flattered by their praise, but did not let it disrupt his concentration. Everything he knew and loved hinged on the success of this mission, and everything had to go just right.

As they sat there, over the long wooden table of the banquet hall, one of the warriors spoke up. "I think it's best, like we have always done, to throw an armed party of men right through the Roman lines, and on to the pirate's cove."

"I don't think that's possible, my friend," Fearghus told him. "Secrecy is far more important in this mission. We shall leave during the night, under the cover of darkness."

Now Irial once again addressed the men. "We are going in search of an ancient and magical spear," he said. "Many unknown dangers may lie in our path, far more fantastic and dangerous than any Romans. We shall be like the great adventurers of old, on a quest for treasure."

At that moment, every man present in the room fell short of breath in awe of the task ahead. Each warrior realized his own importance and worth, and that of his strength, courage and sword. No one, even Fearghus himself, could fathom what lie ahead. Only Colla, and likely his partner Seadna would know of the danger, and the mystery waiting for them upon the Isle of Man.

While Irial hopelessly toiled over the task of coordinating a trip to the *Silverbeam*, Fearghus was allowed to go free. Agnos was waiting outside the main gate of the hall, her ear pressed to the door. When Fearghus greeted her, she staggered back from the building in surprise. "It appears that someone's been eavesdropping," Fearghus said, with a smile.

"Fearghus," Agnos responded, shly, "I think I would be useful on your trip. I know of a few helpful things."

"There is no place for women on my ship!" Fearghus snapped sternly.

"But I'm guessing you've never heard the legend of Osgar," Agnos retorted, holding her ground. "It's a little known tale of a divine spear, passed down through the generations, dating back more than four hundred years from now."

Fearghus was utterly taken by surprise at Agnos's story. "So you think that my magical spear is that which you talk about?" he asked.

"Yes, of course!" Agnos replied. "It was prophecied that the spear, would turn up far in the north of its origin, where the word of God was scarce."

"Don't tell me about your Roman God!" Fearghus bellowed, slapping her face. "I shall heed only to my own gods!"

Agnos backed up against the wall of the banquet hall, extremely afraid. For a moment, Fearghus felt sorry for his foolishness, and beckoned her forward. "We shall each worship in our own way," he apologized, and caressed her. "Please continue your tale."

Agnos's face lit up with relief. "Well I heard it from a young religious boy back in Britain, who I was working with. It is too bad that the man was kidnapped by pirates the day after telling me."

Upon hearing this, something in Fearghus's mind, probably some distant memory, stirred. Fearghus had heard some tale of a kidnapped British boy before, but he did not know from whom. Suddenly, his thoughts were interrupted by Agnos's voice.

"The spear in question," she explained, "is said to be the only item remaining that directly touched the body of the...some hero from way back then. And it is endowed with several wonderful and fantastic magical powers. Namely, the power of healing, the power of strength, and the ability of the item to change form were placed upon it. It was said that only the holiest of men could dare to wield either of them. And also the man said that if the weapon was used against an innocent servant of well...the god of this race, then it would be relocated to its original position, and guarded by fire and brimstone."

"That's my spear!" Fearghus shouted, grabbing Agnos in his burly arms. "I must have it back!"

A strange look of fear, as well as utter reverence and respect crossed Agnos's face. "But I don't understand why you of all people were chosen to fulfill this man's prophecy!" she gasped, staggering back once again.

"That doesn't matter!" Fearghus replied, squeezing her tightly. "You're coming with me to find my lance!"

Right away, each of the men who had attended the initial meeting began to prepare supplies for the journey. Several chariots were tied to their horses, and barrels beyond count were loaded on the wagons, filled with water and fish. In the back of the monastery, Conn sharpened and reshaped every man's sword for the coming journey. The wives of those few of Tuathals's men that were involved caressed their husbands and wept for them. The quest for Osgar would soon begin.

Back at Fearghus's bungalow, Agnos was washing Fearghus's clothes and cooking a meal for them. While she busied herself at this, Fearghus laid his clothes out on the bed, and bathed himself in a shallow tub of water outside. "When do we leave?" Agnos asked, from inside the modest abode.

"We will depart just a bit before the sunset tomorrow morning, allowing ourselves just enough time to reach the pirate's cove in darkness," he informed her. "Don't worry about us. We will have plenty of time together tonight."

When Fearghus finished washing up, he sat down on the floor and enjoyed possibly his last meal at the monastery with Agnos. She had changed into a loose white cloak that one of the other women had given her, and looked dazzling and radiant in the garb. In the past few days, her hair had grown longer and more beautiful, and her eyes sadder and more sincere.

While their other cloaks and tunics dried above the fire, the two of them shared their meal of fish and vegetables silently, almost shyly, or even a little bit distantly. Both of them realized the importance and risk of embarking on the journey just ahead, and each knew of the pain and sacrifice to come. In fact, in every corner of the monastery, the elite warriors who had been selected to come felt just the same way.

When the sun went down over the desolate stone walls of the monastery, casting long shadows across the entire length of the courtyard, Fearghus put Agnos to her bed and set off to talk to Irial. The general had been sitting in the banquet hall throughout the afternoon, planning their trip and counting supplies. Right now, he was still wrestling with the task of boarding the *Silverbeam*. He was relieved when Fearghus pushed open the massive wooden doors and sat down on a chair.

"The pirate ship will be out to sea, likely, when we get there," Irial pressed, looking to Fearghus for help.

"Oh, don't worry," Fearghus said, "We can row out to them on a raft, and have them come back to pick us up. We'd best also bring an armed caravan of chariots to deliver what little fish that they've caught back here."

"I'll get right to that," Irial replied. "Now about that spear…" he continued, once again looking to Fearghus for a response.

Fearghus was quick to answer him. "The woman staying at my bunk house, named Agnos, has heard something about it," he stammered.

"What do you mean?" Irial asked, his face lighting up.

"The tale of my magical spear is a long and twisted one, hidden even to myself. It turns out that my spear has been magically relocated to the Isle of Man by some transgression I committed while using it. It is protected by, as Agnos puts it, fire and brimstone both."

To Fearghus's surprise, the look on Irial's face, though surprised, seemed sinister and excited as well. There seemed a longing in his expression, and a distinguishable look of weariness. "This one javelin," he started, looking at Fearghus long and hard, "can almost instantly solve all of our problems?" At this Fearghus fixed his face to look even more sinister than Irial's, and nodded.

The two men spent several more hours preparing for the journey. When Fearghus finally left the large hall, the last rays of the setting sun were slowly being swallowed up by the darkness of night. This time, the sky above was clear and the stars shone brightly. It was a beautiful way to end Fearghus's stay at the monastery. The odds in the coming days were all against him, but he would try to pull through.

Out in the courtyard, the warriors were lighting up their campfires and bundling up in their blankets. Huddled around the small fires, they looked almost like stout little monks, praying to their single god out in the open. Just like Fearghus, they, too, seemed almost in awe of the world about them. Tonight, there would be no merrymaking, no dancing. Just the lingering fear of losing everything in the adventure tomorrow hung about, haunting even those not involved.

Fearghus crept by them in the shadows, drawing his cloak about him. Blindly stumbling through the bungalows, he finally happened upon his own, where Agnos was curled up in bed, wide-awake. When Fearghus plodded through the door, all she could do was stare at him, the red light of the fire making her eyes glisten.

That night, long after Agnos had found sleep, Fearghus lay awake, still trying to imagine what lay ahead on the Isle of Man. A great number of things crossed his mind, everything imaginable that could occur. In one instance, he envisioned himself falling down a deep chasm of fire, and in another, he saw himself being gobbled up by another great serpent like the one he had battled in his native village. Tomorrow, he really would be like the great heroes of old, as Aodh's hymn had said. He just didn't know if he was up to it. He had so much to prove to his people, to everyone that had sung with him last night around the fire, and everyone that now took shelter behind these walls. He could not fail them. He could not let the Romans win.

Early the next morning, Irial was around waking up everyone who had been selected for the journey. When he reached Fearghus's hut, he was careful not to wake Agnos right away, respecting her peace. However, someone had to get her up, and after Fearghus had dressed and strapped on his armor, he woke her and she put on a long gown and a headpiece to keep out the dust of the wagon ride ahead. As the two of them made their way to the banquet hall for a short breakfast, the warriors that had waken before them were already gathering in the center of the courtyard with their chariots.

Inside the hall, the highest leaders of the monastery were holding council at the head of the table. Fearghus left Agnos to the large pile of salted meats at the side of the table and joined them. The group was deep in discussion and almost didn't notice his entry. Irial was discussing the topic of leadership. "Fearghus and I will be accompanying the men on this mission," he was saying.

Then Conn spoke up. "I'll be a part of the governing council while you're away," he suggested, nodding towards the men there.

"Well then it's all settled," Irial replied, getting up from his seat. "Those of you staying here know who you are."

As Irial strode out of the great hall, Agnos and Fearghus followed close behind. Outside in the courtyard, the group of vehicles set out for the excursion was more extensive than Fearghus had originally thought. "You made that all by yourself?" Fearghus asked, pointing at a small wooden boat.

"We worked all night," Irial responded, beaming. "I thought you would like it."

Fearghus was amazed that Irial had gone to so much trouble to make the little wooden canoe. A well-caulked wagon bed would have done just fine. Of course, Irial was a master craftsman. Just as Conn knew his iron, so too did Irial know his lumber. It was useful to have the two friends around.

Not delaying much at all, Irial showed Agnos and Fearghus to their wagon, and began the final preparations for the exit. Guards and archers were posted atop the wall, swift horsemen were positioned on all sides of the caravan, and everyone in the banquet hall was forced out and onto their chariots.

As the men gathered, there still remained a multitude of warriors present to see them go. Among this group were all the wives, and even a few children. Even so, many of the warriors still slept in their cabins as the group assembled. It was very early in the morning yet.

At length, Irial ordered the gates open and kicked his horse into a walk to lead the party out of the monastery. As Fearghus's wagon was swept into the flow of the chariots, he had one last look back at the monastery, and all the houses within it. He gazed into the puzzled faces of the other villagers, and silently, he wished them good luck and good favor with the gods. Now, however, it was time to look ahead, to look forward to the possible success that could be achieved in the days ahead. With Agnos by his side, he followed the rest of the men out into the black world of night.

As the gates closed behind them, the faint light of the torches in the monastery faded to nearly nothing. Now there was only the guide of the moon and stars above, and the sound of the horses trudging their way through the field. The forest to their right seemed blacker only more than the sky just above it, and to them, it seemed like a great wall of nothingness. Luckily, just ahead, the white cliffs of the valley glowed with the clear light of the moon, guiding them up to the thinnest section of the encircling forest, in the north.

By the time the party had reached the top of the climb, the dawn was coming up in the east, out over the sea. The glassy surface of the water ahead shone with its crimson light, and the world seemed much brighter. With the Romans behind them, the party now wove its way even further northward along the sandy beach, and even closer to the pirate's cove.

And finally, they were there. Fearghus smiled when he discovered that the harbor was completely abandoned, as he expected, and that everywhere, there only remained the black soot of the recent fire to show for all the pirates' hoards. Even the wharves that had been erected out over the water had burned to ashes. And to top off his joys, Fearghus was able to make out the silhouette of the *Silverbeam*, like only a speck in the distance, out fishing in the sea. Soon, Irial had led the entire party down into the loose black soil of the once proud harbor, at least in its own right.

"There it is!" Fearghus shouted, guiding his wagon over to the shore. Next to him Agnos was jolted awake by his yelling. She had fallen asleep on his shoulder during the recent trip. Now she was up, taking in the sights and sounds of the harbor. Her headpiece was off, and she was gripping Fearghus's arm tightly with both hands, looking back and forth curiously. Finally, like everyone else, her eyes came to rest on the ship, a great ways away from the shore.

Someone would have to row out to the ship to alert them of the party's intentions, and Fearghus was prepared for this. Leaving Agnos sitting atop the wagon, he helped the warriors carry Irial's canoe down to the edge of the water. The craft was expertly made, sanded and sawn to perfection, and perfectly waterproof. In days to come it would be useful for scouting ahead, or even, Fearghus realized with an eerie feeling, for exploring water-filled caverns too large for the ship, like the one far south of here where Seadna lived, except smaller.

As the rest looked on, two of Irial's warriors took with them their oars and rowed a good distance away from the shore, until only could be seen the glint of the sun on their helmets. As soon as they reached the *Silverbeam*, it would not be long before the ship dropped its entrance ramp. The men of Seadna's village were tough and strong beyond the slaves that had formerly powered the boat.

As they watched intently, a warm breeze stirred in the south. The conditions would be perfect for a trip east to the Isle of Man. It seemed, at that moment, that everything was all right, that any troubles could be dealt with much later. Right now, Fearghus realized with a sigh, he would be content just to relax upon the deck of his ship, and breathe the fresh salty air of the sea with his love, Agnos.

At length, it became the mood of every man there that the canoe had successfully reached the ship, even though they couldn't really tell. And soon they realized they were right, for in the blazing white light of the sun, the figure of the *Silverbeam* was moving closer. On the soft ashy ground, the chariots and wagons of Irial were quickly moving into a straight, single-file line to board the ship. Everyone's heart was bursting with excitement. Some of the men had never left the land for the sea before.

Soon, Fearghus was able to distinguish the figure of Seadna on the prow of the ship, just as he had two days before. He looked so small against the larger silhouette of his grand ship, and so illustrious and proud. He would have heard of Fearghus's intentions from the men aboard the canoe, and would be happy to tell Fearghus everything he knew about Osgar and the Isle of Man, and about Colla's experience with the treasure.

Before he knew it, Fearghus was at the rear of a long procession of chariots slowly loading onto the ship. Up on the deck of the vessel, there was much shouting and hugging and shaking of hands as the warriors of the monastery reunited again under one cause. When Fearghus, with Agnos by his side, finally boarded the ship, he was pleased to see that Seadna was standing right there, at the top of the ramp, waiting just for him.

"I am quite surprised at this new development," the former pirate said, patting Fearghus on the back. "Now what is this treasure that you are searching for?"

Before Fearghus could open his mouth, Agnos cut in and answered for him. "We seek the great spear Osgar," she replied, in a strong, authoritative voice, uncharacteristic of her usual one.

Suddenly, Seadna's face became grave and solemn. He bowed his head and muttered, "I can't do it."

Fearghus was no short of stupefied at this new side of Seadna. "What is the matter?" he asked, cautiously.

"I know of this very spear," the man blubbered, hiding his face. "And the hammer to go with it."

"Yes, but why can't you help us?" Agnos pressed.

Seadna suddenly revealed his red face. It was full of fear and sadness. "Because it killed all of my pirate friends!" he shouted, and turned to leave.

But Fearghus stopped him. "I think if you help us, we can help you!" he stammered, pushing Seadna to face him.

Now the expression on Seadna's face became more serious, and he brought his head up. "That spear is cursed! It has powers neither of us can control! Only a fool would chase it!"

"But *I* had that spear, just a few weeks ago!" Fearghus retorted.

Now Seadna stepped back, looking up and down Fearghus's body, as if he had never seen him before. "But that is impossible!" he shrieked, groping for the railing behind him. "That spear was locked up on the Isle of Man fifty years ago! No mortal man could possess such a holy item and live!"

"But I did!" Fearghus shouted back, moving closer to his comrade, who was now quivering in fear. But Seadna's fear could not be shaken. Taking complete command of the situation, Fearghus grabbed his arms and wrestled him into his cabin, laying him out on the bed. "Now tell me all about it," he said calmly, holding down the man's convulsing body.

Finally, Seadna calmed down and spoke openly about his travels to Fearghus. "Well one day, Colla and I, upon this very ship even…well, we picked up a young Roman boy from the south of Britain, and he was possessed with strange powers and words as we had never heard before. And the men, save Colla, all wanted to kill the weak little boy. But Colla tricked them into rather selling him into slavery here in Eire, out of pity for the helpless young man."

Now Fearghus was onto something. He had heard a corresponding tale from Agnos just yesterday outside of the monastery banquet hall. She had even spoken with this man, and had heard of the tale of Osgar from him.

As Fearghus thought to himself, Seadna continued. "And so, when the transaction was made, just as we were leaving, the young boy's shepherd's staff turned into a spear, and he presented it to Colla. And the next morning, many strange things had happened to my friend."

Fearghus knew that this was his spear now. Every piece of the puzzle fit correctly. "Please go on!" he pressed, looking intently at Seadna's face.

And so Seadna continued his tale. "Colla was much stronger, and clothed in strange armor. He had become the perfect warrior overnight," he said.

"And then what happened?" Fearghus asked.

"Well then Colla got all headstrong about it, and ran his spear through a man pleading for his life, and the weapon disappeared," Seadna explained. This was just as had happened to Fearghus when he threw his spear through the back of the Roman centurion, in the woods down south!

Then his thoughts were once again interrupted by Seadna's voice. "So he went back to the boy to ask for forgiveness, and by this time he was a Roman monk. And the boy told him about the Isle of Man, and he tried to convince his men to help him at it, but they refused."

"But then what became of your friends?" Fearghus asked.

"They were smitten down by lightning from the heavens. Only Bressel and I were spared. Colla and I tried once, after that, to find the lance, but our mission was abruptly stopped by a great monster."

Now Fearghus knew everything he had to know. He would go in Colla's place to find Osgar. He would once again have it, or die trying. He wasn't afraid of the prophecies, Agnos had told him about. The safety of his people was too important.

Out on the deck, everyone had fallen into a particularly joyful state. None of Fearghus's warriors knew what lie ahead, and anyway, they didn't care. Only Seadna could fathom the adventure that would follow this voyage, and everyone, even including Fearghus, couldn't resist the intrigue and excitement of the sea. Before, he had felt lonely and trapped aboard this ship, but with Agnos and the Sea, two wonderful ladies to his name, he was happy.

Presently, he happened upon Irial, who, in all this excitement, had found himself at home in the very front of the ship. The trusted general and lumberman was taking this experience very well. The skies ahead were clear and warm, and the prospect of a complete victory over the Roman menace, for a moment, seemed possible.

The *Silverbeam* quickly caught a draft of wind from the southwest, and the burly men straining at the oars down below were given rest as the black sails of the ship fluttered in the breeze. The sea in every direction was crisp and clear and clean, just as it should be. For the moment, there was no blood and no dirt, just the fresh salty waves beating softly on the side of the wooden vessel. But still Fearghus remembered that sad day when Colla was taken from him, while aboard this ship, and the day before when he had rammed a Roman ship and saved Fearghus's life. He would forever be curious about the life of this man, this man so similar to himself, and the very deck of this ship haunted him with memories.

Their great pirate ship sailed on and on, quite boringly throughout the day, while the sun raced across the sky with what seemed like amazing speed. Before Fearghus knew it, the sun was beginning to set, and the warriors aboard were bringing out large barrels of ale and mead that they had found in the hold of the ship. Also, to Fearghus's delight, several kegs of Roman red wine were discovered. His men were getting ready for another spirited celebration. Fearghus had already danced around their bonfires, and he now wanted to drink with them and dance on the deck of his ship.

As the darkness of night set in, torches were lit and the deck was cleared. Right away, as the warriors prepared for their celebrating, Fearghus went in search of Agnos. He found her in the back of the ship, her bare feet draped over the side of the vessel. The cool night air was blowing through her hair, and, it seemed to Fearghus, a smile was creeping across her face. Coming up behind her, he snatched her up in his hands and pulled her to her feet. "Come and celebrate with me!" he said, squeezing her tightly.

"Well, I guess I have to, with all the success we've had," Agnos giggled, and followed him to the main deck.

The celebration that night was wonderful. By the light of the torches, Fearghus and Agnos shared their meal side by side. Agnos wasn't shy anymore, as this was, quite frankly, her neck of the woods. Aside from Seadna, she was the only person on board that had been this far from Eire before.

The festivities started with a big toast to Fearghus, and the playing of music. Aodh had been selected to come on the trip for this very purpose, and he did a wonderful job serenading his people with both spirited and relaxed tunes. It was not long before Fearghus and Agnos finished their meal of fish and ale, and joined in the dancing brought on by the music. It was a completely different experience to dance on the hard wooden deck of the *Silverbeam*, but no one seemed to mind.

Agnos was the only woman on board, and unfortunately, she had to speak for every wife who wasn't there to dance with her husband. By the end of the night, the poor thing was so tired, she collapsed in Fearghus's arms. She was able to hold up just for one more slow dance with Fearghus, and then he had to carry her to their makeshift bed of cloth in the back of the ship.

Everyone had to sleep outside on the deck, or in the hold down below, for there were no rooms aboard the vessel, save for Irial and Seadna's cabin. Fearghus and Agnos had chosen a spot up on the deck, just in front of the captain's room, where they could look up at the stars above, and enjoy the soothing sound of the sea all around them. Fearghus, being the esteemed leader of the excursion, was, for now, exempt of taking any night shifts watching for danger. Irial had put that responsibility upon a number of his men, leaving the rest, including Seadna's exhausted sailors, to get some rest.

The deck was a bit crowded when Fearghus and Agnos slipped under their covers. Even so, they didn't mind. Drawing their blankets up about them, they shut out the rest of the world and enjoyed their company, caressing one another.

Many hours later, Agnos was sound asleep by Fearghus's side. Many of the sailors around him were also resting, and the world seemed still and quiet. Not finding much sleep himself, Fearghus turned over on his back and looked up at the heavens. To his surprise, the sky was swirling with gray and black clouds, which blotted out the stars and moon. A storm was brewing, and quickly. The wind that would occur as a result could capsize the ship or even rip it to shreds.

Fearghus had to warn the rest of the men about this. First of all, he lifted Agnos from the deck and without even asking, he burst right through the door of the captain's quarters and set her back down. Irial, who was sleeping in the bed, heard him come in and rubbed his eyes. "What's the matter?" he asked dazedly.

"There's a storm coming!" Fearghus shouted, shaking his friend awake. "We must get everyone down to the hold and put up the sails!"

Without even saying a word, Seadna, who had been sleeping on the floor next to them, burst out of his covers and ran outside to wake his men. Irial and Fearghus were quick to follow. As they got through the doors of the room, a bolt of lightning split the sky with its blazing fury, and a crack of thunder followed close behind. Upon this sound every man on the deck sprang up and began to run towards the stairs leading into the hold down below. As Seadna and his men began to climb the rigging up the sails, a splash of rain greeted them. No sooner than they had begun to pull up on the black cloth, a great gust of wind nearly knocked them off of the ropes.

Meanwhile, Fearghus ran back into the cabin and instructed Agnos to stay put. She had become very confused upon waking inside the room, and was very frightened of the recent thunder. "It'll be all right," he reassured her. "I think we've caught it early enough to save ourselves." As he said this, the ship began to rock back and forth, and Agnos slipped. Fearghus anchored his hand to the bed and grabbed her before she fell. "Now you just hold fast to this bed and I'll be right back," he told her.

Outside the room, the deck had become cleared, except for those of Seadna's men still struggling with the sails up above. The big black sail in the middle had been successfully saved, but the smaller secondary sail behind them had been torn to shreds.

Suddenly, a huge wave crashed upon the front of the boat, spraying water all over the place. Fearghus was jolted back and hit the wall of the cabin hard. Up above him, the brave men of Seadna's village were trying to make their way back down to the deck. As he watched, they all managed to hold onto the rigging and climb their way down, and Fearghus felt much better.

As he turned to go back into the cabin behind him, a voice suddenly rang through the air. Up on the highest point of the rigging of the mast, one man still remained, shouting for help. His foot was tangled in the ropes, and he was stuck. Now Fearghus took it upon himself to rescue the unfortunate fisher, and drew a dagger from his belt.

It wasn't very hard at first, climbing the rigging. Fearghus had to watch out for big jolts in the ship, to keep from falling, but soon he had reached the man. The wind and rain spraying in his face, he cut the ropes loose, and the two men struggled together back down to the safety of the deck. "Thank you so much!" the sailor stammered, scrambling down to the hold.

Chapter 8

The Voyage

Upon regaining his footing on the deck, Fearghus ran back toward the cabin where Agnos was. The rain was growing steadily heavier, and as the boat rocked back and forth, he slipped several times, hitting the wooden deck below hard. He was staggering like a drunkard.

Behind him, hidden behind several sheets of pelting rain, Seadna still remained, holding fast to the tiller of the ship. Only the proper control of the rudder could save them now. If Seadna was to lose it, then the sea would be given the power to toss and turn the ship however it liked.

The look on Seadna's face was hard and strained. One hand fixed on the railing, and the other mechanically turning the tiller according to the movement of the ship, he was the perfect portrait of concentration. He was the only man willing and brave enough to weather the storm, and the fate of Fearghus's mission, as well as the whole effort back at the monastery was weighted upon his shoulders.

Meanwhile, Fearghus burst through the thin wooden doors of the cabin where Agnos was waiting. Inside, she was holding tightly to the wooden frame of Irial's bed, her knuckles turning white in the effort. Upon entering the room, Fearghus stumbled his way over to her and relieved her struggling. Agnos wrapped tightly in his arms, Fearghus prepared to wait out the storm, praying to the gods for the ship's safety.

Many hours passed, the ship still rocking back and forth, and thunder still pounding in the air. In the darkness of the cabin, Fearghus couldn't hardly tell just what was going on outside on the deck. At length, he decided to go out and find Seadna. No man, not even a former pirate could withstand the wrath of the sea this long.

Outside, the deck was slick with rain. Fearghus could hardly see a few feet in front of him. The only glimpses he got of the surrounding world were provided by flashes of lightning up above, and what he saw during these short instances displeased him very much. Seadna was no longer there.

Right away, Fearghus found himself struggling over to the entrance to the hold. At the bottom of the ramp, the light of several torches countered the darkness of the night. The wooden walls of the room glowed red with warmth. When Fearghus reached the bottom of the ramp, he found himself unable to move about. Warriors seeking shelter occupied every inch of the floor. Some of the men were asleep, but many more than that were wide awake, wild looks upon their faces. When they saw Fearghus, a feeling of relief crept through their cramped groups. Their king was alive and well.

Without even attempting to move forward into their midst, Fearghus asked a burning question, one that could easily shape the fate of this mission. "Is Seadna here?" he bellowed, looking back and forth at the faces of his men. Irial, standing just to his right, seemed deathly afraid.

Finally, Finghin stood up and answered him. "He has not joined our company, as of yet," he responded calmly. "Of what importance is this?"

Fearghus's heart sank. Now, he realized, Seadna's life was in danger. He had to get back up on the deck quickly, before it was too late. "Follow me," he told Finghin, and sprinted back up the ramp.

As soon as Fearghus gained the next floor, he dashed into the captain's quarters. Inside, Agnos was still lying in the bed, holding extremely tight to the headboard. "What's going on?" she asked, sitting up.

Fearghus snatched up a sack of provisions and turned to leave. "Don't worry," he assured Agnos. "I'll be back."

When Fearghus found the deck again, he ran straight to the back of the ship. Finghin was already there, with a large length of rope about his shoulders. Confirming Fearghus's greatest fears, he was shouting his master's name hopelessly into the night. Just to Finghin's left, Fearghus noticed, the railing of the ship had been torn away, and the tiller as well. There was still no sign of Seadna.

"He has been washed overboard!" Finghin shouted as Fearghus reached him.

As Fearghus opened his mouth to respond, lightning suddenly blazed across the sky. In that split second that the world was illuminated with blinding light, Fearghus's eyes wandered out to the sea in front of them. Something was out of the ordinary. As the flash disappeared, something suddenly registered in Fearghus's mind. Now he would place all hope upon the rope that Finghin held.

"Tie this sack to the end of your rope!" Fearghus shouted, showing his bag of food. "It should float!"

No sooner had Fearghus said this, Finghin was swinging the sack around his head like a great mace, his rope fastened tightly to his waist. He had also seen Seadna, struggling courageously in the waves ahead, and he sought just as fiercely as Fearghus did to rescue his master. With a skillful toss, Finghin was able to place the sack of food a bit past Seadna's position. The fisher was perfectly prepared for the job, having cast fish nets all his life. Seadna was just a few strokes away from safety.

When Seadna had successfully fixed himself onto the rope, Finghin crouched down and began to pull himself towards the mast. When the thick tether came up on the deck next to Fearghus, he too began to pull on it with all his strength. With his help, Seadna pulled closer and closer to the ship. Planting his toes firmly in the spaces between the wooden planks of the deck, Fearghus did his best to keep from slipping.

Suddenly, a huge wave broke upon the front of the ship. Before anything even happened, Fearghus knew he was doomed. Behind him, Finghin's fingers were stripped across the wood of the mast as he stumbled backwards. When the two men collided, Fearghus at the front, they both hurtled headfirst into the sea, right through the weak wooden railing.

Fearghus hit the water swimming. The cold water of the Irish Sea chilled him to the bone, but his body kept on struggling. Pulling the rope loose from Finghin's waist, he tried several times to cast it up upon the deck, each time falling short. As the darkness of night began to envelope the ship, Fearghus instead cast the rope towards Finghin and began to pull himself towards Seadna, a great ways away.

The waves pushed him back and forth. Sometimes they managed to pull him below the surface of the water, and sometimes they threw him up into the air. Now he would only have his grip to depend on for his life. His fingers no longer had any feeling in them. Behind him, Finghin was having similar troubles.

Suddenly, Seadna came into view. The exhausted man was doubled over on top of the floating sack of food, completely resigned to his fate. Upon seeing him, Fearghus gave a sudden burst of speed. His hands were furiously groping for the rope, propelling him forward amazingly fast. The waves still rocked him back and forth, and the cold of the water still numbed his joints, but all he could see was Seadna, and he unconsciously drove himself ahead, forgetting all else.

At length, he finally reached Seadna. When the former pirate sensed Fearghus's presence, he could only look up at his friend. In awe of the howling wind and pelting rain, neither man could speak. There was nothing either of them could do to survive, except to cling to the sack of provisions and pray for an end to their suffering.

Leaving Seadna to lay atop the sack, Fearghus quickly devised a plan to save himself. In order to survive the penetrating cold of the water, he began to pump his legs and body back and forth, hoping to generate more warmth in his body. He continued to do this for what seemed like several hours, his magical strength lasting far beyond his expectations.

However, his endurance soon waned to nothing. By now, the storm had passed, and the water about him had calmed. The light of the moon above was once again coming out, and the stars behind it. But Fearghus couldn't see this. His body was so thoroughly exhausted, he nearly collapsed onto the side of the food sack. Before he knew it, his eyes were shut and the world was nothing but darkness.

When the light of day next opened Fearghus's eyes, it was burning and bright. His body felt much warmer, and the air smelled sweet. Squinting in the sun, Fearghus suddenly heard a voice. Just above him, he suddenly realized, Seadna was looking down at him. How had they survived last night?

"Where are we?" he asked, struggling to his feet.

Seadna only smiled, embracing his friend. "The current of the sea has led us to this island. This morning I swam us onto the beach."

Fearghus was happy and sad at the same time. Hopes for his expedition were dashed, but still he had his life. He didn't know what to do next. "Where's Finghin?" he asked, scanning the narrow rocky beach of the island.

"I did not know he was with you," Seadna responded, looking down. "I suppose he hasn't made it, then."

Fearghus was disappointed almost to weeping, but the matter at hand was too important. "Where do we go from here?" he asked.

"Back to Eire," Seadna responded, turning to walk down the shore. "It's just a little ways away," he continued. Fearghus stumbled after him, picking his way through the sharp stones of the land. When Seadna stopped, he knelt down to the earth and picked up something. Fearghus was so thoroughly in awe of his surroundings that he scarcely noticed that Seadna was looking through the sack of provisions that they had been floating on. Turning to Fearghus suddenly, he offered his friend a battered apple. "You should eat," he continued.

At length, Fearghus found himself sitting comfortably on a patch of grass, a few paces in from the stony beach. The air of this island was crisp, clean and invigorating, cool and easy to breathe. "I've been here a few times in my life," Seadna sighed, leaning back on the coarse turf. "The Island of No Return."

"Why do you say that?" Fearghus asked, leaning in closer. He was surprised, or maybe even a bit horrified at this remark.

"It was here where what we call "The Revenge of Rome" took place. We call it this because it was believed to have been the wish of a particular Roman slave for my ship to wreck here."

Many feelings, of fear, of intrigue, and even of rage swelled in Fearghus. It was so much, he nearly cried aloud. "Please tell me more," he stammered, curiously.

Seadna drew a deep breath, and his eyes became solemn and sad. "After we sold this boy on the mainland, he cursed our ship to sink, and all upon it perish. As we sailed east to Britain again, the wind stirred and great clouds gathered."

"Might this by any chance, be the boy that gave Colla his magic?" Fearghus asked, already knowing the answer he would get.

However, Seadna was as if in a trance. Looking longingly into the deep blue sky above, he continued his tale. "It was the worst storm I have yet to see," he started. "Our ship was tossed back and forth, and the sea climbed up upon the deck, like a pirate would have done. The next thing I knew, Colla and I were sitting right here, on this island, trying to think of ways to save us. Each of our comrades had fallen to the wrath of the sea."

"But you say that Eire is close by," Fearghus reminded him.

"Of course," Seadna responded. "But we must watch our step, for the god of the Romans might not show so much mercy, next we trespass here. I think we may be granted passage back to the mainland."

"Why do you put it that way?" Fearghus asked, still curious.

"Because the cursed Isle of No Return shows no mercy but to a bearer of the magical armor, what Colla and you have both worn. It is to our advantage that you hold such favor with the Roman god."

In good time, when both of them had rested on the grass for a while, Seadna began to gather up their food. "Come with me to the western shore," he said. Not heeding anything around him, Fearghus stood up and followed.

"You really believe in this god of the Romans?" he asked as they stumbled along the beach.

"All I know is that he spared me of the terrible fate of my friends," Seadna answered, "and that he had something to do with Osgar, your spear."

Fearghus was very troubled upon discovering this. Was this the god that Agnos had spoken about so many days ago? Why was the god of the enemy aiding his cause? Now, more than ever, he was hopelessly confused as to his fate and purpose.

The Isle of No Return was quite small, Fearghus soon realized. It only offered a few rocky beaches and cliffs, and one sparse forest in the center. Everything here was brown, green, or black. It wasn't a very long walk to the westernmost extreme of the land.

When Seadna finally stopped at the edge of the water, Fearghus nearly jumped for joy. Just on the edge of his sight, bright and green and shimmering, he clearly made out the shape of the cliffs of Eire. It was only a few hours away from here! "Do you have a raft?" he asked Seadna, eyeing his friend carefully.

Seadna only smiled, stepping aside. "We won't need one," he responded, signaling Fearghus forward. When Fearghus reached him on the beach and stopped, confused, Seadna nearly broke out laughing. "Go on! Go on!" he urged excitedly.

Still not comprehending his friend's commands, Fearghus cautiously waded out into the water, until he was submerged past his stomach. Just behind him, Seadna had done the same. "What are we doing?" Fearghus asked, exasperated. To answer him, Seadna only pushed him ahead into the water, nearly causing him to fall.

Suddenly, as he looked down at the salty water below him, a great rushing sound filled the air, and a terribly strong wind tore at Fearghus's clothes. The deafening hum in his ears, he stood up to his full height and looked about him. The water around him was rippling violently, and the sea in every direction was shuddering and convulsing, huge waves crashing upon each other. "Keep going!" Seadna shouted behind him.

Fearghus ambled ahead cautiously, trying to steady himself. Then, all of a sudden, everything was clear. As he stared at the surf in front of him, it began to tear apart. As the water about his waist was sucked to either side, he was thrown forward on his stomach. Much to his surprise, he landed on perfectly dry sand.

As he looked up, he noticed Seadna running ahead. "We have to hurry!" he shouted, beckoning his friend forward.

Suddenly, the two were involved in a footrace with the Sea. As they advanced further from the island, the path behind them became blocked, the walls of water on either side sweeping down to cover it. Seadna and Fearghus, thus, were compelled to maintain a steady jog to outrun it. Fearghus, at this point, was most nearly in a daze, stupefied at this new occurrence.

As the two men quickened their pace, so did the water behind them. The closer they came to the opposite shore, the faster the water moved. When the two stumbled down a steep ridge to the ocean floor, the sea cascaded down with them, chilling their legs.

The ground below them was rocky and rutted with cracks and ridges. The sea floor was far less kind than the land above, and as they strove through it, they were forced to climb many hills and slide down them as well. All of this hampered their progress even more, and Seadna soon became slowed by his exhaustion. "Be spurred on by the goal ahead of us!" Fearghus shouted, comforting his friend.

"I am far too old to make this journey again!" Seadna sputtered, his breathing becoming heavier. "Let the Sea take me, as it has my friends!"

Fearghus could see the rocky cliffs of Eire now. In all their ominous glory, they now seemed warm and welcoming to him. He would hear none of this. "Then I shall see to your safety myself!" he bellowed, and slung Seadna over his shoulder.

Subsequently, his progress was only slightly slowed by this new weight. Fearghus's limbs were strong and chiseled, with the strength of the gods. His body would not so easily fail him here. His feet were finding the right holds, and he was very nimble on them. In a short length of time, he had nearly reached the climb back up to the land.

When he approached the impossible ridge, he set Seadna back down on his feet. "What now!" he cried, scanning the cliffs ferociously for a way up. Seadna had recuperated by now, and even in the face of this great hazard, he kept his wits about him.

"You'll have to climb the rock face to the right!" he shrieked, sprinting towards it. "Follow me!"

As soon as Seadna hit the rock, it became obvious that he had climbed here before. Fearghus watched in awe as his hands mechanically reached for outcropping of stone, and he scrambled up the vertical surface with amazing speed. It was all Fearghus could do to keep up with him. Below them, the Great Sea was churning, reclaiming its rightful place on the ocean floor. Before Fearghus knew it, its violent fury was ripping away at the cliffs below him, its salty spray soaking his garments. "We have to hurry!" he cried, nearly slipping on the wet stone.

But Seadna was out of his reach. The former pirate was nearly to the top of the wall now, far ahead of him. Fearghus could see his friend, peering down at him, and a look of horror crossed Seadna's face. "Jump!" he shouted, cupping his hands about his mouth. "It's your only chance!"

Fearghus halted his progress and looked behind him. The Sea, in its foamy wrath, was indeed gaining on him. He could not outrun it. Even now the violent waves were within a stone's throw. In order to save himself from being dashed upon the cliffs he would have to jump into the water.

Just before he jumped, everything slowed down in his mind. Ahead of him, there was only the violent blue Sea, swirling about violently. Every bit if it wanted to have his head; tear apart his body or drown it. Its terrible rushing sound filled his ears, and its salty spray burned his eyes, heralding the ultimate wrath of its source. Now only there existed the jagged brown cliffs about him, and the sea below. And then there only existed the air in front of him, and he jumped.

He collided with the sea trying to swim. Even before he had hit the water, he had thrust his arms forward, ready to struggle his way away from the rocks. The violent water was right there to counteract his efforts, pushing him up and down in the surf, and getting into his mouth. Several times in this struggle he was sucked far down underneath the surface, only to be spat up again by the current. His arms were pulling the water past him like great windmills, and his godly strength endured all while the water rose quickly to the edge of the land.

Suddenly, just as his efforts seemed to be working, though, a great push from the Sea thrust him back to the wall. As the deepening water blotted out the sun above, his head struck the stone cliffs and everything went black.

When Fearghus awoke, just as before, he recognized the voice of Seadna. He had survived after all! Much to his surprise, he also discovered the sound of wagon wheels. "Thank the gods you're alive!" Seadna said, watching his friend come to.

Fearghus immediately noticed a throbbing pain in the back of his head. "What happened?" he asked in a dazed voice.

"We've come back to Eire," Seadna replied.

Fearghus closed his eyes for a moment. They were very sensitive to the sunlight, and worsened his headache all the more. "What'll we do now?" he asked dazedly.

Seadna swallowed. "I suppose we'll just wait for the *Silverbeam* to return," he responded shakily. "I've a mind to ride back to the monastery and wait for them."

Now Fearghus's eyes were open. "By the way, where are we?" he asked attentively.

"We've just left my village," Seadna replied. "And there's nothing left of it. This just gives us an even stronger reason to seek Osgar."

Upon hearing this, Fearghus said a solemn prayer to the gods. Even so strong as he was, he shuddered at the thought of the deaths of so many villagers. This news especially would mean the death of the local magus, the man that had refused to send his warriors to battle so many days ago. Hopefully, the monastery had fared better while they were gone.

The world around them was bright and green. They were clattering down a narrow muddy road, and everywhere there were trees and rolling meadows. Many times before Fearghus had been in such a place, and many times before there had been such a problem as that he now faced. The scenery reminded him of his native village, which now probably lay in ruin a few days' ride away.

The two companions exchanged very few words during the long ride. Both were in awe of the problems ahead, but both still remained confident. The idea of attempting their adventure a second time was pleasing, and brought them hope to endure the hardships of the road.

As sunset approached finally, the dirt road suddenly ended. Just ahead of them, a steep stone path cut over the top of a short mountain. "We will camp here, in the cave just ahead," Seadna said.

Fearghus's heart sank. "We can't seek shelter in there!" he gasped, realizing what cave Seadna was speaking of. "It is cursed with black magic!"

Seadna was already unloading their provisions, most of which had been salvaged in the nearby village ruins. "We'll be safer inside," he replied, choosing not to heed Fearghus's warning. At length, Fearghus realized that his friend was serious, and that he had no choice but to follow him into the cave.

He hadn't realized it before, but he really trusted Seadna, just as he had Colla. He couldn't bring himself to disregard Seadna's judgement, and he felt all the better for it. Seadna was like an old sage, pouring forth wisdom and useful information about the mystery of Osgar.

Upon gathering their supplies, Seadna led them into the small breach in the mountain that Colla had led Fearghus out of so many days before. When they walked inside, the first thing Seadna did was light up a large torch. As the flame flickered to life, Fearghus covered his face. He did not want to see the shamrocks lining the walls or the dead snakes in the water just ahead. However, soon he was compelled to look about.

Just as he had expected, a great phenomenon was taking place within the cave. The walls were covered in shamrocks. It gave Fearghus the chills, to look at them, but as the night progressed, he learned to ignore their presence. There was too much on his mind.

Soon the evening wore on into the night, and the two men lay down on thin beds of cloth, as their campfire smoldered. Now there was only the calming hum of the water next to them, and the cool, fresh air of night. Tonight, Fearghus would not see the stars. Instead, he would be enveloped in the thorough darkness of the cave, hardly able to see from one wall to the other. The only light that entered his quarters emanated from the entrance, and it was the sickly pale luminescence of the moon, eerie and desolate.

Despite his fears, Fearghus somehow managed to sleep. The thoughts on his mind slowly slipped away, until he was completely enthralled in his dreams. In his mind, that night, he saw many visions; some were strange, others were frightening. However, it was only one that he remembered. In this dream, great black clouds were swirling about, like a fierce storm was brewing. Suddenly, there blazed across the sky the Roman cross, just as he had seen it above his fields, before his adventures had begun. As Fearghus looked intently at the blinding light, suddenly another change took place. The cross grew shorter, and each of the three prongs at the top began to spread, like water does when placed upon a flat surface. As it changed, so did its color. In almost no time, Fearghus was in awe of a great shimmering green shamrock. It illuminated the clouds about it, and its brilliance surrounded Fearghus like a warm blanket. As this occurred, he grew ever tenser and his breathing quickened.

Suddenly he awoke in a cold sweat, exhausted and out of breath. The darkness about him had returned, and the night outside still endured. Glancing over to Seadna on the other side of the cave, he covered himself with his blankets, and hid his face from view. He was deathly afraid of this cave now, but he couldn't amend that. Presently, he closed his eyes and concentrated on sleep once again, praying to the gods for aid.

The light of the next morning relieved Fearghus. Seadna led him back out of the cave very early, nearly with the dawn, and before long they were back on their way. The eastern sky was a brilliant orange as they clattered along, and every tree and boulder in their path cast a long shadow west to the mountains. They were heading constantly northward, towards the monastery and the pirate's cove. With the warm morning light shining upon him so brightly, he decided to simply put last night's dream out of his mind and enjoy the scenery of Eire while it remained.

They were making good progress. The ground was smooth and flat ahead, but dusty and dry. To Fearghus now, the sea smelled not fresh, but rather raw and wild. The sun was no longer warm and soothing, but hot and blistering.

By midday, the horses were exhausted. Seadna reined them up to a large grove of trees, and retired to a nearby stream for the rest of the afternoon. Behind him, Fearghus was following closely to his trail, thinking quite hard, once again, about the current situation. His mind was rapidly filling up with visions of happiness and prosperity, but most importantly, and greedily, of land and riches for himself. On the long ride here, he had thought quite a bit about the aftermath of the coming adventure. He dreamed of becoming a great king of his people, and with Osgar, holding supreme dominion over his subjects. However large this yearning was, though, he kept it hidden from Seadna. He was surprised at himself, even, at this new feeling.

The next day, the two men, once again, drove their horses even closer to the monastery. Their goal was still a great distance away, but Eire was a fruitful, flourishing land. From the dawn until the last rays of the dusk were finally squeezed out, they strove on, hoping to beat the *Silverbeam* to the white sands of a beach far away to the north. Tomorrow morning, they would be back on the road with the first light, quickening the pace for the last leg of their journey.

Soon, they were galloping along the dusty shore road, the sun flashing in between the trunks of saplings on either side, their bows forming a lofty corridor, and their trunks like durable Roman pillars. It was all fitting to their triumphant return, and with their helmets gleaming and capes fluttering, they finally came upon the great encircling forest, and the monastery down below appeared august and magnificent.

However, they remained condemned to the sea. Not for a long while would they again pass through the gates of the edifice below. No, only to the glorious sails of the *Silverbeam* would they now heed. According to Seadna, the ship was likely moored upon the coast of the pirate's cove in the north.

The two travelers held a very special reverence for their people as they passed by the valley. If anyone had been peering up at them, to the east, they would have beheld merely the silhouette of two men on a wagon, black against the blinding sun. Their helmets would not gleam, but rather be dark and mysterious to the onlooker. Like gods, imposing and magnificent, they cast a long shadow across nearly the entire basin.

Ahead of them, the white bluffs of the land rose high into the air. The sand, too, was white, and it burned in the undying light. They were rapidly nearing the cliffs of the pirate's cove now, and Fearghus could see plainly, in the face of his companion, a great yearning and sense of excitement.

Suddenly, they were there, and the fluttering flags of the *Silverbeam* were just as grand as the monastery behind them. It was not long before Seadna had guided the horses down the sandy entrance slope, and down onto the black, ashy ground below. On the ship, several men had already noticed their presence. In fact, as Fearghus stared intently upon the row of bewildered sailors, he noticed one faint, his friends catching him in their arms.

Even before the cart had reached the shore, the ramp had been dropped from the deck and a great outpouring of ecstatic men gushed through, surrounding their leaders. Immediately Seadna calmed his men and stood up to speak to them. "Even the terrible Sea has not matched us!" he shouted, to a cheer from his followers. "And neither shall our enemies, of whatever strength!"

A feeling of immense happiness rose in Fearghus. He was completely surrounded with it, and every wave, every detail of the ship seemed to glow with excitement and anticipation. Chants of "Fearghus the King!" rose amongst the celebrants around him, and he was carried down by them from his wagon.

Soon, though, Fearghus's mood once again became serious and solemn. He wished to see Agnos, and, it appeared to him, she was not among the throng of cheering warriors in front of him. Without pausing to speak to any of the men, Fearghus silently made his way to the entrance ramp and climbed up on the deck of the ship. Far to his right, he noticed, with a swallow, the large gap in the railing that he had fallen through before. He would never have thought that he would ever see it again, and it appeared dangerous to him.

His business, however, lie in the captain's cabin, just ahead. He suspected Agnos's presence within it, and this thought drew him closer and closer. Soon, he was to the door. There was the sound of soft, but nervous breathing inside. Fearghus paused. Thinking hard about what to say and what to do once inside, he drew a deep breath and rushed through the opening.

Just as he expected, Agnos was lying on the bed, weeping silently. When she saw Fearghus, she most nearly screamed, and collapsed, limp, into his arms. "Don't worry, I'm back," Fearghus whispered. "Everything has been solved."

Agnos looked up, her face streaming with tears. Her eyes were glazed over, and her face was red. "Never leave again," she blubbered. "I would not be able to bear it."

Fearghus wiped away her hair and dried her face with his tunic. "Do not cry over me," he answered. "This is my purpose, my goal. I must pursue it again and again, even if it shall bring death. You must understand that."

Suddenly, Agnos wiped her face by herself, drawing back a bit from him. "If it is your fate, so shall it be mine," she replied calmly.

Outside, Fearghus's absence was quickly becoming known. The warriors aboard the ship had rolled down every barrel of ale and wine that remained upon the *Silverbeam*, and a great celebration was soon to commence. "Come, let us be off, to celebrate my good fortune!" Fearghus said. And with that, he snatched Agnos up in his arms and plunged down the boarding ramp.

The sun set quicker than anyone had expected. But they were all the better for it. The ground was soft, and easy to the foot. The ash provided a perfect surface to sit upon, and eat and drink. And, because of the fact that the soot was so dark, the darkness seemed fresher, and wilder too. And so it was that Fearghus, reunited with his men, once again celebrated with them, in front of a huge bonfire.

The morning next, when the dawn rent the wispy clouds of night with its brilliant light, the adventurers prepared to embark again. The sails of the *Silverbeam* were filled with crisp wind, and the sturdy oars along side it dipped once more into the shimmering water below. And so it came to be that Fearghus stood upon the forecastle, Seadna by his side. "What lies ahead?" he asked.

Seadna squinted in the sun. "Many trails and tribulations, that will test not only your strength, but your mind. So foolish are we, even to challenge them. But I have faith," he answered, showing an uncomfortably high grade of respect to his friend.

But Fearghus was fearless. He had polished his great sword, and changed his garments. The whole world was his for the taking, and yes, he dared to challenge it. He had come to walk on the dark side, and dance with wolves. He had already secured in his mind that he would never falter, or cower from this task. He could not stop now, and make null and void his people's suffering. "I shall not fail you," he told Seadna, and walked back to the rear of the ship.

Throughout the day, the waters remained calm and forgiving. Seadna, wisely, had chosen to skirt around the Isle of No Return, and not a cloud appeared to darken the sky. When the night fell, the men simply drifted off to sleep, and their safety was not hindered while they rested. Fearghus and Agnos, in particular, relocated the place on the deck where before they had slept, and spread a soft blanket between them. The two lovers stayed up long into the night, admiring the stars and moon, and rejoicing in newfound contentedness. Fearghus's heart was light and happy, and his mind was at peace.

Fog was in the air the next morning. It was thick and mysterious, but seemed to bring no danger. As Fearghus peered at it from his covers, suddenly the figure of Seadna appeared. "Come with me," his dark silhouette said.

Trying carefully not to wake Agnos, Fearghus slid out from under his blanket and walked in the direction of Seadna's voice. The former pirate led him into the captain's quarters, where numerous lamps had been lit to remedy the thick mist.

Inside, the leaders of the voyage had congregated about a round table. Showing Fearghus to his seat across from Irial, Seadna took his own and began to speak in a low voice. "Shall we begin, then?" he asked.

The members of the group nodded, and Seadna leaned in to look at each of them closely. "A great adventure lies before us," he began. "As it is, none of us here can fathom the intensity of this mission, save only myself, having failed at it in the past."

His face in utter horror and distaste, Irial suddenly cut in. "Do we have the resources to execute this task?" he asked, stuttering nervously.

Seadna looked him in the eyes, and replied quickly. "Save only our own swords and armor, all we shall need is this man," he replied, gesturing towards Fearghus. "Fearghus has been chosen to lead us, and it will be his own intuition that will ultimately save us. We must hallow this man among us, and respect his every wish and desire."

Immediately, all eyes were on Fearghus. At first, he felt weak and timid at this new idea, but soon, this only resulted in curiosity. "Tell me more," Fearghus said, slyly and cunningly. "I should like to hear more about my mission."

Seadna drew back and began a complex story about his previous adventures, explaining in great detail the geography of the Isle of Man and also describing the Manx people. "I shall tell you more later, as we continue this long journey," he finished, dismissing them.

As the men went forth that day, each one had a different vision of the future. Some thought of hideous and gargantuan monsters, while others envisioned fire and brimstone. "Knowing Fearghus," one joked, "we're likely to face both!"

The remaining days of the excursion wore on endlessly. Fearghus spent a great deal of his time sitting upon the deck, reviewing various scrolls and such that Seadna had provided to him from the hold of the ship. They were chronicles of Eire, compiled by pirates from a variety of sources, including themselves. Some of the records recounted epic battles, others were poems and hymns, and some were strange and difficult to decipher. One in particular caught Fearghus's attention. It was only a sentence or two, scribbled sloppily onto an animal skin. To Fearghus, it appeared:

With Osgar shall he come, and rule Eire supreme, and his shall be the Lord's land.

This prophecy made Fearghus think hard. In all of this writing, fortunately, he was able to recognize the names of "Osgar," and "Eire," but still he could not make a connection between the two. What relation would his magical spear have to this "Lord of Eire?" Was it he, of all the people in the world, that the prophecy spoke about? Was he to rule supreme all of Eire, yet be subordinate to a "Lord?"

This thought and many more accompanied him as he came closer to his destiny. The time for departure from the ship grew ever closer, and tension also grew. Supplies were beginning to run low, and those warriors aboard the vessel were becoming preoccupied with petty fears and desires. Everyone was becoming steadily more irritable as the illimitable days passed, including Fearghus.

On one such day, Seadna decided once again to call together the leaders of the expedition for further briefing. And so, for the second time came Irial and Finghin and Fearghus to the round table of the bedroom, and in the center, his face grave and solemn, stood Seadna. "Good morning," he began.

"We've got a great deal of things to work out, I'm sure," Irial mumbled.

"Yes," Seadna replied. "First of all, I'd like to establish all of our responsibilities."

"A very important step, to say the least,' one of the sailors commented. "And what did you have in mind?"

Seadna swallowed once, and then began. "Irial shall head the bulk of our ground forces, to begin with. He is an experienced military leader. Then, I was thinking that you, Finghin, shall remain aboard and maintain this ship."

Followed by a nod from both of the men involved, Seadna dove into a much more important subject. "Fearghus and I shall lead the main expedition. Those of you who come with us must be ready to follow every of our commands, and be willing to fight and risk life."

Suddenly, a number of the men bowed their heads to him. "We shall be ready," one of the sailors muttered. Upon this statement, Seadna divided up the rest of the chosen men, assigning each as subservient to Irial, Finghin, or himself. Afterwards, the meeting took a much more serious turn.

"Next," Seadna continued, "I should like to describe some of the dangers we will face. Having failed at this very task in the past, I probably cannot tell of even half the dangers we will face, but I will try my best."

"And so shall we, in your service," one man said.

So Seadna, as the men sat there uncomfortably, began to explain some of the things he experienced during his previous attempt to loose the spear. He told of terrible and hideous things, including sinking sand, poisonous gas, and strange, unsettled apparitions. But, even so dangerous as these things got, many of them, according to Seadna, would shy away from the presence of Fearghus, the rightful owner of Osgar. As Seadna's speech worsened, though, the tension and utter horror of all the men was evident. Before their emotions reached a boiling point,

Fearghus stood up in his chair. "I think now's as good a time as any to end the meeting," he muttered.

After the others had left, Fearghus came up to Seadna, to talk in a more personal environment. "I suppose we shan't be too afraid of this new place, after all," he mumbled absent-mindedly.

"You shouldn't be thinking like that!" Seadna replied, viciously.

"Why do you say this?" Fearghus asked.

"Because," Seadna began, "because, in the end, it will be only *you* to face the final test. We can only help you to a very small extent!"

Fearghus stumbled backwards, horrified. The mission now meant something totally different and unexpected. "Me?" he yearned to say, and make his fears known. However, he couldn't, not now. Before now, he had always viewed himself as a blessed and invincible king, with unlimited power. Now, though, he was brought down to earth in a very understandable way. If he was to gain all of the riches and unlock all of the treasures that he desired, he would have to fight for them, and likely risk his own life, as well as the life force of Eire, as a Celtic nation. The world now rested upon his shoulders, and he couldn't drop it.

"I'll see you tomorrow," Seadna said suddenly, interrupting his thoughts.

That night was like any other aboard the ship. The stars were a bit fainter, and the sea slightly calmer. The air, least of all important, was balmy and thick. However, that night, it seemed to be joyful and intriguing, for it was that night that Fearghus decided, before it was too late, to express once again his love for Agnos. He knew that much was to be risked in the adventure on the island ahead.

Now much is to be said about the unmatched beauty of Agnos that night. Her eyes were deep and knowing, but in them a great yearning seemed to be contained. Her dark hair was tender and gentle. Warm and fair, she was perfect and radiant in Fearghus's eyes. His love for her now was truly real and strong in his heart, and he could see that she felt similarly.

The next morning, both of them found a rude awakening to the prodding Irial. "Meet me on deck," the nosy lumberman instructed them.

"In a moment," Agnos replied, pushing her hair back.

Irial simply turned on his heel and walked back to the stairs. "I'll see you up on deck!" he laughed.

Fearghus quickly sprang to his feet and followed his friend. When he and Agnos gained the main deck, the sky was gray and desolate. Fearghus immediately found Seadna, waiting patiently for him near the side railing. "What shall take place today?" he asked.

"We will land and seek the favor of the natives," his friend responded. "Maybe by dusk we shall gain dry earth, and, with all luck, warm food."

"That is good news to hear," Fearghus responded, and left Seadna's presence.

Throughout that day, the deck of the ship rang with the sounds of swords being sharpened and supplies being prepared for the wagons. Word was out that an end to the voyage was almost at hand, and the heart of every warrior beat faster, and the main deck became like a crowded village square, bustling with people.

Fearghus himself was rather concerned, once again, with the pirates' scrolls. Many questions were to be answered in the next few days, and many fears to come true. Fearghus wanted to know absolutely everything possible before diving headlong into this adventure.

Agnos, on the other hand, was content to busy herself with physically preparing her partner for the landing. She gathered his belongings, including several days' rations of food into a sack, and polished his armor and weaponry. Her gracious aid allowed Fearghus, by midday, to take the time to consult Seadna about various things that could take place on the Isle of Man. While the Sea still stretched as far as the eye could see, Finghin took over the navigation of the ship, and the two friends met once more in the captain's quarters.

"Now," Seadna began, "What did you want to discuss?"

Fearghus swallowed. "I was wondering…about my own participation in the quest."

Seadna knew exactly what his friend was worried about. "From what we have uncovered in our previous adventures, the true secret as to whether or not you will succeed is in *you*, and none other. In the end, it will only be your mind and heart against all of the magic the spear has to offer."

"In other words," Fearghus thought, "I shall have to tame it, and go beyond what Colla could have accomplished."

Seadna took a strong grip about Fearghus's shoulders. "Exactly. However, everything we hold dear, including Eire itself is at stake. We mustn't fail to protect our families from the Romans!"

Fearghus looked his friend right in the eyes. "I shall put my very life behind them!" he bellowed, turning red. "The magic of Osgar shall have to get past my sword before it takes me!"

By the time their meeting was finished, the sun was high in the sky, and the color of the sea was growing lighter. In fact, now, many reeds were appearing. At length, they nearly stopped the *Silverbeam's* progress. "We must be near land," Finghin said, "drop a few men with swords into a rowboat."

The sailors executed his command and the other men watched as they rowed about the ship, loosing it from the reeds with their blades. As far as the eye could see, the sea looked like a flat green meadow, overgrown with thick vines and flowers. Only on the very edge of his sight, Fearghus could see the shine of free water. "Prepare the horses," he said. "We will land soon."

Their progress was menacingly slow. However hard the burly men down below plied their oars, the ship could only move very slowly. When the sun had reached the western sky, back where they had left Eire behind, the ship had most nearly reached the edge of the foliage. "I can see it!" someone suddenly said from above. Indeed, a sailor clinging to the top of the mast had sighted the Isle of Man.

The men aboard the ship had already heeded Fearghus's commands, and every wagon was ready to go, the exit ramp poised to drop from the edge of the vessel. It was at this time that Seadna addressed his warriors for the last time before the landing. "You all know what to do," he began. "Tonight we will find a place to lodge for the rest of the night."

Behind their master, suddenly, everyone on board got their first glimpse of the cliffs of Man. They were gray and brown, and covered slightly with small trees. All about them, black, unsettled clouds swirled around threateningly. As they neared the island, they seemed to grow, becoming larger and darker with every turn of the oars below. At length, lightning was distinguishable inside the dark mass.

"What do you make of this?" Fearghus asked Seadna.

The former pirate frowned with uncertainty. "We are not wanted here," was his simple answer. "The reeds could not stop us, and so we must face the wrath of the sky."

Fearghus's breast burst with excitement. "Then what shall we do?" he stammered, looking back and forth from Seadna to the island ahead.

Seadna did not give heed to him, though. The pirate was running to the hold as fast as he could. Suddenly, down below, Fearghus heard the beat of the pacing hammers grow faster and faster, harder with every change. Before he knew it, the *Silverbeam* was hurtling forward, making a desperate run at the shore of the Isle of Man. "Up with the sails!" he cried frantically.

Fearghus now realized, with a swallow, that Seadna had been exactly right. The magic of Osgar already was attempting to repel the adventurers. As the oars of their ship cut into the water with amazing force and speed, so did the water grow choppier. Now every warrior on the deck was scurrying back and forth quickly, trying to tie down the wagons and horses that had been laid out on the surface. If they did not succeed, then a great deal of their food and supplies would be swept overboard and the railing of the ship would once again be broken. Their only hope would be to run the ship onto the beach, and scramble for shelter.

They were almost there. The ship was being thrown back and forth violently, and the men rowing down below were being pushed back and forth in freezing water. As Fearghus stood on the forecastle, staring intently into the face of the oncoming storm, Seadna joined him. "We are doomed!" he gasped, pointing ahead. The wind freezes whatever it touches!"

Indeed, the swirling black storm had caused the sea to freeze solid just ahead. And it was headed straight for them! If nothing was changed, everyone aboard the vessel would die instantly at the hands of the great menace. Now there was only time for one more word. "Seadna," Fearghus said, clenching his hands in the cold, "it will bow to me, will it not?"

But suddenly Seadna's face was hit with the black fog. Almost instantly, he was like a statue, frozen in his position. The railing in front of Fearghus was covered in thick ice, and as he looked on with horror, the deck of the ship directly behind him was smote with it, and it cracked and shattered. However, Fearghus was unharmed by the terrible mist. He alone would be left to see its destruction.

Suddenly, he realized that Agnos was soon to be hit with the ice! He had to see her once more before she died! All about him, the fair warriors of Seadna's village were frozen solid, covered with several layers of ice, Their faces and hands were sickly and blue, and their eyes were wide, frozen in a state of pure horror.

Now Fearghus was in a race with the mist. He had to get to the captain's quarters before the ice did, and slew his love. All of a sudden, though, his hopes were dashed as he slipped and fell onto the slippery ice. The black fog strove on ahead of him, and rent the walls of the cabin with its fury.

Even so, Fearghus, bringing together all of his courage and resolve, burst through the rigid frozen door and inside to see Agnos's body. To his surprise, she was not dead, but was standing there, shivering in the midst of all the ice and death. "What is going on, Fearghus?" she asked, shouting. "What has happened?"

Fearghus stumbled forward and hugged her tightly. "Nothing," he whispered. "It is all well."

Then suddenly, his sadness was replaced with rage. He wanted revenge on this magic for destroying his men, and making void their sacrifices. Running back outside, he drew his sword and ran to the forecastle. "For Eire!" he cried, and raised his blade to the sky.

As he looked at his proud blade, it burst with red flames. A great beam of burning red light went forth from it, and it split the black fog in half. And suddenly, once again, the *Silverbeam* was hurtling forward to the beach of the island,

and ahead only shone the reflection of the setting sun on clear water. The icy mist was still rushing past Fearghus, on either side of him, but the ship was quickly defrosting, and Seadna, the burning red sword full in his face, was now merely drenched with water, alive and well.

As Fearghus struggled to hold his sword against the strong wind, everyone behind him began to recover from the freezing storm. They were in awe of their master, standing alone against the wrath of Osgar, and many a cheer was made from them while the danger still rushed by. By the time the ship had reached the beach, the warriors were saved and the storm subdued.

Chapter 9

The Isle of Man

Soon, the whole of the party aboard the ship had descended down onto the beach below. Remaining upon the *Silverbeam* only were Finghin and two men of his household to manage the wreck of the vessel. Among the party on the beach was the proud general Irial, with a great host of his strongest men, and of course Seadna, Agnos, and Fearghus himself. All of the men were fully clad in armor and riding upon wagons and horses.

"Where do we head from here?" Fearghus asked Seadna. Behind his friend, the terrible *Silverbeam* was sitting upon the shore at an awkward angle. The ice had ruined the great woodcarvings aboard it. Many of the ropes and poles holding up the sails had snapped, and the walls of the cabin, as well as the deck had been broken and cracked. Unfortunately, the body of the ship had been broken on the frozen water, and the vessel was no longer fit for sailing. Fearghus was still confused as to why the ship had even reached the shore in the first place, without anybody rowing it. All in all, the ship looked like an uneven, rough jumble of wooden planks and poles.

"There's got to be a settlement somewhere down the shore here. But now, I suppose we're stuck here for the night," Seadna said. "Unload the carts."

Leaving Agnos on the seat of his wagon, Fearghus helped the men take down the necessary means of food and shelter from their carts. The horses were given water and grain, and the fruit and bread that had survived the ice storm was passed out to the men. Before long, several fires had been kindled, and the flames did well to counter the cold of the night. The sun was setting below the horizon, casting its red light far across the calm waters of the Irish Sea. The voyage to the Isle of Man was coming to an end, and Fearghus still had Agnos to celebrate it with.

As they sat there, enjoying a basket of fish, Fearghus turned and looked Agnos right in the eyes. "Why did not you freeze during the ice storm, as everyone else did?" he asked.

Agnos looked completely bewildered. "I don't know how to answer you," she responded. "It is a mystery to us."

Fearghus didn't respond with words. Instead, he hugged her tightly and drew a blanket around her shoulders. And so the two lovers watched the sun disappear, and after that their fire burn steadily through the night. Tomorrow, perhaps, they would sleep in a friendly Manx village, under a sturdy roof.

The morning next, the destruction and fear of the previous day could not have been guessed but for the wreck of the *Silverbeam*. Everyone's morale was high, as was their faith in Fearghus. The sun was shining brilliantly, and there was no sign of danger in the immediate future. "Let us be off!" he told his people, and led the way, Seadna and Agnos by his side, down the beach.

The Isle of Man was a truly beautiful place. This particular beach was covered in gravel, and ran along a mysterious green forest. The air was crisp, by the water, and the sea was neither warm nor cold. The horses were forced to ford through many cool and clear streams, and climb rocky cliffs as well as soft hills. At great length, a plume of smoke was seen in the distance. By now, it was nearly midday, and everyone was tired of traveling.

"We are very lucky," Seadna commented. "To find a village this early is truly a blessing."

"I'll go ahead and check out the place, first," one of the sailors said. Seadna approved, and the warrior, accompanied by one of his friends, rode on ahead of them, into the deep green forest.

"We can plan the rest of our journey," Fearghus said, "when we are safe in the village houses."

"Yes, a lull in the storm," Seadna replied, longingly.

The two friends looked intently at the shadowy forest, and complete silence seemed to prevail. Then, all of a sudden, their peace was interrupted as one of the scouts burst back through the branches on foot. He was panting heavily, and there was a bloody gash on his arm. "There is no village," he gasped, doubled over with exhaustion. "A pirate got my friend."

Seadna's blade was out. "Pirates?" he bellowed, his eyes red with fury.

Fearghus also drew his menacing sword. "We'll handle this," he shouted, looking over to his friend. And with that the two leaders disappeared into the forest, galloping side by side. Their blades flashed in the light of the sun streaming through the canopy and the ground thundered with the hooves of their horses. Just ahead, a bright clearing was coming up.

"Who dares attack the company of Seadna?" the latter cried as his steed leapt into the clearing. Ahead of him, just as Fearghus expected, two burly pirates braced themselves against his fury, drawing their own daggers. However, it was too late for their defense. Seadna was quick with his fair Celtic sword, and his steel rang through flesh and bone. In a flash, two mutilated men lay on the ground, their grizzly fur jackets stained with fresh blood, and their tattoos and earrings broken. Seadna had been merciless to his own kind, and he had his gleaming sword to prove it.

Suddenly, a voice interrupted the triumphant scene. Next to Fearghus, a small ruddy man was cowering in fear. "Please spare me!" he pressed, covering his face. Fearghus only put his sword to the man's throat.

"Leave, foul beast!" Seadna suddenly shouted, and galloped forward.

Now the man was upon his knees. "Please! I mean no harm!" he cried, leaning backward.

"Then who is to speak for my dead scout?" Seadna demanded.

"I did not kill him!" the man sobbed.

Now Fearghus was very curious. "Who are you?" he asked.

"He is the Snake, you fool!" Seadna shouted. "Be gone, spawn of demons!"

But Fearghus would not let the man get away from him so quickly. "I am not finished with you yet!" he snapped. "Now tell me, oh Snake, exactly who you are and why you are here."

Now the Snake lowered his arms and peered up at Fearghus. "I have come here on behalf of my captors, the pirates, who are in search of a great treasure of theirs," he whimpered.

"Bite your tongue, thief!" Seadna screamed. "Return to the earth, hideous monster!"

Fearghus didn't know which way to lean. Instead of acting, he pressed the Snake the more for answers. "Could this treasure, by any chance, be the great lance Osgar?"

"Oh yes, yes, that was it!" the Snake replied. At this new idea, Fearghus looked long and hard into the eyes of the man. In them, he could vaguely see some kind of mischief and hate. However, they now seemed so innocent and indifferent that he was compelled to stop Seadna's yelling. This man was a victim of the terrible pirates, and worthy of his aid.

"I am sorry, but the spear now belongs, rather, to me, from Eire," Fearghus said. "But now I shall grant you the freedom to leave my presence."

"No, please have mercy on me, and take me in with your company, lest I should starve!" the Snake pleaded.

"You shall go from here, and leave us be!" Seadna retorted, cutting in suddenly. "Fearghus," he then said, "Do not give heed to this black-hearted sorcerer! He has deceived me once already!"

Now rage rose in Fearghus's breast. "Away!" he shouted, brandishing his sword. "You will not fool Fearghus, the savior of Eire, and Seadna, Lord of the *Silverbeam*! Be gone, before my fair sword pierces your chest! Be gone!"

Now the Snake's eyes had become red, and deep with anger. As Fearghus looked on, holding his blade tightly, he noticed a forked tongue flick out from the Snake's twisted mouth. "Be prepared for your company to fall, and all of Eire with it! I, the terrible and all-powerful Snake, shall have the last laugh. Who dares challenge my power?"

Fearghus was not daunted by this show of magic. "I, Lord of all Eire!" he bellowed, his godly sword singing through the air.

Suddenly, the Snake's form began to change. His skin became a deep black, and his limbs shriveled to nothing. His legs fused, and grew longer. Also, Fearghus noticed, his skin hardened and cracked, while his head grew wider and more hideous. And then, to Fearghus's utter horror, he was a great serpent, very similar to that which he killed in his own village back in Eire. In his mouth shone great saber-like teeth, and his eyes were like burning torches. "Try now, without your precious spear, to take my life a second time!" he sneered.

Fearghus's horse reared. "It will be a pleasure!" he retorted, and his steed leapt towards the Snake. Now, the beast's head hurtled straight for him, fangs out. But Fearghus had improved his fighting skills, in these past days, and just as the venomous spikes reached him, he parried them with his sword, cutting a deep furrow in the fangs.

The great serpent reeled back in pain, and the ground began to shake. "You fool!" he cried. "You fool! This is not the last you shall see of me!" And with that the ground opened up, and the Snake was swallowed by the dark abyss under the earth. With a last terrible shuddering, the land returned to its former shape, only the loose soil evidence of its unrest. And where once a vast black ravine had been, now only was a barren strip of sand.

"Let us return to the company of our friends," Seadna said, interrupting the subsequent silence. "They will be fearful for our safety."

And so the two warriors rode back through the trees, and came back to their followers with gleaming swords. "The pirates have been brought to justice," Seadna assured his men. "Let us continue the pursuit of our goal." Needless to say, Fearghus now realized, the faith of the people in their two leaders was stronger than ever before. However, a different thought burned in his mind. Now, more than before, he felt scared, afraid of the Snake and his wrath.

The party was contented to continue searching the coast of the immense island. The sun was high in the blue sky, and the horses were beginning to perspire. Presently, Irial pulled his horse along side Fearghus. "Everything seems well, as of yet..." he mumbled. "Anything new?"

Fearghus ran this question through his mind, feeling it and kneading it, until he came to an answer to give his friend. "No, nothing," he replied.

"That is good," Irial said. "And so maybe shall the rest of our journey be...with all favor of the gods."

Fearghus looked Irial right in the eyes. "Yes, with help from the gods above shall we ultimately succeed."

As the sun burned its way through the sky, a general sense of futility was quickly setting upon the weary travelers, and the small rations of food that they had brought from the *Silverbeam* were most nearly gone. Each man longed for a warm bed, and even warmer food. There was no Manx village in sight, only the winding edge of the forest and the dry rocky shore. At length, Seadna stopped their progress. "We will make our camp here," he shouted, to the dismay and deluge of groans from his warriors. "I will, however, send forth two scouts with fresh horses to survey the area ahead of us," he continued. "Make yourselves comfortable."

And so, once again did they set up camp on the beach. This time, though, the sighs of relief were replaced by grumbling of hunger and futility. Even Fearghus himself felt considerably anxious about the whole scene. The sea behind them only seemed sinister and cold, and the bright moon was only a mockery of the warm sun that shone during the day. Fearghus could only hope that his followers were not too dismayed, lest they abandon his quest and leave him alone. Hopefully the scouts would come back with good news in the morning.

The sun set quickly past the horizon, and soon enough, Fearghus and Agnos were staring blankly into their campfire, the fire that had not touched any food all night long. But with their hunger also came weariness, and so, with out ever exchanging a word, the two lovers prepared to sleep, praying for better fortune the next day. When Agnos was asleep, though, Fearghus maintained his vigilance, thinking hard, and considering many different things as he did this. Everything had to happen just right in this journey, and right now, he wasn't so sure his plans were coming together.

It was while he did this that he first realized the presence of a peculiar raspy sound coming from the bushes nearby. Of course, he reasoned, this was no time to panic. It was probably a wild animal. Nonetheless, though, he made himself a torch of the dry embers of his fire and threw a few glances over his shoulder. As he expected, he saw nothing but the thorny brush. Satisfied, he drew a thick blanket about himself and closed his eyes.

Suddenly, the raspy sound returned. This time, Fearghus, his ears straining, was able to distinguish a hollow voice, like a whisper. And it was saying something—he just didn't know what. The voice sounded so terrible and eerie, Fearghus shuddered and hid himself behind his blanket, holding his breath. He was seized with utter fear. He did not want to meet this specter, whoever he was. He wanted nothing to do with it. Now he only wished the sun to be up, and all of the brave warriors behind him to be awake.

But the night was young, and the apparition was relentless. On and on, his moaning echoed through the darkness. It was growing louder, closer. As Fearghus's lungs seemed most nearly to burst, a shrill wind filled the air, disturbing his covering and chilling his bones. It was the cold, howling wind of a terrible ghost, likely a poltergeist. Now Fearghus's only hope was to hide, and pray that the spirit had not seen him.

At length, he realized with a pang of uncontrollable horror that the ghost was right upon him. The air was rent with his icy touch, and Fearghus's body was paralyzed with fear and anguish. And as his heart sank, so did the ghost resume his speaking. "Doom! Doom!" he choked, casting about the camp. "Doom to you all! You, who dare to challenge my master, doom to you and your men! Woe is he whose sword should be drawn in defiance of Osgar! Woe is he who should walk the earth in opposition to the Great Serpent! Doom to you all!" he screamed, and with that, Fearghus's body convulsed in terror and he fainted.

When next he opened his eyes, his mind was stricken with fear such that his body shook violently in horror. "Calm down!" suddenly a voice said. It was a gentle, warm voice, and very much the opposite of that of the apparition he had heard the night before. Just as he expected, when he opened his eyes, it was only the fair Agnos there, caressing his face. He was lying down in the bed of their wagon, and it was rolling bumpily down the beach. "It is all well," Agnos said. "The scouts have found a Manx village very close by."

Fearghus sat up and looked around. Indeed, they were rushing down the rocky shore, headed for a small group of circular huts, plain to see atop a rocky cliff. "That is well," Fearghus responded. His body was still tingling from last night's frightful experience, and his heart was beating beyond control.

"What happened last night?" Agnos asked.

Fearghus sat up on his arms and breathed a long sigh of relief. "We had a visitor, and nothing more," he answered.

In almost no time, the warriors were trudging up the rough path to the village. To Fearghus, the settlement appeared rather primitive and crude, but nonetheless, it was thriving. The huts were of thatched walls and roofs, and any other structures were loosely pulled together with wooden poles and lengths of rope. The people here seemed friendly and extremely, almost strangely nice to one another. Though each man bore a spear or club, only would fish and wild animals meet their wrath. Against the shimmering sea and the sweeping hills of the island, the village was beautiful and welcoming.

It was not long before Fearghus and Seadna were bowing to the burly chief of the settlement. Using an interpreter, the leader was first to speak to the men. "You have come a great distance to my village," he observed. "Of what purpose I cannot yet fathom."

Seadna was quick to respond. "Your greatness," he began, "we are here in the pursuit of a great and powerful treasure."

The hefty chief chuckled to himself as he lay back in his chair. "And what more powerful than I shall you find on the Isle of Man?" he asked curiously.

Now Fearghus piped in. In a cunning, defiant voice, he answered, "The great spear Osgar with the terrible Snake coiled about it."

The chief's face suddenly became red and fearful. A growing rage was building inside of him, and his face was strained in intense thought. His bare arms came to rest on his muscular thighs, and his fingers gripped tightly his legs. "Many terrible things have come of these such quests," he replied shakily. "None have come alive from the grasp of this Snake you speak of. I alone of my clan know of what you speak. You are wise, but also foolish to come here to my house."

"But may we implore your aid, in the course of our travels?" Seadna pressed, trying unsuccessfully to retain his humble stance.

The chief sat there brooding as his attendants wiped the sweat from his brow and filled a bowl with water for his feet. Finally, he looked up from his thinking. "Yes, you may seek shelter here," he responded sternly. "Now be off to gather your supplies."

The two warriors thanked him and burst out into the grove of trees outside. In the middle of the village, where they stood, there was only but a muddy drag on which to move their wagons. The villagers were doing all that they could for the warriors, in their struggle to move in, and many thanks were given for it.

For the rest of the day, the men enjoyed the generous offerings of the Manx and the cool refreshing water of the village's stream. There was a great deal of preparation going on for the quest ahead, but also much relaxation and recuperating. As a testament to his love and concern for Agnos, Fearghus vowed to keep her safe with him at every moment of the stay. The two were given to the care of a frail old woman, far beyond the normal age of death in her village. She was wise even beyond her advanced years, and many a tale did she have as her slaves attended to the couple.

As a start, the servants prepared a great basin of warm water for them, and the two were allowed privacy to slip into the steamy bath before the slaves came forward with brushes and sections of cloth to wash them with. They were relaxing in a great wooden tub, sturdy and sealed with pitch. As the maids splashed water over Fearghus's head, he dared to begin a conversation with the old lady. She was sitting there on a stool, with the smooth thatched texture of her hut surrounding her. Her hair was rather grizzled, as she didn't allow her handmaidens to groom it, and her face was gnarled with age. "What have you to say of our quest?" Fearghus asked.

"It is near folly, as I have seen it," she replied quickly through an interpreter.

"Why do you say that?" Fearghus spluttered.

"Once came through here a nasty pack of pirates," she began, "and from my view, 'twas the Snake that killed all of them in cold blood as they climbed the 'Cliffs of Doom', as we sometimes call them."

Fearghus looked her in the eyes. "All but two, as I have heard," he said slyly.

"Yes, if I remember correctly, there were two men that fled from the island, swearing never again to set foot on this land," she remarked.

"Then one has broken his oath!" Fearghus laughed. "For it is my closest friend Seadna who dares with me to reclaim Osgar."

When her interpreter finished speaking, the woman jumped with excitement. "Does he return who bears the armor of heaven?" she asked anxiously.

Fearghus was pleased, really, to boast of himself in this instance. "No, the other," he responded swiftly, but then added: "For it is now I that wears the armor."

Fearghus could tell that the woman, upon this, was pondering prostrating herself to him, and his pride and confidence soared. "It is just as the old days!" she screamed ecstatically. "The gods are kind to give me but one more chance to see a successful quest!"

Across from him, Fearghus could see the delight in Agnos's eyes also, to hear of her partner's praise. Now, her hair was soaking and bunched in front of her eyes, and she was all the more beautiful for it. Fearghus strained to hold her and to see her like this drove him nearly mad. For now, he would wait until their supper to continue his conversation.

Before long, the maids were done with their scrubbing and Fearghus and Agnos were caught up into towels and brought to their dressing rooms. Fearghus was pleased when he reached his room. He was provided with new fresh clothes, and his armor was cleaned and polished. In this small place, there was also a table and a crude chimney. As of right now, though, he was in a great hurry to dress for the feast tonight. He was quick to pull on a loose tunic and a long, elaborately embroidered cloak for the night cold. He strapped his silvery blade to his waist, and flung his cloak over his shoulders, securing it at a gold button on his shoulder. He was now ready to partake of this one last feast before the Quest of Osgar.

The feast was to be held in the middle of the drag, the muddy road in the center of town. There was a great rectangular table set up, made of sturdy wood, and it was covered with a great cloth, and on this cloth was written, in strange mainland symbols, the Chronicles of Osgar. It was here where the great "adventurers of old" as Seadna described them, had recorded the history of the spear. These were the heroes of the Old World, and close to the gods. They knew a great deal more than Fearghus, and their curiosity about the treasure was only paralleled by the number of questions that Seadna and the pirates could answer. In fact, it was Seadna who brought this cloth with him, bringing it as a surprise to the great feast. He had attained it from his spoils in Britain, in a monastery of the Romans.

"What does all of this mean?" Fearghus asked as he looked upon it from afar.

Seadna shook his head. "It is encrypted by strange and terrible pictures of death and adventure."

Suddenly, Agnos appeared from behind them, and her face was evident of intense thought. "I have seen these signs before," she said finally.

"Can you interpret them?" Seadna asked, moving closer to the table.

Agnos bent over the tapestry, scanning it with her eyes. Some hair that hadn't been tied up behind her head fell in front of her face. At length, she looked up and found Seadna's curious gaze. "This cloth encompasses not only the history of Osgar, but its future."

"What does it say?" Fearghus pressed.

Agnos now began a long and detailed description of the tapestry. "It starts here," she signaled, pointing to a strange crest. "This is the signet of a typical Roman governor, but it is very old. It seems to me that it comes from the deserts of Arabia."

"But how does it come to Eire?" Seadna asked.

Agnos looked him right in the eyes. "The spear Osgar has come here to save us, just as it has other peoples. But only the right person can use it for its original purpose."

"Go on," Fearghus told her excitedly.

"Next, the cloth displays the point of Osgar, and its head is covered with both red and white," she continued.

"What does this mean?" Fearghus asked.

"It is merely a symbol of the weapon's great powers. The next symbol, this sunburst here, is also symbolic of the invincibility of Osgar. Inside of it, a skull is shrouded in golden light, and death is defeated," Agnos answered shakily.

"What comes next?" Seadna and Fearghus prodded simultaneously.

"This appears to be the headpiece of a Catholic bishop," she said quickly, looking away from Seadna's confused and suspicious gaze. "And after that, I see the spear Osgar upon the head of a serpent."

"That is good to hear!" Seadna chuckled.

"Yes, it is," Agnos remarked. "And so, the tapestry continues through many more strange symbols. All that remains to be interpreted are this black banner of pirates here, and, at the end, I believe, is a Roman cross imposed on a golden crown."

"This is all very easy to understand, then," Fearghus commented. "But what of the Roman Catholicism?"

Agnos's eyes darted about fiercely, looking around for any nearby Celtic warriors. "The fate of Rome and that of Eire are tied closely together," she whispered to her mate nervously.

Fearghus listened to but rejected her prediction. "Yes, in the way that we utterly defeat them," he replied.

Agnos was compelled to whisper back to him. "No, but in peace and brotherhood," she responded.

Fearghus did not heed her, but instead called together his men. "Let us begin the feast!" he cried, and a multitude of slaves from the huts around him came forth bearing large platters of stew, mutton and vegetables. More came after them bearing mead and ale. Within a few minutes, the whole of the table was laden heavily with food and drink. Fearghus was met well with his subjects at the banquet, and was seated at the head of the table, Irial and Seadna at his sides. As the meal began, Fearghus noticed, quite uncomfortably, that a number of the men had begun to bow to him as they liked, and give him praise he knew was not due to him. As the feast wore on, he waved off a great deal of these attempts and tried to maintain a humble composure.

But none of this could nullify the mood of the great occasion. The meat on Fearghus's plate was soft and juicy, and the ale was chilled and refreshing. Everyone gathered about him bore high hopes for his success, and the dusk was filled with the howls and laughs of joyful drunkards. It gave Fearghus a feeling of control and dominion to have every one of his men gathered around this cause. To see each one sitting at the table just like the others without any grumbling made him very confident. The table was sturdy and fruitful and the air was fresh and soothing on this hill.

When the eating had most nearly ceased, and only remained full mugs of ale, Seadna stood up and addressed his company drunkenly. "Now, let us be to our beds, for tomorrow shall the Isle of Man see our wrath!" And with that, the warriors, with no sense of order, began to return to their cabins and tents. Some stayed behind to drink and talk their way through the night around campfires, but many more realized the importance of sleep. Agnos, for one, was already laying comfortably in their bed by the time Fearghus returned. And so, without resistance or displeasure, Fearghus and the Company of Osgar passed into peaceful rest. In the coming adventure, they would no longer have this luxury, and Fearghus knew it.

The feeling of the next morning was momentous beyond Fearghus's control. There was no time to enjoy the sunrise, or to gently play with Agnos's hair as she slept. Fearghus was awakened long before the dawn, and his chariot and armor were prepared, it seemed, for battle. Now only shone his silvery sword and Agnos's face was only but tired and peaceful. Outside, a cold salty wind disturbed her hair as Fearghus lifted her onto his cart. The sky was dark, but her locks were darker and more beautiful, and her eyes gleamed.

Soon, the muddy drag in the middle of the village was teeming with warriors and their craft, and each man silent, holding reverence for the night surrounding him. The party was assembling quickly but methodically, and soon Irial and Seadna took up their commanding posts at the front. "We shall make our way to the Valley of the Worm," Seadna bellowed. "There, we will plan the assault of Osgar!"

With that, he kicked his horse into a slow trot and led the company slowly down the hills until they gained a plateau low over the rocky ocean coast. Apparently, Seadna knew exactly where he was going, for from here, he turned them into the dark forest with the utmost confidence. "Keep your guard up!" a man by his side shouted as they descended into the dark rocky abyss. They were weaving their way through a maze of stout pillars and fine leafy bushes. Not could be heard even a single sound but the rolling of wheels and straining of man and horse, and not could be seen anything but the glowing orbs of light provided by their torches and the blue luminescence of the distant moon. The stars above were completely blotted out by the boughs of gnarled trees. At Fearghus's side, Agnos was shaking with fear of the dark uncertainty.

"Don't worry," he whispered. "It will be day soon enough, and no one shall leap past my sword."

"I shall not fear, then," she replied, but still her fingers gripped tightly his muscular forearm, convulsing violently.

Just as Fearghus predicted, the dawn soon came, and its pale light began to slice through the canopy of the forest. The company had maintained a considerably low pace until now, but as the ground was illuminated with warm light, Seadna gave the order to speed up. It was now that the forest itself began to liven up. The warriors heard strange and terrible sounds on either side, so much so that Irial posted a guard on either side of the party. But Seadna was quick to stop him. "They are mere poltergeists of the Manx people, trivial minions of the Snake. The only power they do not have is to injure or kill. But keep close ranks lest they dare approach us!"

At this, Fearghus drew Agnos even closer to himself, and kept his eyes peeled and senses sharp for signs of any apparitions. A haunted forest like this could easily drive away the bravest of warriors, but not Seadna. At length, Fearghus finally came upon one. He heard a sinister chuckling in the bushes near him, but the sun was brilliant enough that he did not fear it. Instead of convulsing in horror, as normally he would have done, he plucked up enough courage to draw his sword and address the spirit. As he did this, the cold wind of his opponent swept over him, and the ghost was right upon his chariot. "Be gone, foul specter! Who of your lowly kind dares to challenge mortal man! Be away with you!" he shouted. And as his magical sword swung about, it somehow found its mark, and a red flame seared the freezing air. In seconds, the ghost was screaming like a banshee, leaving them in a hurry. "They will not approach us any longer!" Fearghus reassured his men. "They are cowards, and so shall be their master when we are finished here!"

The warriors about him responded with a small cheer, and the mood was kept high for the remainder of the excursion. Not one gust of cold wind again did disturb their peace, but, nonetheless, Fearghus knew that the specters were watching and waiting, ready to strike should Fearghus leave the group. They feared only but his sword, but the single blade was possessed of magical powers that could bridge the ethereal gap. They would let their master, the Snake, face the shimmering blade, lest it be reunited with its terrible and far more important counterpart, the spear Osgar.

As the sun told them it was past midday, the trees of the forest began to thin. They were now ascending a low hill, and the sun was growing in strength. Now the horses were beginning to tire, and they were in need of grain and water. "We will see the twisting Valley of the Worm soon," Seadna told his company. "Prepare to unload a good night's supply of rations and shelter."

And so, without further struggling, the party came out of the great forest, and the sun was low and red in the sky. Just ahead, the whole island stretched out for miles, and the setting sun made it orange and vast, each tree like a blade of grass, and each pond like a puddle. They were on the very edge of an enormous valley, the Valley of the Worm. The people of the village said that this bowl was carved by the father of all snakes, far greater than even the terrible Snake himself. No one since has seen the serpent, but some say that it disappeared with the coming of Osgar. For now, Fearghus's company would enjoy the favorably clear and soft dip in the land, and prepare for the assault of the Cliffs.

Seadna chose a smooth section of moist, muddy earth, and ordered the group to set up camp. Small tents were thrown up, the animals were fed and watered, and the chariots were prepared for a fast escape, if the need should arise. Irial coordinated a complex guard and scouting procedure for the night's stay, and took the trouble to appoint bodyguards for the three main leaders of the expedition. All in all, the camp was a long shot away from the comfortable surroundings of the Manx village by the Sea. Tomorrow they would cross the Threshold of Doom, as some called it.

"What will happen tomorrow when we cross?" Fearghus asked Seadna curiously as they sat there.

Seadna looked distressed. "When we enter the domain of Osgar, those of us who are unworthy of possessing it are delivered into its power. Only one such as you can bring us in, or for that matter out alive."

"Then, what you are saying is that Colla saved your life," Fearghus said, thinking quite hard.

"It all changes after this boundary, carved by the father of the Snake. When we climb to the other side, we all but you will be possessed of Osgar's power," Seadna continued. "I have refrained from telling you this that you might feel more confident of yourself. We and all of Eire depend on your skill of sword and mind. Good luck."

Fearghus took a shaky step back. Seadna had just told him more than he dared to know. He did not know his troubles would begin so soon. He had been living entirely in the hope that he would not have to engage in such risky activities. He had been ignoring the future, but now destiny was knocking on his door. He knew he would have to be strong now, even stronger than ever he had been in the past. Anyone of his caliber could stand up to Rome, but who could laugh in the face of this kind of magic and evil?

That night the stars were as bright as they likely would ever become, and the mood of the camp was dauntless and vengeful. Everything seemed on edge, in fact, it occurred to Fearghus as he lay there, they all were on the edge, and a great journey lie just beyond the nearest slope. Finally, all of his anticipation would come to an end, and the real Quest for Osgar would come to be.

Fearghus, unusually, was the first person to wake the morning next. He had not slept well the previous night, and anticipation plagued him most of all the company gathered in the valley. When the sun shed its first light on the dark furrow in the land, he gathered his sword and belt to his waist and smoothed out his rumpled cape. Before long the whole of the party had also waken, and Seadna was pacing about the camp snapping at his men. Occasionally, he would glance up and see Fearghus, tired and haggard, standing there perplexed by the whole scene.

The camp came alive. What was once dark was a burning orange hue, and what once was dormant now was alive. "Let's go!" Seadna was shouting, Irial close behind. "Prepare the chariots!"

Like a hive of busy bees, the warriors were quickly assembling the wagons and harnessing the horses. Each man, Fearghus soon noticed, had a shimmering sword tied at his hip, terrible but pure in the light of dawn. It was Seadna, he soon discovered, that had the greatest hand in this. He was trying fervently to tell each of his men to keep well armed, for great fighting would soon commence.

"Assume attack formation!" Irial suddenly shouted from the other side of the camp. Quickly and noisily, the men around Fearghus began pushing their chariots back and forth, putting the craft into an effective crescent formation. The world about them was filled with the sounds of creaking chariot wheels, the clank of idle swords, and the smell of perspiring horses against that of the cool forest. There was no dust here, but instead the soft, gentle earth below them was filled with moist ruts and furrows created by the chariots.

Before long, Irial's attack force was fully assembled. He had engineered a crescent that dipped to the inside, showing two powerful cavalry wings and a stout infantry in the center. They were to rush whatever enemy attacked and catch them from all sides. It was a truly ingenious plan, now that Fearghus thought of it. He wondered who had told Irial about it. It certainly did not seem Roman, but rather barbaric and tribal in fashion.

It was in the tough knot of foot soldiers that the leaders would make their stand. Fearghus still did not know who or what Seadna was preparing them for, but he expected the worst to ensue. Not even the wildest of minds gathered there that day could fathom what Seadna knew would come, and apparently he had taken great confidence in his vast fighting force, far more than ever he had had before, Fearghus reasoned.

Before he knew it, it was time. Fearghus tucked Agnos away in the bed of a wagon close by, under heavy swords and shields. He knew that an attack was sure to come on them right away. Everyone could feel it in the air.

Irial now guided his horse to the center of the crescent, in everyone's view, and shouted with all his might, "To Osgar and beyond!" with the drop of his sword, the whole group plunged after him. Even the foot soldiers in the back were running as fast as they dared. Fearghus, atop his own horse, led them right up to the steep edge of the valley, and began with his men the tough climb up. It was not as rough as he had judged it to be, but nonetheless his steed had a good bit of trouble churning up the slope.

Finally, though, he was there, last of all the host of Irial, and they were all on a flat plain, impressed by the sight ahead. There was a great and terrible mountain looming far away in the distance, and the sun broke off of it in a grand way such that no one in the group could speak.

"That is where resides the greatest power in the mortal world, the instrument of gods and demons!" Seadna shouted over the heads of his men. "But only one of godly stature shall deliver it to us: Fearghus, the King of Eire!"

Fearghus tried to retain his humility as the men cheered his praises as loud as they could. Each man in his immediate vicinity was grinning from ear to ear, his eyes lighting up with renewed confidence. Each trusted Fearghus far more than even himself, and their swords were raised above their heads to his glory.

Now it was his turn to speak. All eyes were on him. "Let us now march with dignity and confidence, and with the divine intervention of Sucellos and his court, let us take Osgar in his honor and name!" he shouted, and the attention of his comrades was once again directed away from him and toward the orange land ahead. With a cheer that no praise had matched yet, the group started forward at a steady and productive clip.

Not did any danger the army see yet, but Fearghus's eyes were divinely strong and wise. He could see further than ever anyone could in the whole world, like a hawk. What he saw though, displeased him very much. He could faintly make out the shapes of strange and hideous bodies wriggling against the rising sun, and they were hunched and terrible. Not could he tell if his sword could cleave their skin or drive them away, or how powerful their wrath could be. Now only he could tell his men to be prepared and calm his nervous breathing. "Hold your ground and positions!" he called to the warriors. "We shall be tested before midday, I fear!"

With that, every man had his sword out and shield raised. They were preparing themselves to intercept any wave of resistance that spilled into their ranks, and slash any creature that pounced from above or below. No one knew what he could expect, save maybe Seadna. It was impossible to know just how bad it would be, but with the sword of Fearghus they dared not despair yet. Seadna himself had once survived this initial foray, had he not? It was not until the Cliffs of Doom that his knowledge would run out.

Knowing this, morale remained high for a great while. The sun was nearing ever closer to the point of midday, and a few soldiers dared to sheath their weapon and slow their pace. Unfortunately, their actions were premature and what everyone had been fearing came true. Just as Fearghus himself was considering resting his heavy shield, a great rumbling shook the earth and his and many other horses reared violently. Luckily, most men managed to steady their beasts, but great horror set upon them as they did. A great cloud of dust was sweeping across the land ahead like an approaching storm, a storm of violence and death. A great army of the earth, Fearghus now saw, was racing towards them, tearing up the ground in their wake.

There were men of earth, horses of water, shields of stone and lances of fire. These creatures first appeared humanoid, but the warriors soon saw that they were assuming many shapes. Before the enemy hit them, Irial reared his horse and raised his blade into the air, shouting his command. As every man drew his own weapon up, Fearghus, alone of all his people, kicked his horse into an all out gallop towards the oncoming enemies. He burst into open ground and swung his sword singing through the air. Just ahead, he could see all the sickly details of the opposing army. Their figures were crude and gnarled, and they did not seem to even have eyes or mouths, just wriggling masses of earthly elements formed heads and limbs. Fearghus hoped his own army could handle them, but for now abandoned them, throwing himself into the very heart of danger.

Somehow, Fearghus knew that the creatures would shy from his sword. As he plunged into their ranks, they scattered fearfully. He had lopped off countless arms and legs and parried even more futile thrusts before he absorbed any damage. Finally, though, his mortal steed was cut from under him, and he was staggering on the ground, not knowing which way the battle was going, but accumulating an enormous stack of enemy casualties around him. Swords zipped by his ear, slicing the air, and lances narrowly missed his abdomen. But the enemies did not seem able to hurt him in the least, for strange magic bound their weapons from his person. It was the magic of his armor, strongest here in the realm of Osgar, that spared him.

He hacked down the masses of earth and water until even his strong limbs were weakened. His face was covered with dust and sweat, and his hands could hardly still grasp the hilt of his sword without aching painfully. Fortunately, though, the battle around him was quickly coming to the end. Irial had commanded his men skillfully, and the Celts held the upper hand.

What had happened as Fearghus slaved away in the center of the battle was that his own cavalry had made a bold rush to the flanks of the creatures' forces. They had not been met well, at first, but eventually the high number of riders proved useful and overran the enemy with javelin thrusts. After that they had been slowly squeezing the life out of the defenders of Osgar while Fearghus continued to eat at them from within. Now only remained intense the fighting within the Celtic infantry. Swords clanked against stone and fire axes, and casualties became high on both sides of this skirmish. The Celts, under Irial's direction, were now making a bold counterstrike, and the vast cavalry now under Fearghus's hand hurtled into the rear ranks of the creatures, trampling over their muddy corpses. When a fair Celtic lance sailed over Fearghus's head, he knew that the battle was coming to an end. Before anymore lance casting commenced, he addressed his followers: "Cease your effort, for the enemy has been too weak to withstand us! We are victorious!"

With that, the last thrusts of sword and shield came to a close, and a great shout rose up among the men. The opposing creatures lay now in rough piles of dirt, charred and soaked both with their weapons. They had come from the ground, and now, under the foot of Fearghus's army, they returned. Even so, a number of Celtic warriors lay dying as well in the heaps of earth. Their blood flowed into the accursed ground of Osgar and their fate was sealed. Seadna was quick to have them all buried there on that bloody field, and to honor their freedom. Osgar had claimed their bodies, but their valiant souls would live forever in the court of the gods. This loss was light, but still a reminder to everyone there of the death and destruction reaped by the Snake and his minions.

The cleansing of the battlefield was brief but meaningful, and soon the company was again on the move, the chariots once more rolling over the magical land. Fearghus, as this commenced, jogged his horse over aside Agnos's, and smiled to see her in good health. "Now you stay there from now on," he told her. "I shouldn't want you to be ambushed and seriously injured."

"I will be fine," she retorted, sitting up in her makeshift bed of cloth and metal. "I've come this far without a scratch, haven't I?"

"Yes," Fearghus admitted, "but you just keep a lookout for danger."

To Fearghus's surprise, Agnos reached into her bosom and produced a leather sheath. In it was a shiny black dagger. "I will," she answered. It was then that Fearghus recognized one of Conn's swords, and just the one that he had handed to Agnos as they approached the monastery many days ago. She had, as he remembered, killed an attacking Roman soldier with it.

"Use that thing only when you have to," Fearghus snapped and turned to leave. Agnos hung the sheath back around her neck, hid it in her tunic, and resumed a position back underneath her blanket. Fearghus chuckled to himself as he rode back to the middle of the group, but there still lurked a fear in his heart, a deep intense fear that he would lose what he most dearly loved, a small spark burning through his breast. He could not bear to lose Agnos, but yet also couldn't bear to be without her.

The position of the sun suggested that it was far past midday, and the edge of night was beginning to set on the accursed land. Camp would soon be set, and some of their rations be consumed. A lively Celtic campfire would put its flames to war with the darkness of the sky, and a multitude of merry drinkers would dare to raise their cups to the great mountain in the distance, taunting it with Fearghus's name and new-found title. Swords would be sheathed and horses be fed, and the company of Fearghus would live to fight another day.

As the first streaks of red stained the setting sun, Fearghus galloped ahead to find Seadna, speaking vaguely with Irial over the use of military formations and types of weaponry. "What's on your mind?" the grizzled veteran asked kindly as he approached.

"I was meaning to ask you about well…the rest of our journey. What lies ahead?" Fearghus asked shakily.

"We have done very well, so far," Seadna said, stroking a small, coarse beard. "I can't see as that we are in any immediate danger. Why do you care?"

"Well, I've been a bit concerned of…" Fearghus began, looking down at the ground.

"Your woman?" Seadna broke in spontaneously. "Well, I see why you're scared, but there's no further need to panic until we reach the mountain. I still think it was a mistake to bring her," he continued feverishly, his tongue moving faster than his mind.

"But I could not stand to leave her in harm's way back in Eire," Fearghus protested.

"Just stay loose and take every day like your sword does," Seadna said.

"What do you mean?" Fearghus asked, completely confused.

"Don't worry about fighting and death until you are drawn out of the scabbard," Seadna replied, and broke off from the conversation. They had just reached a favorable little hollow for their camp. "Break for camp!" the former pirate shouted, and the two friends parted for the night.

Right away, Fearghus found his way to Agnos's wagon. She was asleep underneath a loose cover of coarse cloth and was resting her head against the side of the wagon bed. As Fearghus approached, he noticed a thin smile creeping across her face. Pushing the hair away from her eyes, he picked her up in his scarred burly arms and deposited her on a bed of straw and cloth near to his personal bodyguards. She did not wake as he did this, though, and Fearghus took the liberty to kiss her on the cheek and pull a warm blanket up and over her chest, protecting her whole body from the cold night.

But the night, in fact, had not yet begun. A bonfire was being lit and Aodh pulled out his lyre. A keg of ale was rolled out to the warriors, and a lively tune was struck. "I love you," Fearghus whispered, and bounded off to entertain his men at the fire. They were singing his praises once more, and were becoming rowdy and spirited. Fearghus took a biscuit and a mouthful of ale and sat down near to Irial and the other leaders. Nearly a quarter of the camp, he suddenly realized, had been put out on the edges of camp as guards. Nevertheless, though, the company sang drunkenly into the night the verses of *Fearghus the King*, a tune now far more popular than any to be heard, and far more easy to drink by as the wrath of Osgar closed in around them.

Chapter 10

Assault on the Mountain

The next morning, Fearghus's mood was hardened. He was not so afraid as he was the day before, and accordingly, he was slow to wake up, his mind still lingering in the warm dark realm of sleep. He was far more relaxed today, but he appeared even more haggard. Today he would not sharpen his mighty sword or tighten the straps of his sandals. He was tired, and instead would take Seadna's advice; he wouldn't worry until faced with real danger.

Today the clouds were thick and sad. When the sun rose, it was choked by the fog and only but a dull red glow pierced the terrible grayness. But nonetheless, the company trudged on through the darkness. Seadna planned to get as close as he could to the mountain before the dusk, as the lone peak was a great length away, beyond haunted swamps and forests galore. They were still on the battle plain of before, it seemed, a gentle and smooth incline to the rugged land below.

Now Fearghus thought aloud as they moved along. "The first test, I see, was a trial of military prowess and discretion," he said.

"All the qualities of a good king," Seadna commented, "Will be exercised. The first, put more blatantly, was the display of *military leadership*."

"Yes, and you passed this trial with the utmost ease," Irial cut in. "Nevertheless, it took quite a bit of courage to run out there like that, my friend."

"Osgar wouldn't yet defy its captor. Its magic is a double-edged sword," Fearghus said meekly.

"You fool!" Seadna cried out. "Would not it have a go at you if it had the chance? No, much greater powers than that are present here."

"What do you mean?" Fearghus asked, drawing back.

"Do not underestimate your own power, my friend," the former pirate responded calmly. "You can do anything if you believe you can."

Fearghus immediately felt more comfortable, but confused. He knew very well what Seadna meant, but didn't want to think about it. His armor was no magic at all, without Osgar. He had previously thought this to be true, and it had taken only that to pull him through the toughest of situations. He was somewhat disappointed at this new discovery, but suddenly his breast swelled with pride such as he had never felt in the past. He was a Celtic Warrior.

"What other qualities might a king have to demonstrate?" he asked at length.

"That is up to you," Seadna replied. "No other man can make a king, he must create himself."

"You are right..." Fearghus muttered.

"I do have something for you, though," Seadna said unexpectedly as his friend's head sank.

Fearghus did not respond. He only looked up to see what Seadna was doing. His friend drew close to a wagon behind them, picked up something, and trotted back to them. "What is it?" he gasped tentatively.

Seadna drew a tattered length of cloth from the object he held in his hand. When the sun came upon his treasure, it shone with beauty such that even Osgar in its glory couldn't match. "It is the Crown of the Deep, a great treasure of my people," Seadna mumbled.

Fearghus nearly fell off of his horse in sheer awe. "Where did you get it?" he choked through sobs of joy.

If Fearghus nearly fainted, then Irial nearly jumped off of his horse. "How in the name of Sucellos have you attained such shimmering glory?" he asked slowly, slurring together his words.

"It is the greatest hoard of pirates, worth more than ten *Silverbeams*," Seadna told him proudly. "I will be the last to wear it as the Lord of Pirates, and now I bequeath it to you, Fearghus."

"From the throne of the Sea, to the throne of Eire," Irial remarked behind them, grinning to himself at such use of words.

"Colla's legacy endures now on the brow of Fearghus the King," Seadna added, glancing back at the general.

Fearghus was without words as he held it in his hands. It was not entirely too large a treasure, but it was endowed with glorious splendor. The jewel encrusted helm was fortified with a steel frame and plated with pure gold. Gems without name were set into its front, and reflected the sun's beams in many directions. One in particular seemed to catch Fearghus's eye, and this was the largest one in the center. Its white edges seemed to glow with moonlight, the magic of pirates.

"Go ahead, put it on already!" Irial snapped, interrupting his thoughts. Fearghus looked up and fit the brim neatly about his head, straightening it to be symmetrical with his figure. When his eyes looked up once again, he felt proud, and kingly. It did not weigh much at all.

"Where was it to be found?" he asked Seadna.

"Colla told me about it, a long time ago when we were pirates," his friend answered. "I picked it up on the *Silverbeam* before we landed. I thought I would find it there."

Fearghus pulled the crown to a tighter fit and nodded his head to Seadna. "I thank you graciously," he said.

Suddenly one of the scouts galloped up to their party. "We have reached the forest, sir," he said in a deep voice, then disappeared. Just over the next hill, Fearghus then realized, the dark forest loomed.

"Let us make camp here, for the night," he said. "I think it wise now to wait here before entering."

Within minutes the marching had stopped altogether and the wagons were unloaded. A melancholy supper was attempted by the men, and the afternoon passed rapidly to evening. Fearghus had no further trouble to himself about anything around them, and passed into deep sleep.

They did not rush into the forest the next day. Fearghus was up early with the leaders of the group contemplating the best way to infiltrate it. Irial had the idea of cutting a path through the brush, but the crafty Seadna had other plans to stealthily creep through the area unseen.

"Of course you had no trouble the last time you did this," Irial complained.

"It is too dangerous to just walk in there like it was a forest from back in Eire!" Seadna burst. "The sun never shines and the only creatures that do remain living don't intend to increase their number!"

"Don't worry, Irial," Fearghus said. "We shall *all* make it through alive, or *all* die trying."

"Then it is settled," Seadna said. "We shall go assemble the men to start the journey."

They were upon the outskirts of the trees in no time. "Before we go in, I'd like to give a bit of advice to you," Seadna said sinisterly as they stopped. "When we go in here, I want everyone on their closest guard. There is no light so don't bother keeping your appearance or the time. Have your sword out always, and don't stray from my lead. There will be no lights ablaze but three torches at any time as we travel, so I recommend you hold onto the cloak of the man in front of you, and keep your senses alert for sounds and feelings."

And so the ragged party pulled out their blades and formed tight ranks behind the mounted leaders. Agnos resumed her place in the bed of a wagon, hidden under a pile of metal supplies and weapons. Fearghus kept close to her as they moved forward, and every moment before the darkness hit them he had an eye on her. He had stationed his greatest guards about her position, but still felt sickeningly insecure of her continued safety.

They sifted through the bare tree trunks in triple file, and soon the light of day was waning to nothing and the forest ahead could not be fathomed. "Here we go again!" one of the warriors said, and suddenly nothing was to be seen but the silhouette of Seadna's head and those of two other warriors as they held their torches aloft.

It took a great deal of time for the party to adjust to the darkness, but it quickly became routine to trudge along in the blackness with another man's cloak clenched in your sweaty fist. Of course Fearghus and the other leaders were at a great advantage to this lifestyle, as they were upon horses and nearest to Seadna's light. Fearghus could see with a twinge of fear the dead trees surrounding them, and once or twice glimpsed mysterious shadows in the brambles. There was no hope, though, of seeing a faint bit of sun. The trees formed a narrow corridor with a thick roof of darkness.

The party traveled safely for many hours, and not a word did any man say. Seadna finally chose a time to stop and make camp, and wood was unloaded from the wagons to burn for campfires. The most skilled warriors were placed in a ring about the camp, and supplies were distributed amongst the host of men.

"How large is this place, anyways?" Fearghus asked Seadna as they huddled near a meager blaze.

"Oh, another day's journey, at least." Seadna replied through mouthfuls of bread.

"And what lies in waiting this time?" Fearghus inquired.

"Seadna gulped down a sip of ale and wiped off his hands. "You don't expect to get through without another trial, do you?" he asked sinisterly, as now usually was his tone of voice. "We'll have to see what befalls you tomorrow, and I mean *you*."

Fearghus was taken aback by this statement, but decided not to let it affect him, and went on with his meal silently. His mind was straining tonight to think of what other qualities a good king should have that he might be tested on. Tomorrow the next trial would appear to him.

Fearghus was shivering with the cold the next morning. He had not slept well, and fearful dreams plagued his rest. In the forest as he woke, he certainly was not comforted. A roaring fire was already burning in their midst, and the sentries of last night were gathered about it. One could hardly tell whether it was night or day outside of the forest, really. Even so, Seadna chose now to move once more.

"We must be close to the edge of this blasted forest!" Irial finally said after what seemed like a full day had passed.

"You'd be surprised at the vastness of this wilderness." Seadna remarked. "A man can get lost and go crazy without the proper guidance."

"What do you mean by that?" Fearghus asked quickly.

"Have you ever been lost?" Seadna's sinister voice responded.

Fearghus's heart sank. "Not entirely..." he muttered.

"What are you trying to do, get us all killed?" Irial shouted, his horse rearing. He knew exactly what was going on.

Seadna's eyes, glowing in the weak firelight, turned to the general. "There is no other way," he said calmly.

"Except mine!" Irial snapped, and clenched his fists.

"We must keep moving ahead," Seadna mumbled, turning away.

Irial drew his sword. The smooth blade flashed in the soft torchlight. "You've led us into a trap!" he snarled.

At that very moment, as the operation seemed on the brink of ruin, something occurred to Fearghus. This was no coincidence. This was a test. He had to do something about it quickly, and without hesitation.

Seadna's own sword hissed as it slid out of its scabbard. "I'm the only one who can get you out of here!" he retorted, leaning forward on his horse. The animal whinnied and pawed at the blackness below them.

"Enough of this!" Fearghus began to say, but he was too late. Seadna's blade was notched as it parried a tremendous blow from Irial. Within seconds Fearghus was enveloped in sheer chaos. Decisively, he drew his own sword and opened his mouth. "Stop this madness!" he yelled hoarsely, staying back from the ferocious slashing and thrusts. He could not find a place to enter the foolish skirmish, and only could raise his voice. "In the name of the gods, stop!" he suddenly heard himself scream, and his horse reared.

Miraculously, the two ceased their duel, and faced him, snarling. "Who are you to stop us?" Irial asked curtly.

"I will not have such evil between the two of you. I assume control of this expedition as of now," Fearghus said, his breathing heavier with each word.

But Irial was obstinate, and his eyes flashed madness. "I do not wish to die," he explained. "And I will not have this *thief* make the decisions around here."

Once again, Fearghus opened his mouth and suddenly was halted, for Seadna's sword was up, and Irial was caught off guard. Making a split-second decision, Fearghus thrust his own blade between them, and parried the blow. But the point of his sword was jammed into the face of the general's horse, and before any of the three of them could react, the animal reared and bolted into the trees.

"See what you've done?" Fearghus choked as he watched the crazed animal disappear into the abyss. Irial seemed to be going in slow motion. Fearghus's own sword had not yet even retreated from that point in the air where it had stopped Seadna's killing blow.

Suddenly, everything was stopped. The galloping of the horse became less and less until it was nothing. Now Fearghus's blade went to the throat of Seadna. As blood trickled down the man's neck, Fearghus gritted his teeth. "Now who is the fool?" he asked, jabbing the point shallowly into Seadna's skin. "I can't believe it could have fallen to this!" he continued. "Now I'm going after him, and I expect you to stay right here and wait for me!"

With that, he withdrew his weapon and snatched the torch from Seadna's grasp. Just as Seadna, it seemed, started to weep, Fearghus jumped his horse over a dead bush and was off, his sword severing whatever branch dared to impede him. From this moment, his scope of vision became vastly smaller, and as he rushed through the trees, he could only see a few feet to either side. Even so, he was determined beyond all doubt to find his old friend Irial once more, and did not fear what could come.

When all the sounds and hints of light from the party behind him vanished, Fearghus decided to stop and dismount from his horse. He could only make as little sound as possible, or face the wrath of the forest. But one sound now he did make: "Irial!" he bellowed.

No one responded. The area seemed just as dead as before, and nothing could be seen or heard but the howl of a lonely wind. "Irial!" he shouted once more. This time, something stirred behind him. "It is only I, Fearghus," he told the ominous sound.

When no one answered, Fearghus raised his sword in a defensive position and inched forward with his torch. The sound ceased momentarily, but Fearghus wouldn't let up. Without making another sound, his sword hissed through the air and ripped through the dry brambles, cutting cleanly through flesh. Immediately, he lit up the bush with his torch and strained his eyes to see what creature was burning in the small blaze.

Before it was consumed by the flames, Fearghus noticed what he took to be a wolf. Its face was cleanly cut by his sword, but its awesome teeth were still visible in the now aggressive fire. With this one sight, Fearghus suddenly realized something: wolves hunt in packs.

As if on cue, Fearghus heard something leap out of the darkness behind him. He swiveled around, and caught yet another wolf through the head. They were closing in on his small clearing quickly and in great number.

Yet another wolf lost its life to his singing blade. Then another. He would be overrun soon. In another breath, his horse whinnied and reared. The wolves had taken it. As they momentarily were drawn to the carcass, a great idea appeared in Fearghus's mind. Without thinking much more, he leapt aside and thrust the torch into the trunk of a dead tree. In seconds, the whole clearing was a towering inferno.

"I'm sorry, but I really can't stay!" Fearghus joked, jumping into the dark choked trees behind him. Countless wolves howled in agony as they shied away from the glorious blaze. Fearghus, during all this, found a swampy hollow a safe distance away and hunkered down in hiding. He would have to stay here for a while to rest and find his bearings.

He waited for a long, long while as the blaze destroyed the dead forest. The whole forest was illuminated with ruddy light and the air was riddled with the crack of burning wood and tumbling limbs. Even so, it was not long before the fire began to quiet down. Sheathing his sword, Fearghus finally found it in good interest to explore the deserted clearing.

Fearghus nearly collapsed when he stepped out into the smoldering patch of earth. He could see the sun! His fire had burned a vast hole in the middle of the canopy, and kind, warm rays were streaming down to the scorched ground. The sky above was vast and blue, unhindered by any clouds or foul winds. The stenches of death and smoke were washed away by a cool breeze.

He took this opportunity to have a good look at the wolves. Their coats were messy and matted, and their hair was long. These were not just any wolves, either. Their teeth were razor sharp and quite long, and their eyes were yellow like those of owls. The blood of the wolves he had killed was spilled generously on the ashes. If they attacked the warriors, he wasn't sure if they would have so much luck as himself.

Suddenly Fearghus remembered why he was here, and looked down at his sword in wonder. Where could Irial be? It would be near impossible to find him now. He could be miles away, or even dead! Fearghus had to do something, though. As he pondered what action to take, he only wasted more time. "Irial!" he cried out in vain.

The sun was nearing the edge of the gap above him. He dared not leave it just yet, and despair and hopelessness could solely be countered by the presence of light. There would have to be some way to solve this dilemma, but how? What one thing could be done to complete this test from Osgar?

Soon the sunlight was gone. Fearghus did not any longer possess a light but for the stars, and not a blanket but for his cloak. The temperature dropped greatly, and all he could do was curl up as tightly as possible, waiting for dawn and a solution to this trial.

Miraculously, when Fearghus awoke, a familiar voice found its way to his ears. "Fearghus!" it cried, and its matching running sounds grew close to him. He was in a daze, and the sun above was harsh on his sensitive eyes. For the moment, his body was idle and only his ears strained to hear what was coming.

"Fearghus!" it cried again, and suddenly he identified its owner. It was Irial!

"What are you doing here?" Fearghus gasped, rubbing his eyes with numb fingers.

Irial embraced his friend warmly and sat down next to him on the ground. His sword clanked as he threw it to the forest floor. "I come from the other side of this forest!" he said ecstatically.

"You've reached the other side?" Fearghus asked, staring at his friend as if he wasn't real. "But how?"

Irial's expression fell a bit, and he looked at the ashes under them. "My horse carried me straight out of the trees, without any trouble," he remarked. "It was as if something was guiding it in the right direction. It was certainly a miracle."

"Yes, and something more than that," Fearghus responded, "You were meant to come back to me."

"I just held on and many hours later I found myself on the other side of the trees. On the open plain, I was forced to put my exhausted horse out. Then I saw a great plume of smoke coming from the tops of the trees, just north of me. I knew someone needed my help getting out," Irial explained.

"This is just another test, my friend," Fearghus explained. "I knew there would be some way to get out of it."

Irial snatched up his sword and led Fearghus into the dark trees. "We're close to safety," he explained. They traveled for hours on end without a torch, but made the precaution never to turn or adjust their straight course, and without further struggle, sunlight from the furthest extreme of trees flooded the path.

"We've done it!" Fearghus shouted as they strode into the broad light. A vast plain stretched out before them, and the Mountain loomed in the distance.

"Do you really think that you've completed the second test yet?" Irial asked as they climbed to the top of a great hill.

"Not entirely," Fearghus muttered, "Not until you can be reconciled with Seadna."

"Where do we start in the process of finding them?" Irial asked, disregarding his friend's statement. He was willing but not happy to join the old pirate's ranks once more.

Fearghus thought for a moment, then settled on a quick plan. "The same way you found me," was all he had to say.

"Then we'll just have to hope that they start burning their campfires before dark," Irial said.

And so the two men sprawled out on the comfortable grass and watched the canopy of the vast forest until dark. To their dismay, nothing happened. There were no white plumes of smoke or trembling trees, no shouts or sounds of Seadna's party. "I told them to hold their position," Fearghus mumbled as the sun sank behind the horizon.

"I hope they're not in trouble…" was all Irial said. He was already half asleep, turned away from the forest below. The stars were rising now and nothing it seemed could further be done to help the company behind. Knowing this, Fearghus took a final look across the trees and laid down on the reeds. Now, for the first time in days, he thoroughly examined his life and situation. He considered all that had happened and tried to think of what was to come. As he thought these things over, though, only one thing came back to his thought: he had to get back to the rest of his camp. Without them, his magic would be useless to guide and protect them from hopeless disasters and attacks.

As he lay on his back, thinking, suddenly a familiar sound rang through the air. It was the sad, lonesome howl of a wolf. But to Fearghus, it was chilling. It symbolized everything evil in the forest, and everything that wanted a shot at Seadna and his men. It was a herald of death, the voice of darkness.

Then something extraordinary happened that sent an even greater sense of fear through his tense body. The wolf call, enduring steadily, was suddenly cut short and replaced by a brief yelp of pain. What could this mean? Was it the work of a Celtic blade? If he was right, the wolves had found Seadna's group and the men's lives were in danger.

Or was it another creature? Maybe a boar, or a wild cat? Fearghus could not make up his mind whether to chase after these sounds. If they were the calls of attacking wolves, they could very possibly lead him right to Seadna's camp. He didn't know if he could take the risk though.

"Irial, get up!" he pried, pushing the limp body of his partner. Now more howls were heard. The wolves were gathering somewhere, and he knew it.

Irial was already awake, silently listening to the same howls. When Fearghus touched him, he stood up and smoothed his garments. "Let's go find them," he said, and the two men bounded down the hill, their ears straining for more signals.

When they reached the edge of the forest, Fearghus turned to his friend. "I'll send up some smoke if I need to," was all he had to say, and with his sword gleaming, he left Irial there waiting in the shadow of the trees. He knew very well that for the sake of the expedition, Irial would have to stay behind on the other side of the forest.

He did not have a torch, but his ears, strengthened by the power of the gods, were very useful in picking up a deluge of howls ringing through the night. If he was right about their source, he would be reunited with Seadna, but if he was wrong, he would be paying a visit to a nasty pack of wolves all by himself, and without fire, they would likely tear him apart.

The forest was completely black again, but at least Fearghus knew what time it was outside. He could possibly guess when it would be light enough to put up smoke, and when it would be too dark to communicate. For now, though, all he could do was pick his way in between the trees, keeping his senses keen for sounds and smells.

He ambled on for hours while the sounds grew slightly louder. His limbs were tiring and mood slipping. If the wolves stopped their frenzy, he realized, he would be left to the mercy of the forest all by himself. After this, likely, he would be utterly lost and go mad.

Several hours more passed and Fearghus knew that the dawn would be nigh outside. And now, to his relief, the howling wolves seemed just a short walk away. He began to hear the sounds of their panting and whimpering. He could sense their strong muscles rippling and sharp teeth gnashing. Now was time to act!

"Seadna!" Fearghus shouted, his blade singing. Suddenly, he was dancing his way through a small clearing, and the warm bodies of wolves were everywhere. Their eyes glowed sinisterly like fireflies, and their breathing was heavy.

"It is I, Fearghus!" he cried in vain, and his sword came around his shoulders, ripping into flesh. Now he was one with the violence, one step ahead of every ferocious lunge. His blade was there, but he couldn't see it. It was as if he was telling it to go somewhere, and it was getting there on its own.

Suddenly they were everywhere. And before Fearghus could react, his sword was short and the massive body of a wolf smashed into his side, clawing and biting furiously. His weapon was jolted from his grasp, and his own hands were all that remained to his defense.

It was now that he suddenly realized that he had become a wolf. His hands he unconsciously thrust forward, and in seconds they had found the throat of the animal. "Seadna!" he screamed, and throttled the neck of the wolf. His hands were bloody and body battered, but somehow he won the battle with the beast, and looked up to see who was coming next.

His bloody fingers dug into the earth as he reached for the sword that wasn't there. Yet another wolf was bounding towards him with increasing speed, and its glowing eyes were bobbing up and down vigorously. All Fearghus would do was make his hands into fists and plant his feet in the earth.

Suddenly, another orb of light, this one alone, zipped through the cold darkness. It was almost as if a dream, but Fearghus suddenly recognized the shaft of an arrow. In seconds the shaggy coat of the wolf was aflame, and the bare tree trunks were illuminated with orange light. It was just like that scene he had witnessed with Colla so long ago when they had hijacked the *Silverbeam*.

His sword was right in front of him. Snatching it up, he stepped back into the fight and tried to find the source of the arrow. "Fearghus!" a familiar voice shouted from the trees.

Fearghus had barely any time to look up when a second arrow hurtled into the wolf next to him. "Seadna!" he responded with complete joy. And indeed it was his good friend.

"I've brought help!" the former pirate called, and before Fearghus had ducked completely, several arrows and lances flew through the air, and the clearing was flooded with torches and gleaming helmets. As Fearghus stood up, the battle was abruptly ended.

"What's happened since I left?" Fearghus asked.

"I'm just glad you've gotten back to us," Seadna said. "But sorry that your mission is failed."

Fearghus sheathed his glorious blade. "It has not failed," he said sternly. "I have been to the other side. I was rescued by none other than Irial himself!"

Seadna handed his friend a torch. "I am sorry about our argument," he said.

"Don't worry," Fearghus replied. "It was divinely meant to be."

Fearghus was quick to order a fire started, and was not satisfied until a vast blaze was consuming the trees. He was very confident that the light of day would greet them as soon as the canopy was cleared. From here they would be able to wait and wonder in the broad daylight about what to do next. Now Fearghus could only hope that Irial would make it to them safely and with his bearings.

Quickly now, Fearghus's thoughts, as always, turned to Agnos. With luck, she was perfectly safe and sound in the care of his own bodyguards. It would be a while before the men had rounded up all of the party, but the light of the fire was extremely helpful.

"Are there any casualties?" Fearghus asked, passing one of the warriors.

"Just three men," the gruff fighter responded. "The woman's over there," he continued, pointing to the far edge of the clearing. And indeed she was there, her eyes nervously darting back and forth in search of him.

"Why did you disappear like that?" Agnos asked as he strode towards her.

Fearghus helped her down off of her wagon. "I had to do something," he replied. "We'll be out of here soon," he added.

"That sounds nice," she responded, and embraced him.

They waited for hours, and when the fire had subsided, bright sunlight streamed in, the black dust sparkling in its glory. And in the midst of all this, his sword used not at all, Irial appeared in the clearing, guided by the intense light from afar.

And finally, in all the glory of this his second victory, Fearghus was serenaded with praise and music. And it was then that Aodh with his lyre found a new song:

> *O men of Fearghus, the strong and the brave,*
> *We've fought so far, with Eire to save.*
>
> *Take up your sword and sharpen your lance,*
> *Lest Osgar, our foe, should soon advance.*
>
> *To the mountain we ride, with glorious hearts,*
> *The end of a journey, bitter and far.*

The Serpent we trod, the Romans we crush!
Under the gods we make, the Eire that was!

Now Osgar we take, and make our own,
To the powerful Fearghus, Eire his throne!

Ride now in splendor as fate draws near,
For a king, among us, is soon to appear!

He will forge a palace of riches and might,
A haven of warrior and scholar alike!

It is Eire the kingdom, the empire of old!
The pride of the Celts, the mountain of gold!

And with this song ringing in their ears they burst out into the sun on the other side of the forest. It did not seem so bright as it had in the forest, but nonetheless it was wonderful and seemed to tell in itself of great things to come.

They camped there on the rolling soft hills and another day passed after Fearghus's second task. When next the sun rose, they would be off to the Mountain. But even as they traveled, the looming precipice was more than a few days' ride off. "The legend," Seadna said as they prepared for sleep, "is that the mountain will spew forth fire when Osgar is taken from it. I have, in my travels, heard of other such incidents in the mysterious South, but no such tales as those of the Mountain we see here."

"Not fire or men can stop Fearghus!" Irial laughed, and the three men split up for the night's rest.

The next day, everyone's mood was back to normal and the horses were ready to move again. They started off bright and early, the sun's rays becoming evident in the glorious orange clouds and red cliffs. The wagons were slow in the thick grass, but also there were rocky clearing and steep climbs. To the men now, it did not seem that they were in the magical land of Osgar, but rather their own home, Eire. It was an uplifting experience, toiling through the gentle wilderness of Man.

When they had traveled for two days, Seadna stopped the party. "We have reached the final frontier," he said. "The mountain is for our taking. All that is left is to ascend the path up to the chamber of Osgar."

"Then what of my third task?" Fearghus asked.

"My knowledge stops here," Seadna responded quietly. "My party was slaughtered over there on the south face," he continued, pointing to jagged steep side of the mountain.

"We will not suffer the same fate as your friends, and you can be sure of that," Irial added suddenly, drawing his sword.

"Of course not," Seadna replied coolly, "we will walk right up to the main gate."

"It will be guarded, will it not?" Fearghus asked tentatively.

"Once again, I do not know," Seadna responded, "And I hereby hand over all control of this expedition to you."

They decided to camp that night before the great Mountain, hidden behind a vast pile of rubble. Everyone was to stay quiet, for strange forces lived upon the Mountain, both evil and good. They were the spirits of fallen heroes and burglars, of demons and beasts. In the middle of them, coiled around the pedestal of the spear, the Snake himself guarded that which he could not possess without the help of Fearghus. His ugly head was tormented with thoughts of evil and hatred, and his wounds burned with revenge.

Fearghus was uneasy as he looked upon the precipice of the Mountain that night. He couldn't get over the sheer size and archaic wonder of the great single container of Osgar. He now couldn't be sure if his sword could handle the wrath of this magic, or if the might of the Celts could withstand such ancient and dangerous forces. His mind, for a moment, strayed back to the situation of the warriors back in the besieged monastery, and how Osgar could help free them from the Romans. If he failed here, what would become of them? What would happen to his revolt, and all the women and children it protected?

Before bed, he hastened over to Agnos as she too prepared for sleep. "I don't want you hurt," he said.

"I'll be fine," she replied warmly. "Just make sure you come back to me."

"I might not," he told her nervously.

Agnos placed her arms around his strong shoulders and leaned up close to his ear. "Trust me," she whispered, "I'll see you again after this." And with that, they parted, finding separate places to sleep for the night. Heavy thoughts coursed through both of their minds, and sleep was a welcome refuge as the stars burned brighter above the cursed land of Man.

When the warriors woke the morning next, no one, including Seadna, was in a hurry to enter the place of Osgar. Nonetheless, the task had to be completed for the good of Eire, and the lives of the men could not be thought of for the lives of their families. Now customarily, every sword was sharpened as if for battle and the armor of the leaders was polished to shine with the glory of Eire. Fearghus fixed his golden helm snugly about his ears, drew his shimmering sword of the gods, and swept his cloak over his shoulders. Seadna and Irial did as much, and with the might of all Eire, the party marched like a Roman legion to the base of the Mountain, swords drawn and ready for battle with forces they could not fathom.

The main gate of the chamber was far above them, connected with a network of jagged rocks to the ground. It would not be easy to ascend the path, but many of the warriors were shepherds or builders in their villages, and would be able easily to climb the uneven boulders. Agnos, during this, would remain safe in last night's camp with a good guard.

It was a strange experience for Fearghus, knowing that above him was the most sought-after item in possibly the world. The greatest treasure of the gods: Osgar the Sacred Lance was just out of his grasp, and with it, he would again possess the invincibility and sheer physical power of his previous adventure, and be able to save the besieged monastery in Eire with the blessing of Sucellos and the rest of the gods.

The approach to the base of the Mountain was a bit awkward for the men, being in such awe of the great rock. However, it was not long before they were hurrying up the side of the hill. "I don't expect we'll find the Snake here, will we?" Irial asked Seadna as they reached the halfway point of the journey.

"No, I don't suppose so," Seadna responded with and equal sense of defiance that Irial showed. Nether man had fully recovered from the incident in the forest.

Suddenly, Seadna drew the three of them aside, instructing the party to continue up the Mountain. "We are going to get the spear, just the three of us," he said. "We'll have to scale the south face all by ourselves, and then only can we continue where I left off."

"But where are they going?" Fearghus asked about the rest of the men.

"They're the diversion," Seadna said sinisterly. "We can't hope to pass the main hallway in the first place, since the Snake is there."

"You're leading good men into a trap!" Irial shouted, his face growing red and angry.

"To distract the Snake from us, certain sacrifices must be made," Seadna replied, restraining his comrade. "Don't worry, I've told them to keep their bows nocked."

"The fighting will be fierce in the main chamber," Fearghus added wisely, "but it is all for the better good of Eire."

Irial settled down and they continued their trip to the south side of the Mountain. Not even Seadna could tell what was behind the climb up the wall, for he and Colla had not made it so far when they first attempted to raid the chamber.

And so it was begun. Fearghus figured that the warriors wouldn't enter the main chamber for a while yet, and neither would they reach the alternative entrance to the caves on the south face for a good while, giving everyone a chance to reflect on what they were about to do. For Fearghus, he could only hope that the spear was not guarded, and for everyone else, only the wish to avoid death was present.

Finally, after a long trek, the group of three reached the foot of the south face and began to climb. Just as in the case of the path from the Isle of No Return to Eire, Seadna seemed to know where there were footholds and such, and the other two men followed him up the hallowed place.

As they moved, Fearghus suddenly realized that they were crossing the mysterious place where many pirates had before been slaughtered by the Snake. He wondered why the Snake wasn't here at the moment, but then as if on cue, Irial said, "That'll be them, I suppose." Fearghus hadn't noticed it just yet, but there was a terrible rumbling sound as if the earth was shaking. It was coming from the inside of the Mountain, and made Fearghus cringe. Inside, just as they here moved along the wall, nearly all of his men were doing horrendous battle on the Snake. He could see it now: arrows glancing off of scales, swords plunging into flesh and being torn away, and in all this, the Snake's ferocious fangs eating men up one by one. It was almost too much to bear, but necessary for the three men to cross this threshold safely.

Fearghus would exact terrible revenge on the Snake after this. If it was possible, he thought, he should like to be there right now, his sword singing through the Snake's skin like it was air, and his men rallying behind their leader with renewed hope. But alas, his men would be scattered now, few of them alive, and the main hall of this Mountain would forever be marked with their noble blood.

A great rush of excitement passed through Fearghus's body as he leapt over the edge of level stone pathway on the side of the mountain. Just ahead, there was a small door inside the caves, and Seadna had expertly lead them to it. They had now surpassed even the adventures of Colla, and Osgar was closer than ever to the hand of its rightful owner. Fearghus wouldn't let his expedition suffer the same fate as Colla's, and if he could not, he would die attempting it.

Inside the small doorway the stone was smooth and white, not at all dusty or soft. The tunnel looked as if it had been bored by the Snake itself, but in fact it had not—it was carved by an ancient Manx tribe as a path to the tombs of their kings. The tales of these people had been long lost in the annals of history, but at least this tunnel remained of their existence.

As the rumbling seemed to subside, the three leaders, swords drawn, found themselves creeping as quietly as possible down the corridor, hidden snugly and quite safely in solid stone. Not one of them knew how far away the Spear Chamber was, but they might as well be on the right path. When they reached that sacred place, likely, the Snake would find them there, and make duel with Fearghus, the last hope of Eire. If they were lucky, though, all the straining of the warriors in the main hall had at least put a few cuts and bruises in this worm's hide, or maybe at least an arrow or two.

The path wound back and forth like a wriggling worm, stretching for a great while until, at last, the men reached a small chamber. Seadna had long before lit a torch for them to see, and inside the room there were strange markings on the walls, no doubt memorials or tales of the glory of the tribal kings. Luckily, the snake had not been here, and the inscriptions endured.

The men continued on into the next room, where they found similar markings. If Osgar was here, it would not be too much further. Fearghus's nerves were mounting to the highest degree, because he knew that he would find what he had been longing for all this time within these passages.

Next, they came into a large, sunlight chamber. There was a great hole in the ceiling of this room, and the scent of the great beast that made it lingered on the walls. From here, just as Seadna planned, they had full access to all the rooms of the Mountain.

"Watch out!" Seadna suddenly shouted. Fearghus spun around, his sword gleaming in the intense sun. Behind him, what seemed as two of the soldiers they had defeated on the field before the forest had somehow risen out of the stone floor. They were hideous creatures possessed by ghosts of the Mountain, and they bore swords and shields left by the unsuccessful heroes that attempted to claim what wasn't theirs. Fearghus was quick to parry their blows and attack them, but upon their demise two more minions of the Snake rose out of the ground.

This time Seadna and Irial leapt into the fight with their own blades, Irial clubbing the ghosts with the edge of his shield. Each man, as they fell, became a pile of rubble on the stone. "My blade's been notched!" Seadna said as he dueled with a nasty scimitar, "They're made of stone!"

"Mine too!" Irial added after a bit. However, Fearghus's blade survived the repetitive blows to the rock. His blade was unearthly, and in its slashing, could not be notched, broken or stained.

Suddenly, the battle intensified. Fearghus could hear the heavy breathing of his comrades as they traded blows with the humanoid monsters. The creatures' lifeless faces were angular and smooth, and they all were of one color, a sickly gray.

As their hope dwindled, suddenly something miraculous happened. As one of the stone warriors began to club Seadna ferociously with a fist, it spontaneously fell to the floor dead. When Fearghus had a look at the pile of stones that it became, he noticed an arrow sticking up out of it.

Slaying what seemed like his tenth enemy, Fearghus spun around to find the source of the bolt. When he found it, he nearly jumped for joy. It was a member of their party, and already he had nocked another arrow. "How did you survive?" Fearghus shouted to him from across the room.

"We have driven the Snake from his post at the gate!" the man replied happily, his arrow hurtling into an unsuspecting enemy.

"Where is he now?" Fearghus yelled back, evading blows from yet another stone soldier.

"Deeper in the caves!" came the man's answer, and as he replied, five more brave men came from behind him at the door where he stood and ran headlong into the skirmish. Now the ghosts were picking up swords and axes from the piles of rubble their predecessors had left. As their supplies stretched thin, some now were simply throwing punches and kicks at the men.

The battle raged on until the rays of the sun coming from the hole in the ceiling had moved at least ten paces across the floor. When the last enemy was hewn down by the broken shards of a sword, the men were stumbling over the remains of the creatures. "Let's get out of here!" Irial commanded the remains of his army when they experienced the break in fighting.

Fearghus looked about him. Dust was beginning to rise from the mess of rubble and boulders. For the first time, he was beginning to think of his men as real, dangerous warriors and a threat to anyone or anything that attacked them. "Any casualties?" was all he said to that first warrior that had come to their chamber during the fighting.

"We've lost every man but these twelve to the Snake, and no one in this fight," the warrior assured him.

"What's your name, son?" Fearghus asked, looking about at the bright walls of the chamber.

"Oh, I'm Murchadh," the man replied, looking down.

"Did you hurt the Snake very much?" Fearghus suddenly asked as they reached the corridor leading further inside.

Murchadh's face was red and wrinkled with worry. "I got him in the eye, and that's what did it. The others got their swords in him a few times before he swept them away."

"That was a life-saving shot, my friend," Fearghus told him. "And a brave battle on the part of all *your* men."

"*My* men? Oh no, sir…I'm not the type," Murchadh stuttered, again looking away as if Fearghus was a god.

"Don't worry," Fearghus said, "I'm putting you second in command under Irial and making you the head of a new elite group of men, my Order of the Serpent." And with that, he took one of the pins from his cape, throwing the loose cloth over his shoulder, and placed it on the shoulder of Murchadh. "Now let's go find that spear!" he said, and the two were off through the next hallway, Fearghus with his sword raised, and Murchadh, his bow taut.

Chapter 11

Brimstone and Fire

They pushed further and further into the Mountain, entering yet another vast room that seemed of no particular importance. "What do you say is in here?" Irial asked the small band of fighters.

"To me this looks like a storage room of sorts," one man said.

Indeed, there were a great deal of ancient artifacts. Fearghus noted the presence of a vast number of stone weapons, containers, even artwork. And, just as he observed these things, he noticed another detail of the chamber: there were no doors or windows here.

Apparently, the others had noticed this too. "How do we continue?" Seadna asked himself futilely.

Murchadh suddenly spoke up, his voice hesitant and timid. "I...I think there's something in here that can help us," he said, looking around. "Just another obstacle, but this time of the mind."

"You know, I think you're right," said Fearghus, moving in amongst the jars. "We knew right from the start that this was the only path into the Mountain, and so we must take it to Osgar."

The men searched slowly through the containers, smashing some, gently opening others. Most of them were empty, but in some, Fearghus and his men found dust from ancient foods and liquids that had been stored inside. Suddenly, one of the warriors from where he stood jumped back in horror. When the other men reached his position, they were all taken aback in similar fear. Before them, the rotted skeleton of fallen man, possibly an ancient one, sat clutching at a decaying wooden rod.

"This is a contemporary man," Seadna said, holding up a smooth spearhead from the floor. "I think there is danger in this room just as the last."

Then Fearghus, with his keen eyes, made a momentous discovery. "What's this thing in his fist?" he asked, peeling away the dead fingers to reveal a golden pendant, shining like fire in their torchlight.

"It has to be the key!" Irial shouted ecstatically.

"The key to what?" Fearghus asked.

"Obviously the door out of here," Seadna said, picking up the object. "Now we have to locate the hole matching it."

The men immediately spread out, scanning every inch of the walls with their torches and groping fingers. With all the effort they exerted, it was not long before Fearghus himself happened upon a large group of circular indentations in the wall. "I think we're in for some trouble!" he shouted to his Order of the Serpent.

"What's the problem?" Seadna asked with all the wisdom of the veteran he was.

"It's a trap," Fearghus explained. "Only one of these keyholes opens the next passage."

Seadna gathered the men around him around Fearghus, swords raised. "I'd feel safest if you did this," he told him, and tossed the golden disc to his comrade.

"Be on your highest guard," Fearghus said, and at that moment six bows strings creaked with tension and nine swords swayed in the dank air.

Fearghus looked at the markings within each indentation. In the one on the farthest left he beheld the shape of a serpent. Next to it, to his utter surprise, there was a cross, somewhat like the Roman symbol. And finally, on the other side of this, there was a star. Taking no time to scare himself, he smacked the coin into the star circle and spun around. Nothing terrible happened at first, but nonetheless, no door was opened.

Finally Seadna spoke. "I think that this is the neutral choice," he said. "Try another."

Now Fearghus was feeling a bit better. He had only two choices: the snake or the cross. As his breathing slowed, he became more relaxed and his sword was suddenly lighter in his hand. "This will be it," he told the men happily, and shoved the pendant into the left socket, bearing the symbol of not only his greatest enemy, but of his most valiant men.

It was almost instantaneous for Fearghus to know that he was wrong. The backing up of his comrades combined with the rumbling of the ground below him meant only one thing: doom.

"Get that coin into its right place!" Seadna screamed. Even so, Fearghus realized, there were no enemies attacking them.

"What's happening?" he asked the men as he spun around. Then it hit him. The cave was filling with water! Underground springs that had been suppressed by some type of stone barricade had been mysteriously opened, and the water in the chamber was quickly making its way even to where he stood.

"Don't worry," Fearghus told his men. "I'll have this out in a second."

"If you don't have it in a second we'll all drown!" Seadna shouted. The water had now reached his knees.

Fearghus fit his fingers about the edges of the coin just as he had when he removed it from the star keyhole. This time, to his horror, he could not squeeze it out. The stone had closed the hole on its own, preventing the object from removal. "What's taking you so long?" Irial asked, struggling to turn in chest-high water.

"The key won't come out!" he shouted back. "It's as if enchanted!"

Now the party was in a state of panic. "Go back to the previous room!" someone yelled, but unfortunately, the door they had used to enter was sealed with smooth stone. There was no hope in sight if Fearghus could not coax the key to come out of its bonds. In just a few minutes he would be working under the water, and his heavily-laden comrades would be forced to abandon their supplies and weapons with hopes to swim to the ceiling.

Suddenly, Seadna threw himself at the lock with all his might, stabbing a tough iron dagger into the edge of the constricted keyhole. Only his head remained above water as he worked, and Fearghus was amazed at his determination.

Then, their hopes were dashed. As Seadna moved the blade up and down in the stone, it suddenly splintered. The metal just broke off, leaving a wedge of iron in the crack and a broken blade in Seadna's grasp. "It is a bond not easily broken, but I think there must be some way," he sputtered as the water reached his mouth. "Come, swim up with me that we might last for another second."

The two men stood upon a great stone statue of some mysterious god, waiting for the water to rise beyond this temporary haven. "What do make of it?" Seadna asked his friend, toying with his ruined knife. Around the room, Irial, Murchadh and the rest of the Order of the Serpent were finding similar spots to evade the deathly cold spring water. The stone in the chamber was so clean, and the water so pure that everything in the room could be seen by torchlight through the obstacle.

Now Fearghus gave serious thought to the keyhole situation. "I think I'm going back down there," he told Seadna. "If this ethereal blade cannot cut stone, then it is not worthy to cut the flesh of the Snake."

"You are wise but also foolish," Seadna told him. "When you have your chance back down there, take another look at the symbols on the keyholes. They are not there for decorative purposes, if you know what I mean."

"I shall try to fathom what you mean," Fearghus told him, and slipped down into the cool, clear water. A great ways below him, the floor of the chamber was becoming dark and desolate, as the stone caskets and jars upon it disappeared into nothingness.

It was not long before Fearghus groping in the dark, finally came to the three keyholes, and discovered the one bearing the pendant. Although it was no trouble seeing in the clean water, the light of Seadna's torch far above him was much more dim than he expected.

Suddenly, the torchlight went out and Fearghus only had his fingers to hold him to the position in front of the keyholes. If he lost contact with the wall at any time now, he likely wouldn't again find the same place.

As his lungs began to burst now, he pulled his sword out of its scabbard and clumsily positioned it in the crack that Seadna's knife had left. This was it, he realized. If he couldn't spring the key from this trap it was all over. He couldn't hope to survive much longer underwater, and if his assumption was correct, neither could his men who now could easily be submerged as well, if not dead.

With his last effort, he threw himself hard against the rigid hilt of his weapon, but it did not give way. Then a second time he hurtled towards it, producing similar results. Now his vision blurred and his lungs felt like stone. He began to accept the idea of death immediately, but still his body, strengthened by the power of the gods, struggled on.

With one last tug from the other side of the blade, Fearghus's sword suddenly gave way. He did not know if the key had come loose or not, but his sword was free for the moment. There was only one final chance for him to save the expedition and all the lives of his men: in a way, he knelt down on the stone floor and wiped his arms across the bare floor, searching for the key. If it was here, then maybe in the final seconds of his life, he could at least spare the lives of his men.

Suddenly, his hand came to it. He was victorious! The key was his! He could feel every familiar feature of the coin: its broad edges and smooth sides. And in the same breath he lunged upwards, found the three keyholes, and shoved the coin ultimately into the middle socket, which he had deemed was the Roman cross. At this, his body triumphantly relaxed, and blackness ensued.

Miraculously, in a similar way to that incident a great while ago when Seadna had twice saved him from the ocean, Fearghus woke to the sound of the pirate's voice. "Thank the gods that you have survived!" he laughed, kneeling over his comrade.

"What has happened?" Fearghus asked.

Murchadh, who was standing there, gave him grave news. "A great passage opened on the opposite side of the chamber," he explained. "When the water flowed into the next room and disappeared into a rift in the ground, only ten of the men came out alive, half of them unconscious like you."

"Then we have suffered casualties from drowning?" Fearghus asked, still somehow in a state of relief for the sake of his own life.

"Two brave men," Murchadh replied, "were swept down with the rest of the lighter objects in the room. They could not reach stable ground in time, since they were blacked out, and the current took them."

Fearghus sat up. "I'm very sorry for their loss," he said. "Did you salvage any of our equipment?"

"Just a few things," Murchadh replied, and to Fearghus's relief, he had with him Seadna's golden helm. "I do hope you have your sword," he mentioned as he showed his leader the rest of the rescued supplies.

Fearghus stood up in his wet clothes and picked up a short bow, missing its string, from the mess of wet weapons. Instantly, at his will, it molted into his familiar sword, and he slid it back into its sheath. "Amazing," one of the men commented as the entire party waited there.

"These things are not of this world," Seadna observed. "They are magical tools of Fearghus's mission."

They were in yet another hall like the last two, and Fearghus could see no end in sight. "What do you make of all these trials?" he asked Seadna.

"I think you need to start examining your situation," the pirate explained. "You should be noticing that only the man most qualified will be allowed to possess this spear you seek, and that there is a trend in your hardships."

"What it is none of us can fathom," Fearghus responded, "but I suppose that shall be the objective of this quest."

"I'm sure it shall," Seadna observed wisely, and the group prepared to continue to the next chamber. With luck, the number of tasks before them was becoming small. For now, though, there would always be one last trial to complete: Fearghus would have to slay the Snake for the last time, and take from him the prize of Osgar.

"Let us now continue with renewed courage to take what is ours," Fearghus told the thirteen men behind him. And with that, they pressed into the next corridor, soaking but triumphant, and their feet slipped on the floor as they went.

"Osgar must be near!" Irial said as they noticed the presence of sunlight at the end of this crude tunnel.

"I cannot tell," Seadna added when they suddenly came out onto the side of the mountain. Before them, the entire Isle of Man stretched far and wide. With his keen eyes, Fearghus could even see the free forest beyond the twisting Valley of the Serpent and the calm sea still further. As he looked, he even noticed a plume of smoke from the friendly coastal village they had stayed in and also the wreck of the *Silverbeam* near it on the beach.

They were on an extremely small path, circling around the entire cap of the Mountain, and at the end of it they would reenter the stone caverns and resume their quest. "I feel nothing good for this obstacle," Seadna suddenly said as they began to walk out on the trail, holding onto the rock face. "I say we stop right now and consider our peril."

"You are right," Fearghus replied. "I think I shall throw a stone ahead of us and maybe trigger any traps set for us."

"Your wisdom is impressive," Seadna observed. "You are learning from your mistakes."

Fearghus threw a large rock just ahead of them onto the flat path. Nothing happened. "We will continue cautiously," he told his men.

Fearghus continued very quietly, taking small, careful steps and keeping his sword poised. If they were attacked up here, then they were very likely doomed. Also, they shouldn't want to reach a dead end or a break in the trail, lest the whole mission be suddenly stopped.

"Can you see an end in sight?" Seadna yelled up to his master.

Fearghus squinted his strong eyes in the sun and peered ahead as far as he could. The path, it seemed, was curving up around the cap of the Mountain, and he couldn't see where there was another door. "No, there isn't a change within my range," he told his friend, and they continued on.

When they reached the stone Fearghus had thrown, he picked it up again and tossed it further, but this time only a few paces ahead. He repeated this process several times until they had made a definite turn in their traveling, and suddenly Fearghus noticed a hole in the mountainside, and it was just big enough for one man at a time to pass through. "I think I will go through there," he told Seadna.

"I think it could be a trap," his friend said. "Let me, instead go."

Fearghus moved out of Seadna's way, and the former pirate pushed ahead cautiously. But this door was not meant for him, for at that very moment the Mountain shuddered and the path before him collapsed into oblivion, falling to pieces and tumbling down the side of the Mountain. Seadna himself, distraught by the event, nearly lost his balance and went down after it. If it was not for Fearghus's strong arms coming about him, then the party would have lost a good and valiant member.

The section of the path that was missing was several paces long, and from Fearghus's standpoint, it couldn't be crossed by any man. "What shall we do?" he asked Seadna.

"I cannot cross it," his friend observed, "but there is one alone among us who is meant to go on."

Fearghus knew exactly what the former pirate was trying to tell him. Fearghus could only continue by himself. Not one of his twelve companions possessed the strength to leap across this chasm, but with the strength bestowed upon him by the gods, it might be possible that he could jump such a length. This obstacle in the path was meant to separate the man chosen to possess Osgar from any other adventurers with him. No other party besides his own, and of course Colla's, could find success here.

"I shall go on without you," Fearghus told his men as they stood there together. "Try to find yourselves a path down the Mountain on the outside, for the way inside is sealed."

"We shall try to avoid the fire of the gods," Irial replied, "and maybe come back to Eire in all of its glory with good time."

"I leave you here in good stead," Fearghus told his men, and prepared to make the jump. "May we meet again," he continued, and with that, he ran as fast as he dared straight for the edge of the jump, and when he reached it suddenly was flying through the air, making his own wind as he went.

And so, finally, he fell hard upon the other side, waved to his comrades as they stood upon the brink of the chasm, and continued on without looking back. Just in front of him, the door he had before seen was his for the taking. It was no doubt dark within the tunnel, but he had no fear of what lay ahead. Only the Snake, being an outside faction, could stop the man chosen to possess Osgar, and even then only fate would decide the future of the spear and its captor.

The corridor was nearly too small for him, and his light armor was scratched on the clean stone walls of it. The air within the hallway was every bit as clear as it was outside, and nothing was to be heard or seen inside. Fearghus was well on his way to reaching the goal he so long desired, and nothing the Mountain could do to him could sway his determination.

Finally, the tunnel reached its end. It was still rather dark in this new chamber, but when Fearghus stood up, he noticed the presence of several torches fixed on the walls. They were lit by some mysterious force, which he didn't want to know about, but nonetheless the fire provided light in an otherwise dark chamber.

Now what else could lie in waiting for him to challenge? This room didn't seem to possess any new danger. But yet again, he could never be off of his guard with Osgar so close.

Presently, he located the door and strode towards it. In the middle of the chamber, there was a large slab of stone, and it was in the shape of a circle. As Fearghus walked over it, suddenly a great wind swept through the room. The torches around him were extinguished simultaneously, and the next thing he knew everything went black, and for the second time he fell unconscious to the floor, completely vulnerable, but this time, he was without his friends.

He was in a strange dream world. Dark clouds seemed to swirl about him, and he felt strangely cold. Of course in this world there was a ground, but when he tried to walk, he only stayed in one place. Then, suddenly, he realized that his sword was still hanging about his waist and drew it, the blade glinting in the light of a moon he could not see.

All of sudden, he was attacked. But this was no creature of the Mountain or wolf of the forest, it was a Roman centurion, and he held a strong bow, an arrow already nocked upon its string. His helmet was golden and decorated with red feathers, and he also wore a cape over a strong chest plate. It was just then that Fearghus realized that this was the last man he had fought before losing Osgar. In fact, he had actually cast Osgar into this man's back, and then had lost it.

Then he realized why he had lost Osgar. This man had begged for his life, and Fearghus had taken it from him without considering what evil he was doing. He had disobeyed the gods, committed a great sin, and all of this was his punishment.

Fearghus dodged the first bolt and spun around, his mighty sword swinging around through the air and coming ultimately into the side of his enemy. But the centurion did not fall. Instead, he grabbed the blade of Fearghus's sword and pulled it from him, quickly nocking another arrow.

This shot found its target. It smashed into Fearghus's chest with amazing force, and for a moment he staggered back. The wound the arrow made burned and stung with terrible pain, and suddenly Fearghus realized that this was no ordinary dream. Fearghus was dying at the hand of the man he had killed in cold blood, or at least his ghost. There seemed almost no way out of this horrific dream.

Blood spewed from Fearghus's chest as he fell to his knees. In one last effort, he swung his sword full circle in front of him and miraculously destroyed the bow of his enemy. But the centurion's face was filled with revenge. "In the name of God," he said, "I shall take you now for the last time."

Fearghus was not dead yet, though. Somehow, he maintained some strength, pulling the arrow out of its bloody home. He knew not if he could be killed in this dream, or if his enemy could, but at that moment his sword came up and parried the blow of the centurion's dagger, which was jolted out of the latter's hand, disappearing into the dark clouds around them.

"Do not tangle with Rome," the man taunted him. But Fearghus had every intention to subdue his enemy, for whatever that was worth. At that moment, he pushed his sword straight through the stomach of the Roman, and lunged at the man, his fingers finding the centurion's neck.

But the soldier's hands came up as well, and also fixed themselves about Fearghus's neck while blood continued to soak the clothing of both men. Fearghus slowly began to lose breath, but as he did so he only strengthened his grip on the other man's head.

Suddenly, it was all over. Fearghus's hold was too strong for the man, and as he died, the centurion cried aloud. "My God!" he screamed, "have mercy on me!" And with that, his body disintegrated into a blazing silhouette of white light, which grew too strong for Fearghus's eyes. The sheer heat of the ghost burned across his face, and then all was black.

He was victorious! He had just been given the chance to kill the centurion in a righteous manner, and had somehow succeeded. His crime was avenged, as was the blood of every Celt the man had killed in his campaign on Eire.

The gods were teaching him a lesson. He was being tested concerning all of the greatest characteristics of a king: a respect for life and the moral values that govern the taking and making of it. Now that he was forgiven of this crime, where was Osgar? It must be in the next room, he thought.

Fearghus was disappointed in the next room. Actually, it was a corridor of sorts, long and bare, leading straight to a grand gate at the other end. This was the final frontier of their excursion, and Fearghus knew it well. Behind that door lay the most mysterious and easily the greatest treasure of all the world. His golden helmet would not even match its glory. If he could possess it, then he may rule the world.

Just as in the rest of the Mountain, the walls to this cavern were barren of any markings or decorations. But Fearghus couldn't underestimate the magic protecting this lance: caution would prove to be a great tool as he approached this last fortification.

Taking a deep breath, Fearghus stepped forward, continuing when nothing happened. But as he reached a quarter of the length, the room suddenly lurched to life, and dust from the ceiling heralded a brief shower of pebbles on Fearghus's head.

Before him, the floor had been rent asunder, splitting the walls about it and flinging wide an uneven chasm. Below him, Fearghus noticed something he had never seen before: at the bottom of the chasm a terrible red glow greeted him. The floor of the canyon was running with fire! Just like a river it flowed along, but the heat it produced singed the hair of Fearghus's unkempt face.

What evil was this? A door had suddenly opened before him, and it led to the underworld, the home of the Dead. But how could he pass it? If he fell into the brimstone he would die almost instantly, or else drown in the stuff. He had never seen this substance that the tales told so much of, and his entire body convulsed with fear as the floor he stood on began to warm.

There was nothing, it seemed, inside the room that could help him cross the barrier. If he had his wits about him when the floor split, then maybe he could have leapt across. But now there was no hope.

He was beginning to think that he was doomed, but then his keen eyes spotted something in the left wall that seemed appealing. The stone was cracked and split, and as far as he could see, the surface was filled with deep footholds and ledges. The quaking ground may have made his way for him!

Fearghus did not give any thought to this new discovery. He had almost turned back, and his body was now shivering after almost losing the expedition. Nonetheless, he cautiously stepped out over the fire, fixing his feet into the ruined wall. The burning river below him caused the air to become super heated. He feared that his garments would burst into flame if he did not continue, and it became hard to breathe.

He scuttled along as fast as he dared, not slipping once, but the stone burned his fingers. In some places, his feet were too big to hold in certain cracks, and in others, the holes in the wall were too large or far away. Even so, the gods were kind to him, and he continually found a new ledge to grasp with his fingers.

He had almost reached the other side when, suddenly, his foot slipped on a loose stone. The rock slid out of its place and sailed down to the fire. Flailing,

Fearghus watched it splash into the liquid, and a stream of brimstone leapt into the air, missing his feet narrowly.

Blinded by the intense ruddy light, Fearghus fought for balance. The slip had flung his body back, and had he not such a good hold with his hands, he would have fallen into the river. Now embracing the wall with all his might, he paused for a moment to catch his breath. "Oh Sucellos!" he cried aloud, "deliver me from this death!"

But the glorious king of the gods did not come. The rain of the Celtic gods did not extinguish the brimstone, and the wind of the heavens did not carry him to safety. Fearghus had to prove to them all by himself that he deserved the possession of Osgar, and crossing this chasm included that. If he could not save himself, what kind of King was he?

Now he was tiring, and his body neared its limits as he reached the opposite bank of the river. With one last thrust of his arms now, he fell forward onto the stone, and looked up to see the gate before him, the last obstacle before the chamber of Osgar.

As he stood up, the earth suddenly shook again, and he fell back to his knees. The Mountain was in revolt at his progress, and now would try to expel him.

Now it was a dash to the gate, for the room was collapsing about him. The ceiling itself was beginning to break apart, and the red light of the brimstone spread across it as the chasm widened, breaking apart the room.

But it was too late for the brimstone as it squirmed in its confines, for Fearghus was at the grand gate now. As he turned to push the doors apart, a large section of the hall's ceiling fell down into the brimstone, and where it had been, light streamed into the chamber. It was white light, and it fought against the darkness and the fire. The dust from the falling stones hung in the fair rays, but Fearghus could not stay to admire it.

Tripping a few times as the Mountain quivered, Fearghus planted his feet firmly and pushed open the heavy metal door of the gate, looking down. When he lifted his head, he was amazed. Now this was the treasure chamber: the walls were coursed with writing, the walls were hemmed with gold, and the whole of the hall was cluttered with scrolls, tablets, caskets and gold. The lost tribes who had delved these halls had left all of their belongings here: their treasures, records, even their dead.

Fearghus had not expected to find such precious things in the Mountain. Only Osgar did he seek, and this was an added bonus. Thousands of years of Manx history lay in this chamber, and Fearghus wished dearly to know it all.

But where was Osgar? He did not see any kind of pedestal or altar where he could find the lance. Then again, would the gods have left it in the open for his taking? It would be somewhere in this room, only hidden.

While he rummaged through the artifacts, he stumbled upon a stone tablet bearing a strange hieroglyphic language. As he read it, though, he recognized that it was merely a simple picture. On the tablet he beheld the silhouette of a man. It was a rather crude picture, but he could easily decipher that it was a strong warrior holding a sword. Accompanying him in the art was another form, though, and it was long and curvy.

Then it all made sense: this was a picture of a man battling the Snake, and the man was...him! Suddenly his sword was out, and he spun around to face none other than the Snake himself, coiled neatly in a corner of the vast room. He had not noticed the creature waiting in the dark end of the hall, completely concealed in the blackness.

"Be gone, you foul beast!" he screamed, his body shaking with horror.

The Snake's tongue flicked in and out as he sized up his enemy. His body was smooth and shiny, almost as if by sweat. "Our tales are bound together," he hissed.

"What does that mean?" Fearghus asked, holding his ground.

"You *have* to kill me," the serpent answered in a high, angry voice. As Fearghus watched, every inch of his immense form swayed back and forth.

"But you shall not be killed by any mortal weapons!" Fearghus responded. "I already know that from past experience!"

The Snake's eyes grew large and haughty. Even though they were black slits, Fearghus could see the personality of the beast inside them. "What *mortal* weapons have you ever possessed?" the Snake growled.

Fearghus was taken aback by this statement, but remained firm in his stance. "The gifts of the gods could not kill you in my village!" he shot back.

"It was not then your time to kill me!" his enemy snarled, drawing back his head. "Or *my* time to die!"

"Then I shall take the fight to you now!" Fearghus shouted, and his sword, his greatest companion, soared into the air behind him, narrowly missing the Snake's tail.

But the Snake repelled him easily, snapping the tail quickly to knock Fearghus back.

"That is no more a weapon than my fangs!" the beast cried, and suddenly Fearghus beheld the severed blade of his weapon. His sword lay in pieces at his side.

"What new magic is this?" he asked himself, completely crushed by the occurrence.

"The magic of your *gods*," the Snake hissed, and then Fearghus spied something shining in the beast's grasp. "This is the work of the false gods who have abandoned you," the Snake continued.

Taking up his broken sword, he stood once again to the serpent, shaken but not defeated. "My gods will take you for this offense," he retorted fiercely and without regret.

"Now there is only one ethereal weapon in this room," the Snake said, still jerking back and forth.

Fearghus noticed blood running down his face. His armor was dented and worn. Nevertheless, he would have to finish this fight. "And what is that?" he tempted the creature before him.

Now the Snake confirmed his worst fears. "It is this which I hold here in my coils," he responded slowly and sinisterly. Indeed, fixed snugly in his winding seat was Osgar itself, gleaming in the light let in from the previous chamber.

"So that is what you are hiding!" Fearghus observed, confirming his worst fears.

"Yes, it is," the beast answered, and for a moment looked down at the treasure.

Now was the time to act, and Fearghus had to do it quickly. "For Eire!" he cried once again as he had done in battle with Rome, and hurled his jagged broken sword straight for the Snake's face.

This time the weapon found its mark, and plunged into the scales of his enemy, giving him just enough time to lunge at Osgar with his hands. Venomous blood poured out of the wound he created, staining but not penetrating his armor as he leapt.

Suddenly his hands grasped the shaft of the treasure he had so long sought after. His body was stretched out to full length and doubled over the side of the writhing Snake, but Osgar was in his hands.

"You shall not have it!" his enemy suddenly cried, pulling the broken sword out of its place with his tail.

Fearghus held onto Osgar with all his strength as he was flung back into the wall for the second time. As he hit the wall, his armor cracking, his breath was knocked out of him and he doubled over vomiting. "But I already do," he choked, struggling to look up at his enemy.

The snake looked up as well, dazed and bleeding. "But I have my fangs," he screamed vehemently, shaking off the wound, "and my immortality."

Fearghus backed up against the wall. Before his eyes, the wound upon the Snake's head had spontaneously healed, and now the creature stood before him in full health, his fangs bared.

The unearthly spear of Osgar was now in his hands. If he could run it through the Snake, that was one thing, but if he could escape with it, then that was another. However, the chamber behind them was rent with brimstone; he could not hope to retreat through it.

Maybe there was a way out. Maybe this treasure chamber had a secret door. In any case, if he couldn't find it right now, he would most nearly be dead. Most of his bones were already broken, he estimated.

Suddenly, he had an idea. "You must be quicker, to catch a Celt!" he cried, leaping through the wide gate of the treasure chamber and into the ruined chamber. As he did, the light of the sun above gleamed on his golden helm and the head of Osgar glowed a blinding white.

"How foolish you are!" the Snake cried as he hurtled into the chamber behind him.

"No duel is won until one of the combatants is dead!" Fearghus shot back, planting his feet on the edge of the chasm.

The Snake seemed unaware of the brimstone before him, and his eyes glowing red, he threw his head forward. Fearghus had just the strength to leap out of the way, hitting the ruined wall of the hall hard. Behind him, the beast lost his balance and came to the brink of the chasm, swinging back and forth in complete fear.

Fearghus's knuckles turned white as he fought for his own balance, but his body did not fall. "You shall see me again!" the Snake cried as he fell forward, and as Fearghus watched, his vast body toppled like a tree and fell straight down into the brimstone. As it hit the fire, the flesh was instantly burned to ash, and consumed in flames. The liquid was rather thick, Fearghus noticed, but it was not a long time before the entire body of the Snake had disappeared into oblivion.

As his enemy was consumed, Fearghus suddenly sensed new danger. The Mountain and its brimstone had been disturbed a third time, and this time the force of the quake was tremendous. Stones began to fall about him, cracking upon his battered pauldrons and helm, and dust filled the air.

His fingers were jerked from the wall, but suddenly his legs pushed up, and he threw himself onto the floor, still holding Osgar with a white fist. This time the ceiling of the chamber was coming completely down, and he had scarcely the time he had before to scramble into the treasure chamber. Light streaming down in full upon his bloody arms, he barely managed to save himself from ruin.

Once again safe inside the vast room, Fearghus lay down upon the hoard of gold and listened to the rumbling fury of the Mountain. For now he had a brief opportunity to recoil from this battling, but the Mountain, he knew, was ready to spew forth the fire of the gods, and destroy all memory of Osgar's former stronghold.

It was then that Fearghus, bleeding and bruised, looked down at Osgar for the first time. What he saw amazed him. This was indeed the lance he had carried with him through the forests of Eire, but the jewels upon it were gone. Not the slightest detail remained of the former splendor. The Holy Lance had regained its original appearance, that it possessed many ages ago when it was made. On top of this, none of Fearghus's wounds had healed. He had not noticed this at first when he picked up Osgar, but now he realized the failure of his mission in regaining invulnerability.

Then he realized something that would be more dangerous. Would his men be smart enough to flee the Mountain before it killed them, and with them Agnos? He had to get back down to them before the brimstone came upon their camp.

He struggled painfully to his feet, leaning on Osgar. He would not throw the hallowed tool away, for now, but he was not happy with the results of his struggling. His plan, right now, was to climb out of this trap through the only breach he knew of: the ceiling of the previous chamber.

The once smooth floor was littered with stones and vast boulders. Needless to say, it was quite a struggle for Fearghus to push himself over this obstacle, but actually, it proved to be a good way of ascending to the top of the chamber. Before him, the chasm running with brimstone had widened considerably, and its contents were beginning to reach the platform where he stood.

In order to pass through the large hole in the side of the mountain, he had to painfully pull himself up using only his arms, and when he finally sat upon the exterior of the Mountain, he nearly lost Osgar down the steep slope.

The Isle of Man stretched out before him. Once again, he could see the village, the forest, and the sea, and this time, he was happy to notice the encampment of his comrades a great ways below at the foot of the Mountain. "Help me!" he cried, his plea echoing across the hills and valleys.

Nothing stirred but the Mountain. Behind him, a stream of ash was filling the sky with a terrible poisonous wind. The entire rock was beginning to shudder again, and suddenly Fearghus knew what he had to do: the way down the mountain was steep, but not impossible.

He began by sliding down a loose gravel slope while seated, and used his feet to brake by jamming them against the boulders on either side of his path. Osgar he kept tightly under his arm, and he made slow but cautious progress downwards.

Presently, he reached roughly the halfway point between him and the camp, but still no one noticed him. Then something terrible happened. As he stood up to continue his movement on foot, the mountainside burst open furiously, rocks and debris flying every which way. One small stone cracked on his leg, drawing even more blood, but luckily he went generally unscathed. What scared him, though, was that a small rockslide was headed right for the camp. With luck, none of the boulders would reach the wagon hidden behind a large stone, but still the men were in danger from the raging Mountain.

He was stumbling down the mountainside now, and as he went he tripped over numerous stones; his feet and hands flowed with thick blood and his head was painfully scratched. But he did not care about these things, for he was already dead. All he cared about now was ultimately seeing Agnos again, and maybe leaving this trap, whether dead or alive he cared not.

At last the steep slope gave way and he fell to level ground. The wagon was behind a rock just paces away, but he could not go on. "Fearghus!" someone suddenly shouted. And it was a high, soothing voice, the voice of a woman.

Indeed, Agnos had come to his aid. Even now she was wiping her fair cloak across his mauled face, and stroking his dusty hair. "What has happened?" she inquired at length.

But Fearghus could not speak. His throat was filling with blood, and his eyes clouded. As shouts of "He has done it!" and "Fearghus is back!" filled the air, he held Agnos's hand and fell into unconsciousness.

Fearghus lived in blackness for a long while, but somehow, he woke. The first sound that greeted his ears was not a good one though. He nearly sat up when the sound cracked through the sky; it was the sound of the Mountain destroying itself.

"We must move faster!" one man shouted, and suddenly he knew he was in the bed of a wagon. "What's going on?" he choked. When he moved his head though, a bolt of pain greeted him.

"Stay your excitement," Agnos warned him, "we are in dire circumstances."

Fearghus managed to move his head to the side ever so slightly, and directly before him the Mountain was bursting with fire and brimstone, just as the prophecies had foretold. Even from here he could see the breach in the slopes where he had escaped, and it was far larger than he estimated.

From time to time as he lay there observing the explosion, the Mountain sent forth several large projectiles, and like the fiery catapult of the *Silverbeam*, the Mountain in this way set fire to all of the surrounding region. In addition to this, there were several flying rocks in the air that did not burn, and brimstone began to well up from the heart of the Mountain, flowing down upon the stone barriers at its base. According to Seadna, such events as this had happened before in the lands of Rome to the south, but it was hard to fathom how or why this phenomenon ever occurred. It was as if the fury of the underworld below had found a door to the mortal world, and was rushing through it with amazing strength.

"I have never witnessed such force," Seadna said, pulling beside the wagon. "Except when I'm witnessing your mighty strength. How fare you?" he asked.

With much pain, Fearghus turned to look at his friend. "I am doing better now that I see you have survived," he replied warmly as smoke filled the air.

"That is good," the former pirate observed. "Now we must return to our home."

"Do you expect that they will be in good stead?" Fearghus asked.

"I do not wish to discuss such things, considering your current condition," Seadna replied quickly.

Fearghus noticed Osgar at his side, grasped it, and said, "I don't understand these events."

"Everything has a purpose," Seadna told him, "and this adventure shall have its purpose as well, no matter what the outcome," he wisely continued.

Fearghus looked straight up to the gray sky, now filled with ash. "I am sure you are right," he responded, and closed his eyes.

Fearghus shut the sounds of the Mountain out of his mind and slept soundly while the wagon raced along the hills of Man. Even though he now held Osgar in his hands, he was reluctant to feel triumphant or proud, only shaken and fearful. Before he had held himself to such high standards, but now he just wanted to see Eire again.

Night fell. Throughout the day, the few men remaining to Fearghus had remained considerably quiet, strangely enough. However, as the moon rose, Irial and his men came to congratulate their leader. "You have fought for this honor valiantly," Murchadh said, as the others agreed.

"But still I bleed...," Fearghus mumbled.

"That does not matter," Irial said quickly. "Capturing Osgar was a great feat, no matter the consequences of it."

At length, Seadna joined the group. "We shall now return victorious to Eire and drive away the Roman swine," he said.

"With what?" one of the men burst curtly, looking down upon the simple wooden shaft of Osgar.

Seadna turned about to face the warrior, the hilt of his sword gleaming in the moonlight. "With our strength and resolve," he replied vigorously.

"But what of this quest?" Murchadh asked, toying with a blade of grass.

"We can do no more but leave this accursed land with our lives," came the former pirate's answer, and he sat down amongst them.

At last Fearghus decided to speak, though still he was immobilized upon the rushes. "We have gained much knowledge and skill from this quest," he bellowed, "and I say now we shall all do well to pray to the gods for continued success, and prolong our efforts even as we leave this place."

And with that, the men huddled about their meager campfires and spent the night in thought and reflection, for sleep came not easily after such a difficult day. Each man lay in hunger and thirst, but it did not matter in the midst of this strange land. Tomorrow they would push back to the Sea, and contemplate their escape from Man.

Fearghus was jolted awake twice that night, once by the Mountain and then by his men. The fury of its brimstone had somewhat subsided as they slept, but now suddenly it had renewed its mission, and terrible spouts of fire wrought utter devastation on the foothills behind them. The night was suddenly filled with its red glow and every tree cast broken shadows upon the earth.

"We must move!" Irial shouted as he whipped his horse. "Osgar resumes its battle upon us!"

Before he knew it Fearghus was thrown onto the wagon once again and the weak wooden craft resumed its race across the fields, the dark forest ahead looming closer and closer.

When next the red sun peeked above the horizon, the smoke of the Mountain was heavy in the air, and the brimstone from within it had destroyed nearly the entire length of land they had traversed since the initial explosion. The air smelled foul and deathly, and the wind was cursed with ash.

"Come, we should make good time today in our travels," Seadna commanded aloud. In a very short length of time, thereafter, the whole of his company was well on its way to the forest, marching proudly but humbly in the shadow of the Mountain and its fury. Osgar, Fearghus held aloft as he rode, for he had felt much relief this past night from his wounds.

"How shall we make our path back to Eire?" he asked Seadna as they bounced in the light step of their steeds.

Seadna looked joyous and thoughtful simultaneously. "We shall make new the *Silverbeam* and sail back to our land," he explained. "When we take the fight back to the Romans, they will scatter like the mice they truly are."

"I hope you are right," Irial sighed, pulling up to them. Then suddenly he was taken aback as they came over a great grassy hill. "Have a look at that!" he cried, signaling to each of his men. Ahead of them, Fearghus couldn't believe his eyes. The dark, black forest, before plagued with wolves and death, had undergone some transformation. It was green and beautiful, bursting with light.

It was not long before they were inside of it, and the air was fresh and cool like it was in the forests of Eire. The trail the small group followed was kind and smooth, and passage to the other side of the forest became vastly easier. By dusk the next day, they had crossed the entire length of it, and the old battlefield from before was in sight.

"So tell me," one man asked as they sat about a bonfire, "what was the chamber like?"

Fearghus only laughed to himself as the firelight danced across his face. "It was very interesting," he concluded, "but also very frightening!"

Subsequently, this inquisitive man approached him again as he prepared for sleep. "What do you make of our chances against the Romans?" he asked quickly, passing his leader.

Fearghus closed his eyes. "Let them come," was all he said, and there fell to a calm, untroubled sleep until the next morn.

They reached the village on the morrow. They were met well, like a victorious army returning from battle. The Manx surrounded them in the street with unwanted but still great praise. Fearghus, as they marched, rode his horse amongst the body of his weary men, his spear Osgar hidden within the wagon where Agnos rode. The throng about them was pressing in too deeply for his liking, and thus he hid himself within the ranks of his men, and instead Irial was harried by the rabble.

The sight of the crude huts and crafts of the villagers was nonetheless a warming vision. The sea behind it, the group of shelters seemed to act as a wall between him and the furious Snake, who still festered in the brimstone of the Mountain with anger he could not yet fathom.

At length, Seadna settled the crowd with the Manx tongue, and made a speech to the people in their own words. While Fearghus struggled to listen, he said, "Be still, men of the earth! The curse of the serpent has been lifted from these lands!" And with this, the crowd roared with joyful bliss. "Fear not the hand of the

Snake, for from it has been taken the most sacred of our treasures!" the pirate continued, and thereafter rejoined his men.

When the cloudy sky hastened the darkness of night, Fearghus was again bade to find shelter in the house of the old woman he once knew. With him went Agnos and Murchadh his guard, with Osgar.

Chapter 12

Return to Eire

"You have done it?" the elderly woman asked dazedly, stumbling into the central chamber of her abode.

"Yes, the words of the prophets have been made truthful," Fearghus replied, his face shrouded in the steam of his bath. Beside him, Murchadh stood still as a statue. In his left hand he held Osgar resting upon the earth, and in the other, his naked blade aloft, dripping with the warm mist.

"What divine favor befalls me that I may look upon the instrument of the gods?" the woman cried aloud, falling to her knees before him.

"Do not worship my spear!" Fearghus snapped, waving his hand for her to stand before him. "None shall worship here but to Sucellos himself, or they commit blasphemy!" he bellowed fearfully.

The old woman was taken aback, but nonetheless bowed curtly to him and resumed her ecstatic routine. "My sin has been acknowledged," she admitted quickly, and stared straight into his bloodied face.

For many long hours the maids of the house mended the wounds of Fearghus as Agnos and the vigilant Murchadh looked on. His old useless armor was removed, and the ash was massaged out of his long hair. With time, all three of the company were bathed and anointed with sweet fragrances from the Manx temples. Whilst they cleansed him of his own blood and covered the ribbons of his flesh, Fearghus amused himself by looking across the room to the basin where Agnos in her beauty subsequently was dressed in the greatest ornaments of the village. Her headdress was beautiful as her tunic, and her hair now became soft and radiant.

Night fell over the huts and Fearghus himself was dressed in warrior's garments and adorned with a new sword. It was a short but comfortable weapon, forged of iron and trimmed in gold. Slightly curved, Fearghus decided that the blade was an acceptable weapon for him, and wore it proudly upon a belt of silver. Included in his costume were short bronze tassets, a matching breastplate, and some small pauldrons and greaves. His appearance for the night was complemented by a flowing violet cape and of course his own Crown of the Deep.

It was not long before the party had realized that the villagers were throwing them an encore feast to celebrate their victory over the magic of Osgar. To prepare for this, many pigs and sheep from the village's herds had been killed and many fruits and roots had been harvested from the forest. The table was laden with meat and ale, and large logs and stumps from the surrounding trees were brought in to meet the need for stools, as many more villagers than the last time they were here wished to participate in the festivities.

Once again the tapestry of the tale of Osgar was used to clothe the surface of the table, and the same platters were used to hold the vegetables and cuts of mutton and boar. As they began to eat, a light rain dashed the meal with gentle drops of water, and the trees above swayed in a salty breeze.

Fearghus had just sunk his teeth into a particularly tough cut of mutton when he spied a familiar face at the edge of the ruddy torchlight. Before he could swallow though, Seadna noticed his gaze and followed it to the shrouded face. "Finghin!" he laughed, and leapt up vigorously to welcome his longtime friend.

By now, every man in the company had noticed the arrival of the fisher, who was accompanied by his two servants. "Do my eyes deceive me?" he asked, staring upon the dark figure of Murchadh holding Osgar close to his chest.

"No, they do not," Seadna responded, leading them into the light. Almost immediately a place was cleared for them among their comrades and their plates were generously filled. "How has our absence treated thee?" Seadna asked presently.

"We have done much to save the wreck of the *Silverbeam*," Finghin replied through an oversized mouthful of meat. "We can finish it within just a few days."

Fearghus stood up and greeted his old friend. "I do hope you are right," he said, sitting back down.

The night wore on rather quickly thereafter and the common villagers were drunk by dawn. The warriors, however, kept constant vigilance about Osgar until the next morning light. During the entire feast, not a hand was laid upon the shaft of the spear but those of Fearghus its owner and the newly-appointed guardian of the holy lance, Murchadh.

Midday found Finghin leading them back down the beach to where the wreck of their ship lay. They had a good early start on this final leg of the return journey and reached the place by dusk. Fearghus was amazed at the work that had already been done to the ruined boat; new planks had been fashioned for the underside, a new mast had been fixed into the deck, and already several projects lay just unfinished about the whole beach, and lumber was everywhere. "This work is amazing!" Irial commented as they prepared for sleep on the sand.

In what seemed to Fearghus to be a very short time, the party had settled down in the shadow of the boat, and all the tethers and masts of the craft stood starkly in the light of the setting sun, framed against the burning sky as black lances and swords. That night, Fearghus kept awake, for he was contemplating what the next few days would bring them. His mind was racing with thoughts of death and another appearance by both the Romans and the Snake. Even though he had Osgar, his mind remained troubled through yet another period of darkness.

Fearghus awoke to the sounds of hammers and axes the next morning, all mixed in with the hum of the Sea. The men were beginning to repair the rest of the wreck of the *Silverbeam*. Fearghus himself now joined in the effort, and his ethereal muscles, while not entirely magical or immortal, were good tools as they swung an axe upon the raw lumber lying about.

This work, of course, was Irial's specialty, and just as he was the head of the fighting men, so too was he now the head of the working men. Under his direction, the party operated more efficiently and precisely, fashioning the remaining panels of the ship to exact measurements and such that only Irial could devise.

By sunset on the first day, Fearghus found himself hammering the hot metal skeleton of the ship to the right shape, his body dripping with sweat and his muscles exhausted. When the time to sup arrived, Agnos was instantly by his side to refresh him with water and help him lay down near the fire and food.

"The progress you are making with this ship is amazing," she told him as they shared some mutton and broth.

"I cannot wait to reach Eire again," he said, "and possibly save our besieged comrades."

"You are too ambitious for your own good," she observed, sitting up and staring upon the fire.

"Only cowards are not ambitious," he replied longingly.

"We shall see who is a coward and who is not in the next few days," Agnos continued, and then reclined upon her bed of sand and cloth.

Fearghus was well rested when next the sun rose. He began work straightaway under Irial's watchful eye hammering the last curved planks of wood into the frame of the ship, all while the other men applied pitch generously to the other side of the wall. It was not long before they had finished this project, and by midday a number of the men were climbing upon the ropes to nail in the crossbar of the great mast.

Suddenly, one of the men far above them gave a shout. "A villager rides from the east!" he yelled deeply, drawing the attention of every worker. Fearghus nearly stumbled over the logs holding the ship upright as he bounded to the east side of the craft.

Indeed, a rider from the village had found them. "Let me talk to him," Seadna muttered, for he knew all the languages of the world.

The rider halted his horse and slumped his exhausted shoulders. "We have spotted a Roman vessel near our fields!" he burst, resting upon the slender neck of his steed.

"How far are they from here?" Seadna pried nervously, while the rest of the party looked upon the two, dumbfounded.

"I have ridden all day and all night," the villager responded through heavy breathing. "But still I cannot say that they are more than a day behind me."

"You have done well to inform us of this," Seadna told him, and tossed a few gold coins wrapped in cloth up to the man. "Now, ride back to your village and prepare your defense," he continued gravely.

The man nodded, and as he turned and galloped away, Seadna told his men of what he had just been informed. Instantly, Irial commanded the ship be placed in the water and pulled out to sea. "We will have to work while we flee," he told everyone, and before Fearghus knew it, the ship was afloat, and the men still upon the beach were working as quickly as possibly to fashion oars to replace the few they had lost. The craft, it seemed to him, was a bit off balance in the surf, but nonetheless the workers had spread their pitch well: it floated.

No sooner had they pushed the boat into the water than the whole of the party was laboring in the hold upon their oars, and only Seadna and Fearghus remained above to steer the vessel. "We are making good time to evade the filthy Romans," the pirate observed at length.

"But they will have many strong slaves upon their oars and fire within their catapults," Fearghus warned him.

"We will see how fate treats us when the time comes," Seadna replied optimistically.

They were cutting through the water at a nice speed, due to the efforts of the fighters down below. The wind near the shore was still rather light, but when it picked up, Fearghus knew, it could be harnessed by their mended shield to carry them straight back to Eire.

Slowly, the men below them tired and finally slowed to a comfortable rate. Since the sail of their boat was black, Fearghus knew, the Romans wouldn't so much as notice them if they lit no fires. "We will hide in the darkness," Seadna had commanded earlier that day.

While the rest of his men hid in the hold of the vessel making not a sound, Fearghus alone remained above, watching and waiting for the Roman ship to come upon them. If the need was to arise, he was prepared to load and discharge the fire of the ship's single catapult on the enemy, and blow a horn Seadna had given him to alert the fighters resting far below him.

Tonight the moon was muted by a dense cloud cover, and only could be seen of it a dull glow, illuminating the soft mist. The water all about them hardly reflected it, but nonetheless Fearghus could make out the disturbed state of the sea. Soon Fearghus fell to sleep, his gleaming sword tucked away in his garments, and was not disturbed until morning.

It was a cold day out on the sea this morning, and over the course of the night all traces of the cliffs of Man had disappeared beyond the horizon. The group of weeds that had slowed them so much on the arrival to the island had apparently dissipated as the curse of Osgar had, and smooth sailing seemed in store for the warriors as they hurried back to help their besieged friend.

The Manx villagers had provisioned them well for the journey; packed closely with the rowers in the hold were stone canisters of meat, fruit, and vegetables left over from the victory feast, and many skins filled with water. Even a few containers of ale and mead were given them. In addition, each man had been provided new costume and weaponry from the Manx, and a corner of the vessel was now called "the armory" by some of them.

Yet another grueling day passed. At least now there was enough wind to somewhat relieve the rowers, but still it was light. Even Fearghus himself was forced to help his men ply their oars, and cause the ship to move a bit faster.

For the next few days, Fearghus continually repeated his routine of taking the night watch, all while Murchadh protected Osgar. The Romans hadn't shown their ugly faces yet, but on one day this all changed.

The sky was blue and without clouds on this particular day, but on the horizon, the silhouette of a vast ship was drawing nearer and nearer to them. "The Romans come from the east!" the lookout cried when already every warrior had noticed the omen of doom. Indeed, the vessel giving them pursuit possessed a distinguishable red cross, and likely their own black sail had as well been identified with the pestilence of piracy.

Almost immediately Fearghus devised a plan. "We have little projectile power as it is," he told the men as they counseled within the captain's quarters.

"Then what do you suppose we do about it?" Murchadh asked.

Fearghus gave a moment of thought and then answered the man. "You and the five other archers will do your best to pick off the soldiers as they pull their ship alongside us," he told Murchadh. Then turning to Irial, he said, "You will stay aboard with just two men, throwing your lances and keeping your swords poised."

"Do not worry, my friend," the lumberman replied politely. "We will not forsake this mighty vessel."

Now Fearghus continued. "Finghin will operate the catapult alone," he instructed them, "and all others will leap aboard the other ship and kill as many as we can before either boat sinks."

Now they were all known to the plan, and before long six bowmen had nocked their arrows and gathered in the middle of the deck. When the Roman vessel appeared to be attacking their right side, every man crowded the proper side of the ship along the railing, hiding behind thick blocks of wood that Finghin had put in while they were away from him. Fearghus and seven other men including Seadna positioned themselves in the ropes of the sail, and it was their intention to swing to the Roman ship using the loose chords as bridges to the other side.

Everyone was still as the clearly faster Roman ship approached them. The only sound was of Finghin putting fire to the projectile in the catapult. Fearghus had already drawn his sword, as had a number of his comrades, and all were convulsing with both fear and excitement.

Then it was time to attack. "Go!" Fearghus shouted to the man furthest to his right. At his command, the men one by one swung to the Roman ship as it reached them, each with grace they knew not that they possessed, and fighting commenced instantly upon the deck of the Roman ship even before a shot was fired in either direction.

Fearghus filled in the gap behind the first three of his men as they hacked down unsuspecting archers and dueled with swordsmen. When the whole of their party reached the clearing of the deck, all eight men raced about parrying and thrusting their swords into the Roman legionaries.

Meanwhile, aboard the *Silverbeam*, Murchadh's skilled archers kept their shots low to avoid hitting the Celts. Before Fearghus's eyes, many Roman men fell dead to the terrible bolts, and the fighting Order of the Serpent held the upper hand.

But the Roman ship was armed with four catapults to the *Silverbeam's* one, and as Finghin's shots flew wide, one of the Roman fireballs found its mark among the many sailing through the air. It collided hard with the front deck of the ship, and before Irial's men could stop it, the fire was ravaging this area of the vessel.

The Roman ship was truly vast. Though it sported only one square sail, it possessed a gigantic set of three rooms above deck and a second deck above them reached by stairs. There were two entrances to the hold, and a great mass of flags throughout the rigging. There were no wood carvings upon the boat, but its catapults and thick hull were a menacing sight indeed.

Presently, when all of the Romans on the bottom deck had been vanquished, Fearghus's men, who now numbered five, hurtled up the stairs towards the remainder of the enemy sailors. But Fearghus had a different plan.

Looking about to make sure the coast was clear, he instead made his way to the stairs leading down into the hold. Slipping a few times, he finally stumbled into a vast room, larger than any he had seen but for the great hall of the monastery. Before him, a portly Roman man swung his hammers wide, missing him, and he was quick to plunge his own Manx sword into his stomach. Suddenly, another man, this one a taskmaster, cracked his whip hard upon Fearghus's hand, drawing blood.

"Stay back, you scum!" the oppressor screamed, swinging his weapon again.

Fearghus shielded himself with his arm, and the whip spun about it, catching fast on his wrist. Then he yanked the whip out of the man's hand with a snap of his arm, and the taskmaster tripped and came tumbling down. "You shall never again see the light of day!" he bellowed, and plunged his sword through this second defender.

Suddenly the room was filled with pleading voices. "Please save us!" one of the slaves screamed, pulling at his chains.

"You speak the language of Eire," Fearghus replied, "and so I must free you."

"Rescue us from these oppressors!" the man yelled.

Fearghus wasted no time in swinging his sword down hard on the chain joining them. With this blow, it was broken and the slaves immediately began to pull it through the bonds upon their sweaty ankles, finally coming free from the manacles.

These men were hideous. As they sat upon bloodstained wooden benches, their backs were streaked with sweat and blood together, and their angular frail bodies were weak and broken. Many possessed long beards, and most wore only loincloths.

"Cross to my ship," Fearghus told the man as his comrades scrambled up to the light.

"Whatever you desire, we shall do it," the slave replied, and as he followed the others up, he snatched up the warden's hammer.

Fearghus took one look around the musty hold, with its low benches and barrels, and then bounded up after the freedmen to survey the fight.

The *Silverbeam* was burning. A vast column of fire had crawled up the rigging, but nonetheless the few men aboard were beating it back, including Irial with a great skin of water over his shoulder. Already two Celtic archers had fallen behind the wooden blocks on the other side of the fight, but still four others sent their bolt into the fray.

Now Fearghus turned and leapt up the stairs to the secondary deck, pulling himself up the wooden railing with amazing agility. When he had ascended the next level, he was greeted with a great feeling of triumph. Even as he arrived, the last Roman aboard the ship, the valiant captain with all his golden armor and crimson decoration, felt the sting of Manx iron in his chest. They were victorious!

Then suddenly Fearghus noticed something. The *Silverbeam*, though it naturally was the smaller ship, was markedly lower in the water than the Roman vessel. "What's wrong?" Fearghus shouted to Irial on the other side.

"The new siding of the ship has sprung a leak!" Irial responded, cupping his hands about his lips.

Fearghus was crushed. The ship was sinking, slowly but surely, and they were going to lose it. "Get everyone across!" he commanded the men on the other side, and then cut loose a rope from the sail of the Roman ship, swinging across.

The first thing he did was rush down into the hold, where Agnos stood knee high in freezing water, too afraid to ascend the stairs for fear of a stray bolt. "The fight has ended," he told her instantly, stepping high as he ran to meet her.

"Then let us go from here!" she shouted, a grin across her joyous face.

"We'll have to leave the ship!" he cried, and swept her up into his arms. When they reached the deck, Murchadh's archers were already struggling to find ropes to swing across from. Thinking quickly to solve this, Fearghus drew his sword once again and pried loose a new board from the side of the captain's cabin. As

Agnos watched, he threw it across the space between the two boats, and it barely reached.

"Climb across!" he shouted, and planted his feet to hold the board still as its incline increased.

"The entire hold's full of water!" Agnos suddenly shrieked, peering down into the stairway. "Hurry!" she added nervously.

"Get yourself across this plank!" he shouted to her as the last man scrambled up it. When she had, he tossed it aside and jumped to the ropes, scanning the Roman ship opposite him. Every man just rescued was standing upon the deck amidst the Roman bodies. Then Fearghus noticed something. Not one of them held a lance! Osgar was still down below in the hold!

"I'm getting Osgar!" he assured Seadna who nodded across the way on the secondary deck. Before he had fully grasped the situation, he found himself stumbling to the passage to the hold, but already the water within it had reached the level of the deck, and the floor he stood on was glazed with water.

There was only one thing to do. Wasting no time, he leapt into the cold salty water and swam down into the room as fast as he could. His strong legs churned at their highest capacity under the weight of his armor, and the seawater stung his eyes.

But where was Osgar? He could hardly see what lie about the watery chamber in the light from above, but still expected to see the sacred lance where he had left it; leaning against the wall opposite the armory. Though he groped for, it, he could not find it here or anywhere amongst the rest of the heavy weapons.

Then he realized that the javelin was of wood, and it would float. Maybe it had reached the ceiling. When this idea failed, his lungs were near to bursting and his eyes began to expel blood. Then he looked to his left and right and observed the holes in the side of the ship that the oars protruded from. He noticed that many had disappeared through the holes. Now Fearghus had one more option to explore. Yanking the paddle from the breach closest to where Osgar had been, he pulled himself through it and looked desperately about until, miraculously, he beheld the spear itself slowly sinking by the weight of its head below the belly of the ship. Snatching it up, he put his last strength into his legs and propelled himself up to the air, gasping for it.

"There he is!" Murchadh suddenly shouted, pointing to him. Before he knew, it, the warriors had jumped into the surf and pulled him up onto the main deck of the Roman vessel. Behind him, strangely, the *Silverbeam* had sunk entirely but for the top of its mast, and the once grand pirate ship was swallowed by the vengeful Sea.

Fearghus lay there, breathing heavily, and blood rushed out from his nose and eyes. "Well, my friend," Seadna sighed, "I say we've weathered just about everything by now."

Fearghus could only nod his head and mutter, "but all for the glory of Eire!"

Fearghus stayed there for the rest of the day, shaken by the terrible nautical experience. A cool breeze from the Sea all around them refreshed his burning nostrils, and he closed his eyes, sleeping soundly with Osgar still in his grasp.

When night came he stood up for the first time that day, examining his notched sword, and proceeded to explore his new ship. Osgar he leaned upon, as a sage leans upon his walking stick, for his body ached of exhaustion that hung about his legs and chest like several articles of thick armor.

The prize of the recent battle, that is, the ship itself, was grand and sturdy, far greater than the *Silverbeam* in both speed and size. The deck was immense and open, and the mast was like the trunk of a tree.

However, their journey aboard this amazing vessel would be short lived. Soon the cliffs of old Eire would appear on the horizons, and in a few days the few warriors aboard the ship would rejoin what remained of the besieged men within the walled mission.

Finally the day came. From afar, Fearghus's eyes spotted Eire far beyond them, and to him it seemed only but a rock on the horizon, but beyond that rock there lay the greatest land of all. Upon it were great forests, mountains, rivers and streams, all the work of the gods.

As they slowly neared the land, preparations were made to descend to the beach at the pirate's cove, a flat area covered smoothly with ash. It was not long before Fearghus was squinting against the light of the sun reflecting off of the white bluffs near the encircling forest. Beyond them he could see already the valley of the pirate's cove.

Suddenly he noticed something that caused him to be very alarmed. Merely a flash of light it was, but it came from the very heart of the natural harbor. Almost immediately, Fearghus was back to the chambers of the ship, alerting the few men he commanded. "Take up your arms!" he shouted fiercely.

There was a rustling of men scurrying up to the deck and through the doors of the cabins, their armor and weapons clanking loudly against each other. Unfortunately, there were no horses or wagons aboard this ship as there had often been on the *Silverbeam*.

Fearghus strode back to the forecastle, a grave look set upon his grizzled face. Suddenly, Seadna joined him, giving him a start. "We will make a diversion," he said, for indeed there were evidently many Romans camped upon the land where they likely had witnessed the departure of their quest.

"Lucky are we to have this Roman sail above our heads," Fearghus observed, agreeing to the plan.

"It is a token of immunity upon the seas," Seadna said, looking up.

By then the men were hoisting the exit ramp up in preparation to slam it down and run for it. "Except when you run into the Celts," Fearghus replied light-heartedly.

They drew nearer to the shore, keeping closely hidden signs of nationality or intention. As Fearghus stood concealed near the forecastle, suddenly he was approached by one of his men, accompanied by Irial, and both were dressed as Roman guards having taken the finely crafted armor from the dead aboard the vessel. Irial was wearing a breastplate, interlocking sheets of armor around his middle, and also an undecorated helmet, set of square pauldrons, and greaves, all of Roman steel and polished to perfection. The weapon the two carried was a tall and simple pike, coming to a sinisterly small point high above their heads. It was vastly different from the common Celtic javelin.

"We'll go down first," Irial said. "And when they least expect it, we'll sound our attack."

"May the gods be with you," Fearghus responded, peering over his cover.

Irial nodded as his companion turned on his heel and left them. "We'll be the ones without helmets on," he informed his master, and followed the man.

Fearghus made his way to the back of the boat, just before the vessel stopped alongside the land. There he found Murchadh, and behind him, Agnos. "I'm trusting you with the life of her," he whispered to his captain, and suddenly they heard the creak of the boarding ramp as it allowed Irial and his friend passage off of the boat.

Before the voices of the inquisitive Romans were heard, Fearghus rejoined the remainder of his men waiting silently behind the front cabin. As he arrived, it was suddenly time. The shout of Irial rang through the air as he ripped off his helmet and skewered the soldier before him, all as planned. The blade of his Celtic blade hissed against its scabbard as he drew it to the next Roman, and as he did the swords of all his men suddenly blazed in the sun: Fearghus at the rear, the Order of the Serpent spilled down onto the ground. Behind them came Murchadh standing before Agnos, his bow twanging twice every breath. With him he brought Osgar, for Fearghus in the fight would not dare risk its well-being either.

Fearghus couldn't wait to be back in the heat of battle. Sprinting as quickly as he could, he soon was at the head of their attack, hacking and thrusting down Romans with vigor and grace.

The men staggered from skirmish to skirmish, ending each as quickly as it had begun, but at length Fearghus realized something was not right. More Romans were streaming down the sandy path connecting the cove with the land above, and the size of their endless ranks was beginning in itself to bite deep into the morale of the fighters behind him.

The sun seemed to tear across the sky, and as soon as Fearghus's shadow moved two paces east there came another report from his men that one of their ranks had been taken down by an arrow, or slashed by a Roman sword. By dusk, half of them had either fallen dead or collapsed of exhaustion, and the remaining men formed a tight knot about their fallen comrades, and many were clambering back to the ship.

It was at this time that Finghin had a novel idea. "I'll see if I can get that catapult working!" he shouted across the blood-bathed clearing.

"Certainly we will need more help than we thought we required," Seadna observed, agreeing with this plan.

Fearghus continued to slash the Roman soldiers as exhaustion slowly engulfed his body. Occasionally, he would encounter a curiously skilled soldier, and the two would duel for a while before help from a Celtic arrow or a mistake from his enemy would save Fearghus. As sweat rolled down his face he could only concentrate on one thing: again reaching Eire, where for so many years he had led his flock of sheep through sunny meadows and grassy plains, and where now there lay a besieged monastery needing very dearly his help.

As the efficient world of the Roman military closed in about him, suddenly more disappointment reached Fearghus. Pausing in his fight, he peered back to the ship, where Finghin had made fast his path to re-arm the catapults, and thus spill fire upon the Roman hoard. But when Fearghus looked back, no fire had yet reaped its wrath upon the Romans, but instead upon the ship. The gallant vessel was aflame!

But there was the valiant Finghin, leaping atop the deck and scrambling to his post on the upper floor. His helm gleamed white amidst the ruddy fire, and its wrath encircled him as he was a last besieged hope amidst the flames of the underworld.

Then the mysterious fire of the catapult rained down on the Romans, but it did not burn, for the ground was already burnt black and the corpses of the Roman cause were wet with blood and sweat. Only their clothes burned and consumed them, but in their crowded numbers many would die this way, and Finghin's aid proved its worth.

Dusk made its course, and with it came a final tragedy. Fearghus had since rejoined his men as the Romans briefly regrouped, and as they huddled Fearghus caught a glimpse of the ship, and all its glory had been destroyed. As he looked upon it, he suddenly shut his eyes hard: as one last stream of fire flew from the blackened deck, the burning Finghin fell dead into the water. His body was as if a vengeful dark spirit against the blazing flame that enveloped his body, and great columns of steam from the sea heralded his noble end.

The Romans were proclaiming the death they brought with them. Fearghus and the others could not understand their speech, but it rang cold and chilling in the salty breeze. Agnos and Seadna who heard their words both cringed alike, but neither wavered. "They are reading warrants for our execution," the pirate would finally tell the warriors about him. His voice was both cautious and frightened, both warning and friendly.

At last the Romans withdrew, their losses great, and the four dead men of the Order of the Serpent were briefly lamented and buried under sand and stone from the surrounding area. Few in the company rested that night as they huddled near the water.

Fearghus lay awake for a great while, shielding Agnos with his battered body. For what seemed like eternity he stared at the reflection of the moon upon the calm sea just in front of him, and though he did not sleep, he reached a state of calm, one with the sea and without thought. He did not think of how his men had been routed by the swarm of Romans or what it would take to pass their blockade, he only lay there completely still looking at one spot upon the ever changing waters.

When the pink light of dawn passed above the horizon, Fearghus watched it, too, as it slowly changed but seemed always to stay constant. After much more time, suddenly this tranquil scene was interrupted: the battle cry of Rome rent the air behind him, and the sound of stumbling, charging soldiers followed it.

Fearghus picked up his sword; he had never sheathed it. Barking orders quickly to his men to assemble at the water's edge, he himself raised his sword defiantly to the oncoming assault. When he looked up, his eyes piercing the darkness, he was crushed.

A vast line of attackers was advancing on them in greatly unorganized form, but their numbers were menacingly great and their weapons were protruding from their ranks in all directions like a thorny bush. Those of the Celts that carried shields raised them, and the others could only have their swords or lances out in front of them, ready to absorb the first line of Romans.

When the two forces, the small knot of Celts and the gargantuan line of Romans, came in contact, the result was spontaneous and violent. The first Romans fell upon the Celtic blades and dropped quickly, but then duels sprang up upon the short line, and the Romans on both sides of them closed in, forming a trap.

Two brave Celts fell, each next to Fearghus as he stood, for there the Roman put their bravest. The fighters remained in darkness as they fought for a great while, and at length no man cried aloud, for the fighting was too intense.

Before Fearghus knew it, two more had fallen, and now in a tight knot only Murchadh, Irial, Seadna, and five stout spearmen stood alongside Fearghus and his love Agnos, who shielded her eyes behind Murchadh, her guardian.

That group held their position for a long time until the sun had fully risen, and by then all eleven stood in the freezing water. The sword of Fearghus sailed left and right, up and down, and diagonally as it sang through Roman armor, and a barrier of bodies seemed somehow to slow the Roman advance, if at least a bit.

At length Fearghus was breathing heavily, and before him a warrior was skewered fully by a thin Roman lance, and before him the man's body was defiled many times through with the points of thick Roman weapons. Blood spread through the water about the company's ankles, staining their garments and sandals.

Suddenly realizing hopelessness, Fearghus cried aloud, "For Eire!" and hurled himself into the Roman hoard. Slashing and thrusting, he plowed through the sweaty bodies of the men, knocking more down than he killed. And as he went he grit his teeth and strained his fists, for lances were plunged into his stomach and swords cut across his back. For every sweep of his blade a new shock of pain racked his body, and he winced through much loss of blood, until his eyes grew dim and the light of dawn could not keep pace with the face of death.

At last he fell to his knees before one Roman, horribly weakened and spitting forth blood and flesh. And this one Roman he studied as his eyes struggled to stay open, and the man was the deliverer of death. All other soldiers became obsolete, and only this man, with his shining new armor and soft cape remained. His broad, heavy sword was lifted high above his head in what seemed like eternity, but Fearghus knew it would come down on him at a much faster pace than it had risen.

Fearghus cast his eyes down, welcoming death at the hands of his worst enemies, but before he had lost sight of the Roman he noticed something very strange take place: it seemed to him that the point of an arrow burst through the man's breast, but at that moment he could not decide if it was true, and collapsed unconscious to the soft black ground.

The events thereafter were described to him later in the monastery where he subsequently awoke: Where he had fallen amongst the Romans was in fact the furthest extent of their ranks, for long and hard the men of the monastery had mowed down the rear of their forces with bows and lances, and had luckily come to the pirate's cove on that day. The Romans were hewn down from behind by the superior Celtic numbers and the nine of Fearghus's company were saved quickly after his collapse. Yet another time the Romans had been defeated in battle, but they gathered thickly in the encircling forest and would not give up now. Osgar had since been returned to Fearghus's side as he lay in bed in the monastery, and a great celebration had been sparked outside his door.

The sun shone warmly when Fearghus hobbled out into the courtyard, upon a cane for all the wounds he had suffered. This field in the center of the walled mission was green like the rest of Eire, but the men about had not always felt this happiness. Conn joined his old friend in the middle of the courtyard as he surveyed the building around him, and began to speak of the events since their departure.

"Our halls have been racked with disease and fire," was the first he spoke of.

"How has my absence treated you?" Fearghus asked, leaning upon the smith.

"The Romans have sent fire and arrows over these walls," Conn replied gravely, "but we have remained safely within the whole while."

"I am impressed," Fearghus told him.

"Our supply of food went bad once while you were gone, then half of our men were possessed of a terrible plague," Conn continued, "and we lost a good number of men, though many recovered by work of their wives and the grace of the gods."

"I am very pleased with your condition," Fearghus told him, at length, lamenting the losses and silently celebrating the victories. "But I am afraid that no magic has come from Osgar, though I have retrieved it."

Conn seemed unchanged by this news and supported his weakened friend. "That is nothing to be ashamed of," he insisted. "Rather," he continued, "it is a wonderful and courageous feat of yours, a testament to your worthiness as holder of the spear and Lord of all Eire."

That night Fearghus settled back into the room where before he had slept for many days safely in the walls of the hijacked monastery. It was untouched as he imagined it to be, just as he had left it: a bed of straw and cloth, and a fire pit.

Here were hung new Celtic clothes to replace his bloodstained Manx garments, and a good store of weapons and food.

The next day Fearghus slept soundly to midday, until Agnos, who had awaken much earlier, woke him. This morning she had been given fresh crimson clothes, and had patiently waited for him before leaving to eat in the great hall. Refreshing himself in a pool of cool water, he then followed her there, and met all the leaders of the monastery at the head of the table, which was meagerly laden with bowls of broth and scraps of bread. Fearghus, however, was given a vast portion of meat and ale. "I shall not be treated so highly," he muttered as he approached it. "Spread this evenly among the men."

His orders were promptly followed by his men as if they were his attentive servants, and prostration was, to his dismay, practiced often at his passing glance. The warriors treated him as if he were a god! "The men are talking of a great new age of prosperity!" Irial told him ecstatically as he sat down, ignoring his food. Next to him, Murchadh was solemn as usual, and Seadna looked longingly aside.

"That is good," Fearghus mumbled, "but too fast an assumption."

"True," the lumberman answered.

"We must discuss this new Order of the Serpent," Fearghus mentioned at length, pushing aside his bowl. When he said this, Murchadh perked up, for he was the esteemed captain of these elite fighting men.

"What say you of it?" Seadna asked.

"It will be a useful tool in this war," Fearghus replied, looking directly at his new friend.

As Fearghus looked at Seadna, at his grizzled face and tired eyes, suddenly the pirate's face was set with intense thought, and he opened his mouth to speak. "We will surely have to add to the Order," he reasoned.

"That sounds like a good plan," Irial commented, but Seadna interrupted him.

"We shall create a training course for new members, and thus train the whole lot of these men into fierce fighting men," he spewed out, proud of his idea.

Fearghus stood up, disregarding his hunger. "I commission you, Murchadh, as the instructor of this program. I myself shall oversee the first of your sessions."

Later that day, one of the warriors barked this command out to the men as they gathered in the courtyard, and by dusk, over twenty-five fresh men met in council with their two leaders, respectively Murchadh and Fearghus himself.

There plans were made to train the men in the open courtyard each morning, and thus produce an elite force of fighters to lead the rest into battle against the Romans. Already there were six regarded as highly skilled for their contributions to the Quest for Osgar, and thus the spear itself was delivered specifically into their protection led by Murchadh.

Agnos observed her love, Fearghus, the next morning from afar, as he stood among the men in the courtyard. Beside him, as planned, Murchadh held a lance, and with it demonstrated the proper form of thrusting and slashing. By midday the men were running about the overgrown lawn cracking each other with wooden rods and pretending to stab lances into imaginary Romans before them.

Fearghus did not personally attend the next few meetings, but throughout the day the men sweated and grunted, for their training intensified at each interval. One day as he strolled through the shadows of the buildings Fearghus would see them swinging wooden swords fashioned by Irial and the next they would be taking wild bow shots at rotten fruit. The wise Murchadh had adopted a strenuous daily training program, and each day the men drew closer to his goal: creating the perfect warrior. To the captain, such a man would be skilled not only in the arts of hand-to hand combat and long range attacks, but also in the fundamentals of confidence, bluffing and scare tactics, camaraderie, morality, and courtesy.

Throughout these initial days of recuperation, Fearghus followed a repetitive schedule. He woke each morning and attended a communal breakfast with the men. After this he would retire to his quarters once again and relax with Agnos, or else work to maintain his clothes and armor. Later in the day he would pursue his own personal training, all in preparation for one final battle he had been planning. This was what he pursued as dusk set in; for a while he would pore over drawings of his own design, and on them were his mechanical plans for routing the Romans. He had very little manpower to work with, though, but this did not deter his hopes.

When darkness beset the monastery, Fearghus would often sup alone with Agnos, only rarely attending the communal bonfire dinners in the courtyard. The air was much warmer inside their small quarters, for these nights a cold wind was upon them from the north.

Then, when their fire fell and moonlight streamed through the doorway, Fearghus would sleep soundly in the chilly air with Agnos by his side, and try to clear his mind of thoughts about war and prejudice, entering a dark world of dreams and fantasies.

It was on the fifth day that Fearghus, while eating a meager portion with his companions, was asked by Seadna to attend a specialized meeting concerning hostilities with the Romans, this being in one of the larger buildings at the rear of the monastery where many supplies were stored.

Seadna opened the meeting with a simple question: "How will we get past the Romans to refresh our waning food supplies?"

Fearghus indeed had noticed the recent shortage of water and food. He knew very well that the sustenance of the warriors was running very low, but had not considered the immense task of acquiring more food. Without a ship, it would be impossible to fish for food, and since the Romans infested every corner of the woods and meadows in the surrounding area, it would be impossible to hunt for it. Only contribution from a village could provide enough food to maintain Fearghus's army, but every one south of here had been burned by the Romans, and the northern settlements harried by pirates.

Seadna looked coldly upon his friend and master. "What shall we do to keep alive our efforts?" he demanded, struggling through the common reverence every man held in Fearghus's presence.

Fearghus could not let his people down. He had to think of some solution. Several minutes he spent in deep meditation right there at the table as the other men waited, and finally he came to a resolution. "The only end we have," he answered slowly, "is in attack."

Seadna's eyes grew large and his face wrinkled in disgust. "But we are not ready!" he insisted, pacing back and forth. "We cannot possibly face the Romans now…" he continued tentatively.

But Irial countered. "We must face them in battle either way," he reasoned. "Now we must choose our enemy: Rome or hunger."

Murchadh, as Captain of the Serpent Warriors, was also present. "If it must be done, then I am ready for it," he added.

Now Fearghus stood up and pleaded his case. "We have just tasted victory on the Romans on the North side," he reminded them, "and their confidence is stretched thinner than ours."

Seadna cut in, curtly remarking, "How does one have a low morale when he has food to eat each night? Water to drink each night?"

Fearghus continued indifferently his speech. "We have prepared our men for a few days now," he said, "and with little more time they shall be ready to fight. I say we go for the last killing blow, and for the third time take the victory we deserve from these offenders."

Seadna sat back down and considered the idea. "We shall have supplies to last yet thirty more days," he told them.

"And I will have my men ready in twenty!" Murchadh burst, his eyes wild with excitement.

"Then it is decided," Fearghus concluded. "We will attack when we have decided the time is right, and when we are not starving."

At this time, Fearghus did not realize what he was doing. To make such a move at this time would risk everything the warriors in the monastery stood for, the life, freedom, and religion of Eire.

Thereafter, Fearghus tried his best to relieve his mind of the intense burden that lay upon it. In a short while he would be leading his army against a larger, more efficient foe.

Chapter 13

A New Beginning

The days that passed as they prepared for attack passed interminably by. Fearghus was active in these days, and his body was racked with anticipation and fear. Every day he climbed to the top of the wall and surveyed the encircling forest, where there lay hidden probably hundreds of angry Roman soldiers, eager for revenge and compensation for their losses and the defilement of their missionaries. But Fearghus would not allow them to rule his people. He wouldn't soon let this stronghold fall under his vigilant watch.

One morning when the air was cold and crisp, Fearghus himself called his friends into council. Seadna, the general leader of these meetings and such, was rather surprised. The leaders gathered in the early hours of the morn in the main hall, and Fearghus's countenance was grim and foreboding.

"Tomorrow, we attack!" was all he had to say to set the mood in the now deserted room.

The leaders around him said nothing. All were fixed in deep thought. Death had always been present in their thoughts, but not so much as now. If they didn't attack, they couldn't secure a supply of food, and if they did, they would risk a great loss. Nonetheless, hopes were high that the newly christened Serpent Warriors would become the deciding force in an upcoming victory over the Romans once and for all.

"We will attack hard in the center with our subordinate forces," Irial commented. "With a strong archer front on the wall and a small cavalry charge on one of the flanks we should be able to inflict serious damage on the legions."

"That sounds like as good a plan as any," Fearghus commented. "And what of the Order?"

Murchadh sat up wearily in his seat. "We will stay within the walls until you give your command to charge," he mumbled. "Wait until the enemy has lost some soldiers, and then let my men at them."

"That seems a sound plan as well," Fearghus agreed. "Anything else?"

Seadna was quick to add his wise observations to the conversation. "The Romans outnumber us five to one," he told them, "but if we can claim victory now, their inability to find reinforcements could be their bane."

The leaders then began laboriously to study all of the maps and diagrams that Fearghus had drawn up in the past days, agreeing with some ideas and rejecting others. They discussed every possible outcome of battle, every plan of action to be taken, every detail of weaponry and armor. As they argued Fearghus's anxiety grew stronger and stronger until finally, when the men began to forage for food in the waning store, he disbanded the council and was off to his lodgings to think alone.

In his room, as he expected, he met Agnos, reclining upon the bed, still exhausted as a result of Fearghus's late night working by the fire and nervous fits during the night. Fearghus's fear was getting the better of him now, and though he had fought for and won Osgar, he now felt more vulnerable to death and pain than ever. Agnos did her best to ease his suffering, assuring him of his own strength, but nevertheless he worried endlessly.

Agnos hadn't had her morning meal yet, still waiting for him to return from his meeting. When he stumbled in she sat up, moving to the side of the bed, and smoothed out her clothing. "You must stop your fear," she said sternly, as he proceeded to sit down beside her.

"But I feel I cannot escape it," he replied earnestly, beseeching her comforting face.

Agnos's face in his gaze turned sharp and concentrated. "Not the Romans or any army in this world can measure up to our men," she said slowly. "But in order for you to prove this you have to believe that it can and will be done! A cowardly general is no general at all, but a burden to those he commands!" she added forcefully.

Fearghus drew away from her, frustrated, and began to pace back and forth in the humble room. Words from everyone he had spoken to in his entire life flashed through his mind: words of encouragement, of disdain, and words of wisdom. Each phrase battled the other. On one hand, Seadna was telling him not to worry until danger comes, but then there was his long dead father telling him he was too young to go on a hunt with his older brothers. But then again there was Agnos just as she had been moments before, telling him to cease his cowardice and take up his sword with pride and confidence, and everything seemed all right. Turning to her, he said, "You speak the words of truth. If I shall lead my people into battle, then I shall do so to win."

Agnos stood up and embraced him tightly, and they shared a kiss. Outside in the courtyard, the deep sound of a warrior's voice rang through the chilly air. It was Aodh, a veteran of the Serpent Warriors from the recent quest, and his voice, usually used for singing tunes with his lyre, was oddly robust and heavy. "It has been decreed by your supreme leader Fearghus the King, that attack be carried out upon the Romans at dawn tomorrow morning. Fighters will be briefed on formation and other attack strategies at that time," he bellowed, and at that a frenzied murmur swept through the scattered ranks of the warriors, very loud as Fearghus listened from his room.

The two lovers attended the communal breakfast this morning with the warriors and Fearghus ate sparingly, for his stomach was unsettled with fear. Agnos ate hungrily though, helping Fearghus clear his plate of vegetables and bread, and this so covertly he hardly noticed. She obviously was nervous about the coming battle as well, except in an opposite manner. This last meal, though, was clearly meager as was every other meal they had shared since he had returned, and very inadequate for full satisfaction.

Fearghus tried not to strain his mind today. It was already filled with perceptions of both victory and defeat, and he wished not to add to his suffering with deep thought or further consideration about the upcoming events. On the contrary, he stayed close to his love Agnos, for only in her could he find refuge from the fear that possessed him.

The day, surprisingly, passed as quickly as Fearghus wished it to and the advent of night found him preparing for sleep alongside Agnos, before a dwindling fire. As the sounds of the warriors below the stars upon the courtyard came to an eerie halt, Fearghus still lay awake with Agnos in his arms, frightened as ever. Eventually though, he moved closer to her and there found troubled sleep.

The next morning Fearghus was gently shaken awake by Agnos, and behind her silhouette as he dazedly rubbed his eyes, he made out the figure of the ever vigilant Seadna, who was up early this day waking the men and assigning them to their positions. He tarried only a very short while in their quarters, and then slunk to the building next to them.

While the men gathered outside, Agnos helped Fearghus to put on his battered armor, which, though dented, had been cleaned and polished to shine like the sun. This was the armor of his people, different than that he had been given by the Manx, and it was of tough iron. Everything had been saved for him from the recent quest; there was a decorated chest plate, greaves and pauldrons, a leather fauld, and leather gauntlets. Of course, in addition to this, he also donned the Crown of the Deep, gleaming with the diamonds and gold of the pirates. The shield he used was a short rectangular iron pavise with intricate engravings and rounded corners.

Fearghus then took up a virgin sword, forged for him by Conn himself. It was a blade of tough steel from the far East, and its hilt was adorned with gold and wrapped in soft leather. It was a double-edged weapon and the longest rapier Fearghus had ever seen. He would use it well in the coming battle to slash enemies on all sides of him, and parry the blows of those who might escape his wrath.

The men were assembling quickly in the courtyard, already forming angular ranks. Some of the archers were climbing the stairs in the watch tower to ascend the wall, while others of their kind busied themselves gathering and sharpening their darts and stringing more tightly their bows. Stockpiles of lances, axes and swords were spilled onto the lawn and distributed amongst some of the fighters in need of weapons. Conn, to say the least, had not been idle in his trade whilst the expedition was gone.

Presently, Fearghus was given a horse, clad heavily in armor that Conn had devised and furbished with a comfortable saddle and a leather cylinder of arrows, a bow, and a short axe. Not many other men were provided steeds, for their number was waning within the monastery, but the small cavalry group and each of Fearghus's friends were given mounts, for advantage in the conflict. Fearghus hadn't much experience riding, but was confident he could easily gallop this animal into battle.

And finally, they began. In the time it had taken to dress and arm Fearghus, the men had formed their ranks under Seadna's direction, and as Fearghus walked his horse to the helm of the warriors, he noticed the musician Aodh atop the wall, a horn poised upon his lips. All that Fearghus had to do was give the command now and he would blow it, sending the Celts hurtling into battle with the Romans, who seemed almost as if assembling themselves, across the field, though nevertheless they would be surprised with the attack.

Slowly, sinisterly, the last few moments before battle passed and Fearghus, upon a nod from Seadna mounted behind him, drew his long, untouched blade, brandished it twice above his head, and let it fall. Instantly, the horn sounded for battle and the gates swung open simultaneously, Fearghus leading a desperate charge ahead unto the grassy field. The sound of the blaring horn sent a chill of both pride and fear through the ranks of warriors. In its terrible sound, excitement filled Fearghus's breast and he gasped for air, looking intently upon the border of the encircling forest where the Romans were quickly preparing their defense. Aodh blew three times, each blast louder than the one before it, and all deafeningly loud.

Fearghus's cape was lifted behind him and strained against his shoulders just as did the tail of his steed. A small group of Romans lay just ahead of him, galloping alone in the bright sun, and as he hurtled into them he cried aloud as if he was being stabbed, but it was a loud cry of fury and not fear, and it frightened the Roman foot soldiers near him greatly.

His sword flashed in the light as it sang through the air, first sailing down on the men on one side of Fearghus and then on the other. The Romans didn't have a chance. Their skulls were rent with his sharp blade and blood spewed forth from their helmets. Before the rest of the Celts arrived, Fearghus had slain nearly every man there, his horse literally untouched by Roman steel. Their tall lances he shattered with a sweep of his sword, and their thick armor he shredded with an overhead swing. Not but one lance was thrust into his shield, and its owner he beheaded skillfully among others.

The first skirmish ended as quickly as it had started. When a few Romans sprang from the trees to avenge their kin, they were mowed down with arrows from within the party surrounding Fearghus, and their small numbers were easily reduced to nearly nothing. However, the Roman army here in Eire was vast, and spread heavily in the trees of the forest. As the party regrouped in the center of the field, they kept their shields up to protect from a shower of arrows. The skilled marksmen atop the wall of the monastery noticed this, and put an end to the harassment with their own carefully aimed volleys of projectiles.

Fearghus wheeled his horse around several times surveying the trees for a surprise charge from the Romans, but nothing happened. At last he spotted gleaming Roman armor on the west side and proceeded to make a second charge there. Shouting, he galloped towards the forest.

But then something very evil occurred. As they neared the trees, a surprise attack from the Romans cost them serious manpower. Before they could retreat, twenty soldiers had come out of hiding in the bushes, and they were archers and lance casters. Arrows bouncing off of his shield, Fearghus was forced to turn and run away. His men were not so lucky. Ten men at least fell dead to the group with lances run straight through them, while others cried with pain as they attempted to pull arrows out of their sides or their legs out from under their dead horses. The Romans had just expertly exacted their revenge on the warriors.

Once again Fearghus regrouped his forces in the middle of the field, but there was no refuge here or anywhere but inside the monastery. Nearly a hundred Roman soldiers had now drawn up in a straight line at the edge of the trees, and their heavily armored faces were shrouded with the shadow of the forest. Their armor and weaponry did not gleam but glowed dully, and to Fearghus it seemed their ranks stretched across the entire length of the field. Fearghus couldn't see their lances, but he knew the points of these modern pikes were sinisterly small, and just as dangerous as delicate. The Roman swords, he also knew, were stout and powerful double-sided blades, very dangerous to his men.

Now the Romans attacked in full. Sunlight blazed off of their interlocking armor as they ran forward with a great cry, and every soldier raised his sword and shield simultaneously. They were an awesome fighting force, the greatest in the world. Woe was to him that challenged this type of organized fury, and unfortunately, the Celts were doing just that. Fearghus had heard of the terrible wars of the old days when Rome conquered the Celts of Britain, and there established permanently their religion. He wouldn't let the Romans take Eire, though. He had to keep alive the worship of Sucellos and the other gods under him, and hold the tradition of his forefathers safe from these perpetrators.

Keeping these thoughts in his mind he galloped his horse ahead and smashed into the Roman lines like the blow of a hammer, smashing the fancy Roman shields with their great golden eagles and cleaving the soldiers' shiny smooth armor. His teeth grit, his mouth in a hateful snarl, he grunted with satisfaction as his sword rose and fell, ringing against the helms of lesser men than himself. All the might of the gods strained as one with his ferocious swings, and sweat rolled down his face like raindrops.

Behind him the other men were faring not quite so well. Indeed they had engaged the Roman hoards, but both sides were weathering blow for blow, and though Fearghus was charging through the ranks, the Romans were in some way driving back his men, and the Celts were outnumbered vastly.

But Fearghus could not gamble with the lives of his Serpent Warriors now. He had to wait and see how his standard fighters fared. During this time he was taking great quantities of Romans himself, and around him the enemy began to retreat. They did not wish to face this terrible King of Eire, for in Fearghus's fighting he had taken many more lives than had the whole of his men, and the Roman forces were waning.

At last he did it. The Romans were driven back, arrows still smashing into their rear lines, and their bodies littered the ground. But amongst these there lay vast amounts of Celtic dead. They had fought valiantly, but the Romans, somehow had fought better. Now Fearghus led his thin line of men back to the gate.

But it did not open. Upon the wall, where Seadna was surveying the battle, the former pirate was waving his arms in the air desperately, and when Fearghus looked up, all he could do was point behind them towards the forest. He had noticed something Fearghus hadn't noticed before. When Fearghus looked back though, it was plain to see. The whole of the Roman forces in Eire had emerged from the forest, and they numbered several hundred in size, rank on rank, and included a sizeable cavalry division. Fearghus was literally in awe. Was he to pit his hundred good men against the might of a thousand? Apparently, he was.

Fearghus dismounted his horse, passing it onto one of his most trustful fighters. Drawing his sword, he swung it several times in the air and cried "For Eire!" as loud as he dared. His men, in a tight cluster before him, also drew their swords or hoisted their pikes into the air and cheered. They would inflict as serious a wound as they could upon the Romans now, for the Romans would have no way to regain the men they would lose in this fight. The Celts, on the other hand, if they lived, would be able to recruit new fighters from the villages further west. In this hope they kept their cause alive, for without it they were utterly doomed.

The warriors positioned themselves defensively in a crescent about the monastery gates, as already volleys of arrows from the bowmen sailed to the endless Roman lines. Few fell, but their efforts produced quite a comforting effect for the fighters below them, a spark of hope that arrows maybe could take out the Romans before they even reached the gates. But this was impossible against the thick Roman shields and armor.

Much time passed before the Romans set upon them, but when they did, Fearghus was there to put his hand against theirs. He was standing upon the ground now, and here his sword would be vastly more effective. Instead of attempting to swing his blade low to his side as he would atop a horse, he would now be able to slash it hard across his enemies and thrust it deep into their armor. He was no good at riding a horse, anyway.

And then the first Romans the young and the inexperienced, hurtled into them. These men fought well but foolishly, and Fearghus found that he could only kill as fast as the rest of his men, all holding their ground and already stumbling over the dead of Rome. All the while the archers of the Order picked off as many Romans as they could.

Once again Fearghus plunged with excitement into the tightly packed Roman lines. His sword dispatched men at a horrendously fast rate, and he made his way even to the rear of the thousand men where marched the elder fighters, the experienced ones. He cared not how fared the men at the gate, for now he was alone amongst his greatest enemies. He fervently cut down as many men as he dared, blocking as he had to, but generally taking most blows for himself. He tried to forget the expressions upon the faces of the men he slew as they fell, but as the day progressed he was haunted by these images.

This routine carried on for a great while until the sun, shrouded in thick clouds, was beginning to set below the tops of the trees, and then Fearghus realized disaster had struck. He knew that if the Celts could hold out for the day that they could win the day, but when the strength of the men about him thinned and he began to make his way back to the gate, something was different. While a few arrows from above still fell into the crowd of Roman soldiers, which had in itself hardly gotten smaller at all, the Romans were busying themselves at ramming through the weak monastery gate doors, which, though reinforced with strong timbers from the surrounding forest, were extremely vulnerable to the steady ram that the Romans heaved against them, and not a warrior was in sight to stop them. He was too late!

Fearghus hacked down man after man from behind, but when he neared the rammers he was waylaid with strong resistance and slashed a few times; he was forced finally to withdraw from these tough guards and push his way out of the ranks, all the while deflecting heavy blows and slashing at the Romans. When he reached the edge of the forest where now no Romans remained, he signaled to Aodh and Seadna atop the wall just above the gate. Intensely surveying the hundreds of Romans stumbling over hundreds of their own casualties, the two did not notice him. However, he wouldn't give up now. Quickly dispatching a Roman bearing a torch that was near him, he lit the man's garments afire and waved the burning cloth overhead. Though it burned him, he soon caught the attention of every man there, including the Roman soldiers. He sickeningly knew now that he alone remained of the soldiers originally deployed to attack the Romans, and that included Irial.

Seadna waved his arms once more in a distress signal, somehow telling Fearghus to find his way to the side of the monastery. It was then, Fearghus realized that there was a small door on that wall to let sheep in and out. It had been used numerous times by the men before and would have to serve its purpose once more for him. If he could only reach it!

He was near the forest, and the forest would provide him cover, he reasoned. If any Romans still remained in the trees he would have their heads, though this was unlikely judging from the sheer size of the group crowding the field.

Now he was sprinting through the dark forest, and as he ran the sun disappeared completely, giving way to only the light of the torches the Romans had lit. Fearghus used them as a guide as he weaved randomly through the trunks of the saplings at the edge of the encircling forest. Little to his surprise, he did not encounter any Romans here, and soon he had come parallel with the small door he sought after.

Finally, it was a sprint to the door. Though he could not clearly make it out, when he neared it he beheld the gleam of Celtic armor as one lone warrior held his position secretly in the doorway, almost unnoticed behind a stout shield. When Fearghus came hurtling towards him he readied his sword to defend himself, but then recognized his king and stood momentarily aside to let him in. When Fearghus was safely inside the corridor, the man swung the thick wooden door shut and reset an iron trap of spikes the men had devised to secure this secret passage.

Fearghus felt little change when he dashed out into the courtyard where the Order of the Serpent still stood still, waiting for his command that didn't come. Now they could not have their fight against the Romans, for to open the gate now would invite inside the still hundreds of Romans trying to get in, and to scale the walls would be near suicide, as the Romans had spread themselves out thinly about each wall, their archers ready. All hope seemed lost, with only a hundred men left in the walled mission to protect the wives and children of five hundred.

They had lost the battle. Now Fearghus's worst fears were to play out before his eyes. Scurrying atop the wall, he presently sought refuge in the simple sight of Seadna his faithful companion, whose face was falling with anguish and bitter fear. When Fearghus approached him, he grabbed his friend's shoulders firmly and collapsed upon him weeping terribly. He could not stand to face death or capture at the hands of the invaders, and could not decide whether or not to take his own life now or to wait and let the soldiers do it for him, though they might not.

Over Seadna's shoulder, Fearghus suddenly beheld a heart stopping view of the field before the gate. All the Romans soldiers that had been in this invasion had come to this one place, and their size was tremendous. "It is not over," Fearghus told his friend softly as the hum or battle filled the air. "It will not be over until the last man in all of Eire has fallen to the Roman sword, and all the glorious land has been burned by their wrath. The battle for Eire has only but begun."

Seadna drew away from him, looking up at his face like a child. "You may say this, but there is no hope!" he screamed, sobbing. With a glance over the wall to the Romans he began to panic vehemently, his body convulsing with fear and cowardice.

Fearghus would attempt to escape, though. He could not let his cause die with him, and Eire become the toy of Roman generals. If only he could live, then he could try again! Wild thoughts of revenge filled his mind and he sprinted down the stairs to the courtyard, where Murchadh and his men still stood. "Hold the gate as long as you can and then get out of here!" Fearghus commanded them sharply, and as he dashed to the room where Agnos was, there was a great straining of wood and the immense gate fell to pieces in a cloud of dust. Arrows sang through the air in both directions, some launched at the sky, and other blasted straight through the breached passage.

Fearghus found his room and snatching up Osgar, he cast a glance to Agnos, huddled fearfully in the corner. "We have to go *now*!" he screamed, "The gate's fallen!"

Agnos sprang to her feet, her gaze cast down to shield her glance from the fighting across the way at the gate. The twenty five Serpent Warrior spread in single file across the open gate fought with the vigor and strength that Murchadh had taught them but nonetheless a few soldiers hurtled through them, making attack on the buildings of the monastery.

Now Fearghus had to make a decision more important than any he had ever considered in his life. Would he dare leave vulnerable all of the women still left in the monastery and run for it? Or, rather, could he possibly save them? Suddenly he had a desperate idea and drew his sword. "Agnos," he commanded his love indifferently, "take the women and children into the hall to the sheep gate, and shut the door."

With this Agnos wheeled around and ran as fast as she could to the great hall, where most of the women were hiding together, praying for a miracle. Fearghus, on the other hand, met the attackers headed for him with his sword, and as more and more men filled the courtyard they were forced to reckon with him. He dashed back and forth engaging each man separately, and not letting one of them pass him by.

Behind him Agnos had quickly assembled the innocent women and children and was invisibly escorting them behind the stone structures to the sheep gate, where there was a stout stone corridor and a thick door on not only the outer side, but the inside end. Fearghus hoped that the women would all fit inside the hallway, and luckily they did. By this time, he could hold the attackers no longer. The courtyard, and the great hall and the armory had all fallen to these men, and it was futile to try to fight them longer.

Fearghus dispatched a few more soldiers and dropped into the shadows, though they were becoming few as the Romans proceeded to burn the straw roofs of the buildings. Guided by the light from these blazes, he finally found the sheep gate door and pounded on it enthusiastically, as suddenly he was spotted by a Roman.

At last the women within recognized his voice and allowed him admittance, but before he joined them he swung hard and killed the lone soldier that had spotted him. Inside all the wives of the dead were closely bunched together, and Fearghus had quite a hard time reaching the end of the tunnel where Agnos waited. A horrified look was on her face as he approached her, and he knew that it was because the trap that the men had set in this corridor had proved its worth. Indeed, a Roman soldier lay skewered upon a bed of spikes. Since it was so dark out, the other soldiers hadn't spotted the passageway yet, which was purely lucky on the part of the Celts.

Fearghus heaved the trap out into the dark field surrounding the monastery. Luckily the Roman watch was thin here, and the trees were just across a deserted dark field. If they were spotted crossing this place they would surely die, but it was the only path to safety.

They had saved about thirty women and children, and, Fearghus deemed, it was safe to escort four of them across the field at one time, quickly dashing to the cover of the tress in small groups. Most of them weren't wearing very brightly colored clothing, but the women wearing white robes he decided to save last, in order to spare the others.

Fearghus began to run back and forth with the groups of women, making sure the coast was clear each time, and keeping his hand ever at the hilt of his sword. Agnos, being white-clad, he painfully left behind each trip, but they were making good progress now as the Romans filled the inside of the monastery, ransacking everything. The Order of the Serpent now was dead in its infancy, dashed to pieces by a superior army.

Fearghus ran back and forth several times, his legs tiring with each trip, and soon he was escorting Agnos herself with him across the clearing and into the forest. Behind them a huge plume of smoke billowed up into the sky, illuminated with red light. The Romans were set on burning down even their own structure that had been infested by their enemies. Now nearly all of the soldiers had entered the enclosure, and the fleeing women and children were officially safe from harm.

He then realized that all he had gained in his travels since his transformation, he had lost. Other than the women and children he now protected with his life, he had nothing but the clothes on his back, the weapons in his grasp including Osgar, and also, he suddenly added as he compiled this mental list, he did have Agnos. She was the only thing he held dear now, his only refuge from this madness.

Irial was quite surely dead. Murchadh was also likely slaughtered by the Romans' charge, and Seadna and Conn, his two remaining friends, were atop the wall when he last saw them. Any other men he may have seen in the recent days surely would not have escaped from the monastery, defending their honor alongside the ruined Order. Tragedy had befallen them.

Fearghus, with Agnos at his side, led the women and children quietly through the thinnest part of the forest, very near to the white cliffs he had come to know so well. Soon the whole of their party had ascended to the top of the climb, and the valley below stretched far and wide behind them, crowned with disastrous smoke. Above them a storm brewed, and rain spontaneously descended on them, soaking the remnant of resistance. Steam rose from underneath Fearghus's armor, for so heated had his body become from the grueling battle. Agnos and the other women stayed close to the sparse trees that covered this land, lest they become soaked and fall ill in the cold. Nevertheless, they were soon forced to come forth and follow Fearghus as he trudged north. In seconds they were all drenched with water, their garments dragging behind them and hanging heavily to their shoulders.

The sky was burned with lightning and thunder rolled above, frightening a number of the children who traveled with them, close to their mothers. Suddenly, as Fearghus looked up, a Roman cross burned across the clouds, just as he had seen it so long ago, and indeed it was the symbol of their terrible religion. It was just as he had remembered it, and in its defiant presence he broke down, shielding his eyes, and weeping bitterly for all that the symbol reminded him of. Agnos knelt down and comforted him, helping him back to his feet. "Your adventure is not over," she reminded him, "It has only but begun this day."

The cross was gone in an instant. Fearghus continued to walk steadily forward, towards the pirate's cove, but yet he did not wish to enter that graveyard, now littered with the remains of Romans, pirates, and his comrades. Now only he could hope to locate a village in this northern frontier, and there feed those he was saving. The chances were slim that he alone could maintain such a large group of hungry people in this cold dark world.

They made their camp well away from the valley upon the soft beach beyond the pirates' harbor. Even though they were safely away from the monastery, the ruddy smoke emanating from it still could be seen towering in the distance. They had found some low trees at the edge of the sand that provided them some kind of shelter from the rain, though Fearghus, Agnos, and a few others in their company were forced to sleep under the gray sky, for this room was limited. Fearghus, hoping to save Agnos from the cold water, placed his torn cape over her body as she slept. He lay this night upon his back as the rain pattered on his armor and rusted it, unable to find sleep. Little to his surprise, not one person in their company could fall into a relaxed state that night. Almost all of the married women sobbed continuously during the night for the loss of their husbands, and each peel of thunder only made them weep more loudly. Agnos, during all of this, simply lay there quietly, her face turned away.

The next morning the bashful women of the party were all up and about very early, waiting patiently for their king to wake. Some of them grumbled in secret that Fearghus should be dead alongside their husbands, but mostly, they were all grateful that this one man preserved his life in order to save theirs, and, possibly, those of other people like them in the future.

There were only seven children with them, but their innocence and blissful ignorance of the current situation was enlightening to all of the group. They played jubilantly in the water and chased each other about, genuinely happy. Most of their mothers certainly could not say the same.

They began their journey this day continuing north along the seacoast, for in the south the Romans had moored their great ships. There was still almost all of Eire to explore, but alas, no supplies to last it with. The only chance any person there had of survival was finding civilization or hunting in the forest, Fearghus being the only member of the party fit to do this, but very incapable to do so without getting lost or being unable to find enough game.

And so they walked along the shore, slowed by the weaker members of the party. Fearghus was now bound to the mission of protecting and completely rescuing these women whose husbands he had a hand in killing. The least he could do was escort them to safety.

They continued on, exploring new lands, until midday when something extraordinary happened. Fearghus had entered a kind of daze, paying attention to nothing but the land just ahead. But as he walked he began unconsciously to hear a tapping sound, first very softly, but then more loudly. Before long he finally recognized it. It was the sound of a single galloping horse! The Romans, or worse, were here to hunt them down.

The women, upon hearing this, ran screaming to a position behind Fearghus, keeping their children close. Fearghus, of course, hadn't but a sword to his name, and, to quiet the fearful women, drew it defensively, scanning the horizon behind them. If he could cut down this scout he could buy them some time before the Romans reached them. If not, death would come swiftly. "Get to the trees!" he told Agnos behind him, and she led the village women into a group of trees, choosing a suitable place in the bushes to hide. Now Fearghus stood alone in the open, his weapon poised.

The galloping grew louder and louder as tension rose. At length Fearghus beheld a gleaming helm coming over the crest of the hill they had just passed. He planted his feet and raised his rapier, but suddenly he dropped it and leapt up into the air triumphantly. This rider was none other than Murchadh himself, the captain of the Order of the Serpent!

Fearghus slid his sword back into its scabbard, relieved. Murchadh pulled his horse to a halt, and dismounted. "Thank the gods you are still alive!" he exclaimed.

"I should say the same about you!" Fearghus responded, embracing his friend. By now, the women of the monastery had recognized the sound of Murchadh's voice and Agnos with them rejoined their savior.

"Only ten of us managed to escape, rappelling down the walls in secret," Murchadh explained. "Seadna picked us a good hiding spot while they slew our friends, and at night we made our escape."

"Then Seadna is amongst you?" Fearghus asked tentatively.

Murchadh was very happy to say, "Of course!"

"Hopefully he will know where to seek shelter," Fearghus said, "and revenge,"

Murchadh couldn't manage to laugh, but nonetheless chuckled, "If only he knew where we could find that!"

It was not long before Seadna and nine other men including Conn arrived on foot, for even the horse that Murchadh rode was hard to come by, luckily snatched from the encircling forest. It had been Seadna's idea to go in search of Fearghus, and he had expertly decided that the only way Fearghus could have gone, for safety reasons, would have been north along the coast. Luckily Murchadh had found him there, and with him each of the women that had been rescued from Tuathal's village.

That night they set up camp, again, on the beach, and the newcomers settled themselves in with Fearghus's group. Now a total of about fifty people, mostly women, crowded the shore, blackening the white sand. Fearghus decided, finally, to move everyone onto the dark grass, in case a Roman vessel should still prowl these waters. Fires were to be put out when everyone had decided to sleep, and sentries were posted to safeguard against a surprise Roman attack.

The next morning Seadna was up early, surveying the horizon. "I know of a village north of here," he said when Fearghus approached him, but his face was uncertain.

Their single horse was used to carry their meager supplies as they began to walk slowly along the water. Fearghus and the other men formed a circle about the women and children, keeping an eye out for Romans from the monastery south of them. Upon horseback, a group of Romans could overtake them before midday, and slaughter everyone. With luck, though, the victorious soldiers would be contented to know nothing of their escape.

A day's journey brought them to a warm green forest near a stony coastline, and Seadna was quite sure that the village he knew of was near. Nonetheless, he led Fearghus and two other men into the forest with bows to hunt with, and skins to fill with water from a stream they had discovered near the edge of the trees, flowing unnoticed into the vast sea.

When they were well into the forest, Seadna stopped them and drew his friend aside. Sitting upon a large mossy boulder, he told Fearghus what he thought about his efforts to save Eire. "You must leave this place," he told him solemnly, tightening his bowstring.

Fearghus was distraught. "But why?" he asked.

"There is a place I know of," Seadna responded slowly, "where you can find what you are looking for."

Fearghus, confused and fearful, was taken aback by this statement. What was Seadna speaking of?

"You must leave all of this behind," the former pirate continued, observing the happy green trees all around them. "You must go south alone."

"But *where* must I travel?" Fearghus pleaded curiously.

Seadna would give him no more information. "It is a place not far from my own place of birth," he said, turning. "Just follow the path of the clover to this place of refuge. There, make your revenge as you see fit."

Fearghus sprang up and stopped his friend. "But what about Agnos and the others?" he pried vehemently.

Seadna continued to walk past him. "I have seen a village from afar," he answered coolly. "I will take care of them from here."

Fearghus knelt before his friend, pleading for mercy. But suddenly Seadna was gone. He had disappeared without a trace and without alerting Fearghus. To his right, Fearghus heard a rustling sound, but when he cast a glance to the disturbed trees, it was not his friend Seadna, but a horse, particularly the horse that Murchadh had rode in search of their party. It had come of its own design, and it was fitted with a good leather saddle. The other two men in the clearing in which Fearghus stood were gone as well, and this horse was all he was left with to make his journey.

But Fearghus didn't want to leave them. He wanted to see Agnos again, and grow old with her in a peaceful village. He was tired of this warrior business, and would give anything to hold a staff in his hand once more. But instead, he was holding Osgar.

He made up his mind that not even Seadna could keep him from his dream, and leaping upon the horse, he galloped it towards the edge of the forest where the party was gathered. Numerous branches snapped across his arms an face as his horse plowed through the bushes and trees, but he didn't care. He was going to go back to the beach and rejoin them, regardless of Seadna's warnings.

Suddenly he burst out onto the beach, wheeling around, just in time to catch a glimpse of the rear of the party, which had already departed for the village. He steered his horse towards them, but suddenly the beast reared and whinnied. Fearghus was thrown up and down violently with the animal, but he did not fall off. The horse seemed as if possessed by a strange magical force, and it turned abruptly around, galloping in the opposite direction. Somehow, Fearghus reasoned, Seadna had something to do with this.

But, he realized, if he dismounted the animal, then he could walk to them. With this idea he tried to throw himself off of the horse, but he could not. His legs were fixed firmly to the leather saddle, and though he tried, he could not so much as fall from his steed. When the idea of slaying the creature crossed his mind, he found he couldn't loose his sword from its scabbard or even so much as point Osgar itself at the horse's neck, for it was caught up in the air, also possessed by this strange magic.

He was on his way back to the south, back to the monastery and the villages and the great forest, and completely against his will. Almost immediately the horse turned off into the forest next to him, and began to change direction frequently. No matter how he tried, Fearghus could not remember which way it turned as it carried him away, and was hopelessly lost.

When the beast galloped out of the forest and into a grassy meadow, it abruptly slowed and came to a halt. Suddenly Fearghus noticed that he was free of the horse and that Osgar had fallen from the air and into his power. But now all this was useless, because he was somewhere remote and new. And to try to find his way back to the northern village would likely bring his end, if the magic didn't stop him first.

He made camp here for the night and nibbled on a piece of bread in a sack tied to his horse. The course of events in his life were becoming stranger and stranger, and he had almost no power to control them. Exhausted and confused, finally, he made his bed in the soft reeds and slept soundly and alone.

As he looked up to the stars above, he tried with the best of his strength to forget about Agnos and Seadna and the monastery, but memories of them plagued his mind. Before he closed his eyes this night, he found himself weeping bitterly for the loss of his former way of life.

The next day he pressed on, traveling south through Eire, the dawn burning on his left. He had no map or guide to help him to where he was headed, but he knew that the magic of the gods would bring him safely to wherever the place was. He did know that the place was near to Seadna's village, which he had visited himself on the day of Colla's death, but he couldn't fathom what this magical refuge would look like.

It was a long ride to a place that far south. Fearghus had made the journey once himself, though, with Agnos, and knew a few landmarks along the path. The first, he reasoned, was the ruins of Tuathal's village where in fact he had found Agnos, and the second would be the great southern forest where formerly lived Irial and Conn. From there he would search for a stone mountain near the water's edge, for the caverns of this stone precipice had housed the *Silverbeam* when Colla had led him to his native village. He now remembered how frightened he was of these caves when once he had slept in them, and hoped that they weren't related in some way to his fate.

And so he traveled ever south, the gleam of the sea on one side of him and the hills of the land passing him on the other. He traveled mostly in green fields and muddy swamps, stopping each night under monstrous trees to rest. The ground was sometimes rocky and oftentimes soft and moist, but the air was constantly clear and fresh, and cool breezes soothed the weary traveler.

It was not more than a few days before he reached the black ruins of Tuathal's village, of which almost nothing was left. Fearghus could still make out the two wooden towers on either side of the weak gate that the men had used, and as he picked through the debris he found several black iron swords, particularly the ones Conn had fashioned for him at the first meeting. They had been wielded by the guard of Tuathal's village before the group had all but ceased to exist, and brought painful memories back to Fearghus of what was now truly dead. Even so, the drive to exact revenge on the invaders drove him ever further. Seadna's strange behavior and talk of a place where he could solve his problems seemed very promising.

At last there came a day when he beheld from afar the great southern forest, and even from this distant place he could see the clearing in the center of the trees where once lived the happy lumberman Irial who had died valiantly commanding Fearghus's small army. And beyond this, where the forest ended, the wonderful land of Eire stretched forever into the distance, lined on the left with shimmering water, and covered over with clouds in the far distance. There were mountains and forests and lakes here, and hills and fields in between.

As if plunging into a tasty meal, Fearghus now galloped happily into the tall trees, the broken sunlight dancing across his armor. He had found the single road that halved the vast stretch of trees, and it was clear and open, not dark and narrow like the forest paths elsewhere in Eire and in Man. But it was also dangerous, a thoroughfare used commonly by the invading Romans, as it had been the sight of fierce skirmishes between himself and the bands of soldiers. With luck, they had already left this place behind in the push inland, and he would not encounter danger too great.

When the sun set on this day of travel, he came in thorough darkness to the abode of Irial upon the road, and found that it was still fully intact, left just as Irial had it when he embarked with Fearghus on the road to Tuathal's village. Fearghus had much trouble starting a blaze when he settled down inside of the main house, but eventually he discovered a flint on a shelf and proceeded to illuminate the room from the fire pit in the corner.

Irial's house was very messy, covered in wood shavings and scraps of food and cloth. Fearghus easily recognized the bed where he had slept after a nasty run-in with the Romans upon the road, all covered in blood and surprised at being near death just after the loss of Osgar.

And so he slept soundly under a sturdy roof that night, remembering Irial's happy face. Also this night his thoughts turned to the problem of what exactly his mission was, and why he had been chosen by the gods to be this warrior and not someone else. He remembered everything that had come to pass as of yet but did not dwell on these memories.

The next day he gathered some tools from Irial's abode and, packing them upon his horse, continued on the road to the south, in the cool shadow of the towering trees. It would be a long journey yet to the village in the south, but not more than a few days. He was making good progress to a place he knew absolutely nothing about.

It was a day before he came to the end of the forest, but the road still continued on for a great while, cutting through fields and over hills. Fearghus, though, recalling that Seadna's village had been primarily of the fishing trade, steered immediately to the left along the coast. He would follow this path until he reached the shore where the *Silverbeam* had successfully rammed a ship of Bressel's and where Colla had met his death.

Much more time passed and nothing particularly dangerous befell Fearghus. The weather was mild during the day but was becoming steadily worse as time passed. Fearghus's supply of bread and fruit waned as he traveled near the unfertile shore, but he did not worry about his hunger, for the place he sought for would be near now and he would find whatever Seadna told him to seek.

At last the day came when Fearghus came upon the village of Seadna, which, little to his surprise, had been plundered by the Romans after most of the men had left with him. Most of the buildings, however, were still hospitable, furnished with water, beds, and some dry food that the invaders had overlooked. All this Fearghus enjoyed thankfully as he contemplated what to do next.

The coast was nearby and Fearghus paused for a moment to search for the wreck of the pirate ship that had fallen there. When he spied the shattered vessel in the shallow waters another thing caught his eye. It was the terrible cave he was so worried about, and its mouth was wide open, large enough for two ships to pass through side by side. Inside was a fearful darkness, and the water within it did not sparkle like the sea outside, but instead was dark and frightening.

And Fearghus strode to the very furthest point of the land, even wading out into the water. He scanned the horizon meticulously, surveying every detail of the grassy plain and the trees on every side. And finally his gaze came to rest on the cave, and he reasoned that, being so possessed of magic, it certainly was the place Seadna had told him of, and hesitantly drew nearer to it, remembering that there was a crack in the stone on this south side of it.

The cave was dark and he drew out the flint he had taken from Irial's house and with much trouble created a torch by striking it upon the stone over some dry leaves on the ground, and from there lighting a bit of cloth on the end of a stick he had found. Stepping cautiously inside, he looked around the chamber. Indeed, as he remembered, there were shamrocks growing upon every surface in the cave, like moss. It sent a chill down his spine, since it was so strange. Nonetheless, he strove on, for he had decided before this moment to never turn back, to keep pushing ahead.

He quickly had discovered the water's edge, and then in the darkness sought out a narrow ledge along the freezing river, and followed it cautiously into the cave. Somehow, some way, he was supposed to find refuge in this dark place, and so with strong determination he walked into complete darkness with nothing but a torch, a sword, and an ethereal spear.

Chapter 14

A Refuge of Stone

Fearghus's torch grew dim and nearly went out, but still he walked ahead on the narrow ledge, putting one foot in front of the other. The red light of his torch reflected off of the water and filled the entire corridor, but did not help him see ahead. Even so, it was not long before the ledge widened and he stepped onto a large platform. The place he was looking for would have to be near now, for from the complete darkness behind him he deduced that he had been moving in these caves for more than half of the day.

Now he moved frantically forward, for his torch was going out. If it was extinguished he likely would be lost in this complete darkness and perish. Soon he discovered along the wall that there was an opening, almost a door, and inside of this door there was a deafening sound of falling water. Fearghus could not see the waterfall, but he knew that it was there, and that if light was given to it that it would shimmer with beauty.

Suddenly his torch was out, overwhelmed by the flying water and thin air, but Fearghus could still hear the sound of the water. He knew that the waterfall was at the end of the chamber he was in, and that since the water itself had dug these caves, that the waterfall could possibly be the exact end of the corridor he was traveling through.

He carefully felt his way along the wall, Osgar still in his right hand, and tried not to panic. Miraculously, his efforts proved useful, for, as he predicted, there was a door behind the waterfall, which roared just over his head. Somehow he felt for a handle and found one. When he opened the heavy iron door, ghostly moonlight streamed through it, and his armor glowed.

He found himself in a gigantic valley enclosed on all sides by tall mountains, and abounding with trees and flowers, now closed in the darkness of night. The source of the river was above his head. The water was coming around the border of the valley in a sort of moat, both sides joining as one in a stony trough behind him at the crest of the east "wall" of stone.

And here Fearghus lay down in the soft grass, and fell to sleep in the clear night air. His body was exhausted and here he hoped to find refreshment, and his mind was filled with worry he wished to get rid of. It was a sleep of renewal, and of healing.

When he woke up he felt unusually rejuvenated, and his body seemed relieved of the strain of wearing armor. When he opened his eyes he noticed this and actually did remove his armor, and his body suddenly felt free and alive. He threw down his heavy helmet and sword and stretched his muscles and looked all about him at the tops of the mountains. This was truly a place of refuge and relief.

It was at this time that he had the idea of building a house, for here he could live and recuperate, and prepare for more adventures in the world outside. He began by dragging some dead wood to the center of the field, and then opened the sack of tools he had brought from Irial's house. He had taken for himself a hatchet, a sanding stone, numerous pegs and nails, and a number of other small tools in this bag, and with them decided to attempt to build a shelter. He used the small hatchet to cut the wood into planks and equal lengths, and used the blunt side of the axe to hammer nails into them and fashion a wall. It looked sloppy at first, but he sanded it down and trimmed the wood with the hatchet and finally came to accept this first wall.

In the coming days he repeated this process three more times and then made a frame for a ceiling, covering it with more wood and sealing it with mud and straw from the fields. Also he pulled up the grass from the ground underneath it and laid down smooth river stones as a floor for his abode. During this time he ate the berries and large fruits that covered the valley to sustain him, and washed in the clear water of the river. When he decided that his house was complete, he took up the bow that Seadna had given him originally to hunt in the forest far north of here, and took down a good number of small beasts to eat.

Fearghus stayed here for a great while alone, and he underwent a miraculous change. He grew stronger with time, and his mind came to accept the state he was in. Everyday he woke with the first light, bathed in the nearby stream, and went about gathering food and fashioning novelties of wood with Irial's tools. He grew, in this time, to be vastly better at this trade, and in time he had fashioned all sorts of furniture and trinkets. With more time he even managed somehow to reinforce the walls of his cabin and even build an extension to the single room. In this small area he kept all of his tools, food and other supplies.

At night, Fearghus would enjoy sleeping in the field, under the stars, but when it was stormy he stayed inside, in his little room, and warmed himself with a meager fire. He would think of Agnos at these times in the darkness, but tried exceptionally hard to feel nothing any longer for his previous life, and rather look ahead to his future here.

One day Fearghus surveyed the fruitful land about him and decided it needed a name. He would be the first to name it, and he would make sure that hereafter all would refer to the valley as he decided. After much thought, he had a good look at the great mountains about him and dubbed the place Dún as Cloch, or Fortress of Stone, for it was so well shielded from the world.

Fearghus stayed in Dún as Cloch until the snows began to fall and the air chilled him to the bone. It was winter in Eire now, and the valley was beautiful and white. Fearghus was forced during this time to eat only from his small store of wild grain and the animals he hunted, but he did not mind. He had fashioned for himself warm clothes of skin from the small beasts.

On the day of the third snow, when the air was washed with soft white flakes, Fearghus started the day huddling inside of his hut, surveying the land outside his door. And there came to be a great light, he discovered, that grew ever greater until it nearly blinded him. At first he thought it was the sun, but as it neared him it suddenly went out, and then there was only the snow.

But before long another thing caught his eye: someone was out there in the cold! He could see the silhouette of the person's body as he stumbled through the snow, wrapped heavily in cloth to protect from the biting cold. The man was carrying a small bag of provisions, but was not armed or pulled along a beast. He would surely die if Fearghus did not bring him in.

Fearghus stumbled out into the snow, making his way quickly to the hooded stranger and helping him inside the hut. There was hardly enough room for the both of them inside, but when Fearghus closed the door and rebuilt his small fire, the single room lit up with warmth.

Until now Fearghus hadn't seen the face of the stranger, "Why don't you let me help you with your cloak, sir?" Fearghus asked hesitantly.

"I will take care of that," the man responded, but suddenly Fearghus saw that it was not a man at all. It was a fair lady in a flowing gown, her dark hair hanging down to nearly the floor. Her skin seemed ghostly white, and glowed brightly.

When she turned around to see him, Fearghus caught her eyes and staggered back in fear. They were like blazing candles of white fire, the eyes of a goddess. And he feared for his life, for men were not to associate with the gods.

She bore down on him, as he shielded his face, falling to his knees, and then stopped. "Do not be afraid," she said, in a ghostly, ringing voice. "I have not come to harm you."

The sound of her voice was so comforting, so tempting, that Fearghus found himself peering into her face. In the back of his mind he thought he was hypnotized by the sound of her voice, but he knew he could not resist it. She had taken him into his power.

The lady reached down and touched his face. The moment her finger touched his cheek he was lifted with a great feeling of warmth and happiness, and came to his feet. "You have come a long way, Fearghus" she began, her expression deep and thoughtful.

"How do you know my name?" he asked, not afraid but rather curious.

"I know the names of all who follow me," she answered, and continued. "Now, the time has come for you to know the truth."

"The truth? What do you speak of, fair lady?" Fearghus again asked her curiously.

The woman went straight to it. "The truth," she replied, "is what has caused all of this to happen. The truth will be hard for you to understand."

Fearghus perked up. "I will try!" he pressed, begging from her more information.

"The path you have been following was laid for you by the Lord God," she told him, and he stood back, looking down at her blue gown, and thinking.

"Of course, for that you speak of is the god Sucellos of my fathers," Fearghus observed.

When he looked up though, the lady had changed. Her face had become black as the night, and her gown as well. And the whole room became dark, for the fire was extinguished with a burst of wind. "The ways of your gods are the ways of demons!" she cursed him, raising her arms. And the boards of his house shuddered as he cowered before her terrible presence, weeping.

"The Lord God, who is the father, the son, and the ghost you shall follow!" she screamed, her voice deepening. "Woe to he who strays from the path of salvation! Lowly be the gods of the fields, damned be the gods of the sky! There is only but one creator of this world, and his servant stands before you!"

Fearghus threw himself against the wall of his abode. He had become like a child in her presence, crying and scratching at the walls to escape. The force of her rage was crushing him slowly under an invisible stone, and death he felt was near to him.

And suddenly he heard her voice again. It was much calmer, but still deep and guttural. "You have been commissioned here to build a stronghold for the people of God. Do well with what he has bestowed upon you," she hissed, and with that, she was gone. As she disappeared, the fire spontaneously came back alive, and the shuddering house was calmed.

When Fearghus wheeled around, still convulsing violently from his fear, he noticed that one thing had been left by the lady: a heavy and purely gold Roman cross lay neatly upon his table, and it looked as if it was molten when the firelight danced across it. Upon the base of the cross there was a large cylindrical hole. As if the lady herself had told him, Fearghus immediately placed it at the top of a wooden shaft, creating a sort of staff. He did not know why he did this.

It had become dark outside, and Fearghus slept in a bed of animal pelts near the fire on the floor, curled up tightly in fear. And he thought about what had just happened. What did the god of the lady want him to build here, and for what people? What kind of gift had this deity "bestowed" upon him? All these things he thought about as he fell to sleep that night.

Many days later, the winter waned and the cold began to recede from Dún as Cloch. Fearghus was active once again, and for the first time, he wanted out. Every inch of his body yearned to see the world outside his happy abode, for even the green meadows surrounding him he had grown weary of. And also, he noticed within him, there was a renewed vigor for the life of a warrior, for the thrill of battle. He felt again like the shepherd boy he once was, standing on a grassy knoll with his sheep.

As he prepared to journey outside, Fearghus thought about what he was to do. Would he go back and find Agnos and Seadna? Or did he dare? It had taken him a very long time to let go of his attachment to them, and if he went to find them now he would ruin his mission.

And so instead he thought about the words of the ghost who had visited him. She had spoken of building something here. Certainly, he reasoned, he could not build this without help, and he created for himself a mission of finding other men. Indeed, he would defile Dún as Cloch with this such action, but surely he could not keep it to himself.

He packed his things quickly and silently, provisioning himself only with a bit of food, his arching equipment, his new staff, Osgar, and of course his sturdy sword. It was a blustery and cold day when he finally turned to the iron door in the mountainside where he had entered so long ago. The ground was soaked from the rain and still laced with snow, and sank under his step.

When he opened that strange door he held it open with a stone, for it was dark inside the stone chamber. The roar of the waterfall therein blasted full in his ears when he stepped inside, holding a torch, and the sunlight from the valley outside made the falling water glimmer. His staff shone like to the torch itself in its light. Osgar he had left in his house in the valley, for he did not dare take it with him on his adventures.

Fearghus followed the narrow path along the waters edge for a great while, fearlessly and purposefully. At length his torch went out. The wood he had used for it was too young, and the moisture left in it prevented it from burning further down. He stood there momentarily in the dark, and tried to decide whether or not to attempt to go back to the valley, or to press on.

Suddenly, his mind was made for him. He willed his torch to come back to life, and as he willed it, suddenly his staff burst with light and the entire cavern was blasted with it. Fearghus could not stand even to look upon the golden cross as he walked ahead, and shielded his face from it as he picked carefully along the gray ledge.

And so, with much ease, he reached the end of the watery cavern, and when sunlight touched the cross, its luminescence was extinguished. This world, to him, was very familiar. To his left the wreck of the Roman vessel was no more, for in the freezing cold it had broken apart and fallen to oblivion. To his right the trees were still barren, but the buds of their leaves were showing already. The remains of Seadna's village were still lying lifeless on the ground, but the plants were beginning now to swallow them up. A whole new world lay before him.

He walked inland by day, hunting every two days for food and drinking in the streams. He reasoned that the Romans had not infiltrated any villages in the inner land, since they were a nautical force primarily. He was confident that he would be led to the right place.

After ten days of travel he finally observed from afar the smoke of a small village. The land around it was soft and treeless, and he was seen by the villagers many days before he reached them. The village, he saw, was composed of about fifteen structures, all of wood and thatched roof. The huts were arranged in a circle, sort of a defensive formation, and in the center were kept all of the beasts in a large fenced area.

"We welcome you with open hearts into our homes," the chief of the village said, greeting him warmly with a bow. "But may I ask what business you have in our peaceful hamlet?"

"I have come in search of friends," Fearghus answered him quickly, his face composed.

The man stepped forward and embraced him, laughing heartily. "Then you have come to the right place!" he chuckled, and led Fearghus to the quarters they had made for him.

Later that night, Fearghus joined the villagers in a communal celebration for his arrival, and it was about a great bonfire. Fearghus was seated near to the chief and the rest of the warriors in the village. The women mingled with their husbands in a circle encompassing completely the flames, but still their numbers were vastly limited. Even so, these were friends of Fearghus's.

After a great while, one of the warriors engaged him as he sat nervously by the fire. The man was old and grizzled, and many scars lined his face. "You are Fearghus?" he asked anxiously, drawing nearer. "Fearghus the King?"

Fearghus drew back from the man, and simply uttered, "Indeed I am he."

The old warrior wrung his hands enthusiastically, grinning. "I have heard much about you!" he pressed. "You have fought these invading Romans?"

Fearghus was very curious about this man. "That also is true..." he replied hesitantly, "but what business have you with them?"

But then Fearghus noticed something that put an end to his curiosity. The old man had just drawn a short black iron sword from his belt, and it gleamed dully in the ruddy firelight. Only a few men carried these swords that he knew of, and most of them had died at the monastery—they were warriors of the village of Tuathal, men who had taken the swords forged for them by Conn the smith. Fearghus could see the skillful design of the weapon as Conn's and also he could see that the warrior knew he saw this.

"You escaped then?" Fearghus asked.

The man laughed. "Oh, I not only escaped!" he answered, "I've spent many days fighting the swine on many fronts throughout the land! And I hear that you have as well!"

Fearghus forgot his fear of this man and opened himself to him. "Certainly," he responded, "but let us not talk of that now. That is finished. I have another mission this time."

The man leaned closer to him and listened as he told him everything he had experienced since his demise, about Dún as Cloch, and the ghostly lady, and the origin of his staff. The man jumped back when he set his eyes upon the thing, for he had seen this symbol of the Roman god before. Fearghus learned from him at this time that his name was Dunchad, and that he was older and nearly as wise as Seadna himself.

Dunchad wanted very much to see Dún as Cloch. The cross, Fearghus soon realized had had a strange effect on him, but it did not worry him too much. This man could convince others to come to Dún as Cloch and help him build whatever he was to build there.

The next day when Fearghus woke, twenty men waited outside of the hut he had been quartered in. All of them were laden heavily with food, weapons, and tools, for Dunchad had told them all of their mission, and had before the dawn prepared all of them to depart immediately. They were to leave the women and children behind, explained one of the young men. They would wait and see what happened next before bringing them.

Fearghus examined the village passively as he prepared to leave it. The people here were different than any he had ever seen. They were kind and humble, and quite simple. Only the colorful Dunchad was unique to his fellow townsmen. Fearghus decided that this was entirely as a result of their distance from the great tempting sea; they had little to do with shipping or trade with other groups of people.

A horse was provided to Fearghus, though the town possessed only five, and the other men followed, carrying their supplies upon their backs. Dunchad as well, as their provisional leader, accompanied Fearghus on mount, and Fearghus noticed he had fashioned a scabbard upon his back for the sword of Conn.

And so they began their journey to Dún as Cloch, where, as Fearghus hoped, he would build what the Lady had instructed him to. The going was rough to start with. Fearghus found himself lost at times, and the men trudged through mud and stumbled over stony ridges. The cross Fearghus carried, though, seemed to lead him back to his green valley, and in a few days of travel he beheld from afar the cliffs of the walls of Dún as Cloch. Certainly this journey had been easier than his path to Dunchad's village. The men about him had provided much food, protection, and shelter.

The next day, Fearghus led the men into the open field before the sea, where once he had battled pirates under the hot sun with his new warriors of Seadna's village. The remains of such, every man had noticed, lay rotting near the other corner of the field. And once again, Fearghus himself noted, the wreck of the Roman ship Colla had sunk had disappeared below the surf.

The men became suspicious when Fearghus led them to the watery cavern. Once inside, Fearghus thrust his staff ahead and it suddenly shone with white light, blasting the walls of the chamber with its own fire. Some of the men stumbled backwards in their fear of it, but, as Fearghus half-expected, they had soon fallen under its spell and gathered behind their leader, Dunchad at their helm.

Fearghus walked briskly through the passage he had already twice traversed, and the men followed. The roar of the waterfall, at its end, guided him, and sparked his desire to once again behold the glory of Dún as Cloch. With time he indeed came to this waterfall, and the light of his staff in it made it into a thousand crystals that blinded him and sent him reeling nearly into the water. The other men could not be further lured by the staff. They, too, shielded their faces with desperate vigor, looking down as they followed Fearghus to the iron door, which was yet still ajar as he had left it.

And so without much trouble the men of Dunchad entered one by one the paradise of Dún as Cloch, and themselves sampled its ethereal glory that Fearghus feared was only meant for himself. But yet nothing befell the men that day, as Fearghus had hoped. The valley had welcomed them into its fruitful interior.

Fearghus allowed the men to make camp on one side of his house in a grassy field. Also he hesitantly gave them permission to have at the fruits and straw he had amassed for this purpose, and as well the sparkling stream for baths and drinking. He wished in secret that they would not defile the land by their presence, and kept a selfish eye upon them.

They all slept there on the soft grass rather quietly until the morning, but Fearghus was awake with apprehension, for so long he had been without the company of men. Tomorrow he would confront them again and commission them all to build a city, for the construction of a city, he had deemed, would be a suitable interpretation of the Lady's command.

When the soft dawn alighted on the craggy eastern bound of Dún as Cloch, Fearghus sought the council of Dunchad, and before the broad light of day they had come to an agreement. Dunchad was going to build the *city* of Dún as Cloch, or in his eyes, more of a fortress by that name. They were going, in this task, to take down only a few of the magical trees of the valley, for Fearghus had convinced Dunchad to find his lumber outside of their new home. Also, as Fearghus heard, there was much talk of stone-hewing, an art known to only two of the men, but also very promising.

At several points throughout the discussion Fearghus wondered why the men were willing to give so much of themselves to him. When asked, Dunchad would claim the debt of his life to Fearghus for all his effort against the Romans. Fearghus, though, suspected the magic of his golden cross as the cause of the strange loyalty. He had seen men walk towards his staff already, and beheld their mesmerized eyes in its presence. This was the one tool the Lady had given him to do her bidding, and cunningly it had worked in him, and brought these men here.

They began work that very day, and their determination spurred them onto furious progress. Though Fearghus could have left himself out of their toil as their leader, he decided instead to aid them with his immeasurable strength, taking up the axe in the forest around the village ruins near the Sea. All the stout trunks he felled were floated with surprising ease through the watery cavern and into the valley. Some Fearghus was forced to halve that they might pass through the iron door and into Dún as Cloch, though all of the timber eventually was cut down as it lay in the field.

By the end of the first day, miraculously, enough wood had been harvested by the men to build an edifice three times the size of Fearghus's house, and the men had done much to strip it of its bark and fashion it into planks. When Fearghus laid himself to bed that night long after dusk, his body was exhausted, but his mind jubilant. His vision of the future had changed drastically since his arrival here.

The strong men of Dunchad worked long into the night, even after their leader had fallen to sleep. When Fearghus awoke, he found them standing beside two expertly fashioned wooden walls, two stories high. "You've done so much for me already," Fearghus praised Dunchad. "I thank you with all my heart."

Dunchad surveyed his work. Next to the two walls there stood an immense pile of wood, and the two stone hewers had already set up their own camp near an area of the mountains where a great deal of boulders lay about. "I see a wonderful future in this city of yours," he responded, wringing his rough hands. "The stronghold of Dún as Cloch shall be a thing of tales, of legends! I am honored to be the builder of it."

Thus began the second day of the construction of Dún as Cloch. Under Fearghus's watchful eye, there then came many more, and when the balmy nights of spring had set themselves upon the land, three massive structures towered above the fertile valley. Each had high ceilings in their many rooms, and all the men who had built them slept in their halls. Dunchad and Fearghus had in this time grown to be lords over the men, and kings of their great green valley.

The buildings were crafted to be especially sturdy. Fearghus spent a great deal of each day examining the work of the men, which was always continuing day and night. At times he would fancy himself at fashioning furniture and fencing for the group of buildings. He was beginning to enjoy his life in Dún as Cloch.

Now the buildings were made with long planks of wood, cut from the trees outside the valley. They were surprisingly even and sealed meticulously with mud and straw, as was necessary to aid the men against the bitter cold of winter. The corners of the edifices were reinforced with sturdy poles, and the windows, doors, and roofs were trimmed with smooth wood. The roofs, respectively, were covered in animal skin, as Dunchad had intended, to waterproof them, as well as they were thatched with straw above. They had acquired the pelts for the roofs from many days of hunting in the nearby forest.

These first buildings of the city had many rooms upon two floors each, though one had but a high ceiling over just two main halls, instead of two stories. Fearghus liked to call the primary chamber of this building the great Oaken Hall, since Dunchad had furnished it particularly for feasts and Fearghus's own throne, and provided it with many tall windows and supporting beams above. Subsequently, Fearghus dubbed this room the seat of his power in Dún as Cloch, as more massive structures rose before him. The interior he would eventually fill with gold, statues, and fine garlands.

Now Fearghus was filled with excitement. And it was now that he realized something important: he needed more men. He wanted them to be stone-hewers, for he had seen already the work of Dunchad's men who had made blocks for the foundations of the buildings. Dún as Cloch, as its name implied, was rich with stone on all sides.

Trusting Dunchad with the care of the valley, Fearghus himself decided to make this trip for more manpower. With him he brought his staff with its cross, and Osgar as well, for he yet did not trust any other man with this greatest of all treasures. He still did not know its purpose, but detected its importance.

Fearghus traveled upon his horse with just two of his most trusted men. They galloped quickly through the countryside, for so light was their load and number, and for so important was their mission. Instead of going inland, this time, Fearghus made the decision to travel south along the sea. He suspected there could be villages unknown to him in this region of Eire. The North, he knew, was still held strongly by the Romans in the monastery he had lost. He dared not attempt to find Seadna and his men again.

They traveled for many days, and their supplies ran low. "Where exactly are we going?" one of the men asked on the fourth day.

Fearghus only looked ahead as they approached a great steep drop into a valley before them. With his keen vision, he suddenly spotted what he believed to be a man-made clearing in a grove of distant trees. Also, as his eyes strained, he saw what he expected to find there: the thatched roof of a hut. "We are going down there," he told the man, throwing his staff forward towards the village. His two followers only looked bewildered.

Fearghus kicked his horse into a gallop as he set his eyes on the village in the distance. His horse whinnied and stumbled as it slid down the hill, but it did not falter. The other men followed him at a slower pace, but nonetheless the three of them were virtually soaring across the country towards their goal.

The closer Fearghus got to the village, the more was revealed of it. Only three broken huts lay in this clearing, he soon realized, crestfallen. Slower now, he finally brought his horse to a halt in the middle of the shelters, shouting aloud for survivors. Just as he had expected, the buildings were a blackened mess, each one partly consumed by fire. One hut, though, was still mostly intact.

Fearghus drew closer to this house, carefully as though he was afraid of finding someone's charred body laying inside, still writhing in pain. But this hut was different from the others. It had survived the fire, and he was somehow drawn to it.

Pushing away a ragged cloth from the door, Fearghus peered inside the mysterious hut, his vision piercing through a screen of smoke inside. The eerie rays of the sun were evident in the gray smoke, and they fell upon one thing in the very middle of the shelter that caught his attention. It was a pile of cloth, or rather more of a hump covered in cloth. As he neared it, suddenly he was taken aback. It was a young girl, and she was weeping bitterly.

Fearghus knelt down and placed his hand on the child, whispering into her ear softly. Certainly, he reasoned, her parents had either been killed or had fled this village, leaving her behind. Feeling pity for the girl, he picked her up in his arms and stepped out into the clearing where his two companions waited.

Suddenly, the girl nothing short of woke up in his arms, and wiggled out of his grasp violently. "You fool!" she cried in a childish voice, pointing straight at Fearghus. But as she finished her sentence her voice lowered and became frighteningly guttural. And at that moment Fearghus noticed a fiery blaze in her eye, and hers were the eyes of a snake!

As if he had expected this, Fearghus drew his menacing sword as quickly as she had jumped from his arms, and in almost no time brandished it in front of him. But the girl, or rather, the Snake, pounced upon him before he could react, and ripped the hilt of his long sword from his fingers, clubbing him across the face with it and jumping high into the air.

By this time Fearghus's companions were grappling at their own swords, stumbling back in fear of the girl. But she was too fast for them. Before Fearghus noticed, the Snake had engaged them, running each of them through the stomach with the blade he had stolen from him. And Fearghus was suddenly alone against this his worst enemy.

As the Snake slashed and stabbed the bodies of his comrades, Fearghus sprang to his feet in a fit of desperation. He had to save Osgar from the Snake. If the creature managed to take the spear, then all of his struggles until now, all of his pain would mean nothing. And, he realized, his entire cause would fall to dust, and all of Eire be laid waste in his absence.

Fearghus was too fast for the Snake this time. The girl had been too busy with his friends, that he was able to lunge ahead and snatch the shaft of the holy lance in his fists as it lay across the body of his horse, and fall to the earth with the prize in his hands.

By now the Snake had become his normal self. In the time Fearghus had taken to gather up the spear, he had grown into the sickly long creature they both knew him to be, and that Fearghus was ready to engage. "So we meet again!" the Snake hissed as he rose above his foe with a menacing stare.

Fearghus planted his feet firmly in the ground and raised Osgar, the one weapon that could destroy the Snake. "I will never bow to you!" Fearghus screamed, swaying back and forth on his heels. "I will be the last man you see upon this earth!" he added haughtily, ready to thrust the spear into his enemy and inflict true damage.

But the Snake would not be shaken. He simply reared his ugly head and then plunged it down to Fearghus, his fangs bared. Fearghus struck a glancing blow on the side of the beast's head as he jumped aside, driving a furrow along the Snake's head and into its right eye. As he expected, the wound burst with blood, but it would not stop, because it had been inflicted by Osgar.

The Snake reeled backwards, angered at the loss of his eye, and retreated into a tight coil as his face bled. Fearghus, spurred by his success, suddenly had an idea and took up his golden staff in his other hand, thrusting it forward as it burst with blinding light, just as he hoped it would.

He had survived! The Snake was literally knocked back by the force of the light, and as Fearghus watched, he disappeared literally into thin air in its glory, screaming in his terrible voice louder than anything Fearghus had heard. And suddenly he was gone, and the venomous blood stain he had left was absorbed into the earth.

Immediately Fearghus tended to his fallen friends. But they were not to be saved, as both had died. He used a knife and some stones to bury both of them there, and was quick to leave the place where the Snake had been with the three horses. He remained still firmly resolved to continue on the mission he was on, and find more men to help him build his city. Sheathing his sword and tethering the horses of his companions firmly to his, he set off again, going continually south, with the calm blue sea at his left.

That night he made his camp in a shady glen. He could not sleep, or eat, for so much was he afraid of everything around him, as if the very trees over his head were winding serpents. He simply existed that night, and leaned against a stout tree, shivering in the cold.

The next day he continued his journey alone, thinking of nothing but the task he had set before himself. The three horses he brought with him followed without a sound, and he felt very alone, having been with other men for such a long time. But yet he did not suffer too much from this, for as well he had indeed been alone for a similar amount of time when he first discovered Dún as Cloch.

Many more days passed as he traveled through the great green hills of Eire. He had not known that his homeland was so empty, so untouched and pure. He almost enjoyed the absence of man, as his horse trotted along.

Finally, when even the nights had become sweltering hot, Fearghus spotted a very large village. Like Tuathal's settlement, it possessed wooden walls, and seemed incredibly preserved from the outside world. When Fearghus galloped up to its gates, the heralds atop the wall shouted down to him, obviously having seen him beforehand. "Who has come?" one of them asked in a low but loud voice.

"I am Fearghus of Dún as Cloch!" he responded, trying to sound like an important nobleman.

The herald opened the gate, and shouted back to him. "I have not heard of this Dún as Cloch!" he told him.

"You surely will!" Fearghus informed him, letting down his noble disguise. Before him, the gate was wide open and the women of the village were hurrying to meet him in the central square of the town. They brought with them many gifts of fruit and bread, and with them, surprisingly, came the king of the town, decorated with a golden circlet upon his head. He seemed a very old man to Fearghus, but yet very wise.

"My people welcome you," the old king said. This man was not a magus, Fearghus observed. Only the smaller towns he knew were led in such a religious manner, his own being one of them.

"I thank you for that," Fearghus said.

The king stroked his chin. "Why have you come here?" he asked.

"I come seeking help, and men," Fearghus answered him, looking into the king's wrinkled face for an answer. The man's countenance, however, revealed nothing of his inner thoughts.

"We will see about this, inside," he replied, and turned towards his hall in the very center of town. In a very short time Fearghus's horses were attended to, and he was led by two tall guards to the king's table within his hall. The long table was modestly furbished with the usual of feasts including bread, meat, and ale.

"So tell me about this Dún as Cloch," the king asked him as soon as he sat down.

Fearghus told him only what he felt was necessary to convince the king to allow him some of his men. He described with much detail the valley itself, and also the work already being done there to create a city. What he didn't reveal to the king included information concerning the Lady, and also the Snake, Osgar, and the Romans.

After hearing this, the king thought for a long while, and left the table for a very long time to consult with his advisors. After a while Fearghus became fearful that he would not return and possibly was insulted for some reason by him, but to his relief, the ruler returned and sat back down next to him. "I have given much consideration to your proposal," he started, "and would like very much myself to visit this valley with forty of my fighting-men. We will discuss how they aid your cause when we arrive."

Fearghus was ecstatic, this so much so that he found himself unable to eat for the remaining duration of the feast. He wanted so badly to return to Dún as Cloch, he even asked the king when they were to depart. The old man assured him it would be after only but one day of preparation. The king himself was excited.

Throughout the next day, the forty warriors of the village commissioned to help Fearghus prepared their beasts for travel, and gathered their tools, weapons, and clothing. Fearghus hoped that there would be enough room for them all to safely make camp in his green valley, but with the progress of Dunchad's men he was not worried.

Finally the day came for them to leave. Fearghus made sure with the king that the men should go on foot, because he could not allow forty beasts to ravage the fair fields of Dún as Cloch. Also, he inspected carefully the tools they brought with them, for he had seen the instruments Dunchad's men were using and knew much about the trade of building, as surely these warriors would not.

They left the village at midday in two columns, with Fearghus and Conaill, the old king, at the front of each. The men walked quickly behind their leader, for rumor of a great fruitful paradise had reached them all by now. Fearghus, during this time, kept the head of his staff hidden from the men in a pouch hung across his shoulder, and instead held Osgar itself as a standard for his small army. He had tied a crimson ribbon about it to make it suitable as such, and held it high next to the red banner of Conaill.

When they made camp that night they were surprisingly organized. The men formed into groups of ten and gathered about four campfires, each group sharing a single lamb from their small herds and some water from their skins. Conaill's warriors were a rare occurrence in Eire: they functioned in an orderly and courteous manner, as more of an army than a drunken band of war-mongers.

Fearghus drank ale with Conaill around a separate fire, and the two were given the choicest lamb of the bunch to eat. Just as he did two nights before, Conaill ate greedily the meat he was allowed, and filled his cup with ale as he pleased. Sharing his vigor this night, Fearghus was pleased to find himself in the mood to eat and drink heartily with his new friend. He felt he was with friends again, a feeling he had not felt entirely since he left Seadna and Irial in the North.

They traveled in a uniform style for all of twelve days before Fearghus recognized the mountains around Dún as Cloch. They were gray and pointed, but somehow seemed so even and perfect. Conaill was pleased to see them as well, for he knew as well as anyone that they would be perfect walls for an unbreakable fortress.

When Fearghus led his horse to the mouth of the watery cavern, he was pleased to find that Dunchad's men had completed a floating wooden bridge of sorts running along the side of the inner wall, and had decked this wall with iron rings now holding numerous torches. Also, he could see, they had busied themselves in constructing a hefty wooden gate for the entire mouth of the corridor over the sea, so that no intruding ships could enter the cave. At the moment, this project was only partially completed. Conaill certainly was pleased to find at least this evidence of a settlement here.

Fearghus and his forty men walked in single file across the floating logs and eventually came to the iron door at the end of the tunnel, where Dunchad's torches illuminated the waterfall with golden light and also where there stood a well-armed guard of his. The man was happy to see his master returning successful, and held the door open for the warriors to pass with their heavy loads.

Dunchad gave Fearghus a tight hug of approval when they met. When the two men separated, Fearghus introduced Dunchad to Conaill. The two leaders eyed each other skeptically, but soon came to an agreement to collaborate their efforts in the construction of Dún as Cloch. By nightfall, the forty men had found shelter in the buildings, and made friends with the twenty of Dunchad.

Before he retired to his own house, Fearghus approached Dunchad again. "See to it that the men are trained in the processes of breaking stone," he told his friend, and walked away.

But Dunchad stopped him. "What has happened to my men?" he asked curiously.

Fearghus decided to lie. "They were slain by thieves," he answered in a sad tone, bowing his head. "I am truly sorry."

Dunchad climbed into his bed. "Thank the gods that you escaped!" was all he said with a longing sigh, and turned away.

Fearghus went immediately to the house he had built for himself so many long days ago. It was hardly big enough for him alone, but he had grown too familiar with it to leave it for a room in the other buildings.

The forty men of Conaill did not begin work immediately. There was a vast amount of training and planning to be done, and thus it was allowed that Dunchad's men become their teachers in the ways of construction. These men were warriors, certainly not workers. But there was promise in their strong bodies and open minds. Dunchad, Conaill, and Fearghus alike agreed to this.

Fearghus talked to Conail as they ate breakfast the next morning in the Oaken Hall. Conaill was very impressed with the beauty of the valley, and with the buildings already constructed, of which there were now four, as Dunchad had made yet another while they were yet far from Dún as Cloch.

"It is just as you have said before," the king commented happily.

Fearghus only smiled. "I thank you for believing me then. Do you, as I do, see what may come to be in this paradise?"

"I do, and I wish to join your settlement," Conaill replied, grinning. "I simply shall send one of my men back to the village to appoint a new leader and recruit more settlers and workers to your cause."

Fearghus perked up. "Do you tell the truth? Are you really willing to settle yourself here, in Dún as Cloch?" he asked.

Conaill nodded. "Just find me a good place to stay, and I shall see about bringing even more help for you to build your city. I'm through with all this power and responsibility. I name you my lord until my death." And with this the old king knelt before Fearghus, bowing his head.

But Fearghus knelt as well, and looked Conail straight in the eyes. "There will be no lords and vassals here, I tell you," he said, "only good men working for one cause." And with that Conaill stood up upon his feet and followed his friend out of the Oaken Hall, for there was much work to be done that day.

Fearghus subsequently thought very much about Conaill's actions. He had given up the throne of a large walled village to serve him. What was his motive? He said he was tired of playing the role of king, but Fearghus suspected yet another reason. It was a decision determined by fate. Fate brought all these men here, and fate had brought Osgar into his power. What then, was his own ultimate fate? Was it to be here, in Dún as Cloch? Or instead was it to take place somewhere else? He very much wanted to know, but he knew he would not for a very long time hereafter.

After ten days, the forty men were put to work. They worked quickly and efficiently, from Fearghus's standpoint. Under the direction of Dunchad's men, the speed of the erection of buildings in the valley was doubled, and then tripled. Also, the quality of work was increased, as a good number of Dunchad's men were commissioned to work as judges and overseers of the project.

To Fearghus's delight, his desire to create a fortress of stone was beginning to prove true. The two stone-hewers of Dunchad had trained Conaill's men expertly in their trade. Already ten men had cut several blocks from the inner mountainside, and were pulling them in vast carts to the building site. There was talk of a huge stone hall in the very center of the valley, and it would be known as the Rock of Sucellos, as a temple to honor the king of the gods. Its foundation had as yet been laid already, but it covered a large area, and so the shrine itself would take a lifetime to complete with just fifty men.

By this time, Fearghus had perfected a daily routine for himself. His day still included helping harvest wood from the forest outside the mountains himself, but he was also beginning to view himself as a leader over the common man. In this sense, he spent an equal amount of time in the Oaken Hall approving building plans and being attended by two particular slaves from Conaill's village.

At times, Fearghus would think about the life he left behind when he left the village in the North. His mind would wander to thoughts of Agnos, and her love, and also of Seadna, and the lost Irial, and all their military might that now had been laid to waste. He thought of his experience thus far, and of his adventures upon the Isle of Man. What would all these things come to if he didn't once more seek his friends out?

The city of Dún as Cloch rose to amazing heights all around him. Every man now had a dry room to sleep in, and a hall to feast in at night. Now, not four but ten huge edifices filled the entire green valley with their spires and balconies. A town twice the size of Conaill's had been constructed out of more than half of the forest around Dún as Cloch.

At last Fearghus stood before his great and very own kingdom. It was far larger than he had thought it would be. And through all this, he noticed, the stream around the valley and the wonderful plants within had not been violated by the sixty men who had built the city.

Fearghus was proud as a victorious king takes pride in his riches and victorious knights. But he was truly sad, he realized, as well. In the days before this moment he had spent several nights dreaming of Agnos and what she was for him. He remembered her soft hair and skin, and her knowing eyes staring deeply into his. She would be the only woman he ever loved, and he had to see her again.

It was then that he decided his masterpiece was finished. The refuge Seadna had sent him to find was here in front of him, and he would like very much to share it with his old friend. Dún as Cloch was better and safer than the monastery he had hidden in before. He had to find them again!

That night it was very warm, and there were no clouds in the sky. The stars were shining brightly above the highest tops of the mountains, unimpeded by the red glow of fire dancing across the stone walls of the Rock of Sucellos. It was here where Fearghus came this night, and lay on his back on the very top of the unfinished temple, looking straight up into the endless sky.

With the desire to find his old friends again, there also arose in Fearghus the desire to take the fight back to the Romans at the monastery. Were there not sixty able-bodied men below him in the valley who were willing to fight? This time he would be the aggressor hiding in the encircling forest. He would exact revenge so swiftly, the Celts would sing of him hereafter as Fearghus the Great, and the Romans call him Fearghus the Terrible. And so anger consumed his heart in unison with longing and sadness.

Fearghus kept his plans secret for many days, because he did not expect his companions here to agree with him. He would have to think of something to convince them to come with him, and of course he would need even more men than this. There would be hundreds of Romans in the monastery, all equipped with stout horses and long javelins.

Fearghus knew he would need a miracle to make his army so great, and many days later when he woke, one came.

Chapter 15

Return to Glory

Fearghus was working outside the valley chopping wood when he noticed on the horizon a very large ship. He could not make out exactly whose ship it was, but nonetheless the sail was white in the distance.

Soon enough every man around him had noticed the sails, blazing in the dawn, and the ten or so laborers gathered behind him and watched the horizon with equal interest, though Fearghus knew they could not see the ship as clearly as he.

They waited in such a position for a great while, and at length the ship came into clear view. When it was close enough for Fearghus to see, his expectations were confirmed. "It's a Roman vessel!" one of the men cried out behind him. And with that the whole lot of them ran into the trees, keeping a close eye on the incoming invaders.

Fearghus followed them into the forest but did not hide. "We have a real chance here," he told the man nearest to him.

"What do you mean?" the worker asked, bobbing back and forth from the cover of a stout tree trunk as he spoke. "We shouldn't let them see us!"

Fearghus crouched behind an adjacent tree. "You know what I mean," he said sarcastically.

The man shook his head. "What could you possibly have in mind?" he whispered, for the Roman ship had drawn up to the shore.

"We can capture the ship!" Fearghus answered quickly and without fear.

His friend looked confused. "With just this?" he asked, holding up his hefty axe.

Fearghus drew his menacing blade quickly and silently. "Don't worry," he assured the worker, "I'll take care of that part."

The two men moved quietly through the trees and alerted the other men. Only two of them had brought their swords with them, but this did not worry Fearghus. The rest of the workers carried light hatchets and daggers on their belts.

Fearghus gathered them all behind a large bush. "Now if I'm correct, then I think they'll send the majority of their men ashore when they land here. Those of you who are brave enough can follow me out to get them."

Most of the men, Fearghus knew, were warriors of Conaill's village, and had not forgotten about their training in hand to hand combat. All of them agreed to a stealthy plan involving concealed weapons and swimming to the Roman ship to take it, and Fearghus was pleased. Fearghus concocted a nasty plan in which he would risk his life by approaching the Roman men alone on the beach.

Before he left the woods, Fearghus sent his friend to the small door on the side of the mountain to warn Dunchad and Conaill of the coming danger. The Romans, he knew, had seen the sturdy door blocking the entrance to the caverns and were very suspicious.

Finally, he put his plan into action. The Romans had run their small boats ashore with more than fifteen men, most of them soldiers. Fearghus knew that with the element of surprise he could take all of them with just his ten men, but just as well he was very nervous about this prospect.

The Roman armor gleamed in the sun as Fearghus stood up and casually walked out of the forest, his sword and scabbard behind his back. The soldiers were in a good fighting formation of two columns as they gathered upon the beach, and each man looked the same as the other. The warriors would have no trouble deciding who was friend or foe in the fight ahead.

Fearghus glanced back and saw his men take their last positions in the trees as he neared the Roman column. He diverted his revealing gaze not a moment too soon, for as he turned around the leader of the Romans acknowledged him. Now Fearghus had learned a few words of Latin from Agnos when they were together in the monastery. When the Roman shouted something at him that he could not understand, he simply shouted back, "Hello, my name is Fearghus," and strode forward as quickly as he dared.

The Roman seemed pleased by this, and allowed him to move even closer. Before he knew it, Fearghus stood directly before the mighty Roman captain, with one hand behind his back holding a massive sword. Any time now and he would strike, and send the entire troop of men into chaos.

Not wasting any time, he suddenly shouted his favorite battle cry, "For Eire!" and out of nowhere his sword swung down from behind his back and sailed straight into the gut of the captain. In that split second, ten men burst from the forest, screaming on high. The Roman soldiers next to Fearghus were cast into disarray, pulling their swords out.

But Fearghus was too quick for them. He would not leave his ten men with knives to face fifteen with broadswords. Jerking his sword out of the captains stomach he leapt into the air, and in a flash was upon them, all alone. His sword rose and fell, and was drawn in and out of flesh. Before the men reached the soldiers he had taken four of them, and their blood spilled across the ground, seeping into the sand.

Two of the men, particularly those with swords ran to the side of the fray and dove headlong into the water. They were skilled veterans and Fearghus had commissioned them to capture the ship for him, as there would be hardly a soul aboard the vessel.

Now all of the men had hurled themselves headlong into the battle, swinging hatchets and axes through Roman necks and into Roman chests. They had a slight disadvantage of weaponry, but yet the advantage of surprise and of determination. The Roman soldiers were hacked down so quickly under their blows that Fearghus almost immediately ran out of targets to strike with his own terrible blade.

The sound of ringing metal from the ship led them all into the water, their arms spinning like great windmills. In a flash Fearghus had found the anchor line and had pulled himself onto the deck of the vessel, his sword never leaving his grasp.

There were yet five soldiers defending the fair ship, and the two men Fearghus had sent aboard to engage them were having quite a bit of trouble with it. One of the soldiers was trying desperately to cut the anchor line and get the ship to move again, but as Fearghus watched him suddenly one of his men hopped onto the deck and slew him. In a very short amount of time all enemies had been defeated.

Fearghus dropped the bodies into the sea near the old wreckage, and steered the ship towards the cavern. Just as he did this, to his pleasure, the men of Dunchad who had built the great gate upon it opened the passage, and the ship rolled into the stone harbor under the power of the twenty slaves below, who Fearghus discovered were mostly of the Celtic race, and from both Britain and Eire.

Fearghus and his men departed the ship when they were safely inside the watery cavern and the gate had swung shut. This chamber was continuously lit with torches as was the entire corridor, and the liberated slaves from the hold below were impressed with the structure.

And so Fearghus had his ship. With it, as the men of Seadna had done with the *Silverbeam* before it, he could raid the coast, trade with distant villages and cities, and even land an entire army of men wherever he pleased. The free men from the ship would help his building effort, if any of them agreed to stay, and the capturing of the ship would invigorate his existing men with a strong desire to fight the Romans and battle abroad. Fearghus also now had a medium to safely travel north to find his friends again, which he had decided to do long before.

Fearghus now decided to reveal his plan to the leaders of the building effort, and hopefully they would agree that the time had come to take the fight back to Rome. They would start slowly, and then pick up speed. Of course, Fearghus knew, he would need more men to attack the monastery outright, but he knew where he might find some, and he had the ship to reach them in.

At supper that night, as the men laughed and drank about the vast table of the Oaken Hall, Fearghus paused in his eating and looked up at Conaill, who sat next to him at the corner of the table. "Think you that I have done a good deed?" he asked cautiously, studying the face of the king.

Coniall replied quickly and with resolve. "I would have nothing to do with it," he said harshly. "Your folly has led nearly to the death of ten men!"

Fearghus looked horrified. As he opened his mouth, though, Conaill continued. "But as long as no dirty Romans survived, I see no harm in it," he said under his breath and with a chuckle. "Just don't take another risk like that again!"

Fearghus drew back. He knew he had to reveal his plan to the king soon, but he could hardly muster the courage now to do so. "I will see to it that I don't," he answered, and pushed back his chair. "Good night to you," he told Conaill politely, and set off to the other end of the table, where at the head sat Dunchad, a very amiable but also very easily manipulated leader of the men.

When he approached him, Dunchad said, "Well now, how are you doing, Fearghus?" and straightened up in his seat.

Fearghus did not sit down. He was too nervous. "I wish to speak with you," he said, and pointed to the door.

Outside, the two men walked towards the temple in the center of the valley, looking at the stars above them, each one bright and clear, unhindered by the red light below. "I've been doing a great bit of thinking in recent days," Fearghus began, looking at Dunchad.

"What do you have to say?" the old man asked.

"You know," Fearghus said, "that I used to be a great warrior in the North."

Dunchad nodded. "Men from the forests up there sing of you as a great hero among men," he said. "Thus I am honored to be in your presence."

Fearghus frowned. "I am afraid I have not been entirely honest with you," he said. "There are some things that happened in the North that I have not told you about."

"What might this be?" the friendly warrior of Tuathal asked.

Fearghus had nothing to hide. "We have suffered recent defeat," was all he said, and indeed as he expected the expression upon Dunchad's face changed dramatically.

"To what extent?" he asked curiously, his countenance wrinkled and distraught.

"We managed to save the women and a small band of men," Fearghus assured him, "But we were unable to hold our ground."

"Then the rumors are true that the Romans gather their forces unchecked in the North?" Dunchad asked.

Fearghus bowed his head. "We have made a great fight against them, but they have proven to be too strong."

"There must be some way we can stop them," Dunchad said enthusiastically.

Fearghus's face lit up with this comment. "I was considering that option myself," he told him.

Dunchad seemed excited. "This shall be our new stronghold, and we will finally deliver the killing blow to these Romans," he nearly shouted.

Fearghus seemed hopeful now as well. "We will begin to amass our fighters in a few days," he warned Dunchad, "do not reveal our plan to anyone else here, just yet."

Fearghus was beginning to put his plan into action. At least among the two leaders he had spoken to, one had agreed with his thinking. But not so badly as he wanted to defeat the Romans, he knew, he rather wished to break from his war-bands and seek out Agnos and Seadna in the hills north of the encircling forest where once he had held such high ground against his enemies.

The men continued to work for two days while Dunchad and Fearghus held their secret. The city of Dún as Cloch looked to be nearly complete in this time, though the laborers had worked only but a half more than an even hundred days, and the heat of the summer days was still set upon the green valley, which did not show the worse for it.

The great city seemed empty, since only sixty men were present to fill its five hundred rooms. Fearghus knew he would need more men to make the stronghold great as well as its army. As he had heard, the king Conaill knew much of the land around his native village, and would be a great help in this task.

The Rock of Sucellos was still far from completion, but nonetheless stood out among the other buildings in the city as great. The base was an arcade of great doors and pillars, and it was made of massive blocks of stone from the mountains to be unshakable, even in the most terrible of storms. The rest of the temple was composed of flat stones, laid as bricks upon one another, and they were glued together as bricks. They were placed in rising stories as up to a point at the top of the temple, where would be placed a great likeness of Sucellos, far above the towers elsewhere in the city. Dunchad had commissioned his greatest builders as the constructors of this shrine, and even now it looked beautiful and strong. No where in Eire this day was there such a building. It was the beginning of a new age of architecture, led by the gods.

Finally the day came when Fearghus decided to reveal his wishes to the men, and their leader Conaill. He asked Dunchad to do this for him, so that he would not possibly lose the trust of the king, but all was fine when Connaill in fact agreed to consider the idea of attacking, and engaged Fearghus directly about the idea.

The two men then created a plan of attack, involving most importantly the stolen ship. "I will be able to have a hundred men here in five days," Connaill told Fearghus as they sat in the Oaken Hall. "We will be able to attack in ten."

"When we go up there again," Fearghus asked, "will you allow me to take a small company further north to search for a few friends of mine?"

"Of course you may, if it wins us the support of more men," Conaill answered.

Shortly after their conversation, a caravan of twenty men left for Conaill's village on foot, there to acquire horses and ride to the five villages on the outskirts of the coastal plain. From these places they would recruit as many men as possible to Fearghus's cause, and march them back to Dún as Cloch with arms. Fearghus, in the meantime, would prepare his ship for carrying the men and chart his course to battle.

The wait for the men to arrive was very long, and Dunchad and the others grew impatient. But just as Conaill said, after five days a vast column of men was seen by the lookouts atop the mountains around the valley and hastened into the now completed gate. It was a bright morning when they came into the heavenly valley of Dún as Cloch, and Fearghus had just risen from his slumber.

He hurried to strap on his old armor and girt his sword, and by the time he was out of his cabin the men had organized themselves on the open field before the Oaken Hall. Stumbling a bit, he finally came into their view, standing on the doorstep of the great hall, the new standard of Dún as Cloch in the hand of the guard at his right.

The sun blazed off of the helmets of two hundred men, and Fearghus noticed that each of the helmets were different. Some were open-faced and made of iron, others were closed or made of leather. Some men did not even wear armor on their heads, or for that matter on their entire bodies. Fearghus could see many of their faces, and he saw both of the looks of youth and age, and of exhaustion and strength. The general weapon of choice for the party seemed to be the short crude lance, fashioned of iron and wood, but also Fearghus beheld many archers and swordsmen amidst the masses of irregular spear heads. These warriors were like to any that he had seen in Eire from the time of his childhood. They were dirty, unorganized, and ill-behaved, but yet also confident, courageous, and very well-trained.

The men remained quiet as Fearghus addressed them for the first time. "If you do not know why you are here," he began in a loud voice, "then soon you will. The Romans have come here to impose their religion, their way of life upon us. They come with swords and terrible lances from the south. Now I ask you, can we let them take over our land?"

The crowd of fighters erupted with shouts of "No!" in many different Gaelic dialects, also with many crude bellows and whoops. The spears above their heads stirred like reeds in the wind, and the great masses mulled about in common agreement. The captains and magi among them tried to settle them down, but it was no use with these men from so many different places in southern Eire.

Fearghus stopped them, though. With his heavy voice he silenced them with a great cry, and continued his speech. "The Romans have one thing that we don't have," he told them haughtily, and now he had their attention. Before anyone there could ask what it was he was speaking of, he continued. "They have an organized military."

The men talked amongst themselves but did not become unruly at this comment. "In order to defeat them, we must join together as brothers!" Fearghus shouted above them to numerous cheers. "Whatever differences you may have, put them aside now!"

It was now that Fearghus was to mold these men into an invincible fighting force. He had devised a number of steps to help them get along better. "Divide into your own village groups!" Fearghus told them first. In a very short amount of time, five blocks of men, some larger than the others, had formed in the field. Within each group the weapons and armor were similar, as was the dialect, clothing, and otherwise appearance of the men.

Next Fearghus did something very questionable, but also very wise. "Form into groups of five, with one man from each town!" he shouted, and immediately the sixty men of Connaill and Dunchad drove into the two hundred men and assisted the chaotic task trying to be accomplished. The five enormous groups had collided on the field, and men ran every which way. "Completed groups shall come to the Oaken Hall!" Fearghus now cried, and one by one, groups of five and four men clambered up the steps of the hall, until the crowd upon the field was halved in size. At length, luckily, all two hundred of the men were herded into at least groups of two or three, and the great Oaken Hall was filled.

Fearghus sprinted to his throne at the head of the table and began barking more commands. "Each group shall be furnished a room in the city to sleep in," he told them, "and each group shall be served their share of food and water there." But he added, "Ten groups shall stay here with me," and instantly ten groups of men wove their way to the front of the room and joined Fearghus at the throne. The remaining one hundred and fifty men were shuffled out of the hall and to their rooms, as one of Conaill's men accompanied each of them. When the buildings at the helm of the city were full, the buildings behind them were filled until five of the huge structures were occupied. There yet remained over ten towers more with yet other smaller buildings than this, but to Fearghus, the city seemed alive.

And so the Army of Dún as Cloch was formed by integrating different groups of warriors into one body. This was the first real army Eire had ever seen, and Fearghus was confident it would be a fine antidote for the wrath of the Romans in the North. It would be the tool for breaking the Roman military presence in Eire, and keeping it pinned to the sea at least. If he could capture the monastery, he knew, then he would really defeat the Romans once and for all, and send them back to the shores of Britain, where long before the Celts had lost a terrible and bloody war to them.

With the fifty men Fearghus had left to himself in the Oaken Hall, Fearghus suddenly threw a great communal feast, and it was to be the first of many more. He himself sat among the men as they ate wild game and fruit from the surrounding forest, and drank ale from Conaill's village store. The meal ran long into the night, and by the end of it the men were very drunk and very happy. Also, as Fearghus had designed, they were very trusting of him and ready to follow his every command.

For the next three days Fearghus threw this same feast thrice, alternating the rest of the two hundred warriors into the Oaken Hall and meeting many interesting men. During this time the other men would be trained in the arts of war by the men of Conaill and a number of their own superiors, this from the dawn to the dusk. Each day Fearghus watched them in the field through the great doors of his hall, for so great was the gate of the Oaken Hall.

On the fifth day Fearghus prepared his men for travel. He was up early in his little house and dressed in his armor, which had been shined and polished meticulously before this time. He gathered unto himself his sword and Osgar, and went straight to the Oaken Hall where Conaill and a number of the magi from the army had gathered long before this time, when it was yet dark. They had devised a preliminary plan of attack, but needed his approval before mobilizing the warriors in the city around them.

Fearghus strode to the head of the long table and leant over it, examining a map in front of the leaders. Conaill was the first to speak. "A hundred and fifty men will march from the south on foot, and they will arrive later than those aboard the ship," he explained. "We will bring fifty upon the vessel with us, and attack from the north, while fifty more will ride upon horses from my village and appear in the west, to block the Roman retreat inland."

Fearghus examined the sketch Conaill made on the paper in front of him. The monastery was denoted by an circle and the great southern forest was represented with stripes in between them and their goal. Fearghus then picked up the brush the king was using and made markings for the pirate's harbor, the houses of Conn and Irial, and the villages of Tuathal, Seadna, and even the one that he intended to find in the hills north of the monastery. He was very concerned about detail, and nervous about the coming siege.

Suddenly, the thunder of four hundred feet rattled the beams above them. Immediately the guards at the door swung the immense gate open, and Fearghus beheld through it the gathered forces of one hundred and fifty men. They stood in neat lines as in mockery of the Romans, and their armor had been cleaned. Their ranks were organized by their leaders into specific ranks. The spearmen stood in vast columns in front of and in a thin line around their comrades, since there were so many of them. Behind them stood the swordsmen with their light shields, and further behind them were the few archers of the group, their quivers bursting with newly fletched arrows of iron and stone.

When Fearghus dashed out to the front of his hall to look them over, a great chant rose among them. Fearghus was pleased that his method of integrating the diverse peoples had worked. The magi had taught them a battle cry, and they chanted it in nearly perfect unison before him, and their words echoed through the stone valley with amazing impact. They said something Fearghus could hardly imagine, for such it was : "For Eire!"

Instantly Fearghus drew his terrible blade and rallied his men, brandishing the weapon several times in the air. And behind him the standard of Dún as Cloch fluttered in the morning breeze. It depicted in hues of silver, blue and green the great mountains and streams of the valley, and an image of Osgar in the middle, striking in the intense light of dawn. And Osgar itself Fearghus lifted into the air, though the men knew it not, and he gave a great cry of battle, like to the cries of the ancient warriors of this land, and raised his face to the sky above.

The men stayed in their ranks, but burst with support of their master, shouting aloud through the valley. Some there thought they were so loud, the dead could hear them below the earth. And with this they were off, marching in a single column through the iron gate. Fearghus watched them as they disappeared from him, and when the guard finally closed the iron door he returned to his hall, still shaking with excitement, and drew a chair to calm down in.

"The horsemen have left with them," Conaill told him when he subsided.

"Them all we have left is the fifty men to board the ship," Fearghus said. "When will we depart?"

Coanill leaned back in his chair. "We will depart at dusk, that we might not arrive too far ahead of the greater force of warriors."

"So shall it be," said Fearghus, and he swept his cape up behind him as he left his seat, and dashed out of the hall to the sunny world of morning outside. He had nothing left to do to prepare for his next great adventure. All he could do was wait until the sun set, and then he would be off to be reunited with his old friends.

Now he bounded off to the iron door himself, for he wished to board his boat. He walked quickly down the wooden path in the cavern until he came to it, and when he did he rejoiced. Leaping onto the deck, he delighted himself in exploring the rooms and the now empty hold. He stayed here in the warm light of the cavern's torches for a great while as the sun outside traveled all the way across the sky, only returning to the city when it was nearly dusk.

The city seemed deserted. Only sixty men were left in the entire valley, and their presence was not well felt as they lived in the closed buildings. More than half but not all of the men were of the original band of laborers in Dún as Cloch, but each nonetheless had become friends with the other.

As the sun passed the tops of the mountains encircling the valley, Conaill sent the guards in amongst the buildings to rouse the remaining men. They were going to board the ship and sail north to the monastery, and they would be there in only a few days.

The men lit torches as they gathered in the field where that morning two hundred others had congregated. Fearghus did not rally his men this time; instead he joined them. He rode a horse at their helm and led them to the iron door with the standard, waiting there until all had passed into the cavern. Ten men under the supervision of Dunchad were left behind in Dún as Cloch, so as to maintain and guard it during the expedition.

The rest of the army was already a full day's journey north of them, but they likely would pass them in their speedy ship, even before the full night had taken its hold of the world.

The ship dropped a bit in the water as fifty heavily armored men climbed onto its decks. There was room for only half of them in the hold as oar-turners, and thus thirty men were now forced to make the main deck their home. They laid out on mats on the hard wooden floor while Fearghus and Connail moved into the main cabin.

The two guards at the heavy wooden gate pulled upon ropes to open it, and allow the passage through it of the stolen ship. Beyond the sturdy timber of the gate, the water was darker than the star-studded sky above it. Nothing could be made of the land around them as the moon remained covered by clouds. As the twenty men down below slowly propelled it out into the sea, the guardsmen drew up torches and ran along the shore, guiding the men at the rudder. When the ship had turned completely left and sat parallel with the land, the men with torches signaled to Fearghus to proceed forward with caution. As Fearghus gave the command to move, one of the guardsmen ran ahead to a rocky cliff further down the shore and held his torch aloft for the men on the ship to see.

Soon the ship had passed this man and the warriors were well on their way north to the monastery. It was dangerous that they were moving, though, because the dangers upon the shore such as rocks and shallow fields of water were invisible. Even now, several men were leaning over the railing of the ship at its front and side, holding lanterns and torches close to the water.

Fearghus and Conaill had the pleasure of speaking outside on the small upper deck above their room, since there weren't any strong winds to blow away their maps and rain to destroy them. They brought a lantern and two guards with torches to their table at the top of the stairs, and enjoyed the fresh air of the sea, very different from the sweltering and humid air of the land.

Now Conaill looked over the map they had drawn before in the Oaken Hall. "We will wait near the pirate's lair for your return, and give time for the army to arrive," he said, for Fearghus had yet informed him of his intentions upon landing in Eire.

"Thank you for that," Fearghus answered. "I should not be too long, if we land in the correct place."

"I hope surely that we do," said Conaill.

Suddenly they were interrupted, for one of the men on deck cried aloud, pointing towards the land. Just to the left of them on the beach, a hundred campfires glimmered like the stars. In their light the two-hundred men of the Army of Dún as Cloch were visible, their silhouettes black but evident in the firelight. What little light the stars could give in the absence of the moon reflected off of the smoke from their fires, and a great gray cloud seemed to hang over their position near the water, where they had marched in nearly an entire day. Conaill and Fearghus watched them until they were gone, for they had nothing more to say until they landed far north of here near the monastery.

The rest of the night wore on routinely as the men below slowed their pace and took turns at the oar, moving the ship sluggishly ahead into the foggy night. Fearghus slept soundly in the cabin of the ship adjacent to Conaill, and kept Osgar near to him. He did not know why he held the spear with such determination, why he strained to keep possession of it. It had not helped him ward off the Romans before, and thus he could not fathom how it would prove to help him. He thought maybe he had used up its power as if it was a well, but nonetheless maintained it.

The next morning brought a brilliant dawn on the blue horizon to their right, and a helpful breeze. All fifty of the men were able to relax in the air above the hold for the duration of the day, and the white sails were let loose, though the Roman cross upon them was not well liked by the warriors. At least, Fearghus knew, the sails would disguise them when they landed on the beach, and lead the Romans to believe that more men had arrived to reinforce them.

Fearghus spent the day further preparing for battle. He had not engaged the Romans for a great while, and he was eager to exact his revenge on them with his three hundred men. He did not think that there were yet more Romans than this in such a remote place as Eire, but he was foolish enough to want to find out. The great battle that destroyed his first army had weakened their presence enough, that with so little men he thought certainly he could destroy them.

Fearghus sharpened his sword and polished yet again his great golden Crown of the Deep, and kept to himself for the duration of the day. At last after the day's travel, the sun yet again pressed to the mountains of Eire, and the men prepared to sup atop their proud vessel. The men had brought with them provisions for five days of travel, and this night they used some of these to fill their stomachs for the next day, when they probably would land.

Fearghus ate with Conaill and a number of other men at their table on the upper deck, and feasted upon bread and meat from the hogs, all with fine Roman wine from the hold. The meal was long and fulfilling, and some of the men again became drunk as they had in the days before.

Fearghus finished eating early and before the others, and decided to walk down to the deck below, where the men were stretched out across the deck, some relaxed, and others wild with happiness and confidence. Fearghus walked through their ranks as a king walks among peasants, and finally came to the front of the ship, where he looked ahead into the night, scanning the darkness to their left for the land.

He could not see the shore from here, and it troubled him a bit. Yet he did not worry himself about it, for the men at the rudder, he believed, were skilled enough for such work. Apparently, he was wrong.

Suddenly Fearghus saw a great precipice looming ahead of them, and they were doing nothing to steer from it. He ran to the back of the ship where the men at the tiller sat, but they were not there. The men had tied the mechanism off to drink with their comrades. He opened his mouth to scream for help, dashing to the rear of the ship, but he was too late.

Fearghus was knocked off of his feet as he wheeled around to see a great white stone smash into the front of the ship. It was an impact worse than any he had ever felt, even during the ramming of other ships. The wood squealed and cracked as it was pushed further into the ragged cliff, and the deck was tilted as the entire vessel ran up upon it.

Quickly regaining his feet, Fearghus sprinted to the entrance to the hold, peering down the stairwell to the floor below. The wooden planks, as he feared, were washed with water, deep enough to enclose the knees of a man. "Get off the ship!" Fearghus screamed as loud as he could, running back and forth amongst his panicking men.

The warriors near him somehow found the beach to their left and began to file down a crooked ramp to the land below. Fearghus first ran to his cabin to save Osgar and then followed them, looking every which way to supervise the evacuation of his men. Behind him, five men were swimming in the sea, and from their faces he recognized the men from the upper deck, who had been knocked into the waves by the initial collision. Conaill was one of them, he knew, though he could not recognize the king's face.

Fearghus ran down the ramp to the beach below, and leant against a pale white stone in the sand. Gasping for breath, many other men joined him in this place, until their noise had subsided and the evacuation was complete.

Fearghus immediately stood up and tried to determine their location. When he did, something immediately caught his eye, and he knew they were close to their destination. They had crashed into the white cliffs on the north side of the pirate's harbor. He could see the blackened remains of the cove even now, as he stood on a sandy hill far above it.

Luckily, Conaill had survived. He staggered to a position behind Fearghus, and grunted a bit to let him know of his presence. "I am sorry we have failed so terribly," he muttered, his head bowed.

Fearghus placed his hand on the king's shoulders. "We have not failed," he said painfully, his body bruised and tired. "Look below us into the ruined home of the pirates."

"I see it indeed," Conaill responded. But suddenly his expression changed. "Let us be down there now!" he shouted, for quite suddenly he had heard the sounds of many men coming from the south. They were coming from the monastery. Their armor made a racket that resounded off of the mountains, and even now they had gained the top of the valley.

Fearghus led the fifty men down the rough sandy slopes of the cove, and all at once the lot of them slid down the hill on their backs, coming to a thrilling halt at the very bottom of the harbor, on the burnt plain. And not a moment too soon did they do this, for above them the feet of what seemed nearly as many men were heard.

The group crept into the long shadow of the vertical wall of the harbor, moving out of the light of the moon. The group of Romans were here to investigate the wreck of the ship, probably having seen the friendly sails of it on the horizon near the monastery. Though their mission was not to behold the wreck, that is what drew them nearer.

Suddenly Conaill whispered in Fearghus's ear. "We must take our chances now!" he pressed, his eyes glazed over in the dull light. "If we can face them now, then we will not have to deal with them with a wall between us!" he added, and rolled out into the clearing, looking straight up to where the column of soldiers stood, their armor white in the moonlight. He knew they could not see him down here, and took every necessary liberty to get a closer look at their ranks.

At length he rolled back into the darkness. "There are not many of them," he said, "but it will be a tough skirmish."

Indeed, a third of the Celts here had not rescued their heavy weapons from the ruined ship when they left it, though most carried swords. The twenty or so Romans above them would be prepared with lances and thick shields.

Conaill warned the men before attacking. He went in among them in the darkness and told each of their peril, and the task that was required of them. As Fearghus watched, five archers moved into a comfortable position at the far side of the harbor and notched their arrows. The rest of the men began to move up the wide path of sand near them in the corner of the harbor, their swords already drawn.

Fearghus followed cautiously behind them, and when they stopped behind the cover of a large stone, he positioned himself in the front of their group, keeping his sword masked in shadow so as not to draw attention from the Romans directly in front of him.

After much preparation, Conaill finally gave the signal. Waving his hand to a man at the rear of the party he said, "Tell the men to shoot now," and crouched back down. Soon after he said this five well-aimed arrows flew like owls into the Romans, taking down three and wounding another. Their onslaught was so quiet, so sudden that the Romans did not know what to do. They immediately fell into a state of panic.

Then it was time to fight. Without making a sound, Fearghus was upon them, and his sword flashed in and out of the light of the moon, quickly becoming bathed in blood. He jumped high into the air and hewed the Romans down violently, and then recoiled on his landing to slash a good number more, in all dispatching six men. By this time the rest had run into the fray, bearing down on the Romans with their spears and daggers. They washed over the remaining soldiers like water covers the beach and within their ranks the Romans fell to their deaths, run through many times with iron. And all this was done with hardly a sound, for the Roman monastery was near, and certainly would be known to the echo of the sound of battle in this place.

Fearghus did not tarry here a minute. A horse had been saved from the fight that a captain had been riding, and Fearghus was very quickly given it to ride. "Cleanse this place of the stench of death," he told the men waiting there. "Wait here in the harbor until my return."

And with this the men lifted their weapons into the air as a sign of obedience, and held their ground as Fearghus wheeled his horse around and galloped off in search of the village where he knew he could find his old friends. He had never actually seen this place that Seadna had spoken of in their last conversation, but he knew he could find it if he tried.

His horse was a jet black color, and it was a very fast beast. Its feet were light on the barren ground. As he rode forth into the night, Fearghus kicked it into a rapid gallop along the moonlit beach, his cape lifted behind him and his face blasted with a cool night wind. At this rate he would find the village very quickly, for it had not been too long a journey for the defeated men on foot.

He galloped without end for a great while, his eyes searching constantly for familiar signs. Of particular importance to him was the forest he had departed from so long ago, for from a hill just outside of this group of trees, Seadna had seen a village where he planned to bring the rescued people of their rebellion.

Before he rode too far, Fearghus stopped to make camp. But what he actually did was halt his horse under some trees and tie its reins about a sapling. Here he gathered his cape into a roll and laid his head upon it as he slept in the soft sand. The salty and now cold breeze of the sea tossed his hair about as he finally found sleep, and the world became darker.

He was rudely awakened by the sound of many horses galloping towards him. When he opened his eyes he noticed that it was still nighttime, and this alarmed him very much. Drawing his sword in the blink of an eye, he wheeled about, looking for the enemies that were after him. But he could not see even the mountains around him in the darkness of night. The clouds in the sky had thickened and covered the moon, and he was surrounded by complete darkness.

The hoof beats grew louder as he backed into the trees, his sword still swaying in front of him. His own horse began to stamp its feet as it heard them coming, and Fearghus did not know whether to slay it for the reason of quieting it.

But it was too late. Suddenly the torch of a rider rounded the corner of a large rock, illuminating all of the surrounding area, even into the trees where Fearghus hid. Finding shelter in the shrubbery near him, Fearghus hid his entire body and listened for the rest of the horsemen to come. Soon he recognized the Latin voice, and became very angry.

The Romans gathered near the beach, looking into the trees for signs of life. Fearghus did not know why they were here, but he certainly did not want them to be here. He sat for a long time pondering whether or not to attack them, and tentatively convinced himself to stay his rage.

But certainly he was fated to fight that day, for a moment later the Romans discovered his horse. Fearghus could only lay on the ground frozen while the riders advanced on his unsettled beast. He knew that if he didn't take action now that they would find him, and connect the appearance of his horse with his presence. And so he got into a crouching position, ready to pounce.

The first rider dismounted and stepped boldly into the dark forest to locate the horse. Fearghus, seeing this, jumped up into his view and hewed his torch in half, grabbing the throat of the man with his other hand, so that he might not alert his comrades of his danger. Subsequently he slit the man's throat and dragged him behind the bushes, ready for more.

The next man to venture into the grove of trees was already dismounted, and held simply his torch in front of him, seemingly unaware of his friend's terrible end. He walked even further, passing Fearghus's position, and waited foolishly in one place while Fearghus crept up behind him.

In a flash he leapt out of the darkness and swung his blade over his head, aiming for the man's neck. But his sword never found its target, for suddenly a splitting pain met his back, and all the strength was gone from his arms. He fell headlong into the man instead, and the man had already known of his presence, for he jumped aside, swinging his torch around to see his assailant. Fearghus, wincing with incredible pain, was quite sure an arrow had plunged into his lower back and fell motionless to the ground, giving a great cry of defeat.

Fearghus had no memories from the time that passed between this instance and his waking up in captivity. The only recollection he had from this experience was waking up in chains near the waters edge, his back still throbbing with pain from his wound. Luckily it had not been fatal, but it had caused him to lose consciousness and thus the battle with the Roman horsemen. They had cleverly placed a trap for him, having seen one of their own disappear at the edge of the trees. His willingness to fight had been the end of him.

The Romans nearest to him noticed his gain of consciousness, and began to curse at him, kicking him in the stomach and pulling on his chains. He could not understand their speech, and very certainly didn't want to. He would tell them nothing of his plans and thus they would gain such from his capture.

Fearghus groaned in pain as the men tortured him, the arrow in his back not yet removed. He strained to prevent the shaft from being shoved further into his flesh, and luckily the soldiers did not note this, lest they should have pained him further. They simply mounted their horses, and forced him to stagger behind them in his manacles, his wound becoming infected and bloody.

The dawn was coming as they rode back to the monastery. Fearghus was happy with the new light, but it did not do him any good. Now he would be walking under the hot sun. He could now still feel the coolness of the night on his clothes, but soon he knew his armor would burn with heat.

They traveled for a very long time along the beach, and Fearghus, though he was tired, became very excited that they would reach the wreck of the ship that he had arrived in, and then of course the fifty men of Conaill near it. And indeed the soldiers passed this way, but just as they neared the white stone that the ship had crashed upon, they turned into the west, and passed it unknowingly, heading to the stony pass back to the monastery.

But Fearghus was confident now that he could shake these men off. He noticed that the man holding onto his chains was mounted, and that he was not paying a great deal of attention to his prisoner. If Fearghus could muster enough strength, he knew, then he could swing his captor off of his horse and get a start on the rest of the men, hopefully managing to escape to the pirate's harbor, a little ways behind them.

Slowly Fearghus calmed his nerves and staggered further ahead, reducing the tightness of the rope in the soldier's hand. When he decided that the man was sufficiently comfortable with the situation, he suddenly stepped back and planted his feet. When the man felt the chain in his grasp pull away from him, he tightened his grip. At that moment, Fearghus yanked the chains around his wrists with all his might, and the soldier did not let it loose quick enough. In effect he was pulled right off of his horse and down into the sand violently, stunned by the sudden snap of the chain.

Fearghus jumped forward and snatched the tether in his hands, swinging it around to the soldier's neck. After doing this he pulled on the chain as hard as he could, and the Roman immediately fell dead, his throat bleeding and marked with chain links. Fearghus then drew the man's short broadsword with his clasped hands, and stumbled back, sizing up the remaining riders, of which there were four.

Fearghus instantly knew that he had made a mistake. He could not parry the blows of a pike with this small dagger, much less swing the weapon. His chains, but more drastically his wound, put him at a serious disadvantage in the face of these men.

Fearghus braced for a killing blow when the horseman nearest to him dismounted his nag and drew up his nasty round shield. He advanced on Fearghus slowly and confidently, and soon had reached him. Fearghus, in response to this, raised his sword over his head and leapt forward in one last effort, the weapon in his hands cocked behind his head, ready to swing down and split the soldier's helmet.

But the soldier only pushed forward his hefty shield, and the sword was knocked from Fearghus's tied hands as he struck hard metal. And suddenly he gave a great cry of desperation, hoping the men of Conaill would hear him. But he was too late. The Roman's shield went back, and then came straight at his forehead.

The next thing Fearghus knew, he was on the cold hard floor of an immense room, a room he then identified as the dining hall at the monastery. He recognized the long table that now was but a plank of wood compared to the one in his Oaken Hall, and he recognized the cross at its head that he was told represented the religion of Rome. And all of this disgusted him.

Then he heard a loud voice in his own tongue. "I see you have waken," it said haughtily. And then he noticed that it was a Roman centurion, the captain of a hundred men. He had dealt with the likes of these men before, and he did not fear them.

"What do you want?" Fearghus snapped back, sitting up in the corner. He then noticed that the arrow in his back had been removed, and his wound bandaged.

"You are a prisoner of war," the captain said rudely and advanced on him. "And as such, you are entitled to a few special privileges."

Fearghus hunched into a tight ball. "And what might those be?" he asked.

The man strolled over to a table and picked up something that enraged Fearghus. It was his sword, and the man swung it about as if it was his own toy. "This is a fine blade," he remarked, eyeing his prisoner keenly.

"Far better than anything you've ever seen!" Fearghus shouted, and spat in his face.

This display only enraged the centurion. He began to swing the long sword back and forth, expertly slashing Fearghus's clothing to shreds, and then cutting a shallow gash across his face. "Think twice before you do that again!" he snapped harshly, and pressed the point of the blade into Fearghus's neck until it drew blood.

But Fearghus remained steadfast, and glared at his captor, blood running into his mouth. Now the centurion made his case. "Now I believe you have some information for me!" he hissed, the sword still swaying back and forth before him.

Fearghus drew back, bringing up his hands to shield his face. "There is nothing I can tell you!" he retorted. "I am but a lowly vagabond."

Instead of dealing Fearghus more damage with his sword, the centurion also stepped back, revealing the table behind him. What Fearghus beheld upon that table both frightened him and angered him greatly. Side by side, both Osgar and the Crown of the Deep sat on the table, and the centurion pointed to them, his eyes red with fury. "How does a lowly vagabond come by treasures like this?" he screamed, and slapped Fearghus across the face. Thick red blood spattered on the wall.

Fearghus gathered his strength and climbed to his feet. "By killing men like you!" he shouted, and leapt to the side, quickly dashing out of the dining hall. The Roman made no pursuit, luckily, and Fearghus found himself being stopped instead by a passing foot soldier, who led him through a crowd of other soldiers to the back of the monastery.

Luckily, none of the men recognized Fearghus as he was dragged through the dusty courtyard. None of these soldiers had identified him as a great slayer of their people in the recent war, and thus he was treated as only a captured peasant, and not as a criminal.

Speaking words of Latin, the soldier opened a heavy wooden door upon one of the houses, and pushed him angrily inside, slamming the door shut. There were no windows in this room, Fearghus suddenly realized, and despaired. Leaning against the wall in the dark, unable to see anything around him, he relaxed and waited for the door to open back up.

Chapter 16

Revelation

Fearghus found sleep in his dark prison after some time. It was difficult for him to do so in the troubling blackness, but he made an effort to relax and accept his temporary surroundings. He could not make an escape attempt or do anything at all in here, so he just waited.

He was awakened by a loud bang. The door to his cell was kicked open and nearly fell off of its hinges as a Roman soldier walked in, holding aloft a long lance. He began to bark out orders in Latin, prodding his prisoner with the sharp tool. Fearghus could not understand what he was saying, but nonetheless stood up and allowed the man to force him out of the room and then into the courtyard, now painted with the red light of dusk. Fearghus had been locked away for the length of one entire day, he now realized. He had not been able to keep track of the time while he was in captivity.

The Roman soldier behind him motioned for him to walk to the tower at his left. Soon he was forced into the structure, and began to climb the winding stairs within. At the top of these he found the catwalk of the wall, and it led to the crest of the gate, where stood someone Fearghus feared the most of all in this place: the Roman centurion who he had spoken with earlier today. And he appeared to be very angry.

Fearghus was suddenly struck from behind and fell upon his face before the man. The cold stone under him scraped his chin and blood ran down into his shirt. The centurion looked down at him with disgust. "Get up!" he snapped, and watched Fearghus painfully come to his feet. "Now why don't you have a look out there," he said, pointing over the parapets.

Fearghus peered out over the wall, looking down to the land below. Nothing did he see at first but the green forest and to the left of it the sea, lit with red fire from the sunset. But then the glint of metal caught his eye, and he noticed before him a single rider near the edge of the trees, and above him waved the standard of Dún as Cloch. The man was atop a horse as black as night, and from observing this, Fearghus knew that his own steed had been recovered from the forest.

His eyes scanned the horizon for evidence of more men, but there were none to be seen. As he did this suddenly he was struck again from behind, and fell to the ground before the centurion. "Now I believe we have some negotiating to do!" the soldier snarled, and roughly pulled Fearghus back to his feet.

The rider below suddenly perked up. "Fearghus!" he cried, and reared his steed. "We have come for you!"

But the centurion pushed Fearghus violently back. "You cannot have him!" he screamed.

"Then let us discuss your terms," the warrior countered, and rode into the open.

Fearghus watched the men all around him in the monastery. If there was a trick to be played, now was the time to do it. Also he kept a close eye on the centurion, for already his mind wandered into the possibility of escape.

Then the voice of the soldier rang out over the green clearing. "We shall take whatever you have to offer, if it is enough!"

The rider turned his horse to the side. "Then we will offer you all the gold in our camp, for just his life!" he shouted, and held aloft the hilt of a golden dagger, as well as a golden cuff from Conaill's costume.

The centurion smiled as the golden treasures gleamed. "You must value the life of this man far more than I thought," he observed slyly. "But yet more valuable than anything you have to offer is the helmet that he was wearing. He must be your king!" he laughed, and struck Fearghus again, this time across the face.

Fearghus leapt to his feet, and suddenly noticed something to his right. A column of Roman soldiers was moving into the trees, heading for Conaill's position! Even now Fearghus could see their rustic armor within the forest. Their swords were drawn, and they crept like mice to surprise the warriors.

Now was the time to do something. He had to think of something quickly, but all his mind could muster was attack. And that is what he did. Jumping upon the centurion in front of him he shouted, "Attack!" and the two fell hard to the floor, Fearghus's fingers biting into the man's flesh and drawing blood.

They rolled about on the stone floor for a while until Fearghus reached the hilt of his own sword. Quickly he drew in and plunged it deeply into the man's chest. The blade flashed in the sunlight as he flung it out wide, catching the soldiers who had run to their leader's aid. The centurion, his eyes bulging with surprise and pain, let out a terrible scream of defeat and expired, his body convulsing violently, covered in blood.

Fearghus gained his feet very quickly and hewed down the two guards upon the wall. "To your right!" he shouted to the rider below, who had already retreated to the forest. But he did not need the warning, for in the trees there already was a great rustling, and men screamed as the Celts plowed through the weak line of fighters.

The rider brandished his blade triumphantly and rejoined his men, as Fearghus wheeled around to stave off another onslaught by the men on the wall. The first swung a mighty axe above his head and missed his target narrowly. Fearghus ducked the hefty blade and the suddenly broke the shaft of the weapon with his own sword. The soldier had little time to withdraw from the fray before he was dead. Fearghus then parried a blow from another's broadsword, and dashed down the winding staircase of the tower to the courtyard.

The men walking in the square were taken by surprise when Fearghus dashed through their ranks. Not one of them drew his blade, but only watched with confusion as the Celt sprinted by. Fearghus first found his way to the eating hall, where upon the table yet remained his two greatest treasures. He donned the Crown quickly and then snatched up Osgar, but by now the men had noticed his presence.

The point of a Roman sword drove a deep gash in his shoulder. He wheeled around and stabbed the man who directed it so, but he was not the only soldier in the hall. The guards had closed the heavy door, and suddenly Fearghus was surrounded with angry fighters, all at the ready.

But yet he knew he was armed, and jumped up onto the table. "You shall not have me yet!" he shouted in his own tongue, and danced across the long table, dodging swords and lances from all directions. He then broke into a swift sprint, and the table creaked as he flew across it.

His amazing strength propelled him faster and faster until he had gathered enough speed for his purposes. When he abruptly reached the head of the table he leapt high into the air, and crashed headlong into the wooden door, driving his shoulder right through it. The impact was so great, his pauldron was dented.

But he made it out of the eating hall, and found himself very near to the secret passage, where so long ago he had led a whole village of women and children to safety in the woods. The door over its entrance he threw open before anyone noticed him, and immediately he was safe.

He ran overjoyed into the forest and soon had sight of his comrades closer to the gate of the monastery. The fighting here had already subsided, luckily, and he came upon warriors as happy as he. Even Conaill had journeyed here to the monastery with his men, and embraced his companion happily. "You are very lucky that we heard your cry for help when you passed us at the harbor," he remarked.

Fearghus was surprised. "You actually heard me?" he asked.

But abruptly they were interrupted. "I don't think you are lucky at all!" he said. "We've got a real mess on our hands!"

Fearghus looked beyond the man's shoulders and saw behind him the doors of the monastery gate swing open slowly. Then the marching of a hundred feet was heard within, and another great Roman centurion pranced out into the clearing on his horse, carrying a standard bearing the eagle of Rome. He did not say anything, but looked keenly at the group of men before him in the forest.

Fearghus's sword remained drawn. He immediately ran to the helm of his own forces, a scattered troop of tired warriors in the trees. "We must fight to the last man!" he shouted to them. Then he brandished his sword above his head and charged, whooping and yelling, his cape flying behind him. He knew that his fifty men would have to fight now before more help arrived, because the Romans had chosen this time to fight. They would not withdraw.

The warriors behind him followed, and the two forces fell together simultaneously, the Celts sifting into the Roman lines, though the strength of their numbers remained on the outer edge of the Roman column. The Celts and Romans rubbed together like two sandstones, each gradually wearing away to nothing. However, if like stones they were, the Romans comprised a boulder, and the Celts were vastly outnumbered.

Fearghus hurtled deep into the ranks of Romans, breaking their shining armor with terrible crushing blows. He ran through them like a single stream of wind through the reeds, and left behind him a trail of death. He realized with a sinking heart that his own men were horrendously outnumbered in this fray, and hoped by his own effort to somehow make amends.

The fighting remained at a constant level of fierceness and aggression for a great while as the warriors of Fearghus dwindled to nothing. Fearghus suffered much injury in his courageous fighting, but yet was met with tougher resistance as he progressed. His body quickly became weak and tired, and at length his only purpose was to stave off death for only but the remainder of the evening.

The dusk drew into night, and only the faint light of a muted moon maintained the battlefield. Slowly but efficiently, the Romans were now beginning to withdraw into their fortress, though Fearghus and a few warriors persisted in pursuing them at close quarters. The enemy archers on the wall of the monastery now began to drive off the crippled Celtic forces with their arrows, and the twenty men that remained to Fearghus and Conaill withdrew deep into the encircling forest, as the wounded groaned upon the bloody field.

Fearghus, in his fighting, managed to push all the way to the gate of the monastery, but alas it was closed, and he was prevented from damaging the soldiers further. Reluctantly he turned to the forest, and became to creep back to his own position, picking his way through fallen bodies.

Suddenly, a stout horn blow rang through the air. It was the even note of a Roman bugle, and atop the wall Fearghus himself now beheld the herald who was creating it. The sound of his horn was a comfortable and audible blast, but yet it was foreboding of death to come to all enemies who heard it. And then in its midst, the thunder of soldier's feet was renewed, and the gate began to creak open once more.

"They come again!" Fearghus screamed to his men in the trees. "Run into the trees! Do not let them have you!" he continued, drawing his blade. The Romans had not retreated, he now realized, they had regrouped and added to their force, and now were commanded to deliver a killing blow in the dead of night.

Fearghus dashed to one side of the gate, hiding himself from view. He would now fight to the last, and give his final gift to the people of Eire, that maybe they might not fall to the mighty Rome. He stayed in the shadow of the wall until the deafening sound of the men marching out reached him, and enveloped him. The Roman column marched neatly straight into the field, and not one amongst them lost his place.

At the helm of their impressive ranks the centurion rallied them on horseback, barking orders and waving his weapon. He commanded them to stop, abruptly, and they halted before him, their overlapping armor gleaming row on row in the white moonlight.

Now was the time to strike for Eire. Fearghus gave a great cry that pierced the silence of the night, and leapt into the rear ranks, swinging his sword back and forth desperately. The Romans were dismayed but not shaken, for they remained still, and only those men he threatened turned to defend their lives. They were not successful.

Fearghus was so vicious in his assault he did not notice when the centurion gave the command to attack, and when he looked up next, the whole crowd of

Roman soldiers was lumbering across the field. The world seemed to vibrate as they made their charge across the clearing, and their racket was full in Fearghus's ears.

The Romans withdrew from him like frightened dogs for they could not best him, especially without their companions surrounding them. These rejoined their group nearer to the field, whilst the braver among them fell violently to the long sword of Fearghus.

Fearghus was awestruck as the Roman forces filled every gap between the trees. No one of his company would be spared this night, if only himself. He was left to keep to himself in the very center of the field now, and suddenly realized the hopelessness of his campaign. He could only stand here and watch his men being slaughtered, his sword lying loosely in his arm, which was racked with exhaustion.

The Romans drove deeper into the trees, and only their furthest back men represented them to Fearghus. They would cleanse the encircling forest of all his comrades, and spread wide their great forces in the chase. Now Fearghus thought of escaping, and finding his larger army in the south. If tonight they arrived somehow, the fighters would be saved and the Roman effort be laid waste, if not completely destroyed.

Fearghus listened to the screams of men as they were discovered in the bushes and killed, and heard the terrible sound of the Romans running through the trees. They had taken control of and fully infested this land near the sea, and it was hopeless for Fearghus to try and break them.

The night wore on endlessly, as the stench of death filled the air. Even the wind could not conquer it, and the once happy valley was possessed of a great evil in this way. And as Fearghus experienced this, he heard another horn blast in the west. It was faint and distant, but yet he heard it clearly. He decided now that the Romans had sounded their victory over his scattered force at last, but then the horn sounded again. And it was closer.

He listened intently for the horn again and again, and as it neared him he suddenly drew a daring conclusion. This was not the sound of the Roman trumpet, but instead the fearsome blast of a Celtic battle horn, ringing clear and loud through the cool night air. The Army of Dún as Cloch was coming! They certainly had traveled very fast to come here, though.

Fearghus waited excitedly as the muffled cry of distressed Romans drew closer and closer. Their thundering feet now sounded of retreat and fear. Their vast ranks now filled the gaps of the trees again, but this time they were advancing towards him, and very quickly. The sounds of a renewed battle filled the air behind them, and men screamed once more for their lives.

Fearghus had not yet sheathed his blade, and now lifted it triumphantly to absorb the impact of the Roman stampede. His proud sword sang through their flesh again and again, and as he always did, he accumulated a great number of fallen soldiers at his feet, so that movement was difficult.

The Roman lines waned quickly as they hurried past him, and soon his position was near to the end of them. And when he looked up from his battling, he saw something wonderful and magnificent, something he had never seen in his life, but yet that he recognized immediately. And in its presence he fell to his knees.

What he beheld, gloriously framed in the full moonlight, was the banner of the Serpent, or rather, the Order of the Serpent. It was a great green snake on a fiery red and orange field, laced with gold and blue. And the men under it wore smooth silvery armor and carried long gleaming swords, their faces shrouded by their helmets. And in their midst also was the galloping of horses, for many of them were mounted, and held great pikes to slay men upon the ground.

Fearghus let them pass him by, and watched them as they pushed the Romans back into their fortress speedily, exacting a great victory on the foes of Eire. Soon the fighting had ceased, for the Roman guards at the gate were forced to forsake many of their men to securely close the gate. The valiant men of the Order, then, had pinned these men to their own walls and dispatched each of them brutally.

When the rear of the forces drew up, Fearghus saw that the remnant of Conaill's men were with them. Only fifteen men remained unscathed, but they bravely remained in the skirmish. "I am glad to see that you survived," Conaill said when he approached his friend. "These kind men have rescued us from complete destruction."

Fearghus was overjoyed. "Don't you know these are my men?" he asked with a hearty laugh, and Conaill became very confused. "Long ago," he explained, "I founded this organization of fighting men in the North."

Conaill surveyed the one-sided fight with equal satisfaction. "But I bet you didn't know that they would do this!" he replied.

Fearghus agreed. "They are exacting their revenge on the Romans for a battle they lost long ago," he said.

"As are we," Conaill responded, and the two jogged ahead to meet their saviors.

Fearghus was the first to speak when they met the huge mass of men. "I thank you for your services," he started. "Your fine efforts have saved my men from death."

Suddenly there was a great commotion in the crowd as one of the men pushed his way to the front. "Are you who I think you are?" he asked dazedly, rubbing his eyes. He seemed to look different from the rest of the men, as if higher ranked or more greatly honored.

Fearghus crossed his arms and eyed the young man casually. "I certainly think so," he answered smoothly, feeling proud that one of them recognized him.

The warrior whooped for joy as he screamed, "It is Fearghus the King! It is the King returned from the South!"

The other warriors remained in a confused state as the man dashed in among them and informed them of Fearghus's identity. None of these recently recruited men had any idea who Fearghus the King was, though they had probably heard of him. Fearghus, during all of this, hoped desperately that the news of his return would reach Murchadh or even Seadna, who likely were in command of this elite force.

And it happened exactly as he hoped, for just then a tall man in a blue cloak stepped forward, one of the men whispering in his ear. At his side was girt a lengthy sword, and a quiver of arrows was strapped about his back. When he looked up, Fearghus recognized his face as that of Murchadh, the Captain of the Order and the greatest bowman of his Quest for Osgar.

"It is good to see you, friend," he said immediately upon recognizing Fearghus.

Fearghus sheathed his weapon and embraced his friend. "And also you," he said, in a stately manner. He was trying to sound like the king every man here thought him to be. Murchadh had not seen him go, he now realized. Only Seadna had wished him goodbye last fall in the north of here.

Now Murchadh addressed the issue of why Fearghus left him. "Seadna would not tell me where you went," he said. "Would you like now to tell me?"

Fearghus hesitated, but then another voice cut into the conversation. "It is fine, now, for you to tell him," it said, and then the old and wise Seadna joined them.

"So we meet again," the former pirate said slyly, but then embraced Fearghus. "Back from your adventure so soon?"

"Yes," Fearghus replied tiredly. "I think I have been to this place you spoke about."

Seadna stroked his chin. "Have you done the bidding of the gods?"

Fearghus nodded. "I do not know if it is the bidding of the gods, but if it is, I should say that I have done their will. I have constructed a great city in a stone valley and named it as Dún as Cloch, my fortress of stone. There I have established many buildings."

"I see," said Seadna. "But you have not done their bidding yet."

"Why haven't I?" Fearghus asked.

Seadna shook his head. "You will know, in time," he answered.

"Now let us ride back to our residence in the north," Murchadh said suddenly. "We may speak more of this fortress of stone there."

"I agree," Seadna remarked, and they set about gathering their massive forces.

The Romans were long gone into their walled abode when the huge Order of the Serpent marched victoriously to the white cliffs north of the encircling forest. Fearghus was given his black horse and rode at the helm of them, and also Seadna, Conaill, and Murchadh joined him with the other leaders of the Order, as had been appointed.

They marched in the silvery light of the moon along the beach where Fearghus had traveled before. Many footprints were made in the white sandy beach where they traveled, though later they would be washed away by the tide. The men did not carry very many supplies with them, Fearghus noticed, so certainly their home was not too far from this place. They'd established a stronghold very close to the stronghold of their enemies.

"Where did you find all of these men?" Fearghus asked Murchadh as their horses struggled through the soft sand.

"They came mostly from the two villages closest to here," the captain answered. "The rest are from a few settlements in the far north that Seadna knew of. We've recruited a force of nearly a hundred as of yet."

"And do you train and feed them like an army?" Fearghus asked curiously.

Murchadh nodded. "Just as we trained those men in the monastery so long ago," he replied.

Then Fearghus revealed his plan. "I've got two hundred men coming from my city in the south," he told him. "I think it's time to take back what is ours."

Murchadh's eyes lit up with amazement. "What?" he exclaimed. "You're really planning something big, aren't you!"

Fearghus laughed at his friend's reaction. "They'll be here in a few days," he assured him.

Murchadh shouted up to Seadna, "He's got more coming, Seadna!"

But the old pirate merely acknowledged him with a nod. "And so have we!" he shouted back pleasantly.

They had now come to the last hill that Fearghus had seen before departing. From here Seadna had claimed to behold a village from afar, and had whisked Fearghus off on a crazy horse to Dún as Cloch. Indeed there seemed a good valley below them when they reached the top of the hill, though this place could not be distinguished in the darkness of night.

They marched in a fashion similar to but not completely mocking the style of the Roman legion. Unlike the ancient warriors of the past, they were disciplined and organized, and wore armor like to the interlocking plates of the crafty Romans. The Order of the Serpent had been molded into an elite army of Celtic warriors, intent on breaking the Roman fortress in the monastery.

Soon enough, Fearghus saw the entire village appear below them, and in fact there were a few lights, dimly evident in the windows of the buildings. There were quite a few huts here, Fearghus saw, and the village was surrounded by a sturdy wall of earth and stone, though it was low and weak compared to the straight walls of the mission. The gate was a tall archway of oak, and the men passed under it silently, as the town about them awoke, and the square was filled with light and people.

Seadna pulled his horse near to Fearghus's. "You are a hero here," he said under his breath. "The people have heard many tales of your bravery and adventures."

Fearghus slowed his horse to a walk. "I am honored to be in their presence," he answered, and glanced down at a group of children, who were giving him curious looks, not recognizing him as a warrior that they had met thus far. At a wave of Seadna's hand they ran off laughing, and their mothers caught them as they entered the small square, marked by a well in the center of town.

Now the warriors broke their formation and ran to meet their wives, which many of them had. The reason why so many men had been recruited from here resulted from the fact that many of the husbands and fathers had volunteered to fight, since the Romans posed such a great threat to them.

Suddenly Fearghus's mind turned to something that had been plaguing it for some time now. In fact this thing was the entire reason he had come here, if not to fight the Romans. He wished to see Agnos again, for he had been without her for the entire duration of the winter here, and she was sorely missed.

Fearghus was ushered into the greatest hall of the village, where in the seat of power was the magus here and beside him Seadna and Murchadh, who had become great heroes under him. The table they sat at was furnished with a modest feast, and all the warriors sat down at their respective places. Another chair was provided for Fearghus now, and he sat next to the druid, who wore lavish gold jewelry all about him comprising a crown, necklace, and bracers. It was richness such that even Conaill had never seen, though the Crown of the Deep atop Fearghus's head was truly the better.

The plump druid sat before a large cooked pig, and looked up with surprise when he saw Fearghus approach him. "Whom do I have the pleasure of meeting?" he asked politely, and got to his feet.

Seadna walked up behind Fearghus and took his seat. "This is Fearghus the King, the founder of our great army," he informed the druid.

"A king you say? Well then he deserves a feast fit for a king!" the jolly magus responded, and clapped his hands.

"Do you celebrate a lot of feasts?" Fearghus asked Seadna, whispering.

Seadna nodded. "Every time we go on a major raid of the monastery, we come home to some very happy villagers," he replied quietly. "The magus here is living proof of that!"

Fearghus laughed secretly and took his seat. Instantly his plate was piled with meat and his cup filled with ale, and the hall was filled as well with laughter and mirthful singing. Fearghus ate quickly and greedily. But for how hungry he was, he was also anxious to see Agnos again, and remained nervous and thoughtful for the duration of the feast. When the eating portion of the meal was concluding and the general drinking stage of the merrymaking was beginning to take effect, Fearghus excused himself and crept out of the hall secretly, while the men of the Order inside remained distracted by their drink.

Seadna had pointed out a small hut on the left side of the village when they arrived. His face when he did this had seemed to hide something, but the wrinkled countenance would give nothing more away than the mere existence of something notable. Fearghus couldn't wait to see his love after more than half of a year. He was beginning to miss Agnos.

Finally he walked through the door of her hut, which was left ajar. He knew Agnos had not been informed of his coming by anyone, since the feasts were so routine. She was standing at the far end of the room bent over her bed when he walked in, and did not notice him right away.

He took a few more steps and she looked up, her face lighting up with joy. "Fearghus!" she shouted with the happiness of a child, and danced over to him, embracing him tightly. It was then that he noticed something different about her, something unseen at first but now quite evident.

He stepped back and studied her. She was wearing a very loose dress, and a thick cloak that covered most of her body. But this could not hide the obvious. "You are with child," he observed, and frowned suspiciously. He was very surprised, and the sudden change in her expression informed him of a change in his own.

But she stopped him, placing her hand over his mouth. "Do not be worried," she assured him, "It is of your blood."

"But how could this happen?" Fearghus asked, stupefied. He did not think of these things at night when he thought of her. This changed things in his life drastically.

Agnos did not seem too worried about Fearghus's reaction. "It happened a long time ago," was all she said, and went about her work indifferently. But Fearghus advanced on her, and put his arms around her.

"I understand," he told her lovingly. "It must have happened a very long time ago." And the two shared a long and wonderful kiss, and forgot about all of the things that troubled them. For one moment all of the warmth of Fearghus's love for her was renewed, and she fell into his arms as only she had a great while ago, when they traveled together through the troubled world.

At length Agnos drew away from him, and pulled her cloak all the way around her. "Where have you been?" she asked with intense curiosity.

Fearghus stood still and lowered his head. "I have been to a great refuge, a sanctuary for my troubles," he answered. "And I have there built a seat of power and raised an army. My army will arrive soon to right all the wrongs of these accursed Romans."

"But Fearghus," she pressed, drawing in near to him, "What has happened to the days of old? Should we now continue our wrathful quest for power?"

Fearghus stayed his anger towards her remark, and placed his hand over hers upon his cheek. "It is not a quest for power, but a quest for purpose, and for Eire!" he said, and stepped out of her grasp. "I am sorry if you have a conflict with who I am."

Agnos fell to her knees. "I have no conflict with you!" she exclaimed. "Only for now, spare me your anger and your pride!"

Fearghus turned and leaned against the wall, on the verge of tears. "I am sorry," he stammered. "Tonight I will stay my troubles for you, if you will stay yours."

Agnos leapt to her feet. "I certainly will," she said, and closed the door.

Fearghus hugged her tightly in his arms and kissed her on her head. "There will be time for worrying tomorrow," he said. "Now let us find sleep while there is time."

Fearghus left her in bed there and walked back to the feast to speak with his new friends, who now would be wondering where he was. When he took his seat back next to Seadna he leaned over and said, "Then have you seen her?"

"Yes," Fearghus replied. "She is as beautiful as the first day I saw her. It is good to see her again."

There was a look of hidden thoughts upon Seadna's face again. "That is good," he said, and glanced over at the druid, who was leaning back in his seat, heavily drunk and filled with food. Only the bones of his meal remained before him, and he seemed quite content on a full stomach.

Slowly the jubilant men left the hall, some of them with much trouble, and when Seadna prepared to leave, only a few men still remained, listening to a sad tune of the lyre. "Good night to you, Fearghus," the old pirate said before he left.

Fearghus then returned happily to the quarters of Agnos. She was inside in the darkness, lying awake in bed waiting for him. When he walked in she turned to him, and he lied down next to her. He could see how large her baby had grown to be in the faint light. He had been gone for too long. But yet, he was simply happy to see Agnos again. He held her hand and kissed her. "I am not sorry that this has happened," he whispered to her.

Agnos grabbed his shoulder and leaned towards his ear. "I am not sorry either," she said, and then her arms became limp, and she fell asleep rapidly, in his arms.

The next morning, Fearghus woke with the sun and stepped out into the village square. Not far behind him, the other leaders of the army woke and dressed themselves, congregating near the well. Seadna was among them, and he beckoned Fearghus towards him. "We have come to discuss your battle plan," he said when Fearghus briskly reached him.

"That is good," Fearghus replied. "We should send some riders to the Army of Dún as Cloch soon to inform them of our cooperation and plans," he continued.

"That is an idea fair and necessary," Seadna answered him. "After our discussions this morning, we will send some of your men to do that."

The men cleared the table of the great hall of the village and sat about the head of it. Seadna unraveled a detailed map of the entire area, provided by the druid. It was detailed beyond any drawing Fearghus had seen yet in his life. Even the walled stronghold of the Romans had been added. Seadna then produced a brush and drew some arrows on the map. He drew a large one for the Army of Dún as Cloch, then two smaller ones for the Order of the Serpent and the riders from Dún as Cloch, as Fearghus had informed him of. "This is our position thus far," he explained to the men there. "We should apply pressure on both the north and south walls," he continued, signifying the two points of greatest manpower in their arsenal.

Then Fearghus piped in. "The riders in the west should wait for our word before attacking," he said. "They can come as reinforcements and also to block the Roman retreat."

Seadna pointed to the arrow west of the monastery on the map. "That is a good plan," he observed. "We will catch them in a trap. On three sides will be our men, and on the fourth, the impassable sea. No supplies will come in or out of the place, and certainly no Romans." The other men, mostly captains and guides in the Order of the Serpent, nodded their heads in agreement. There exactly were ten of them, and each wore a distinguished blue cape to represent his position. They carried swords with hilts of gold, and wore closed helmets that hid their expression.

At length, Fearghus finally stood up, satisfied. The other men were impressed when they beheld the sheer size of his sword, a sword that Conn had forged for him. The smith was not present at this meeting though, but yet lived in the village at his own new forge. "We should have a look at the monastery," Fearghus said finally. "There are some high cliffs I believe we could climb."

"A good idea," Seadna replied, and disbanded the men. "We will go have a look."

When Fearghus exited the large hall, someone suddenly shouted "Fearghus!" and Agnos appeared, running across the dusty square.

When she slowed to a halt and spoke to him, her voice was urgent. "I must speak with you," she pressed, grabbing firmly his arm.

"I believe I have some time on hand to speak with you," he answered gingerly, and she pulled him by the arm back to their hut, leading him like one leads a horse by his reins. Immediately she drew a chair up for him to sit in, and sat herself down upon the bed, trying to calm down. She was beautiful sitting there, with her long hair draped over her shoulders. Her skin seemed to glow with a happy radiance, and in her eyes Fearghus could see deeply into her soul.

At last she spoke. "I have been hesitant to tell you this before," she said, "but I think now the time has come for you to have yet another revelation."

Fearghus opened his ears and his heart, and became very interested at this remark. "Tell me everything," he said.

"As you know, I am a Roman Catholic, and I worship the God of the Romans," she began nervously. When Fearghus nodded, she continued. "I believe our fates are entwined in more ways than one," she said.

"How is this so?" Fearghus asked calmly.

"I have been given a task by my God recently," Agnos said. "And it involves you."

Fearghus was very confused. "Your God?" he asked, exasperated. "What do I have to do with your God?"

Agnos drew back a bit, but held her ground. "My God has spoken to me," she warned him, in a fearful tone. "He has crossed our paths for a very important reason!"

Fearghus leapt out of his chair and began to pace the room. "Your God doesn't exist!" he yelled. "I should have nothing to do with Him! Or you!" And with that he threw up his hands and snarled at her.

Somehow, though, Agnos was not afraid of him. It was as if she was possessed by another being than herself. But she yelled back at him. "Didn't you ever wonder who gave you all of your gifts?" she screamed. "Didn't you ever stop and ask yourself why you were selected to have them?"

Fearghus tripped and fell against the wall. "Yes," he stammered like a frightened child. "Yes I have."

Agnos's fury subsided only a little. "Those gifts were given to you by the Lord God, the creator of all the universe," she seemed to whisper, and advanced on him as he crumpled to the floor. "He picked you, and only you to carry out his plan here in Eire," she continued. "Do you understand?"

Fearghus began to weep. He would not answer her. He could not open his mouth and speak to her. His mind did not have the capacity to hear all of this that she was saying. As he cried he felt physically weaker and then he felt helpless before her.

Agnos finally stood back and regained her seat on the bed. When she spoke next, her voice was ordinarily soft and comforting once more, and so Fearghus heeded it. "I have been commissioned as your guide and companion," she said. "I am obliged to tell you of all these things you wonder about, and to help you to complete the task that God has given to you. The gods of your people are no more. If you follow in their path you will defile the work of the one God who created you, and destroy the advancement of his word unto your people."

Fearghus stopped his crying and remained sitting against the wall. His body was racked with exhaustion and his mind filled with confusion. "I cannot understand what you are saying, but I will try," he told her more confidently, and looked at her intensely, trying to comprehend her.

"Understanding God will be a difficult task for you," Agnos said, "but accomplishing it will start with a single step." And with that she reached out and held his hand, and helped him to his feet.

He sat next to her and wiped his face dry. Then she began to talk again, looking down at her lap. "What we have done is a great sin in the eyes of my God," she said. "I cannot reverse what has happened, but I can make some amends for it," she sighed, and looked into his eyes.

Fearghus looked back into her eyes, and there found a solution. It was to him as if the answer had been placed directly into his head, and he opened his mouth to speak. "It will be I who makes the amends," he said, and then embraced Agnos tightly. Lowering himself below her, he then took her hand and said, "Would you like to be my wife?"

Agnos's face lit up with joy. Before she even opened her mouth, Fearghus could see the acceptance in her smile. "Yes!" she burst, and nothing short of tackled him to the floor, her arms coiled tightly about his back. There, as he lay on his back, he shared a long kiss with her, and held her soft face in his hands.

When they were finished, Fearghus sat up and said, "We shouldn't waste a moment! Let us be wed now!" And he found himself bounding out into the square to find Seadna and told him what he desired. Seadna laughed heartily at first, and then his face became a bit more composed.

"Do not worry!" he chuckled. "There will be time to prepare all day for this! For now at least, lend me some of your time to survey with me the coming battlefield."

And so Fearghus mounted his black horse and the two men trotted out of the fair village, and in the distance beheld the white cliffs near the monastery, from which they could see all of the valley below them. Their horse moved along briskly in the bright morning light, and enjoyed the coolness still left behind from the nighttime. There wasn't a cloud in the vast blue sky, and the color of the world was vibrant and bright.

"I think now we have a better chance than ever we did of defeating these pesky Romans," Seadna said as they moved along.

Fearghus nodded. "They will soon leave our kindred alone, and be satisfied with the land they have already stolen from the race of Celts."

Seadna slapped him on the shoulder. "Now that is the outlook of a king!" he chortled. You've certainly come a long way from that young fellow I met sailing with Colla so long ago!"

Fearghus laughed with him, and relaxed in the beautiful world that surrounded them. Indeed, he had progressed quite a bit from the condition he was in a year ago, when the campaign in the monastery had just begun. He remembered when he met Seadna and his kinsmen, and fought off the pirates on the field outside Dún as Cloch. He did not know if those were happier days than these.

Now they stopped their horses before a towering white stone, that hardly they could look at without squinting, for so reflective it was. But they persisted in their efforts, and after dismounting found a vein of sloping stone, covered in dust and pebbles. And here they clambered up the cliff in single file, slipping seldom but feeling always the danger of falling down the stone face. Fearghus was the first to reach the climax of their climb, and stood up to his full height atop a level length of stone on the summit. Seadna joined him, and used his hand to shield his eyes from the sun as he looked across the valley below them. It was filled mostly with the trees of the encircling forest, but the monastery, in its respective clearing of the forest, shone like a jewel in the sunlight.

The two men stood in awe of this view of Eire for a great while, but then suddenly Fearghus spoke. "I think I see the Army!" he shouted. "They are near now to their goal."

Seadna sighed. "What amazing eyes you must have!" he observed, and strained to see what his companion already witnessed. "Don't worry," he assured Fearghus, "Our riders have already been sent to intercept them, and inform them of our plans. We will gather our forces again and move into a position to attack tomorrow. Any sign of the mounted men?"

Fearghus cast his long gaze to the west, and scanned the hilly land further away from the sea. "No, I cannot see them," he replied, and frowned.

Seadna crawled to the back of their perch. The wind was starting to pick up. "That is fine," he said. "They are probably a bit delayed. Now let us go back to our own stronghold and proceed with our plans."

Fearghus cautiously followed Seadna back down the cliff, and easily regained the ground, where their horses waited. Fearghus excitedly mounted his and the two began to gallop back to the village, for there they would begin preparations for Fearghus's wedding. It was a special thing, getting married in Eire, and so there was to be much preparation during this day. Tomorrow they would be preparing instead for war, so today was the day for Fearghus to be wed.

And so finally, they came back to the happy village where Agnos waited for Fearghus to return. Instantly when Seadna rode into town, he ordered the great hall and the town square to be decorated for a royal wedding. Fearghus, in the meantime, was whisked away to one of the huts to be bathed and dressed.

Fearghus spent the whole afternoon washing in sweet smelling oils and by the end of it all, he was given a great crimson cloak and certain articles of golden jewelry as his costume. When warriors were married, he knew, they were still dressed as if for war, to signify their importance as a fighter in society. Thus, he donned his own battered armor to complete his appearance, and wore a golden circlet upon his brow.

All the while, the great feasting hall of the village was cleaned and prepared for yet another, greater meal. The walls were accented with fresh boughs from the trees and flowers from the fields. And many candles and torches were placed throughout the village and lighted when it grew dark.

The enticing scent of food filled the air as the women cooked sheep and swine from their herds. Fearghus was very excited to smell these in the air, and sat in his dressing room nervously, anxious to attend the ceremony. It would be a druidic wedding, he had decided, so as not to offend the villagers, but for the sake of Agnos, they would not name a period of engagement for the couple during the ceremony.

At last the evening had come. Seadna and the other men had been busy all day preparing for both the attack and the wedding, and when the time for the ceremony came, all were exhausted and ready to proceed and begin the greatest feast of all.

Seadna came to get Fearghus out of his hut, and laughed when he saw the battle-hardened warrior shaking with nerves. "Relax, my friend!" he said. "It is as good a step as any man can take! You should be proud!"

Fearghus finally conquered his fear and left the room with his friend, and walked to the middle of the town square. He was the first to arrive, and after he did, the other men and women came in small groups to join the festivities. The families of Fearghus and Agnos were not there, so others volunteered to help them.

At last the druid arrived who was to mediate the joining. He was dressed in his flowing violet robes laced with pure gold, and carried a book of words to say during the ceremony. He seemed very happy for the occasion, and stepped lively to his position before Fearghus. The torches all about them were lit and their golden light illuminated the entire square as the rest of the guests arrived.

Fearghus's nervousness mounted as Agnos's arrival was delayed. But soon after the square was filled with people, she appeared from her hut, and she was dressed beautifully. Her hair was tied up in an elaborate fashion, and it fell lightly about her shoulder, shining in the firelight. Her skin was smooth and shiny, and her eyes glowed with happiness. Her dress was the most beautiful garment Fearghus had ever seen a woman wear. It was light blue like the sky, and girded with a wreath of lilies from the river far from here. It was also laced with shimmering gold and jewels, and flattered her attractive form. It dragged heavily upon the ground as all dresses should, and was hemmed with golden thread. And also Fearghus noticed that she, too wore a golden circlet atop her head, though set in it was a dazzling diamond that accented her brow with white reflected light.

Agnos held a bouquet of flowers as she approached the druid, and the smile on her face outdid anything else comprising her appearance. With her pretty brown eyes she looked into Fearghus's blue ones, and the two shared a special moment before the magus began to speak.

He named many of the gods as the witnesses of the ceremony, but for each time he did, Agnos did not show her disapproval in any way. At length, he asked both Agnos and Fearghus if they had come of their own free will, and if they intended to serve one another and love each other as was good and right. Both Fearghus and Agnos responded with "Yes" and "I do," as was required during the many vows, naming the four cardinal directions, the seasons, and the gods and goddesses representing each. Fearghus helped Agnos along as they were obliged to walk in various directions within a circle of onlookers. At one point, Fearghus and Agnos were asked to share a kiss, and they did so beautifully.

And finally the time came for the handfasting. By the command of the druid, Fearghus and Agnos formed a circle by holding each other's hands right in left and left in right. And after some more speaking, the other people participating in the ceremony formed two other larger circles, and the druid stepped forward. Then he produced two red cords and tied each of them about the wrists of the couple, binding them together.

After this, as was customary, the couple spent the rest of the ceremony awkwardly tied together, and even proceeded to the feast as such, for in many cases the married couple was required to stay bonded for the whole day of the wedding. But as the night wore on the cords were cut, and Fearghus and Agnos finished their meal together at the head of the table, drinking and laughing with the common townsfolk.

When all the processes of getting one's self married were completed, Fearghus and Agnos left the banquet hall energetically and retired in privacy to their enormous quarters for the night. They drew quite a bit of good attention as they made their way to the house appointed to them, and closed the door with finality when they were inside. Fearghus had at last managed to master his fear, and now he was relieved and excited about the results of his wedding.

Chapter 17

The Battle for Eire

Fearghus awoke late the next morning. Agnos was still asleep at his side, her head resting on his arm. He tried not to wake her when he arose, but his movements caused her to open her eyes. "Fearghus," she mumbled, coming in and out of sleep, "is it already morning?"

Fearghus sat on the side of the bed. "Yes it is, and a beautiful morning at that. Did you get a good night's rest?" he asked, pushing her hair out of her face.

"Of course I did," she muttered, stretching her legs. "But I seem to have a headache."

Fearghus allowed himself to fall backwards onto the bed. "I've got one too, and I think I know where it came from," he said, "Are you going to be alright?"

Agnos gave him a kiss on the cheek and hopped out of bed. "I think I'll be fine," she answered briskly, and straightened out her robes. "What've you got planned for today?" she asked.

Fearghus then became very serious. "I should have told you about this earlier, but I've got quite an important thing scheduled for today," he told her.

Agnos's face became mildly troubled, and she sat down in a chair. "Nothing that big, I hope," she said.

Fearghus stood up and walked over to his armor, on the table. "I do think that it is *that* big," he responded, and began to pick through the miscellaneous metal panels. He was disappointed with himself to have to tell Agnos about the coming war so soon after their marriage. He wished he could have a longer time to enjoy it with her, but that simply was not possible. "Today, we are going to take the fight back to Rome," he informed her, and turned away, that he might not see the distress in her expression. But then he remembered the events of yesterday and asked, "Do you consider it against the laws of your God to battle the Romans like this?"

At this Agnos became very thoughtful, and paused before she gave an answer. "No, I do not," she replied. "Eire was not meant to be won by force, as the Romans intend. It was meant to be won by the compliance of all its peoples to the word of God. In attacking them, you avenge your kin and maintain the peaceful island of Eire. Your purpose, I believe, is to prevent the conquest of Eire that Rome is attempting. It is the will of God that you destroy them and halt their evil campaign. Wheels too immense for you to ever imagine have been set in motion"

Fearghus understood everything Agnos said, and agreed with it in full. "You are wise beyond your years," he said, "and by your wisdom, I justify the defense of Eire, for the good of its people."

Agnos dressed herself quickly, donning a white gown and a red hooded cloak. "Then you are off to war," she concluded, brushing her hair.

Fearghus was nearly done strapping on his armor. "Indeed I am," he answered her. "My army from the south will arrive today. We must attack while they are yet unnoticed."

Agnos hugged him tightly. "I understand," she said, and the two of them walked out into the sunny world together. Outside, many of the men of the Order were finished with their breakfast and had gathered in the square. Each of them was covered heavily in silvery armor, and as well each was girt with a long sword and leant upon a lance. Some were mounted upon horses, and their presence was very strongly felt. Their faces were shrouded in shadow by design of their helmets, and only their mouths could be seen. When he approached them, one gave a short bow and said, "King Fearghus, are we ready yet to leave?"

Fearghus shrugged him off saying, "We will be off very soon," and continued on to the great hall to seek out Seadna. Agnos reluctantly followed. Inside, only a few men tarried at their breakfast, and Fearghus informed them to join the rest outside. At the head of the table, Seadna, Murchadh and Conaill all sat speaking with one another.

When he saw Fearghus, Seadna stopped in mid-sentence. "And here they are, the king and queen of Eire!" he joked, leaning back in his chair. And then he looked at Agnos with seriousness and said, "I hope that our plans are fitting to you!"

Agnos sat down at the table and nodded. "They are satisfactory," she replied softly.

But Fearghus was in no mood to sit down and eat. He was excited about the war, and ready to fight. "So shall we be off?" he asked. At this the men, without words, left their places and filed out of the great hall slowly. Agnos remained at her seat, staring at the wall and thinking.

Fearghus shared one last kiss with her. "I will be back every night to see you," he said, "so do not worry about me going out there. I will think of you during the toughest parts of the battle."

And with that he followed Seadna and the others out of the hall and was gone. Outside in the square the troops were completely assembled, and only the presence of their leader was needed to depart for war. And soon that need was fulfilled, for Fearghus was atop his black horse, and his sword was flashing out in the air. Every man there saw it, and heeded his command. "You will travel to the northern side of the valley," he shouted to them, "and wait there for further instructions. I will leave to fill the command of the Army of Dún as Cloch, and my friends Seadna and Murchadh will rule in my absence."

They left in two rows under the arch of the gate, Fearghus at the helm. He carried his sword aloft next to the twin banners of the serpent and the fortress of stone, and his cape floated behind him in a lively breeze. The leaders of the Order rode in perfect harmony side by side, and when they'd cleared the fortifications of the village, they began a spirited trot, with the men jogging behind with only their weapons to carry. They had been trained to move quickly in a large formation, among other things.

When they reached the white cliffs that yesterday Seadna and Fearghus had climbed, the men were given time to rest and recuperate. The encircling forest was in their view now, and the monastery within their reach. But they would not attack yet, they would have to remain hidden until the Army of Dún as Cloch was prepared to strike with them. For this to happen, Fearghus was to rendezvous with the Army, and so he now broke away from their company and galloped out to the open beach above the valley, where he would have safe passage to the other end of the forest. The breeze incoming from the sea was salty and refreshing, and he was quite confident as his horse raced through the white sand.

Soon enough, he turned off onto the stony land, and then moved into a grassy field. In the near distance he beheld the modest Army of Dún as Cloch at their camp in the hills, and very quickly reached them, waving his unique sword in the air to alert them of his coming. And he was well met. "Good to see you again, sir," one of the young fighters said, greeting him.

"And good to see you," Fearghus said as he passed the man. Subsequently, he directed his horse right to the front of the group of a hundred and half men, and spoke to them clearly and loudly. "You have finally reached your destination," he boomed. "We will attack later in the day, when I give you the signal. You are to hide in the trees before you attack."

"And what will be the signal, master?" another one of the warriors asked.

Fearghus looked down at the tired boy. "We will wave the standard of Dún as Cloch from the top of that great rock, over there," he answered, and pointed behind him to the white cliff at the north end of the valley, below which the comparably sized Order of the Serpent now rested. He decided that he would like to be with them for the rest of these great battles, though his true post was with the force of his creation. "I will return at times," he informed his men now, and wheeled his horse around to depart. "Attack with only ten men at first, and try to tempt them into open battle," he said before he left.

He followed his route back to the Order of the Serpent on the north end of the forest, and immediately gave the command for the standard-bearer to climb to the top of the cliff so that the offensive could begin. Seadna he sent up with the man as well, so that he could plan the major troop movements and survey the battle as it happened. He was too old to fight now, but was a skilled commander of men.

After a while, the standard bearer signaled down to Fearghus to let him know he was there. Fearghus waited for a great while after this, but then finally yelled up to him, "Now!"

And so the magnificent banner of Dún as Cloch appeared in the striking sun over the valley, and flapped in the breeze. Now the Order of the Serpent crept stealthily to the rear of the fortress, and waited for the battle cry of the southern army to herald the initiation of a battle. The Romans likely were expecting a fight, and the Celts weren't going to disappoint them.

They waited and waited, and no sign of an open battle. The evening was nigh when the blast of the Roman horn greeted them, and the sound of sailing arrows echoed across the stony valley. It was a perfect time for the Order to strike, because the low sun did not reveal their position as they crept in the shadow of the trees, and then in the shadow of the wall. They would try to penetrate the open gate, or at least block it, so that the Army could move in and destroy the Roman ground forces that were sure to come. The invaders would have no chance of retreat, and thus no chance of living in the face of such strategy.

The men crept faster and faster as they neared the gate, where the marching feet of the Romans was heard. Above this, the voice of ten men in the field was heard, taunting the Romans and tempting them to fight. And the men of the Order fed upon this crafty trick, and moved quietly into position at the corner of the wall. And then there was the sound of the gate swinging shut and this was followed by a great silence, in which the Romans halted and drew up their arms for battle, ready to bear down on the Celts like a crashing river. And it was now that the Order of the Serpent chose to strike. They began with a blood-curdling battle cry that frightened and confused the Romans greatly. Soon all of the more than one hundred soldiers were cast into a state of chaos, and they began to run about randomly, running for their lives. And in this time, most of them turned to look upon the advancing men of the Order, and did not notice the Celtic movement at the trees.

The Army of Dún as Cloch suddenly made their vicious charge, smashing into the Roman ranks as they remained distracted by the Order. Now the Romans were being attacked from both sides, and they had not supplied themselves with enough manpower to sway the ruthless onslaught. Three hundred soldiers were massacred in this one-sided surprise attack, and the Romans were hopelessly defeated.

Fearghus played his role in the battle as well. He stayed behind the men of the Order of the Serpent and then leapt into the fray when he pleased, hewing through flesh and bone with all the wrath of the Celts. But yet in this fight he found himself a bit more reserved, and less reckless. He now had a wife to take care of back in the village, and he wished very much to come home to her after these such battles unharmed. And so he did not this time hurtle headlong into the Roman lines, and exact his terrible damage to them. He ran along through the lesser battles and gave aid to the weak and the frightened Celtic warriors, instilling in them the confidence of kings, and in many cases saving their lives.

The battle turned heavily in the favor of the Celts, even though they were outnumbered. And the tide of war never returned again to the side of the evil Romans this night. Their bodies were bruised and even smashed as the Celts stumbled over them, advancing further on the core of Roman power. And the corpses were marked with many horrendous wounds, for the way of the Celtic warrior was brutality and pride. It was not long before the ragged men of the Army and the proud men of the Order began to fight side by side, meeting each other at the center of the blood-stained battlefield. Fearghus soon fought his way to their position in the middle, and there declared utter victory over his enemies. His men lifted him onto their shoulders and he cried "For Eire!" wildly, his sword flashing each time he said it, gleaming with the pale light of the risen moon, which was both beautiful and ghostly.

A great cheer arose within the ranks of two hundred and fifty fighters. The battling subsided quickly now, and the remnant of the soldiers were smashed back into their own gate, which could not be opened to save them. Blood was spattered upon the very wood itself, and this as a testament to the prowess and determination of the Celts that day. Now Fearghus regained his jet black horse and rallied his men back to the trees. They had delivered the first blow to Rome, and littered the clearing with the dead.

As Fearghus galloped his horse triumphantly to the north, he spied Seadna and the standard bearer atop the rock, whooping and jumping for joy. When he passed under them, Seadna called, "Victory for Eire! Victory for Eire!" and then disappeared behind the edge of the cliff. Fearghus and the men of the Order he had led in battle walked slowly out of the valley, for there was no need for speed now. They were exhausted but relieved, and the wounded Romans could not hurt them any further this night.

It was not long before they beheld the village once more, and marched under the archway of the gate. Fearghus was filled yet with more energy this night as he returned, and looked for Agnos anxiously around the town square. In a moment he found her, and dismounted his horse quickly, running to catch her in his arms. "Thank God that you are alright!" she sighed when they embraced, her chin on his shoulder. "I was worried!"

Fearghus lifted her off the ground with his amazing strength and looked her in the eyes. "I can never leave you," he assured her, and then brought her down into his tight grasp. "You are a wife and soon to be mother," he said, "And in my eyes, a queen."

Agnos then turned to tears for so happy she was to see him, even after only an evening that they were apart. She sobbed bitterly, her face turned into his chest, and held onto him for several moments. Then she withdrew from his embrace. "I have got quite a large task before me," she said. "Come with me into my room, and we will speak more about our entwined destiny."

Fearghus allowed her once again to lead him by the hand into their house, and took a seat in the chair she produced for him, trying to open his mind to her words. He seemed as if hypnotized by her, but blamed his actions instead on their love. He would listen to whatever she told him, for in this world of brutality, she was the only constant of goodness in his life.

"In order for you to accept me, I must use in your presence a word that once I considered forbidden," she said finally.

"And what is that?" Fearghus asked immediately.

Agnos sighed and braced herself for his reaction. "I must try to convert you," she replied.

Fearghus laughed and relaxed in his seat. "Convert me to what?" he asked her smoothly, eying her with only the slightest suspicion.

Agnos seemed pleased at his response. She now saw a path of hope in her conversation, and thought carefully about her next response. "I must convert you to what is just and righteous in the world," she answered impressively. "With my guidance you will find the true meaning of life and love and goodness, and in me your task will be fulfilled at last."

Fearghus took sudden interest in her words. "Will I discover my purpose, and solve the riddle of all of these strange happenings?"

Agnos nodded, with a grin. "All you have to do is open your heart to me," she said.

Fearghus held her once more. "I have done so already," he responded in a whisper.

But Agnos came out of his grasp. "Then you have already taken a step to conversion," she said. "Next, I must tell you of who my God is." And for a great while during the night, Fearghus listened to her speech with interest as she elaborated on the definition and identity of her God, the God of Rome. But by the end of her speaking he was convinced somehow that He was not the God of Rome, but the God of all man. And many of the moral values expressed in his own pagan doctrine were evident in hers. He listened attentively as she even began to tell him of some of the lore of her beliefs, as there were many stories in his own religion as well. But hers seemed to have the ring of truth, and strayed more often from the epic elements of war and strife.

During this time, Fearghus's mind strayed to think of things that had happened to him in the past. He thought of the disappearance of Osgar, and of the Lady of Dún as Cloch. He mind even reached back to the night of his transformation, when an old man had been killed for the mention of Sucellos before the snakes. Why had the snakes been there that night? What were they running from? And then his mind shifted to his memories of the one and only Snake, and of all his adventures and trials on the Isle of Man. They now all seemed related.

After much discussion Agnos stopped her speech, and became weary. She was already dressed for sleep, and wished her husband a good night before reclining in bed. He followed here there as quickly as he could, and extinguished the candle on his table. Under the covers of their bed, he held her in his arms and closed his eyes with relief, trying to clear his mind now of all his thoughts.

But he did not pass that night smoothly, though he soon slept. Midway through the night he abruptly was awakened, and his eyes he uncomfortably opened into an intense light. It was green at first like the light of many of his miracles before, but then it grew to be an intense white light, that blinded him and surrounded him entirely. He could not make out its source, but he deduced that it was in the corner of the room. He struggled to his feet and planted them in the floor, as if the light was pushing him away from it. He scarcely now could see his bed next to him in all its glory, but did not worry. He pushed through it, and soon recognized the corner of the room. And then he remembered something: he had placed Osgar here in this corner when he arrived! Now he leapt forward and felt in his hands the hilt of it, and then all the light vanished.

Then a noise from the bed. Agnos was awake, sitting up. "What are you doing?" she asked him.

"Oh, I'm sorry," Fearghus stammered, and looked down at the weapon in his hands. "I couldn't sleep," he lied. Osgar seemed different to the touch. He moved his hands up and down its shaft, and then came to a drastic conclusion. Excitement welled up in his chest as he stumbled over to his table, and grabbed the candle upon it. When he lit the wick in the dying embers in the fireplace, he couldn't believe his eyes. The spear that he held was changed completely, though it was not unfamiliar to him. The shaft was plated with gold and jewels, just as he had seen it so long ago, before he had lost the spear entirely. Many colored spots of light danced across the wall of the room as he held the candle to it, for gems of every size and color were set in the gold of the handle, extending to the very point of the spear, which seemed to be made of glowing silver.

The reflected light reached Agnos as she sat on the bed. One of the red gleams ran across her face and she cast a curious glance in Fearghus's direction. "What is that spear you are holding?" she asked dazedly, sleep still heavy in her eyes.

Fearghus ran to her side, bringing the candle with him. "It is Osgar!" he replied triumphantly. "Osgar has returned!"

Agnos was wide awake now. "Osgar never left," she reasoned, still looking curiously at the treasure. The expression on her face was one of confusion but also of pure joy, for she knew that this miracle was sent by God. Her efforts were being rewarded.

Fearghus smiled as he showed her his prized possession. He held it in front of her with the interest in it of a child, and cherished it deeply. "I have not seen the spear like this for a long time," he informed her, hoping to change the still confused expression on her face. "It is a miracle that I see it once more with this beauty."

Agnos smiled and embraced him, pulling him back into bed as he replaced Osgar in the corner. The two fell back to sleep quickly after that, grins stretching across each of their faces.

The morning came quickly after that, and the couple slept well into it, resulting from their vigilance the night before. When Fearghus finally opened his eyes, he routinely prepared himself for the day, and leisurely donned his armor and weaponry. He examined more closely the jeweled Osgar, and waited for Agnos to wake before leaving their quarters.

The village square outside seemed deserted, as was the usual, when war was not nigh. But as Fearghus advanced to the well for a drink, an old friend greeted him. "Well hello!" a grubby-looking man said, and waved to him. It was Conn, the blacksmith from the southern forest, come to procure more water for his forge.

Fearghus was delighted to see his friend. "It's a pleasure to see you again," he said, "and in such good health, too!"

Conn lumbered over to the well with his bucket. "I see you've kept that spear of yours safe for all this time," he observed, motioning towards the wondrous Osgar.

Fearghus remembered the time when he offered Conn his spear in exchange for a horse to pull his wagon. He'd taken it back again later, by design of some kind of odd magic. "Why yes I have," he answered proudly, looking once more at his fondest possession.

"That is some kind of spear!" Conn remarked, looking even more closely at it.

Now Fearghus changed the subject. "Have you found good work here?" he asked.

"It is not like back home, but yes, I have," Conn replied a bit gloomily.

"Well, cheer up, my friend," Fearghus said. "You are providing some of the greatest warriors in all of Eire with their weapons."

Conn bent over the stone walls of the well and retrieved his bucket, filled with water. "Indeed I am," he sighed, and said farewell to Fearghus, returning to his forge nearby.

Fearghus then proceeded to walk to the great hall, where surely Seadna or the others were gathered. He wished to inform them of his new discovery. He had achieved a goal now that he had hoped to achieve on the Isle of Man. With this golden spear there came strength, confidence, and hopefully, invincibility. Had that not been the reason he embarked on the journey to Man? He was happy now to have fulfilled his quest at last, but felt guiltly about it. He knew now why he had not discovered this spear on the Isle of Man, and he felt strongly opposed to his previous actions. Nonetheless, he would be sure now to tell Seadna about this miracle.

As he expected, the former pirate was still at his breakfast in the hall, at the head of the table where always he sat. He had become quite accustomed to this lifestyle as of late. When Fearghus approached him, there was upon his face a look of exasperation and boredom, but his expression changed when Fearghus produced Osgar. "Where did you get such a beautiful artifact?" he asked, stunned.

Fearghus could hardly restrain his happiness at revealing the identity of the spear to his comrade. "It is no simple artifact," he warned Seadna.

"Then what is it?" Seadna asked almost angrily, though his innocent excitement shone through his face the most.

"It is Osgar transformed," Fearghus said proudly, and held it aloft. "It has returned to a form I knew it to be a long time ago," he continued.

Seadna drew back in amazement. "Does this spear possess the properties that you spoke of before we left to reclaim it?" he asked.

Fearghus frowned. "My purposes were wrongly chosen then," he said. "It has returned as my honor has returned, and it shall be used only for the cause of goodness, rather than greed and prejudice."

Seadna seemed to understand what Fearghus said, and nodded. "I had come to that conclusion long ago," he muttered. "But only in you has it truly become apparent to me. I commend you."

Fearghus smiled. "I am glad to hear that," he said. "And I thank you for all your services."

Seadna stood up and proceeded to leave the hall. "I must say the same to you," he said, and reached the door. "And by the way, we will not attack today," he said.

Fearghus was very happy at this remark. He did not wish to go to battle again for a long time. Instead, he planned to ride back to Dún as Cloch with Agnos and show her all the wonders of his new home. And so now he dashed out of the hall to catch up with Seadna, and informed him of his intentions. Seadna seemed surprisingly agreeable to his plan, but gave him some warnings. "You should ride swiftly," he said, "and return quickly. We will hold out here for some time and wait for your return, though I cannot tell you definitely that we will not fight. Have a safe journey!" he continued.

Fearghus wished him farewell and ran off to his hut to find Agnos. Inside, she was already dressed and prepared for the day. "What tidings do you bring from the meeting hall?" she asked when he stepped inside.

Fearghus gathered all of his things together quickly. "The men are to hold out here for many more days in a dormant state," he informed her. "But we are going to leave this village and travel to my home in the south."

Agnos was curious at his remark. "Your home?" she asked.

Fearghus nodded. "My grand city of Dún as Cloch, hidden in a secret valley," he replied. "I wish to take you there, that you might behold my proud accomplishment."

Agnos swept her thick traveling cloak over her shoulders, and tied it across her chest. "I should very much like to come with you and see your great city," she told him.

Fearghus lifted a great bag of rations and supplies over his shoulder, sufficient for the ride of a few days. "Then it is settled. We must leave immediately and with speed," he said. "We cannot waste much time on the road, for I am needed as commander of these fighters in this terrible war."

Agnos ran out into the village square quickly, and raced over to the paddock where the horses were tethered. She immediately selected a milky white mare, and also found Fearghus's black horse, leading both by the rein. Once back in the square she hopped lightly onto her own steed, and watched her husband board his. "Let us be off then," she said, smiling, and kicked her horse hard in the side.

Fearghus, upon his fearsome black stallion, could hardly catch her as her horse galloped out into the hills. She was a skilled rider, apparently, and a far better one than he. Soon enough he was chasing her across the brilliant white beach, the valley of the monastery passing by rapidly. Her hair and her cloak both whipped out behind her as she rode, and her face was radiant in the morning light.

Finally they came to the hills south of the valley, and Agnos slowed her tiring mount. Fearhus pulled up beside her and looked upon her jubilant face, now a bit winded from the ride. "You should rest," he said, slowing his horse to a walk. "When you feel up to it we will gallop again, but for now let us move with reserve."

Agnos nodded her agreement, crossing her arms and taking a deep breath. "That was fun," she laughed. And the grin never left her face.

"Indeed it was," Fearghus agreed, and their steeds walked slowly ahead for much time, as the great southern forest neared. Soon they would reach the ruined village of Tuathal, and there make their camp for the night. It was there where Fearghus first found Agnos, hiding in the burnt rubble. She was left behind by the Roman soldiers, though did not particularly enjoy their company, as she later explained. Fearghus had nothing short of saved her life when he took her into his company, for a death of starving or thirst was imminent. Now, he reasoned, it was an action he was meant to take, one determined by fate.

It was not late in the day when they happened upon the village ruins. But Fearghus knew that they couldn't continue into the inhospitable forest until tomorrow, as there wasn't enough time left in the day to cross it completely. And so they stopped in the middle of what once was the village square, and ate a quick meal of fruit and bread, as such they had supplied themselves with. Even before the dusk, Fearghus began a warm campfire in the center of the clearing they were camped in, using the wood from the destroyed wall.

There, as they waited for the day to end, Agnos once again set about educating Fearghus in the ways of her God. She told him many full length stories of her religion, and explained each in great detail, highlighting the faults and morals involved in each. They seemed to tell of a very distant land, unlike Eire in almost every manner. Fearghus listened attentively, but remained confused at many points in the speech. When finally the sun began to set, he stopped her talking, and asked her a very important question. "Are you trying to change my religion?" he asked.

Agnos did not hesitate to answer him. "Yes I am," she answered shyly. "But what you call your religion, you must understand, is false. I do not look to change you, but rather to enlighten your knowledge of life, and morality. You must comply with my teaching in order for you to complete your journey."

Fearghus somehow did not seem convinced by her response. He felt alone, and afraid. "My journey?" he asked. "What is my journey?"

Agnos responded quickly. "Your journey is a journey to save Eire, and to spread the goodness of God peacefully within it. Among all the young men of Eire, the Lord has chosen you as his first messenger. You must listen to me!" she pressed, her voice growing louder.

But Fearghus was not hypnotized by her voice this night. He was allowed his own free will, and became hotheaded in her presence. "How can I trust you?" he yelled. "You are a Roman!"

Agnos stood up, and stepped back. "That is true," she hissed. "but I am also your wife, and trusted companion!" and with that she lifted her hands to the heavens. Then she cast a cold glance upon Fearghus, and said, "I did not think I would have to show you the power of my God, but now it has come to this." And as she stood there, her arms outstretched, the sky turned black before Fearghus, disturbed like the sea. Suddenly a great bolt of lightning came down from the sky and smote their campfire, its many fingers running back and forth across it. And then its arms seemed to jump out at Fearghus, and wrapped themselves around him. For a moment his entire body convulsed with energy and he shook violently, but then the bolt was gone from him and he fell to the earth hard.

He struggled to his feet and looked upon the wrathful face of his wife. She looked similar to how the Lady of Dún as Cloch had looked many days ago in the winter. Truly, she was sent to him by a force too great for him to comprehend. "The lightning," he mustered. "It comes to me again."

Agnos fell to her knees and comforted him. "You have seen such power before?" she asked him, holding his face.

Fearghus nodded. "Now I am convinced of the power of your God," he added. "These wonderful miracles I may now trace to him."

Agnos smiled and helped him to his feet. "You have passed the test." She assured him. "Now reap the reward." And as they embraced, a wind suddenly came up from the east, and engulfed them. Fearghus felt changed as he held onto his wife, and abruptly let go of her, looking down at his body. Upon it was the ethereal armor that he had been granted before, but now, he noticed, it was new and shiny, made of pure gold. His costume that had become so battered in all of his adventures was rejuvenated and remade miraculously, and so was his body. He felt refreshed and alive, and strong beyond his previous capacities. He felt as he did many long days ago when he was first transformed. "Your God does wonders beyond imagination," Fearghus said to Agnos, as she looked at his costume. And then he noticed that she was changed as well; her old riding cloak had become like the cape of a queen, and she wore many articles of gold jewelry about a pretty white gown.

"We should be thankful for these gifts from God," Agnos said. "But also, let us thank Him for all that he has created for us in this mortal world," she added, and knelt to pray to her one God. Fearghus hesitated for a moment, and then knelt beside her, searching innocently for this God in his mind. He did not know if he found Him as he knelt there with his eyes closed, but he felt very happy and relaxed as he did this.

It was a warm night. Fearghus allowed the fire to burn down to nothing in the dark, and slept soundly with Agnos near it, dreaming of things that had already happened, and that he expected would occur. Osgar he kept close by him, to ensure that he would retain it until the morning.

Agnos awoke before him the next morning, and prepared the horses for another day's ride. She gathered their supplies into Fearghus's bag before he even opened his eyes. When he did, though, he was quite pleased. "We will ride through the forest today he informed her. "In just another day we will reach my friend Dunchad in my hidden valley."

Agnos was already atop her mount. "That sounds wonderful," she replied, and waited patiently for him to board his nag. "I have never traveled through this forest," she added when their horses began to trot.

"You will like it," Fearghus assured her as the trees loomed ahead. "The road here should lead us in safety through it," he continued. Their horses moved quickly down the dusty thoroughfare, and Fearghus recalled all of his memories from this road. He remembered his duel with the centurion, his dealings with Conn, and his near death at the hands of Roman archers, resolved by the intervention of Irial. And as he thought about these things they passed the abode of Irial, which was deserted but yet untouched. "That is the house of my friend, Irial," Fearghus said as it disappeared behind them.

Agnos frowned. "I remember him and mourn his unrighteous death," she said.

They moved faster and faster as the road widened, deserted before them. Agnos even got up the courage to gallop her horse, and the two raced through the green forest joyfully. They moved as one, side by side, until the end of the road was nigh, and the hills of Eire again were evident. The land took a tremendous dip before them, and as they stood upon the height of this land, they could see all of the southern region of this land. Fearghus, with his vision, even saw the peaks of the Dún as Cloch valley far away on the horizon. When he pointed them out, Agnos said, "I see them too," and looked to the far mountains.

Fearghus was amazed. "You can see my home?" he asked. He did not think that she possessed the same physical capabilities that he did.

Agnos looked into his eyes. "I can see whatever you can," she answered, and smiled.

They broke into a new gallop, sweeping down the grassy slope and into the hill country. The land was wide and open before them, and the sun shone brilliantly upon them. It was then that Fearghus realized how fast they were traveling, looking up at the sun. "It is only just past midday!" he exclaimed. "We may yet reach Dún as Cloch before dusk!"

And so they continued on their jubilant ride, and the great mountain in the distance grew nearer and nearer. Soon they were into another, smaller forest, and it was the last obstacle before they reached the ruins of Seadna's village, as the Romans had left it. "Finally we are here!" Fearghus shouted when the halted their horses at the ruins.

Agnos seemed confused again. "Where is your city?" she asked.

Fearghus dismounted and pulled his black horse to the face of the stone mountain, and found there a door, set on the inside of a large crack in the stone.

It was made of wood but reinforced with iron bars, and appeared to protect this entrance very well. He rapped upon it three times, and shouted, "I am Fearghus, back from the North!" And with that, the door swung open, and a burly guard set himself in the opening, holding his pike aloft. When he saw Fearghus, though, he stood aside, and greeted him.

"I am coming to bring you good tidings from the Army," Fearghus said when they were inside. "Only for a short visit am I here," he added. The guard stood still and proud, and nodded to him. Fearghus helped Agnos and her mare through the door and the closed it. Inside this chamber there were many shamrocks growing in the torchlight, and they seemed very strange indeed. Next, they found the wooden walkway that spanned the watery cavern inside. Leaving their horse in an enclosure at the door, they walked excitedly down it, until the sound of rushing water filled their ears, and the glimmering light of the waterfall met them. Here at the iron door another guard recognized Fearghus, and held the door open for them to pass into the hidden valley.

Agnos's face lit up with joy when she beheld the sunny valley before her. "I did not think that your city was this wonderful!" she gasped, hesitant to advance any further into the great place. "It is grander than any town of the Romans that I have seen!"

Fearghus laughed. "I would say that you have not seen very many Roman towns, but I'll take your word for it!" he chuckled.

Agnos walked out into the field in front of the city, looking back and forth across it. "It is wonderful!" she exclaimed. "Are there many people living here?" she then inquired.

A happy old man walked out of the Oaken Hall, directly before her. "There are some," he said. "A few have moved in from the surrounding villages recently. Now who are you?"

Agnos turned to him and replied, "Now I could ask the same of you."

"I am Dunchad, the head builder of this fine place. Now why don't you tell me about yourself, dear lady," he responded.

Agnos acted like a stately queen before peasants. "I have heard of you, proud Dunchad," she said. "It is a pleasure to meet you. I am Agnos, the wife to Fearghus."

Dunchad bowed to her, then perked up suddenly. "Fearghus you say? Is he back?"

Fearghus appeared over the hill and saw his friend talking to Agnos. "Dunchad!" he exclaimed and ran down to meet the former warrior of Tuathal.

Dunchad embraced him. "I am glad to see you unscathed," he remarked, and then looked up and down at Fearghus's costume and weaponry. "But where did you get all of these treasures?"

Fearghus smiled. "From a friend," he answered.

Then Dunchad gave him a slap on the back. "I didn't know you were married!" he laughed. "Congratulations!"

Fearghus nodded to him. "Thank you," he replied briskly. "Now, about the campaign in the North."

"Oh yes!" Dunchad exclaimed. "How had that been going for you?"

Fearghus smiled. "We have already experienced a victory," he explained. "The Romans have lost quite a few men, but just not enough."

"How did you do it?" Dunchad asked.

"Well, I discovered that the men who fought with me before during our terrible defeat have been recruiting some men as well," he said. "Our combined forces crushed the Romans in open battle."

Dunchad grinned happily, and sat down on a log. "So you have won?" he asked, wiping his hot face with a cloth.

Fearghus shook his head. "It is not that simple," he explained. "The Romans, I estimate, have yet more than a thousand more men in their fortress."

Dunchad was surprised and drew back in disbelief. "Then it is hopeless!" he cried, slumping down in his seat.

Fearghus knelt to his level. "I do not think that it is," he said. "The Romans are a conservative group. They will be afraid to risk all of their men at once in battle. Besides, they are besieged at this moment, and will run short of supplies with so many mouths to feed."

Dunchad looked up. "I certainly hope so," he stammered. "But for now, it is good to see you again."

"We may meet many more times before this is over," Fearghus told him, and left, seeking out Agnos, who was exploring the town. He found her near the center of the city, where the great temple to Sucellos stood towering in the sky. She stood in awe of its architectural beauty, and did not notice him when he crept up behind her.

"Do you like my home?" he asked her, giving her a start.

"Of course," she answered, and the pointed to the temple. "But what is this?" she asked.

Fearghus was very embarrassed. "In recent days," he admitted slowly, "my men set out to build a great temple to the gods here."

Agnos did not show her horror at this discovery. "It is a great temple, no matter its allegiance," she pointed out. "Maybe I can help you solve this problem," she added, and looked at the stone walls of the building. "There can be made some minor improvements to the representation of religion here."

"I think I know what you mean," said Fearghus. "Will you come inside with me?"

Agnos grinned. "I think I may," she replied, and followed him inside the huge structure. Dunchad's men had made some improvements to the temple while Fearghus was gone. There were massive stone pillars supporting the walls and ceiling, and stone benches had been installed around a great altar and fire pit. The single room of the temple was massive, larger than even the Oaken Hall. And before them, to Fearghus's dismay, was a great golden statue of Sucellos, like to the one he had seen in the temple of his own native village.

Fearghus ran down to it, and stood in front of it, hiding it from Agnos's view. But Agnos had already seen it. "It is a mark of the ignorance of your people," she said, and stepped down to the floor where the statue stood. "And like the other things here, it can be mended," she said, and suddenly as her foot touched the ground, the statue in front of Fearghus burst into a million fragments, showering the floor with pieces of gold. Fearghus had to jump aside to avoid being showered by the sharp pieces.

"What magic is this?" he shouted, gathering his feet again.

Agnos helped him up. "It is not magic," she told him. "It is the power of God."

Fearghus looked down at the slivers of gold. "He truly is the one and only power in this world," he said.

Agnos scraped the pieces of gold into a pile with her foot. "You should save this precious metal," she said. And as Fearghus gathered the little pieces of gold, she told him another story about the history of her religion, about a time thousands of years before. She told him how the people of God strayed from Him and built themselves a statue such as this one, and how as punishment, they were forced to wander in exile for many years. She told him to remember it as a lesson, and that later she would tell him all about the conclusion of the story. According to her, stories such as this were passed on through the generations, and used as tools to help people become closer to God. Each one had a moral, and related to the present state of the world.

Fearghus poured the shards of gold into a leather pouch and brought them out of the temple with him. "This gold will be put to good use," he stammered, and passed it off to one of the men walking by. "Make it into a plate for my table," he said, and then rejoined Agnos as she strolled gingerly through the streets of the city, admiring the immense buildings.

"It is a miracle, how fast you built this city," she remarked.

"Yes, it is," Fearghus said, and looked around at the uniform buildings. Each seemed perfect in its own way. The boards making up the structures appeared to be smooth and spotless, and they fit together nicely, with no holes in between. There were many floors to these buildings, and many rooms. It would be a great place for good people to live, and make their homes. In recent day the men of Dunchad had begun to lay down stones in the fields between the buildings as walking paths, though no horses or wagons would find passage here. Fearghus wished to fill every room here with honest and good people, and take them with him on his journey to be closer to God.

Presently, Agnos discovered Fearghus's own small house, or more of a shack, as he now would put it. But it was here where he lived for most of the time they were apart, and he had a special attachment to it. When he came to it, Agnos was bustling about inside, examining his things. By the time he reached the door, though, she was finished with this, and came back out of the hut with something in her hands. "Where did you get this?" she asked, holding up the golden cross that the Lady had left to Fearghus.

Fearghus reached out and held the cross. "A fair lady left it behind," he replied. "I had forgotten about it."

Agnos looked it over in his hands. "It is the symbol of my faith," she told him softly. "This must have a been a fair lady indeed."

Then Fearghus asked yet another burning question that plagued his mind. "What does it mean?" he inquired.

Agnos stepped closer to him, and held his shoulders. "Long ago," she began, "the Roman Empire was lost in the darkness of a pagan religion, much like yours. And in those days, before they worshipped God, there was another race of people, whom I have already spoken of, that knew and loved God. But they strayed from Him again and again, and soon God needed to bring them back."

Fearghus looked deeply into her eyes. "And what did He do?" he asked curiously.

Agnos drew a deep breath and sat down on the bed Fearghus had built for himself. "He came down to the earth in the form of a man," she explained, "and as a mortal, He began to help them back to God."

"But what does the cross have to do with that?" Fearghus pressed.

"Before they came to follow Him, the Romans and even the chosen people of God all hated him bitterly," she said. "And because they were jealous of Him, they killed Him."

Fearghus then perked up. "I think I may have heard of this method of killing," he said, looking down at the cross. "It must have been a brutal practice."

Agnos nodded. "Crucifixion was a terrible and barbaric punishment," she said. And then Fearghus listened further as she elaborated on the story of the man. She explained how the selfless sacrifice of His life saved the race of man from evil, and how it was the defining example of the love and goodness of her God. After much discussion, she finally said, "and this has been the foundation of our faith for all these hundreds of years since."

But Fearghus was curious still. "And what happened to Him next?" he asked.

She smiled and reclined on his bed. "He rose from death and conquered it, proving once and for all that he is the one true God of all creation," she answered in a kind tone.

Fearghus sat there and thought about these things for a long time, and came to a conclusion rapidly. Now decisively and proudly, he regained his feet and said, "I should like to become a part of your faith."

Agnos stood up, and they shared a kiss. "One day soon I'm sure you will," she assured him. "For now, though, let us deal with the matter at hand."

Fearghus was reluctant to break away from her as she sped to the Oaken Hall. But suppertime was nigh, and the few builders and guardsmen left in this happy valley were in need of a good meal. Agnos was acting strangely, as if hiding something from him, so he followed her to the hall, and took his place at the head of his table. The men of Dún as Cloch sat along each side of the massive table, some of them accompanied by their wives and children. Other women, whose husbands were fighters, sat amongst them, and a solemn meal was served. Next to Fearghus, Agnos ate voraciously, somewhat ignoring him as she helped herself to more and more food. She was a sort of riddle for him to figure out this night, and he sat there thoughtfully, picking at his large serving of food.

Chapter 18

Rome Crumbles

After supper they made their way back to Fearghus's hut, but he turned away. "We will spend the night in one of the rooms," he told Agnos. And so they turned back towards the city, and traveled to the furthest building of the valley, where surely there would be no inhabitants. The structure they selected was fresh and new, just furnished with beds and other furniture. Agnos was pleased with it when she entered, and ran about through the upper rooms. Finally she found the one that suited her, and ushered Fearghus up the stairs to it. Inside there was a large bed and a fireplace, with an earthen chimney. Also there was a round table and one chair next to it, and a window on the east wall, with an overlook of the stream at the edge of the valley.

"I love it," Agnos said as they entered. "This place is a miracle in itself."

"Yes," Fearghus sighed, "it certainly is." He was tired now, and wanted nothing more than to pass to sleep. He removed his golden armor carefully, and then climbed into bed and immediately closed his eyes. He felt Agnos join him much later before he fell asleep, but did not wake to speak with her.

The following morning, Fearghus and Agnos elected to tarry another day in Dún as Cloch. They were already ahead of their predetermined schedule, and decided to take the pleasure of remaining here longer. Dunchad was also pleased at their decision. He came to meet them at breakfast in the Oaken Hall. "Did you have a good night?" he asked the couple as they finished their meal at the head of the table.

"Yes, we did," Fearghus replied. "Living in your building is quite luxurious."

Dunchad sat down next to them, and helped himself to some vegetables, peering across the table at Agnos. "Very good, very good," he mumbled. "So, what are you up to today?"

Agnos glanced at Fearghus, a curious look on her face. Fearghus knew that she was risking quite a bit by opposing the religion of Dunchad and the others, and also that many would not be pleased to learn of the new allegiance of their leader. And so he answered for her. "We would like to explore the valley some more," he replied, "and be better acquainted with the city."

Dunchad looked inquisitively from Fearghus to Agnos, and then his eyes returned to his meal. "Very well," he responded.

Agnos and Fearghus left the Oaken Hall shortly after that, and the sun was bright and breathtaking, illuminating the city before them. And as Fearghus looked on, a distinct golden gleam greeted him from the pinnacle of the temple. The gray columns of the building still remained in shadow as the massive structure towered above the other edifices, but atop them, there was something wonderful and golden, burning in the light from the sun that had just risen above the valley's mountain walls. The dawn had only just but conquered the immense peaks surrounding Dún as Cloch, and the barriers drew a line between the light and the dark on the opposite mountains. This line, Fearghus noticed, was cut just below the shining treasure he beheld, and in its reflected light, all else in the city was diminished. Beside him, Agnos had a glorious expression upon her face, if only polluted by a bit of arrogance. The object atop the temple, Fearghus now knew, was the Roman cross.

"How did that cross ascend to such a position?" he asked his wife, as they stood there in awe of it. It was then that he noticed a number of scrapes and bruises on her hands and forearms. "You didn't—"

Agnos nodded. "That artifact has strange powers," she said. "I ventured during this last night to explore them. I have placed it where every man can behold it now."

Fearghus glanced back to the cross, which yet seemed to be the only thing in the city graced with sunlight. "Your schemes will never work," he scoffed. "What should become of us?"

But Agnos was not looking at him. Her gaze had shifted to the working men, who, though in small number, had scattered themselves across the field. One by one, the golden cross caught their attention as well, and they stopped their struggling to stare unrelentingly upon the blazing symbol. Not many words, as Fearghus could hear, were exchanged among them, but they somehow slowly congregated in the center of the field, their wives and few children drawn to them silently. They crept towards Fearghus like shy children, but when all had stopped behind him, he turned around and appeared the more distressed.

"What is happening?" Fearghus asked shakily, turning desperately to Agnos.

But Agnos seemed to be in a trance as well, and uttered only one sentence: "They are seeing, and believing."

Fearghus cast his gaze back to the cross, and then to the thirty or so villagers behind him. At last he clambered back up the hill and almost to the steps of the Oaken Hall, and turned back to the people. Then he began to speak. He had been intending to address them in some way, but the words that he spoke to them now seemed almost as if they were not his, as if they came from another source, far greater than him. But yet he approved of them and understood them, so he did not worry. "We have suffered many long years," he began, "under the watch of the terrible and dark gods of the past. They have retained their hold upon us for hundreds of years, since the days of the old heroes and monsters." And at this the people seemed not moved at all, so he continued. "But now they are broken!" he shouted in an angry voice. "Their spell of evil is lifted from this land!" At once the people drew back in awe and fear, but continued to heed him. "They run away like the wolf runs from the shepherd as he protects his flock from it," he continued. "Our new faith shall be to this shepherd who protects us, this single brave man. Like the wolves, our gods, run in a pack, He stands alone before them with his staff, and is in Himself superior to them all. We are his sheep as He drives the wolves away with a single swing of his staff, and thus we must be near to Him, to avoid the lure of the wolves. We cannot stray from Him!"

He noticed Agnos at their helm, smiling up at him. And then he remembered the tale that she had told him of the cross, and what it meant. "Now this cross!" he boomed, looking over the top of the hall to behold it, "This cross is the symbol of Him, the symbol of the greatest story ever told!" And with that he told them quickly about the life of the man Jesus Christ, as Agnos had told him. He mentioned every important detail of the story known the world over, and was pleased with himself, finally concluding his speech. He half expected the men below him to disagree with his views when he rejoined them all, but it was quite the contrary. They smiled upon him happily and returned to their work, speaking amongst themselves in happy as well as inquisitive tones.

Agnos came to him immediately. "You truly are worthy of the task He has given to you," she told him. And then, "I told you there would be no problem with your peers. It only takes the consent of one man to speak for his people. You have my approval, and my gratitude for your efforts."

Fearghus glanced back up to the cross. The sun had come more fully upon the valley, now, but it seemed duller: dark clouds were forming at the very edge of the sky, and their predecessors, which were rolling white clouds, had finally choked the sun of its warm rays, preparing the land for a violent thunder storm. Judging from the look and color of the nearing storm clouds, Fearghus guessed that it was to be a terrible storm, and hastened the doors of the Oaken Hall to be closed.

He dashed to his hut and gathered a few personal items before retreating to the sturdy hall. Inside, all of the men and women he had just spoken to were sitting about in various corners of the room, and Dunchad was among them. "It will all be fine," the grizzly old man assured his comrade. "I have sent men to the stables to calm the horses, and to the storehouses to secure our food. I have weathered enough storms in my life to tell you again that we will have almost no trouble."

Fearghus sat down. "Thank you, my friend," he replied, and at that moment a distinct whistling sound was heard all about them. The winds had picked up, and with them, the sound of rain violently being hurled upon the wall of the hall. But this storm could not be as terrible within the walls of the valley, Fearghus deduced, because there were mountainous walls blocking the ruthless onslaught of gusty winds and pelting rains. They would only experience a fraction of the furious storm, as could pass through the circular top of their abode.

Fearghus passed the storm chatting with others around him. At length he finally relaxed, and looked at the massive doors of the hall as they shuddered in the wind. Little did he know that at that moment they would be hurled open to reveal a soaking wet warrior, his head bowed, struggling to push his way into the warm room. He looked to be exhausted, and his hair and clothing were thoroughly windswept, as if he had been riding a horse very fast. When he finally was given a chair to sit upon, he drew deep and troubled breaths, his eyes darting about the hall wildly. "I am here for a man named Fearghus!" he bellowed at last.

Everyone's attention instantly fell upon Fearghus, who got to his feet, and strode across the room to the mysterious fighter. "I am Fearghus," he said convincingly, standing before the messenger, who looked to be sporting a blue cloak, and the armor of a Serpent Captain.

The soldier looked upon the golden armor and helmet Fearghus was wearing. "I have been sent by Seadna, my lord," he said, bowing. "He has sent me with a message from his village in the North, to my ultimate master, the King Fearghus."

Fearghus eyed the man suspiciously. "I am here," he replied. "Give me your message, before you forget it."

The man bowed his head as he kneeled before Fearghus, and spoke. "My lord has sent me with grave news," he said. "The Romans have captured his stronghold village in vast numbers, and they further move to the north in his pursuit, as he has been forced to flee."

Fearghus seemed very troubled at this news, and became prodding. "And what of the Order?" he asked the man frantically, holding his chin. "And the Army?"

The messenger did not make eye contact with this man he so revered. "Your great Army, sir, battles the Romans even now in open combat," he said. "But the Order has fled with Seadna to the north, leaving only a small vanguard to defend their flank. Things look grim for both forces, with no sign of reinforcements."

Fearghus staggered back, completely crushed by this news. Many people could have died in his absence! Now his worst fears were confirmed: the Romans *had* decided to pursue war with all of their men, utilizing the enormous remnant of an entire legion to completely trample the village of Seadna, and recently, he realized, of Agnos. He felt suddenly sick to the stomach and sat back down upon his chair, looking ever to the man who informed him of these events. "Get this man to the fire!" he snapped at one of his attendants at the door, noticing the condition of this messenger. He was annoyed and distraught.

This changed things quite a bit. His Army likely wouldn't stand up to even half of the Roman forces for very long. If only they could hold off the Romans while he made his journey back to the North. His life would be put in a great deal of danger there. He would have to go alone, and...

Agnos nudged him. "You must return to your people at once," she panted. Surely she had not realized the magnitude of this problem until now. "I will stay here," she said now, relieving Fearghus's mind of the task of telling her this.

Fearghus had dressed himself in his armor already. Now only he needed to dash to the other end of the hall and procure Osgar and his sword, and then he would be off. Outside the hall, the storm seemed not ready to let up. He had been mistaken about the effect of the mountains around the valley; instead of lessening the gusts, the barriers captured them and bottled them up inside of Dún as Cloch, creating a dangerous swirling windstorm inside, that only the great architecture of Dunchad could withstand.

Fearghus was nearly knocked off of his feet as he traveled alone to the iron door, which one of the guards hastily opened for him as he, too, tried to survive the force of the blasting wind. There was another guard inside, and the waterfall next to him seemed to be overflowing, spilling onto the stone floor and extinguishing a number of the torches. But yet it was cozy and fairly calm in this chamber, and Fearghus was relieved to be walking behind these natural walls of stone. The water continued to flow under his feet as he walked over the wooden walkway, if a bit more lively.

At the end of the cavern he met up with the heavyset guard at the door, and was given his horse. The guard held the door open for him and stood out of the way of the nasty rain as Fearghus left, and waved his farewell to him. Fearghus's proud black horse he mounted quickly and kicked into a gallop, and soon he was off, running steadily against the wind, though it tore at his garments and blasted his face with ice. His horse seemed destined to carry him in safety through it, and he held tightly to his steed.

He was moving far faster than ever he had been traveling with Agnos. He was firmly resolved to ride constantly throughout the rest of the day, even into the dark forest at night. Trouble was brewing in the North, and death was at its heels.

He rode on and on, finally reaching the great southern forest as the storm faltered. Here he slowed his horse to a trot, but moved yet further, for the sun shining through the broken storm clouds seemed to be reddening, as dusk approached. In a moment, though, he could not see it beyond the trees all about him, and felt somewhat relieved by the hue of the sky above, not wanting to watch the sun set. He knew that this road moved ever in a straight line as he took it, and that even in darkness he might still navigate it and remain safe from the beasts of the forest.

The hue of the sky steadily darkened above him, but still he drew confidence from the gradualism of this process. Even when the sun was beyond the horizon, he knew, he would be guaranteed another length of daylight after to further his journey through the forest, which was quickening as he grew wary of the darkness.

At last he gave a yell and kicked his horse into a fierce gallop, and the forest began to rush by. He noticed now how dark the world had truly become since his entry into the forest. He was once more racing against time to find the other side of the trees, and apparently, as he had hoped, he was winning.

He burst out into the hills on the other side of the forest, just having passed the house of Irial. The world out here was darkening quicker than he imagined; the moon had risen already, and the pink dusk was nearly gone. Over to his right he could see a stone mountain framed against the purplish sky, and he knew that it was the one he had traveled upon in the company of Irial before the sacking of

Tuathal's village. The ruins of this place were just ahead of him, but he could not tarry there.

Instead, he rode around the miscellaneous burnt pieces of the village walls, and then remembered the walls of the village that had been just captured in the North. They were similarly made, as he recalled, but much thicker and sturdier than these which lay ruined at his right. Presently, he passed the clearing in the rubble where just two days before he had camped with Agnos about a warm fire. Those times seemed much happier and also quite distant, and he felt sickly again when he realized the importance of his current trip.

He quickly took to the beach as the moon rose and grew in intensity. The sky had cleared of the thin clouds left over from the recent storm by now, and Fearghus wondered whether or not there had been a storm in this place, so far from Dún as Cloch. But it was of no consequence. He was granted favorable conditions as he traveled north along the shore, and felt comfortable with them.

He grew tired as his horse trotted endlessly through rocky and sandy beaches, and grass-covered cliffs over the water. He did not realize it when the sky lightened finally; he was dazed in his loneliness and exhaustion. But when his horse slowed in the white sands of a familiar beach, he managed to look up, and noted with joy that the new and fresh dawn was shining upon the white cliffs of the monastery valley in the distance. Now he became quite alert, for the sounds of a one-sided battle echoed across the valley, and greeted him with a ring of evil to come. He heard men cry aloud in both anguish and relief, and heard metal weapons crash upon each other, like the thunder from the last day. And above all this he heard the buzz of rushing feet and rattling armor, the buzz of battle.

His horse broke into a gallop as the battlefield opened before him. Two great masses of men looked up in awe to see him as he passed, and at their forefronts, archers pulled back their weapons to their chest, and sent two waves of arrows in both directions, which met each other in the middle of the field, and then passed by to sail to the enemy lines. In the breaking sunlight, Fearghus saw on the south side, the great banner of his own Dún as Cloch, and on the other, he could hardly make out the standard of a Roman legion, a golden eagle glinting in the dawn. Before he passed them, their horns were sounded both to signify a charge, and the two groups of men proceeded to run across the field, their swords and lances raised so that they, too, gleamed in the fresh light.

Fearghus steered hard to the left, and raced past the white stone that overlooked the valley. He began almost immediately to see in the distance the village in question, and sped towards it with determination such that he had not seen in himself for a long while. His speeding horse covered the distance from the rock to the village much faster than he imagined was possible. When the village neared, he realized with a pang of hope that it was very lightly guarded, since the Romans had left in pursuit of the Order.

He did not stop to dismount his courageous steed, nor did he slow his pace as the walls of the place neared. He saw out of the corner of his eye there a gaping hole in the fortifications such that the Romans would have made, and his horse leapt through it expertly as the heavy sword of Conn rose from its scabbard impressively.

Indeed, there were few Romans in this place. His long sword had no trouble swinging low to catch two of them from the start, but a well placed lance from the steps of the great Village Hall caused him to jump gracefully from his mount and continue his desperate fight on the ground. The first thing he did was charge the man at the Village Hall fiercely after this, and then he was dancing through the hall itself, holding Osgar in his left hand, and his sword in his right. There were quite a few straggling soldiers in this hall that defended themselves against his onslaught, but they were no match for his Celtic rage.

He had nearly cleared the hall when one of soldiers took a risk and lunged at him, succeeding in slashing his high chest, near to his throat. Fearghus leapt aside and finished him quickly, but felt himself bleeding just above his chest plate, where only the pins of his cape shielded him. His thick red blood ran down the front of his golden armor, and he paused momentarily to look down at it.

All of a sudden, Fearghus noticed the flow of blood down his chest stop. He looked wildly back at the wound where it had been coming from, and then gave a shout of joy. Just as before, when he yet still possessed Osgar in this form, he was immortal! His wound had healed itself.

With a rush of confidence flooding his body, he bounded out into the square, his eyes wildly looking for more Romans to destroy. In a moment he had found more, who had hastily gathered off to one side. He rushed at them, brandishing both of his fearsome weapons, and parried their coordinated blows. Then he spun around and unleashed the blade of his sword upon all of them simultaneously, somehow killing two of them and merely grazing the others. But the two remaining men did not have time to strike, for in another moment the tough shaft of Osgar knocked them heavily to the ground, and the two blades in Fearghus's hands came down at the same time, straight into their chests.

Fearghus drew his weapons out of them quickly, and spun around defensively once more. But these two were the last of them, and there was no more fighting left for him. He had won the city back, if only for a moment. He looked around at all the deserted huts and houses around him in the square, and was on the verge of tears. He tried to push the fact that he had been married here out of his mind, and instead imagined Agnos safely living in Dún as Cloch. His horse had remained standing in the square near the gate, and now he realized the situation of his time. He had to find his way to Seadna quickly, or else his pursuers would catch him. And so he leapt upon his horse and galloped out of the forsaken village, turning his steed to the North.

How far could they have traveled since he left? Judging from the time of arrival as well as the essential task of the messenger who had met him at Dún as Cloch, Seadna would have left at least three days ago, five at the most. They would have been on foot, he reasoned, so they would not be too far from here, if he rode hard.

He desperately scanned the horizon for any sign of them, and he knew that there was a twin village somewhere here. He just had never seen or visited it. Then a novel idea occurred to him: the villagers had spoken of a river in this northern region, and of its importance as a last line of defense. Since all rivers emptied into the sea, he reasoned, why not find it along the coast and then follow it to Seadna? The river banks seemed to be a perfect place to dig in and plan defense.

He redirected his horse off towards the rocky beach, and soon had gained it. From here he rode ever North along the shore, looking for the obvious signs of a river, which included trees, bushes, and men. None of these did he see as he galloped further, but then he found it: off in the distance there was a thin line of trees and other plants, most certainly running along a source of fresh water like a river or stream. He broke off of his path alongside the briny sea now, and headed off in the direction of the trees, where he found a calm and clear river, lined with sedge and cattails. The path of the river broadened as it continued towards the sea, but narrowed in the direction that Fearghus looked.

And so he trotted along the south bank of the river, always looking to the north bank at his right. It was a long path he followed, and he passed over long reeds as well as black mud on the river's edge. His horse was beginning to show his exhaustion from being constantly ridden for so long, but nonetheless carried Fearghus along at an acceptable pace, until Fearghus began to see some signs of other men.

He stopped his steed abruptly when he came to them, fresh tracks in the mud, and all made by the same boot. The Order of the Serpent had passed here most definitely. When Fearghus looked up, he noticed the land to the north dip a bit, so that his view of it was obstructed. But his view of the south was fine. There was a large hill behind him. When he looked upon it, though, something gave him a fright. Just as he looked, there was the thunderous sound of many feet at its crest, and he saw what he believed to be quite a large number of men walking to the west along it, their helmets just visible. By their oddly crafted lances, he knew immediately that they were Romans.

He crept behind some of the reeds and bushes near the bank, and led his horse into the shadow of the trees. Waiting until the marching men had passed, he then cautiously mounted his stallion and steered it towards the North. Luckily, the hooves of the creature did not make a sound as it wheeled around in the soft mud, and he remained undetected until he was sure he was out of earshot of the column of soldiers.

Now he led his horse into the current of the river, and guided the tired creature carefully through the water, which clouded up with sand when the horse attempted to ford through it. Once again, Fearghus was lucky that his steed managed to clamber up the other bank, and then he kicked it into a great gallop that found him hurtling down a hill at incredible speeds. And then his heart raced, for just ahead of him, in a camp under a group of trees, was the Order of the Serpent, their armor shining revealingly in the midday sun. Fearghus advanced to them quickly, raising his spear Osgar as a sign of friendship, as they all reeled with surprise. "It is I, Fearghus!" he called to them.

Straight away, Seadna appeared at their helm, and greeted Fearghus as he dismounted. "I knew you would find us," he remarked as they embraced. "As you can see, we're in a bit of a mess."

Fearghus looked at their vast party, including all of the women from the village as well as the children and the elderly. It would be impossible to move these people faster than the Romans. He wasn't sure how Seadna had gotten this far unharmed. "I should say you are," Fearghus replied. "This because I have just seen the Romans behind you on the opposite bank!"

Seadna shuddered with fear at these words. Fearghus had never seen him so alarmed, and so he patted him on the back. "Look," he said briefly, holding up Osgar his lance. "I can use this to distract them, for now."

Seadna nodded his shaky approval. He suddenly looked older than he was, though he was quite old, and very wrinkled indeed. Fearghus turned to him once more before departing. "I've cleared the village," he said. "You should flee to the south and to Dún as Cloch at once!"

Seadna struggled to smile at his friend, and went back among his warriors to tell them of their plans. Fearghus, meanwhile, had jogged back to the hill, tying his black horse to a nearby tree. He waved back to his men, and then disappeared behind the crest of the hill, where the river ran quietly along.

Now he himself forded across it, waist deep, and then he crawled up behind a tree on the south bank. The Romans, somehow, had chosen here to stop, and he could hear them speaking amongst each other at the top of the next hill. Slowly but surely now, he moved to the east. He didn't want the Romans to see his advance in the north, or even the east where Seadna was moving. He believed he could find some trees to hide behind and come from the south or even the west, and use his gift of immortality to distract and kill a number of the Romans, so that they would be confused and unable to move.

As he hopped from tree to tree, hiding behind their stout trunks, he realized the importance of distracting them from the west. They would consider him a spy instantly, and would advance further in this direction, hopefully moving far enough away from the sea, where the refugees would be running for their lives.

It was a risky business, hiding behind trees. Some were just too thin to keep him concealed correctly, and between others the gap where he was to cross was too small. A few times Fearghus considered himself purely lucky not to have been spotted by the idle Roman soldiers as they washed in the stream. Soon enough, he had completely passed them by, and found cover behind some rock bluffs on the completely west side of their position.

He waited there momentarily until he could see in the far distance the Order of the Serpent moving along the sea's edge. The Romans did not notice them so far away, but Fearghus could see them with his keen vision atop this hill, especially without the trees in his way. Once they were far enough along he could attack, and then they would break into a frenzied run down the beach, alerted by the raucous sound of displeased Romans.

Finally the moment came to attack, and Fearghus took it in stride with all his adventures. He leapt into the air with Osgar aloft, and no sooner had he done this than he drew his sword. Just ahead of him, a number of the Romans were jolted awake or stunned by his entry, and no one had yet thought to react. But Fearghus was determined to distract them as best he could, and so he hurtled into their ranks, slashing the Roman armor to ribbons and parrying their weak blows every now and then with the golden Osgar, which was not notched by this use. Ten, then twenty Romans were dead, and yet the Romans as a whole had not yet begun to move, conceitedly thinking that they remained safe from this single man.

But then some of the men caught a glimpse of the hysteria and death Fearghus was spreading, and began to retreat, effectively alerting their comrades of the ensuing danger. However, the five or six hundred men there could not be swayed to turn back by just these thirty or so. But their leader had become aware of Fearghus's presence by now, and he was using his horse to make his way over to the site of the skirmish. When he finally reached Fearghus's position, he laughed. Then he began to shout more orders in Latin, and more soldiers jumped in to help their comrades. Fearghus was quickly overwhelmed, and began to stumble back, deep gashes and bruises appearing all over his body. But yet, as he had planned, the Romans were beginning to mobilize, and were heading west after him, as the rescued villagers moved further and further away from him, to safety.

He now began to run back to the wide open hills behind him, and the Romans, in their heavy armor, pursued him like dogs. Of course he managed to outrun them now, but he found himself on a spot. He had to somehow lose their sight, and sneak away from them safely while they continued to march unknowingly west, judging him to be a spy. His plan was being put perfectly into effect, he now only needed a distraction so that he could jump into the trees he had come to. He slowed his pace and looked about desperately as the thunder of Roman feet filled the air, but there was nothing.

It was then that he prayed innocently to God, and asked him through words in his mind whether or not he could save him this day. And as he sat there, praying, the Romans spotted him again and began to lumber towards him as one great ensuing darkness. But as he beheld them, holding his ground, he noticed truly that the world was filling with darkness, and that the sky had just become black like it had been the day before. At that moment, as Fearghus cowered behind his sword, a great bolt of lightning like to the one he had seen many times before rapidly pierced the ground ahead of him, and the Romans at the front of the column were thrown back forcefully into their own men, and the very earth was thrown into the sky.

The dust from the blast was so thick in the air that Fearghus saw his chance. The Romans would not see him as he broke into a spirited run, and dashed behind the rocks and trees near him. When he did, though, he noticed that this cover was flimsy. He had the entire open land of Eire before him, and the Romans still back there lost in the darkness. And then another prospect lifted his heart. The neighing of a mighty horse filled the air, and out of the dust in the north Fearghus's black horse came to him. He sprinted to catch it as it passed him, and then leapt onto its back, feeling the exhilarating sensation of escape.

He rode with joy he could not measure, and rode swiftly, as though his horse was the very wind itself. And in his favor, as he left the sight of the Romans, the weather returned instantly to its former condition. He then found the beach to his left, and slowed his mount to a trot, as the pirate's cove neared him. He was plainly sure that the Order had found refuge here; after all, it was the perfect hiding place for Conaill's warriors when they wrecked here recently.

Fearghus's horse somehow managed to scramble down the sandy slope to the clearing of the harbor. Indeed, as he expected, what seemed to be two hundred people, half of them Serpent warriors, lay quietly in the shadow of the cliff. Directly in front of him, Fearghus spied Seadna and Murchadh, as well as Conaill behind them. He greeted them quickly and dismounted his horse. "I have distracted the Romans for now," he told Seadna.

The old pirate murmured his approval. "We all owe you our lives, Fearghus," he said.

And then one of the warriors piped in, saying, "Some of us twicefold!"

Fearghus laughed as he sat down in the sand. "We must rest here while we can," he told them. "We will move out when the sun begins to set."

Seadna sat down next to him on the cool ash. "That looks to be as good a plan as any," he remarked. "I should like, at last, to see your impenetrable paradise."

Fearghus leaned his head back against the stone wall and rested his eyes. "That is all good and well," he said, trailing off a bit, "but destined for a time after I have a nap."

Fearghus could see Seadna and the others chuckling as they too prepared to sleep, also having been denied this privilege the previous night. Before Fearghus fell completely asleep, he heard an exhausted Murchadh yawn quite lengthily, and then slump down into a heap of sand.

Fearghus was nothing short of jolted awake that evening, when the sun was only half submerged below the horizon. It was Seadna who waked him, and he seemed rested and refreshed. From the look on his face, Fearghus concluded, he was ready to leave immediately, and quite anxious to do so at that. "It is time to go," he said hastily as Fearghus opened his eyes.

Fearghus had fallen asleep in his armor, his sword still sheathed at his side. Osgar, in fact, had never left his grasp. And so he had no trouble staggering to his feet and finding his horse, mounting it reluctantly. Finally his steed clambered back up the sloping sand, and the others followed respectively as darkness fell, the other three leaders also mounted. Fearghus was a bit groggy as he looked out over the valley of the monastery that night, but his outlook changed drastically when a sudden realization reached his mind. When Seadna pulled along side him subsequently, he burst, "The Army has had a nasty battle with the rest of the Romans this night! I do wonder how they fared!"

Seadna gazed upon the white cliffs and the tops of the trees of the encircling forest. "As would I," he remarked. "But we shall soon know, I'm sure." And with that he pointed towards the plain beyond the valley, where the conflict had taken place.

Soon they were traveling across the high beach above the valley, trying desperately to stay from the view of the fortress below them. At times, Fearghus fearfully herded them into the freezing surf, doing everything possible to prevent detection. But the monastery seemed dead as he beheld it passing them. The Romans had left it idle, their armies wandering outside of its walls this night. Yet Fearghus did not dare attack at this time, for the task seemed too daunting, even in the current state of the place. He still, he pointed out to himself as he trotted along, hadn't discovered the outcome of the recent battle here.

More time passed as his stomach shook within him, and he was near to vomiting. If any Romans lay camped on the plain tonight, they were sure to see them and come running to kill them all. Only the faint chance of victory he clung to as they passed, and he held his breath as the sound of a galloping horse echoed across the land.

The whole of their company breathed a massive sigh of relief as one of their own, a Celtic warrior of the Army, came to meet them. "You have won?" Fearghus asked in disbelief.

"Yes, my lord, we have been victorious against an enormous foe. Your grace of appearing to us this morning before the battle has somehow allowed us to claim victory over four hundred soldiers. But we have suffered heavily for this, of course."

Fearghus had been preparing for this outcome since this afternoon, though it had seemed unlikely to him then. He merely waved his hand, and twenty Serpent Warriors joined the messenger as he waited before him. "Take these with you and capture the monastery *tonight*," he instructed the man. "Burn it to the ground if the others return and attack you," he added quickly. "However," he continued with a thoughtful expression, "I should also like to have some of your remnant forces accompany me back to Dún as Cloch."

The man nodded. "We have just under a hundred left, sir," he said with the bow of his head. "It shall be done as you command."

Fearghus motioned for his group to continue ahead at a more lively pace as the messenger galloped back to his warrior forces, completely safe in this place tonight, since the other Romans were marching aimlessly in the far north. Fearghus winced as he watched him go, for in the plain ahead there were hundreds of bodies scattered randomly about, surprisingly near to the campfires of the Celts.

Nothing more happened that night as they trudged towards the forest. This except for the coming of thirty battle-hardened warriors from the Army. The men, though they dressed differently, seemed to fit in well with the refined Order of the Serpent, and held conversations with their new friends as the party wearily continued on, using the cover of night to their advantage.

By the dawn, they had found the remains of Tuathal's village. Fearghus instructed the villagers to find hiding places in the buildings and such all about them, and then consulted his friends inside one of the places where there were still four walls in tact. They used the fallen ceiling as a table and sat on piles of stone around it, all while the white dawn filled the room with light.

Fearghus began the conversation with a pressing point. "What will we do if the Romans manage to defeat the Army, and then follow us to Dún as Cloch? We will certainly have no way of fighting them then, and no way of feeding the refugees, once my storerooms are empty."

"We must consider that the Army will fight valiantly against them, mustn't we?" said a very curious Murchadh.

Fearghus swallowed. "Yes, we must think that they will," he answered. "That should win for us some time and also diminish the Roman forces, but what does that say for all of their lives?"

Now Conaill's voice entered their argument. "We have been fighting this war too long, I say," he remarked. "I think that we cannot tamper with their fate any more, as it has already been sealed. They are destined to face death for the sake of Eire, and for the sake of all these refugees. Let us then assume that they will try to stop the Roman onslaught as best they can!"

Seadna glanced over at him uncomfortably. "That idea has merit," he decided, "and it shall have to stand. We cannot save them, nor can we advance them."

Fearghus stood up to his full and fearful height, slamming his clenched fist on the stone slab before them. "Then it is decided! We will leave immediately for Dún as Cloch this day, and pray for our doomed comrades in the North."

The leaders then decided upon letting the rescued villagers rest in their hiding places until midday, and were firmly resolved to cross the forest before the day's end. Fearghus was wide awake, though, and planned more of his ongoing war with the Romans in private, until the sun appeared directly overhead.

The villagers were reluctant to gather behind them on the road. All were very tired, having walked throughout the night, but in addition to this they were eager to find the safety that Fearghus promised them. None of them had very much trouble gathering their things after such a short stint in the village, and before Fearghus knew midday was gone, they had passed into the forest, the trees unable to shade completely the dusty road. They walked in sunshine for a great while, and passed Irial's house quickly.

When the sun could no longer cast its rays fully on the road, Fearghus knew that they had reached the late afternoon, and that the end of the great forest was near. He was jubilant to have finally passed it, but still anxious and nervous all the same.

It was dusk, or rather twilight when they exited the trees. Fearghus now permitted them to make camp for the night before coaxing them on, though he had until now been very pleased at their rapid rate of progress. It was now quite impossible that the Romans were in their pursuit. Even if they had returned from their westward wandering, they would be waylaid at the monastery, and would be in no mood to march south, after nothing they knew had definitely passed that way. All in all, they had successfully evaded their Roman pursuers, who were the only soldiers remaining from an entire mighty legion of troops.

Fearghus sat about a campfire with all of his familiar friends, still holding Osgar tightly. He wasn't hungry this day, nor did he think he ever would be again. His mind was clouded with thoughts of the war against Rome, and the triumph of their escape seemed overshadowed, in his mind, by the prospect of the hundreds of Roman soldiers still present in his homeland. He brought these thoughts to bed with him that night, and allowed sleep to relieve him of his troubles temporarily.

They began their last leg of the journey to Dún as Cloch in the late morning, when Fearghus noticed it was near to midday. The villagers were refreshed and rejuvenated now, and they walked happily behind him, if not a bit slower than usual. The hill country they were passing through was marked by many steep slopes, but it was generally a kind region to their feet. As they traveled they kept close to the beach, and Fearghus kept his eyes peeled for the mountains of Dún as Cloch in the distance, soon finding them at last. "We are almost there!" he called to the column of people behind him, and veered off towards the ruins of Seadna's village, the latter following close behind.

The two friends steered their horses onto the coastal plain where before they had battled pirates. Seadna looked over to their left and saw the door in the mountain. "Ah," he remarked, "There is the secret entrance to paradise."

Fearghus dismounted his horse and walked over to the door, pulling the dark stallion along behind him. He knocked three times on the wood and iron, and the heavy guard at this door allowed him in without suspicion. When he saw who Fearghus's company was, he let out a sigh of relief and surprise. "Your city will be full before we know it!" he joked as the villagers moved in behind their master. Seadna waited behind them with his horse, surveying the people.

Once most of them were inside, Fearghus walked over to the floating path. "Follow me!" he boomed, and then turned to walk down the path, in the view of all of the people. He could hear them follow him in droves upon the log path, and their footsteps echoed throughout the cavern.

Fearghus reached the iron door quickly, and the guard upon it looked inquisitively at him as the other villagers filled the waterfall chamber. "They are my people from the war-torn North," he assured them warmly. "They have come to settle our fair city and reap from it unlimited safety."

The guard smiled back, and opened the heavy door. "You are truly a king of men," he remarked as his master passed.

Fearghus waited at the left side of the door as the ragged people of the northern village passed into his blessed realm. Many of them stopped when they looked upon the sunny and enormous city, but others were eager to run into it. All in all, it was a fine experience of Fearghus's to see them rejoice like this. He waited there, greeting many of them, until he noticed Seadna and the other leaders bringing up the rear.

"It is fairer than when last I was here!" Conaill most nearly shouted when he walked into the field, for their was a loud racket in the valley from all of its new inhabitants.

Seadna, who was the last man to see Dún as Cloch, approached Fearghus, grinning obviously. "This is indeed the place I spoke to you about," he said.

Fearghus patted him on the back once more. "You are wise and loyal," he replied, "and very worthy of living here with me."

Seadna glanced up at the Roman cross on the temple, but said nothing. As the two walked into the Oaken Hall together, he had quite a strange expression on his wrinkled countenance.

But Fearghus had no time to pay attention to his friend's face. Someone had just screamed "Fearghus!" from the opposite side of the hall, and in another moment, Agnos was pushing her way through the crowd to meet him. She walked especially gracefully for her condition, and threw herself into his outstretched arms. "I was worrying about you again!" she said in a laughing and airy voice.

Fearghus kissed her. "I thought you might do that," he responded light-heartedly, and they sat down at the long table, still holding one another's hands.

"How has the war been going?" Agnos asked quickly and curiously.

Fearghus tried to remain cheerful as she studied his face. "We have had yet another, larger victory," he stammered nervously.

Agnos stroked his long hair, which he hadn't shortened for many days. "Then why are you so troubled?" she asked innocently, moving closer to him.

Fearghus frowned. "We were able only narrowly to escape the rest of the Romans and come here," he answered. "I fear that they have yet enough men left to crush us!"

"But what of your Army? And the Order?" Agnos asked.

"I have brought most of the Order and some of the Army here with me," Fearghus said. Agnos looked about the room and recognized some of the Serpent warriors about the room. "However," he continued, "a small remnant of the Army still remains up there in the North, as the Romans march upon them with five times their number."

Agnos shuddered at this news. "They will be doomed!" she observed hopelessly.

Fearghus embraced her. "I know," he whispered. "But that has become their fate."

Agnos tried to push this idea out of her mind as they prepared to sit through a melancholy feast. Warriors and villagers alike gathered on either side of them, and looked at them pleasantly through their dull eyes. Many of them still could not draw their gaze away from the golden lance Fearghus held aloft.

At last Fearghus stood up at the head of the table, and the hall fell silent before him. "You are safe now," he began. "And you are now my guests, and my dearest friends. I invite you to be safe here in my halls, and to rid of all your troubles, which you have so luckily eluded." The group cheered heartily at this, and every man had a drink of ale. Fearghus continue now, a bit more confidently. "Now many strange things have come to pass in recent days. I'm sure you have noted the Roman cross in the center of town." At this a murmur arose throughout the people, who looked both uncomfortable and curious at the same time. Fearghus did not even dare to look at Seadna and the others. He only looked ahead, at the doors of his hall. "I have recently undergone a conversion to Christianity, the way of the Romans," he said, to the communal gasp of many there. "I know you are frightened," he added quickly, to amend this. And then he did something very strange. "To show you the power of God," he said, "I will perform this miracle before you. It is a miracle of much fame and importance in the old teachings of God, and hopefully it will convince you of my righteousness."

One of the women next to him screamed. He had just laid Osgar down upon the table, and it had turned instantly into a long serpent, which proceeded to slither down the table towards the other end, where Seadna sat. When it reached to old pirate, it raised its head defensively, its tongue flicking in and out. Seadna's hand immediately went to his sword, but Fearghus was too quick for him. Holding his hand aloft, he called to it "Osgar," and the snake flew into the air, and returned to his hand as a golden spear. "And there you have the power of my God," said Fearghus defiantly, trying to avoid looking at Seadna's snarled expression.

The people there were too scared to cheer or even respond. But nonetheless, they gave their attention to him. And then he rehearsed again his speech naming God as a shepherd of them, and sat down nervously. "Let the feast begin!" he then bellowed, and clapped his hands for the servants to come. In that instant, the hall filled once again with the voices of happy people, and everyone busied themselves at eating their supper.

Next to him, Agnos leaned over to say something to him. "Once again," she whispered, "well done." But then she cast her gaze down to the other end of the table. "I do not seem to trust Seadna any more!" she seemed to whisper, for so low she kept her voice.

Fearghus looked straight ahead of him as the angered Seadna looked down at his meager plate of food. "I think so too," he said in a normal voice, as Agnos turned back at him. "I should speak with him soon."

The feast continued in a muted sort of joyous state, and Fearghus ate only a small amount of food, for so full was his mind of trouble. Agnos tried to comfort him as he sat there that night, but even her caressing could not ease his mind. He thought of many things, including Seadna, the Army, and of others, which came together to form a dark abyss in his mind, one which he seemed about to fall into.

The people came and went during the feast. Dunchad was busying himself outside trying to find them their accommodations, and he was constantly entering and exiting the Oaken Hall. Fearghus watched lazily as the great doors opened again and again, and soon had come into almost a trance as he stared at it. But then it opened once more, and Dunchad did not walk through it.

It was the exhausted messenger of the Army in the North, and his face was tired so that Fearghus could not fathom what his message was. Immediately one of the Serpent Warriors at the door referred the herald to him, and he rushed to meet the warrior, holding his breath again. When the messenger reached him, he bowed upon one knee to deliver the message, as had become customary. "The men of my company in the North have sent me ahead of them to inform you that—"

"That the Romans have bested you and you are retreating to here?" Fearghus burst, trying to ease his suffering.

"No sir," the man replied. "Not at all sir!"

Conaill leaned over from his chair at the table. "Well, then get on with it, boy!" he snapped.

The messenger remained kneeling. "I have been sent to inform you that the Romans have been defeated."

"*Defeated*?"

"Yes, my lord, the Romans have been destroyed completely."

Fearghus staggered back, and one of the kind old village ladies drew a chair up behind him just as he fell down into it. "But how did you do it?" he spluttered.

"We have received aid from over three hundred horseman of the south," the messenger responded, looking up at his master with inquisitive eyes.

Fearghus let out a long laugh, and hardly could calm himself down. "The riders have appeared?" he asked. "But I only sent for fifty of them!"

The messenger got to his feet, no longer afraid of Fearghus. "All the strength of my village has come," he said. "After their king left, they grew restless, and joined the men we sent back to them, who were looking for horses."

Fearghus was amazed. He looked to Conaill now, who sat their grinning. "It was a very fierce battle," the herald added. "The whole lot of us were up all night in the monastery listening to them coming."

"The riders?" Fearghus asked.

"No, sir, the Romans. They came with five hundred men down from the hills, and sounded their horn. Obviously they knew that we had captured their fortress."

"And what happened then?"

"We waited nervously as they surrounded us on all sides. They'd already begun the siege when we saw the horses coming," the messenger recalled. "We were about to burn the place down like you said, too. After that, it was all just one big storm of dust outside in the field, and the horsemen came out of it alive. We did not even have to leave the monastery!"

"Outstanding!" Fearghus shouted. "Remarkable! We are victorious!"

Back at the table, Agnos spoke to him once more. "Yes, the corruption of Rome has been lifted from this land. They disappear over the sea, never to return. All across the world, these things are happening. Their borders fall to madmen and pagans. Rome crumbles."

"Rome crumbles, you say? But I should note that its legacy does not," Fearghus remarked.

Agnos looked more thoughtful than she had at any time previously. "You can be sure that the power of God could never crumble," she said. "You are far more wise than I judged you to be."

And they feasted happily into the night.

Chapter 19

▼

The Iron Door

It was a happy night when they retired after that feast. The villagers had all, at one time or another, been assigned to their new homes, and Fearghus and Agnos had also been allotted a large room in the front of the city that they could call theirs. That night they moved into it, and slept soundly in the same large bed, near a window overlooking the field.

In the morning, Fearghus looked at his armor with a strange expression, one of relief but also of longing. He had enjoyed being a warrior for the sake of Eire. It was what he had wished for, was it not? Now he missed it genuinely. But yet, he realized, he had many more things to worry about now. He glanced over at Agnos still asleep in bed, and noticed how swollen her stomach was. He would have to pay much better attention to her one day in the future, and by the looks of her, that day was not too far off from the present. This coming child seemed to be his gate into a quieter life, and a life closer to God.

He dressed in his golden armor once more today, for the valiant fighters of the Army would arrive soon. He would appear as their king until the end of his days, and many elements of this protective suit were necessary components of a king's costume. Now he picked up Osgar and tied his sword about his waist, and sighed as he climbed down the stairs to the field below, with the Oaken Hall directly before him. Inside he was greeted by many of his trusted men, and their wives. They were all eating calmly around the table, and gave a cheery welcome to him.

As soon as he sat down, one of the Serpent Warriors approached him. "I have been thinking of your words last night," he said brightly as Fearghus turned to him. "And I know that we would all like to be a part of your faith."

Fearghus swallowed a large mouthful of fruit with an audible gulping sound. "I am pleased to hear that," he replied. "And I shall one day see to it that all of you do."

But the warrior was not done yet. He sat down next to him and looked into his eyes. "The old gods are too brutal and demanding. I am ready to praise a new God, one that is almighty, and one that does not demand sacrifice. I want his principles of goodness and love to be the foundation for the rest of my life."

Fearghus looked down at him. "Then you shall be the first," he said. And as he said it, he suddenly noticed that this was the very same fighter to whom he had spoken to in the courtyard of the monastery, a whole year ago. It was right after he had demanded that the monks of the monastery be spared, and had killed two of his men to ensure it. The warrior had come to him innocently then with these such words, just as he did now.

"The first to what?" the young man asked as Fearghus looked away.

Fearghus did not know how he managed to answer him, but he turned to the warrior and said, "The first to be baptized."

The warrior looked confused, but so did Fearghus. And so they parted then, and Fearghus went back to his breakfast, his mind filled with strange ideas. In the back of it, a warning had appeared. It was almost as if it had been inserted into his mind, but it did not confuse him. He knew then that this day would be a very eventful one in his life. He just could not fathom how this would happen.

He left the Oaken Hall late and went back up to his room to find Agnos. He found her brushing her long hair in the reflection of the window in their immense room. She was sitting on a cushioned chair. As Fearghus looked around, better observing the room, he noticed that in addition to their wide and soft bed in the middle of it, there was also a grand fireplace of hewn stone, and a long table to his left, decorated with an assortment of gold cups and plates, and in addition to this a large assortment of sweet smelling candles and an enormous basin of fresh water in the corner. There were fresh flowers on the table.

"Hello again," he said, trying to catch the attention of Agnos.

She spun around in delighted surprise, and ran to hug him. "Well, you've done it!" she exclaimed. "What is there to do next?"

"We'll have plenty to do soon," he remarked. "But for now, I have some victorious warriors to greet."

Agnos kissed him again. "I know you do," she laughed. "And then all your troubles will be over with."

Fearghus lifted her in his arms and laid her back down on the bed. Looking across at Osgar on his table, he couldn't help thinking that there still was one more task he had to complete, one last challenge waiting before the end. But here with Agnos, he could not even imagine what it was. "Now get some more rest," he told her, turning to leave the room. "I'll be back soon."

He left just as the men in the Oaken Hall were gathering in the field before it. Apparently, there was quite a major event happening down there. The mounted warriors that defeated the Romans obviously had returned to their home. Fearghus had very little time to dash to the steps of his hall before they were there, marching in single file through the iron door, and stopping in rows before him.

He raised his golden spear before them and they cheered thunderously. He knew that he had spoken to only a quarter of them before, but all of the many warriors seemed to him to be just like the others he had rallied to battle. He spoke to them now with a confident and loud voice, briefly mentioning the cross on top of the temple and congratulating them for defeating the Romans. He did not wish to waste much more time here in front of them, and so he invited them to eat in the Oaken Hall and the fields around it, for not even this hall could hold so many men.

Inside, Fearghus sat at the head of the table and dined yet again on roast pig among other things, and nearly half of the incoming warriors joined him at this table. Outside in the fields, the other warriors sat in the soft reeds and were served similar foods, until the storerooms and pens in Fearghus's valley were almost entirely empty. But it did not matter to him. He was very pleased at their accomplishments battling in the North, and had to treat them to a good meal.

Much time passed during this time, and Fearghus wondered what was about to befall him, for the day was waning quickly. Halfway between midday and the dusk, the feast abruptly ended, and then Fearghus was left alone to himself, sitting further back in his throne, as the men bustled outside, finding themselves rooms in the rear of the city. By now, Fearghus thought, the city would nearly be full, and his wish of populating the valley was fulfilled.

He sat there, listening to the men outside, and became bored. But he knew something was coming that would cease this lull, and soon it did. It was something that Fearghus had half-expected, but also feared very much.

He was considering going back up to see Agnos when the great doors to his hall creaked open. He thought it to be one of his attendants at first, but when he saw the gleam of a drawn sword, he quickly got to his feet. Ten men entered his throne room now, and each had a bitterly evil look upon his face, so that they looked like attacking wolves. They split into two columns as they crept around the table, and eyed Fearghus carefully, watching for him to draw his own sword.

To his right, Fearghus recognized someone he thought to be his friend. He was of course the leader of the others, since he beckoned them forward. "Hello, Seadna," Fearghus said without making the slightest move.

Seadna gritted his teeth furiously, his knuckles white as he clenched his weapon. "I have come to end it," he snarled, his sword lifted to the side of his face.

Fearghus still did not move. "End what?" he asked haughtily.

"You know," Seadna barked, still advancing slowly, his eyes wild and having perhaps a frightened look in them.

Fearghus remained tauntingly calm, his arms wide of his belt, looking back and forth at the other men. They seemed to be honest enough warriors to him as he saw them now, but he knew each of them was troubled inside. "What?" he teased. "My new faith to God?" he asked smoothly.

Seadna was near to the point of bursting. "You betray Eire!" he howled. "You betray me!"

"I don't know what you are talking about," Fearghus retorted, his own hands now in fists. "You betray Eire with your false gods!" he then screamed.

There were no more words Seadna could speak. He now lunged at Fearghus, swinging his sword over his head, and missing. Fearghus himself jumped into the air, and flung and outstretched hand towards his throne. Osgar, his lance, flew into his grasp, and he had barely enough time to bring it down in front of him, parrying a fierce blow by Seadna.

The others had joined the fight now. Fearghus was forced to leap onto the table to dodge a swing by one of them. He then jumped back off of it as a sword passed under his feet, and he plunged Osgar into the nearest man to him. The warrior crumpled to the floor holding a bloody wound, and Fearghus sprinted clear of the rest of them, his sword screeching as he drew it from its scabbard. He was in a corner, though, and it took both Osgar and his blade to block the next series of blows, which he returned by dispatching two other men.

He pushed his way out from among them as more of the rebels joined their comrades. He advanced toward his throne, and then turned to engage them. Three more men fell to his sword as they fought him together, and his weapon was stained heavily with blood.

Seadna came to the helm of his remaining three comrades now, and his sword he swung faster than Fearghus could see it in the air. It was all Fearghus could do to block his blade and dodge what certainly would have been killing blows, but he somehow managed to strafe to the right, and dispatch yet another of Seadna's companions with the long shaft of Osgar.

Fearghus decided to use his speed to escape Seadna now. He ran in circles around the great table, and in one great bound jumped over it, and struck again, finally destroying the last two of Seadna's men, as the warriors screamed and howled in pain, finally to die there on the floor in a pool of blood. But Seadna did not relent. He was nearly as fast as Fearghus and also nearly as strong, his skills with the sword vastly superior. His days as a pirate suited him well for this kind of combat, and Fearghus knew it.

As Fearghus evaded him, Seadna was able only to deliver a few blows to Fearghus, who blocked them expertly and continued to dance around the room. At last Seadna stopped in one corner, and relaxed a bit. Fearghus stopped as well, and they looked at each other for a moment. Then Seadna spoke. "You cannot win, Fearghus," he bellowed. "Who do you think you are that you can challenge the gods?"

Fearghus looked hard at him, never blinking an eye. "I am Fearghus, of course," he said. "I thought you knew that."

But this crack only enraged Seadna the more. "You do not deserve to live!" he screamed. "As the gods as my witnesses, you shall perish from this earth!"

Fearghus raised his sword. "And as the Lord God as my witness, I shall cleanse this place of your evil!" he yelled back, and then jumped into the air. He found himself flying high over the table suddenly, and he raised his sword as he landed straight before Seadna, who staggered back in surprise. There they dueled furiously, Fearghus seeing each of Seadna's blows before it came, and Seadna the like. Their swords could scarcely be seen as they swung in the air, and this for a great while, until somehow Fearghus knocked the sword loose from Seadna's grasp, and in the same motion hurled him against the wall.

Fearghus pointed the point of Osgar straight at Seadna's throat. He almost thrust it in right there, but then thought better of the situation. "You have lost," he told Seadna.

Seadna looked up at him, his face weakened with fear and his eyes watering. His mouth curled into a helpless frown, and he slumped forward, pleading for his life. Fearghus could not hear what he muttered, but withdrew his spear. As he stood there one of his memories raced through his mind again, and he recalled the day a year ago when he was traveling in the forest, and was attacked by a Roman centurion. He remembered the terrible struggle that followed, and how the Roman was unable to take his life, and tried to run away. And then he remembered his terrible sin that cost him his immortality; he killed the centurion by throwing Osgar into his back. *That* was his greatest mistake.

Fearghus took Osgar back into his hands, and stepped away from Seadna. "You are free," he said, and looked own as Seadna acknowledged his kindness. When the old pirate looked up though, he was looking past Fearghus, and a look of horror crossed his face. "Don't do it!" he stammered. "No!"

At that very moment, a long spear sailed past Fearghus and plunged into Seadna's chest, blood spattering on the wall. Fearghus spun around, and there saw one of the warriors he thought he had killed earlier standing on the other side of the table, a malevolent grin coming across his face. "That should finish him!" he cackled, and threw back his head to laugh. But Fearghus was not laughing.

"What have you done this for?" he asked innocently, casting a cold glance upon the man. "I thought you were on his side—"

"I am on my own side!" the warrior shouted.

Fearghus was filled instantly with anger. He wanted revenge. He wanted to kill for Seadna's sake, to avenge his friend's death. And so he jumped once again over the table, and sunk his sword into the stomach of the man.

The warrior staggered back, clutching his wound, but did not fall. Instead, he drew the sword back out and just as skillfully, he spun around and threw it into Fearghus's stomach. Fearghus immediately felt a killing blow. His whole body weakened by the wound, he fell against the table, blood spurting out from under his armor. Then the warrior cackled again. Fearghus noticed that his wound had healed almost instantaneously. And then his memory warned him again. This was no man. This was a Snake!

"By now, I think you know who I am," the Snake said maliciously.

Fearghus was still leaning upon the table, gradually feeling better. "This will be your last day alive!' he retorted, still giving the impression that he was mortally wounded. The sword in his gut slid around uncomfortably as he spoke.

"What's that? I think you are forgetting who has the sword stuck in them!" the Snake shot back.

Fearghus stood up and drew his weapon out, throwing it on the table. "And you are forgetting who has the Holy Lance!" he yelled, and flung his hand back. Osgar leapt into his fingers.

The Snake backed up against the wall, horrified. But a smug look came across his face as Fearghus brandished the weapon before him. As Fearghus watched, his skin slowly darkened, as he had seen it do before, and his body was elongated. His head grew larger, and his arms and legs melted into one. He was returning to his true form, terrible and ugly. It was then that Fearghus noticed something; he had no sight in one of his eyes.

Fearghus decided to play this game with him. "One of us is going to have to kill the other eventually!" he boomed. "And there is only one weapon that can do it!" And with this he twirled Osgar proudly in the air.

But the Snake seemed not afraid. "You foolish little man!" he hissed. "You should not anger your greatest enemy!"

Now Fearghus wanted to end it. He planted his feet, his arm sweeping back, and prepared to throw Osgar. "And neither should you!" he retorted, and his whole body he threw forward. The Snake was quick to react. His head he flung to the side quickly, and Fearghus knew that he *would have* missed him, if he had actually thrown the spear. But he hadn't. He had instead tucked into a roll, and somersaulted into striking range. Now he was behind the Snake, who was stretched out across the Oaken Hall, thinking still that he had dodged the spear and that Fearghus was now doomed. But instead it was he who was doomed, for Fearghus leapt upon his back, and sank the silvery point of Osgar into his neck, near to his head.

With one huge scream of agony, the Snake's body writhed in pain, throwing Fearghus off of it. Fearghus hit the ground hard, but retained Osgar. He rebounded quickly, seeing that the half-blind Snake had thrown his head back one last time, before it came down again to the floor. Then Fearghus dashed to it, and plunged Osgar once and for all into the Snake's head.

He had nothing more to say. He stepped back, surveying the great dead Snake, and sat down upon a chair. He felt very tired now, after such a terrible night, and wanted nothing more than to sleep right there. He watched the Snake for a moment, and then it began to change color, to more of a greenish tint. Before Fearghus knew it, a great wind had come into the Oaken Hall, and the Snake's body began to shake violently in it. Soon enough the entire corpse was spinning in a whirlwind, and rapidly dematerializing.

In a flash, it was gone, and Osgar with it. The treasure had served its purpose here, and it had gone back to wherever it came from. Maybe this place was nowhere, beyond the realm of the mortal world. Whatever the case, all that was left from it was a tiny green emerald, which Fearghus had seen fall from the wind to the floor. He picked it up and examined it, and then tucked it safely into his belt.

He sheathed his sword and wiped his sweaty face with his cape. He was opening the great doors to the hall when suddenly, he heard a scream echo through the valley. A woman was in distress! He most nearly drew his sword again as he stumbled down the steps, but then a short village woman stopped him. "Do not worry!" she said. "There is nothing wrong! It is only your son!"

Fearghus paused for a moment. "My *son*?" he asked. And then he remembered: Agnos was ready to give birth at any moment! He had to go see her, and quickly! He broke into a run, and quickly found the door to the building where they were staying. He dashed up the stairs so fast, he nearly knocked down one of the housemaids, and stumbled, falling onto the floor. When he lifted his head, he heard an incessant crying coming from the room next to him. A newborn baby was crying. His baby.

He struggled to his feet, and entered the room. Agnos was lying on the bed. In her arms, squirming around, was the baby. "Are you alright?" he spluttered, running up to meet her.

Agnos pushed him away briefly. "I am fine, Fearghus," she said. "You needn't have to worry over me."

Fearghus tried to open his mouth to explain, but she stopped him. "I know what happened," she said. "And I understand. You may hold him, if you like," she whispered.

Fearghus outstretched his arms, covered by golden bracers, and cradled the newborn baby in them. He was a bit embarrassed by his appearance, but when he looked down at his son, he felt much better. "Now don't become too attached to him," Agnos joked, taking him back from Fearghus, who was at a loss for words. "You two will have a lot of time to play together later."

Fearghus bent over and kissed her forehead. So this is what he had seen coming today. This was the major life-changing event that he had foreseen. He felt happier than ever he did before.

It was already night outside. Fearghus had not noticed the darkness when he'd run up here, but the sun had already set. After he had spent some time with Agnos, he hurried back down to the Oaken Hall, where some of the men had already discovered the bodies of Seadna and his rebellious warriors. As they carried them out one by one, Fearghus gave instructions concerning their burial. Mostly he told the men to consult the families of the men or simply to send the bodies to their native villages, but for Seadna he made an exception. "Bury him by the sea," he said plainly, and the two men holding him nodded, and started for the iron door.

Fearghus surveyed the work that was done to clean the Oaken Hall throughout the night. His mind was still racing from all the events that had occurred to him. When at last the dawn came, Fearghus decided to go back and be with Agnos. But he stopped Conn in the field before he did, and produced his small green emerald from his purse. He gave the smith a few instructions, and then set out for his home again, where Agnos and the baby were probably asleep.

Indeed they were. When he found them, Agnos was fast asleep and one of the maids was standing guard over a bundle of blankets, in which the baby was also slumbering tenderly. Fearghus dared not wake them, but nonetheless pulled the cushioned chair up next to the bed, and fell asleep himself, sitting in it.

Agnos was the one to wake him up. She was very awake for someone in her condition, and very anxious to talk to him. The maid was still sitting in the corner at their dining table, with the baby in her protective grasp. But Agnos did not notice her as Fearghus did, she was too busy trying to get his attention. Finally he turned to her, and she looked him in the eyes. "What should we name him?" she asked pleasantly.

Fearghus racked his mind for an answer to this question. He had not given much thought to this since he had known that Agnos was expecting, and now, frankly, he was at a loss for words. "Come on," she coaxed him lovingly, "something nice and Celtic."

Then he had the answer. "We will name him Cian," he replied.

She looked across the room at the baby, who had begun to cry. "That sounds like a very good name," she said. "Then we will name him Cian."

Outside, the sun was rising rapidly. When Fearghus looked back on his grand city, he once again saw the rays of the dawn touch the cross on top of the temple. The golden light of it was cast all across the valley once more, and he felt the same sense of elation that it had caused him before. Once more, the people of the city seemed to gather about him as he stood in the field where once he had slept in the soft grass, and they surrounded him in every direction, for their number was so great. During the past day alone, many wives and elderly people had journeyed to his city from their own villages in the surrounding area, mainly to find their husbands and sons of his Army, but also to become permanent residents here. They all came to him now, and stood in awe of the glorious symbol.

They maintained this position for a while, until one of the guards at the iron door was alerted. He came into the crowd and found Fearghus, beckoning him towards the door. "There is a man here to see you," he said as they approached it. "We would not allow him to pass, because he is not like any of us. I suggest you talk to him yourself. He seems gentle enough."

Fearghus allowed the man to hold the door open for him, and glanced back at the crowd behind him. Inside the waterfall room, the other guard at the door had heard of this visitor too. He pushed Fearghus on curiously, wondering about this man that they were all talking about. Fearghus started to jog when he reached the wooden path, and very soon reached the last chamber, which was filled to capacity with horses, some of them on a wooden raft in the water. The riders from the North certainly had brought many animals into the place.

When the burly guard at the door noticed him, he stood aside and opened it for him, revealing a tall man in flowing robes on the other side. "Please, come in," Fearghus said politely, motioning for the bearded fellow to come into the warm reddish room. When the man ducked down a bit to go through the opening, he lowered his staff to fit through the door. Fearghus noted immediately that it was, though plain, decorated on the top with a Roman cross, much like the one on his temple.

"Why thank you," the mysterious stranger said when he was inside. He had an odd sort of headdress on that was also decorated by the cross.

"I am pleased to meet you, ah—"

"Patrick," the kindly man told him. "I am Bishop Patrick, and I've come here in search of a particular Fearghus, if I am correct."

Fearghus bowed. "I am Fearghus," he replied, "though I do not know what a bishop is."

Patrick chuckled. "It just means that I am a faithful servant of God," he replied. And then he noticed the shamrocks growing on the walls of this chamber, the ones that had given Fearghus such a fright before. "You see those?" he asked Fearghus suddenly.

Fearghus gulped. "Yes, I do," he replied.

Patrick broke one of the clovers from the wall, and showed it closely to Fearghus in the light of the torches. "Did you ever notice that each shamrock has three leaves?" he asked. When Fearghus nodded, he touched one of the three. "Just like the Lord God is three things combined as one."

Fearghus was confused, and Patrick could see it upon his face. "And may I ask what they are?" he said.

Patrick touched the first petal. "There is the Father," he said, moving to the next one, "the Son," he added, touching the third, "and the Holy Ghost. All these wonderful things He is, and we call this the Trinity."

Fearghus nodded. "The Trinity?" he asked shakily, trying to understand. And then he showed Patrick to the wooden path in the cavern. "Any servant of God is welcome here," he stammered, bowing once more.

"Then I have come to the right place," Bishop Patrick said. He walked calmly behind Fearghus, who seemed rather jumpy this morning, and who struggled to walk properly without revealing his excitement. When they came to the door he allowed Patrick to proceed through it first, and then followed.

"You have done a great job building this city!" the Bishop exclaimed as all the townspeople looked at him questioningly.

"Thank you," Fearghus replied. "Would you like to have some breakfast, maybe?"

"I would like that very much."

Fearghus led him to the Oaken Hall, and told his attendants to find some more food. He let Patrick sit down in his respective chair at the head of the table, and sat next to him on his right. In another moment the servants were back with a platter of food, including fruits and meats and breads for the visitor. Patrick ate them ravenously, but politely allowed some leftovers for Fearghus. He was too nervous to eat though, and refused. Instead, he began to question the Bishop. "Did *He* send you?" was the first question.

Patrick gulped down some milk. "For lack of a better answer, I think *He* sent both of us," he replied cleverly. And with that Fearghus felt much relieved, and began to discuss many things with the Bishop, who answered all his questions beautifully. When the meal was ended, he waited for Fearghus to cease his questioning, and then said, "Shall we begin?"

Fearghus knew better than to rudely ask, "Begin what?" and instead, he followed Patrick out of the hall until he'd reached the very edge of the valley, where a stream ran in a circle. The curious people in the field joined them silently, and he smiled broadly as they came. Agnos was among them, for recently she had mustered the strength to come down to the field. She held little Cian gently in her arms.

It was then that Fearghus had an idea. "Are...are you going to...to baptize us?" he asked innocently, stuttering a bit in his nervousness.

Patrick looked down at him with wise and loving eyes. "Do you wish to become a Christian?" he countered.

"Yes indeed," Fearghus answered.

Patrick waded into the water. Then he looked upon the masses of people there, and pointed to one particular warrior. "Come," he said to him, and a young man appeared. "You have been granted the first position in this line." Fearghus knew it too. He had told the man this when they talked yesterday.

When the warrior stepped into the stream with Patrick, he anointed him with water over his head, and blessed him in the name of all three elements of the Trinity. When he was done with the ritual, he said, "You are now a Christian. Go with God."

Once again, only Patrick stood in the cool water. "Now I should like to have your son," he said to Fearghus, and Agnos came over to him. Patrick took Cian in his hands, and repeated the baptism on the baby, repeating his name without having to be told of it. Then it was Fearghus's turn. He felt very proud and honored to become a Christian, and even a bit weak as he approached the Bishop. But the ceremony was the same as it had been twice before, and he felt the water rush over him, relaxing him and making him feel safe.

Fearghus joined Agnos on the bank when he was freed. He thanked Patrick and then stood aside as the other men and women rushed to be baptized after him. As they gained the field, a massive line had formed behind them, and they both were delighted to see their countrymen act in this way.

The baptisms continued for the rest of the morning. Fearghus and Agnos watched from the window of their new room, and the day continued uneventfully. Patrick was gone in the evening, and the whole city went to the temple in the middle of the valley after he left, and prayed to God. Patrick had called this building a "church" before he disappeared, and Agnos, of course, knew what he was talking about. The two of them followed the warriors and the women into the huge stone citadel, and communally worshipped their new God with the best of intentions. The warrior who had been baptized first stood in the center of them that night, and claimed that he saw a vision. Fearghus unknowingly named him their "pastor," and was not sure what he had just said. He did know that it meant that the man was some sort of a leader for them, though he was unsure. But yet again, Agnos understood this word, and shared with the community all that she knew of these strange things.

The next day, Fearghus was relieved of his struggles at last. The warning in his mind that trouble was yet to come was gone, and he spent the morning with Agnos in their home, many things filling his mind. Conn had visited them this morning, and now he had a surprise for his wife. She easily detected his unrest, and asked, "What are you thinking of now?"

Fearghus reached behind his back and produced a gleaming golden ring. "I have had this band made," he said, "for Cian here. I have set in it the emerald stone that appeared to me at the time of his birth two nights ago."

Agnos grinned. "It is beautiful!" she remarked. As she held it in her fingers, green light seemed to fill the room, sparkling on the walls. "Do not worry," she then said. "I will keep it safe until he is old enough to wear it."

Fearghus stood up. He'd left his armor hanging on the wall behind him, and he felt vastly more comfortable without it on. "You do that," he told her, and kissed her.

Now the task of the men in the city had become improving the place. Dunchad had commissioned his loyal workers already to begin work on another structure, and was pleased with the reaction the men gave him. All day long they chopped down more trees from the outside and brought them into the valley, and by midday they were working on walls.

Fearghus only busied himself with being with Agnos during this wonderful day. She enjoyed his company as well, and they explored Dún as Cloch some more together. By the end of the day, they were both as happy as they could possibly be, though Fearghus felt more fully the absence of war. He missed being a warrior somehow, but still felt triumphant as his kingdom entered an age of prosperity.

When the red dusk was seen over the high mountains of the valley, something awoke in Fearghus. He felt strangely that he had to do something, and the next thing he knew he was doing it. He left Agnos preparing for bed in their room, and walked all the way back to the construction area for the next building. There was Dunchad, commanding his men happily, surveying his fine work. Fearghus approached him silently, and distracted him from his work. "Would you come with me?" he asked the old man.

Dunchad grinned, and followed obediently. "What can I do for you?" he asked.

Fearghus started off towards the front of Dún as Cloch. "You can come with me," he answered.

Dunchad agreed to walk with Fearghus through all the great buildings of the city. As they went, Fearghus spoke to him of their beauty, commending him for his fine work on them. "You are a true friend," he said several times, confusing Dunchad a bit.

"Thank you, but—"

They had come to the iron door. The guard opened it for both of them, and the two friends walked into the waterfall room together. Dunchad turned to look at Fearghus, even more confused. "Where are we going?" he asked. "It's almost dusk."

Fearghus had an odd gleam in his eye as he turned to Dunchad. "We aren't going anywhere," he said.

Dunchad looked around nervously. "Then why are we in here?" he pressed.

Fearghus opened the iron door himself, for there wasn't a guard posted in this room tonight. Dunchad caught a glimpse of the fair valley of Dún as Cloch as he did this, and smiled briefly at it. But the thing that happened next left his mouth wide open in surprise. Fearghus had ignored his question, and only his head was visible as the door closed over him. "Good bye, my friend," he seemed to whisper, and then closed the iron door behind him, disappearing from view.

Dunchad stepped forward and tried the door, but it would not open. He began to shout for Fearghus to come back, but the King did not return. When he tried his hand on the knob again, it suddenly vanished, along with the entire door.

He screamed as loud as he could for Fearghus to return, and looked up sadly at the waterfall, which was illuminated with orange light. He did not want to think that the water was lit by the torches in the room, which he himself had placed. He convinced himself that it was the light of the sunset, coming directly to it through the valley of Dún as Cloch.

He instantly knew that he would never again see the city that he built, and came to the verge of tears. Why had he been left out? What had he done that caused this to happen to him? He could not imagine what it was. To him, this wasn't a privilege, nor was it an honor. He wanted to be with his friends, and live forever in the valley with them. But this just wasn't so. He turned towards the wooden path to the outside, and sadly started down it, not knowing what else to do.

When he reached the final chamber, he looked back down the tunnel he had just traversed. Though the torches in this room stayed lit, the lights lining the cavern had suddenly been removed or extinguished, and he peered into the darkness curiously, but fearfully. In this last room where he now stood, there was nothing left but the torches and the door. The horses had gone, and with them the guard, and it was only him here, by himself with the mysterious clovers. And so he finally pushed himself to swing the wooden door open, and looked outside to the field from within the chamber. As he did this, the torches in the room went out, and only the faint light coming in from the doorway provided him with light.

He walked outside, forced out by the darkness, and as he expected, the crack in the stone vanished behind him. When he jogged out to the sea's edge and looked for the entrance to the watery cavern, it had disappeared as well. There was only a solid rock face here where there had once been a gaping hole, and it seemed to him like it had been there for eternity. Judging from the surf below it, though, he could see that the stream pouring out from the interior of Dún as Cloch was still there, since a strong jet of water was pushing up from the depths of the dark sea.

Dunchad set out for the main road as the stars and moon appeared above him. It was hard for him to believe that his friends were looking up at the same sky, but he knew they were. After regaining his bearings, he proceeded to travel north. He had heard of the monastery up there, and wanted very much to see it at long last, if it still stood. As he walked along, he finally came upon the answer to his burning questions, and it seemed obvious to him—he was left behind to tell the tale of Fearghus and his valley, and to advance the ideals of him. The legend of these things, as well as the Catholic religion, were meant to be spread, and by Dunchad himself. He felt suddenly honored to be this one man left out of the valley. He would be the first man to tell the story of Fearghus, and the first in all of Eire to worship this different God.

Not much more than this is known of the legend of Fearghus the King. Of his Order of the Serpent there remains only that—a legend. The days when people worshipped the gods in Eire passed quickly after his disappearance, or so the tales go. The coasts abounded with new monasteries after his time, and they were said to be exactly like the one that Dunchad traveled to, the one that was such an important place in this tale. They filled with the followers of Saint Patrick, and from them the word of God spread all the way to the far west of the island. Some think that Dunchad was the first Christian of his time to appear in Eire, while others disagree. He line seemed not to appear thereafter in Irish lore. Many doubt that he even produced children.

Of Cian there is a more interesting tale. In a small village next to a mountain there is a legend that once in the days of revolution on the mainland of Europe, there came a young lad from the sea. He seemed to have swum up from the very sea itself, and alighted on the shore. From there he came and settled briefly in the village, which the elders say was built on the ruins of an ancient settlement. He moved on shortly after, but the people there still claim that one thing that they all knew him to wear was a golden ring, with an emerald stone set in it. They also claim that he married one of their young women when he was there, and he had five children by her. Now in many places throughout Ireland, five cities to be exact, there survive families who claim to be descended from these children. Only one of them is said to be of the direct line of Fearghus, for Cian only had a single son to carry on his line. The family lives in Dublin these days, far from the sea, and it is widely known that another young Fearghus has sprung from them.

And that is the tale, as is best recounted by word of mouth, of how Fearghus the King saved Ireland from the Romans. It seems odd that he would have to do this, since the Irish abide by the Roman Catholic religion, but yet the storytellers agree that never again did a Roman soldier come to the island. Only the Roman monks came in their absence. And from the time of Fearghus to the present, the great land of Eire has remained one of the most steadfast centers of Roman Catholicism in the world, unflinching in the face of war and other evils.

A Word From the Author

Thank you for reading my very first novel, *The Battle for Eire*. I began writing this story when I was still in the eighth grade, and I finished it shortly before becoming a sophomore in High School. I'd been casting about trying to come up with a theme and name for a novel for months, as I had only ever written short stories before.

When I began to write, I was aiming to compose something of a fantasy epic, though now I do not know if I have. During the writing process I referred to my novel as fantasy and even historical fiction, though it is far from historical. In fact, the plot of my writing diverges from fact in countless ways, ranging from the actually false invasion of Eire to the details of life in the fifth century A.D. I do not claim at all to be a historian or an expert on the Irish Celts. This novel, in fact, I wrote independently of almost all known facts of its environment. I wrote down my thoughts as they came to me, and shaped them to fit the plotline.

My style of writing is quite simple indeed. I haven't done any research or made any international trips, or even written an outline. I tried to to write the story as if I was the main character, thinking of what would happen next. All I armed myself with was a vague idea of the beginning, middle and ending sections of my story, and allowed myself to fill the gaps in between however I liked.

When my dream of a fantastic setting materialized as Ireland, I sought out a source for the miracles and strange happenings in my book. Immediately my mind shifted to God, who remains surely the most powerful force today in the Irish culture. I began to use Him as others would use witchcraft and other magic, as the higher being that governs the path of the main character. I feel no regret for this, since the Lord has performed many miracles in countless works, especially the Bible.

In the next few paragraphs, I will try to the best of my ability to evaluate my own work, and describe for you the inner working of the plot. The many parts of my novel relate in a great number of different ways, though you are open to draw your own conclusions.

Osgar is a perfectly fine Gaelic name (for a person), but I have chosen to use it to denote, in fact, an object. The meaning of it is "champion," and the Norse interpretation is "divine spear,"so I figured it to be suitable. The Holy Lance has been used literarily many times before in a similar manner as I have. It is supposed to be the very spear that a Roman soldier plunged into the body of Jesus Christ on the cross, and thus is said to be blessed with many special properties. In my tale, I portray it as a thing that is granted freely to Fearghus as part of his destiny, and something also that he loses and must struggle to regain. The Quest for Osgar is most nearly the center of my story, because it is on the path to his conversion. Note that his invulnerability, which is a quality identified with his possession of Osgar, did not return until he had proven that he believed in God and His righteousness.

The role of Agnos began as a love interest for Fearghus, so as to complement the fantastic style of the book. Her importance to the story only increased as he grew closer to conversion, since she was a Catholic herself. The reason why the Romans invaded, as it is given, is in fact determined by her father's wrongful death (or more of the same) as a missionary. Agnos's position is filled out by marriage and motherhood, but most importantly the discovery of her own divine selection as Fearghus's guide to Catholicism. She becomes literally the key to his success, and the personification of his less violent and more thoughtful side.

Of course, maybe even more of the plot is dedicated to Seadna, the former pirate from a village near Dún as Cloch. He is the friend of Colla and a wise member of the first Quest for Osgar, and thus becomes even greater than the other characters as he helps Fearghus along the road of military leadership and adventure. But there is a difference between the roles of Agnos and Seadna, displayed fully in the last chapter. Seadna is unsure of himself, and corrupted by piracy and death. Indeed, he is Fearghus's guide, but also falls short of his friend in many ways. He, or more accurately Colla, is described as a man similarly treated as Fearghus. This may lead the reader to believe that Colla wasted the same opportunities as Fearghus was offered, by failing to convert and find the true reason for the miracles. But truly this is not so. Seadna, as Colla's friend, was rather destined to meet Fearghus. Seadna is, in fact, provided as an obstacle for Fearghus to conquer, and one of the facets of his journey. His decision to stray from the beliefs of his most trusted companion, even to the point of mortal peril, is one of his toughest.

Seadna can hardly compare to Fearghus's greatest adversary, the Snake. He was made as part of the spontaneous beginning to Fearghus's divine journey, but later on the Isle of Man, he becomes the worst enemy to him. The Snake is not a man, though he could appear as one if he wished. He is rather more of a thought to Fearghus, an idea. As a serpent, he is an icon of evil and untruth, as truly he is meant to be. It may be argued that the Snake is the personification of Fearghus's pagan beliefs, those which he has to defeat before he truly can become Christian. His struggle to find the truth behind his adventures is summed up in his apparent battles with the Snake, which are like his battles with his own beliefs. Also, there is much to be said about his immortality, which the Snake shares with him. When they both possess it at the end of the story, only Osgar can be used to kill either. Since Fearghus has already at this time won the battle with his paganism, he is able to employ Osgar to kill the Snake. Thus, the true Quest for Osgar lies in this one question: will Fearghus be able to use Osgar, or will it kill him? He can answer this only by his response to God. But yet, Osgar is there only to help him convert, as the miracles in the Bible usually are. His real battles are fought only in his heart and mind.

The object of Fearghus's war with Rome is to rid himself of hate and evil. In itself, the bloody war is evil, but by the design of the Romans, who have wrongly chosen to strike with military might, rather than missionaries. Fearghus is chosen by God, then, to set Rome straight. The goal of Catholicism lies in peace and brotherhood, things that Fearghus actually advances as he moves against the legion of Rome. In his path, involving vanquishing these offenders and also converting to their religion, he not only rids Eire of Rome's evil intentions, but advances the idea of the peaceable spreading of God's Word. Osgar, Agnos, Seadna and the Snake are all, in themselves, the challenges he faces in this tale, and the way he responds to each of them decides the outcome of his important mission from God.

Lastly, there can be much speculation about the selection of Fearghus by God. He could have been chosen because of his willingness to battle Rome, or something else in his character. I will say that he was selected not only because of his restlessness and desire to be a warrior, but because of his open mind, which is reflected in his reactions to all situations involving Agnos. Also, God sees his wandering mind. In this light, maybe, it can be said that he was selected because of his unwillingness. His folly in the forest with Osgar and near the monastery with a captive monk reflects his attitude. One of his greatest feats, though, is realizing these mistakes, and making amends for them.

Once more, thank you for reading all the way to the end of my novel. It is good for a sixteen-year-old to know that someone actually respects his writing abilities. In the future, if all of this works out, I hope to write many more adventurous and fantastic stories. The success of this novel, my first, will help me achieve even greater things to come.

978-0-595-36860-0
0-595-36860-3

Printed in the United States
39601LVS00005B/10-30